The Pirate Devlin

The Pirate Devlin

MARK KEATING

GRAND CENTRAL
PUBLISHING

New York   Boston

First published in the UK by Hodder & Stoughton Ltd, February 2010

Grand Central Publishing
Hachette Book Group
237 Park Avenue
New York, NY 10017

www.HachetteBookGroup.com

Printed in the United States of America

First Grand Central Publishing Edition: July 2010
10 9 8 7 6 5 4 3 2 1

Grand Central Publishing is a division of Hachette Book Group, Inc.
The Grand Central Publishing name and logo is a trademark of
Hachette Book Group, Inc.

ISBN: 978-0-446-56390-1
LCCN: 2009942016

For John Roberts and James Montgomerie,
who always wanted to read on.

Pride, envy and avarice
Are the three sparks
That have set on fire
The hearts of man.

Dante Alighieri,
The Divine Comedy, 'Inferno': VI, 74–5

Prologue

The West Coast of Africa, April 1717

*T*he Frenchman's boots were filling with blood as he cracked his way through the wet coarseness of the undergrowth. As daylight faded into bladed shadows, the jungle pulled him deeper into its crushing green.

His breaths rasped through the heavy heat, stretching the pain along his side. The pounding of his heart engulfed his body.

Bereft of sword or pistol, his only hope was to push himself ever on, spurred by the shouts of the pirates echoing from the beach.

Desperately he dodged across the uneven ground. Stumbling upwards in one step, falling the next, grasping for purchase, the wet jungle slapping his face with every cursing breath.

Without a glance behind, he arrowed away from the triumphant yell that signalled the first sighting of his bloody trail spotting amongst the waist-tall fronds; his pace slowed with the strange coldness of his own blood seeping down his leg.

Away from the sand and the mud now, he found himself wading through lush boot-high grass and shadowy palms.

Enough of the green flaying him weaker. Enough beating him back. He crouched to draw breath, to slow the beat of his heart pushing his life from the hole above his hip and staining wine-black the worsted blue of his Marine Royale doublet.

The sweating forest was reminiscent in his near delirium of a mansion house back home in Orly, a maze of corridors and echoes.

Now, passageways of mossy trunks, instead of green flocked halls, opened up into insect-humming, fern-filled rooms, each one sealed off from the other until he broke through its emerald door.

He crouched in one of these dark chambers, his insides cramping, his own will trying to pull him down into the soft, welcoming grass. Sleep awhile and hope his pursuers would pass him by, give up, return to the boat.

When the longboat had landed, and all had jumped into the surf to drag her in, he too had leaped clear and seized the moment of the struggle against the tide to back away and then bolt free, pounding up the beach, clumsy against the sand underfoot.

He had stumbled the short distance to the breach of the wild mass of twisted white branches protecting the jungle, when one of them had got off a lucky pistol shot that had slammed into his hip, and he found a powerful desire to keep running from the wicked laugh that followed it.

Now, as he sucked at the moist air, he heard no noise around him save for the chattering of black beetles, the endless chirrup of the cicadas. The mocking calls and whistles had faded, he was sure. He reached up to a friendly branch and heaved himself along as quietly as the jungle would allow in its pity.

Staggering through the swathes of enormous leaves fanning his brow, he came into another clearing, as polished as a bowling green, as peaceful as the hour after mass. In the centre of the dell, disturbed in his foraging by the interloper, a lone crow bobbed, glistening black against the vitality of the green. There was a moment of judgement as the bird cocked his head to the sweating Frenchman. He cawed once, softly, to question the intrusion.

The Frenchman hissed to his companion for silence, but the black bird merely chuckled at his impudence then, as punishment, sprang into the air, with his laughing war cry pealing around the trees like a plague bell. A dozen of his brothers followed with their admonishment, breaking through the roof of the trees to form a black cloud over his sanctuary.

The shouts of the pirates rose with the cries of the birds, and the jungle danced with the crash of their approach.

The Frenchman pitched forward, drunkenly pliant. The imminence of his own demise gave at least some promise of rest. He collapsed gratefully into the coolness of the damp grass as the seven brutes came through the green curtains into his world.

'Well, well, Froggy,' panted the quartermaster, Peter Sam, standing over him, sweat running off his shaven head, filtering through his red beard. 'That's quite a run you gave us there, boy.' Throwing his cutlass aside, he joined Philippe Ducos, the unfortunate young man from the Marine Royale, and sat in the grass, his chest heaving.

The other half-dozen gathered round their prisoner, who stared straight up, gasping his last breaths to the blue sky breaking through the lacy canopy of trees.

Hugh Harris gave a swift kick that belied the daintiness of the red and white silk shoes he had taken from the French sloop only the week before, now soaked and salt-stained.

'So, there's no pig farm on this island, then? Eh, Froggy?' Another kick to the black wound.

'What'll we do with him, Peter?' William Magnes, the old man of their group at forty-five, put his hanger away, never willing to be the killer.

'We'll do for him sure enough.' Peter reached for his cutlass, stood up and wiped his head with a dirty kerchief. 'Makes no sense to take him back. But we'll not go back empty.' He snapped his fingers to a young pock-faced lad. 'Davies, go with Hugh and Will. Back to the boat. Get the muskets. See if you can scout down some goat. The ground's right for pigs at least.'

'Aye, Peter.' The lad and the old standers went off with slaps and swearing.

'You two.' He pointed to Patrick Devlin and Sam Fletcher, who were new hands, weeks new, a couple of navy 'waisters' still learning the sweet trade. 'Go through the Frog's pockets for yourselves, lads, then end him. I'm going to scour for fruit. I wants his jacket as a sack. Gets it off him, then come and gets me with it.' He grabbed the arm of the remaining pirate, a young, black-haired, moon-faced lad. 'Thomas, come with me.'

Devlin, Fletcher and the Frenchman were now alone in the gloom.

Philippe Ducos's eyes were closed. He had been drifting away to Peter's growling voice. Now he jumped awake as he felt the quick hands of the pirates running through the pockets of the blue tunic his wife had lined two years before.

'Stop squirming, Frog!' Fletcher cackled. 'Aye, Pat? Don't it make more sense to shoot him first then relieve him?'

'Maybe,' Devlin murmured, his face lowered to avoid the pleading eyes of Philippe Ducos.

Fletcher had been a deserter, had leaped into his pirate life with glee a month before Patrick Devlin had been dragged aboard.

To Devlin, who had spent years amongst the king's ships, manservant to Captain John Coxon, the pirate ship was but a passing inconvenience. He had signed their articles without protest and kept his distance from the ones he had beaten back and striped with blade when they had chanced upon the *Noble* in the North African straits.

Of all the officers and sailors of the *Noble*, the pirates marvelled how it was the tall, black-haired servant who had carved a circle of defiance in front of the cabin as the others ran and the deck burned.

They had laughed as he stood before them in his shabby, ill-fitting suit and danced, against Peter Sam no less, who had strode forward and twisted the sword from Devlin's hand as if plucking it from a child.

He would bide his time. Keep low. He did not mind the men themselves, for some of his old days amongst the fishermen of St Malo had fringed along the blade of the '*écumeur des mers*', skimming off the surface of the sea rather than underneath it. But this was not his life. Merry enough, but too short for his liking.

From Ducos's pockets they pulled out an empty tobacco tin, a small flint wrapped in a strip of white leather, a thimble, a handkerchief and just the bowl piece of a clay pipe.

The Frenchman resisted more as he realised that death was closing. He began to struggle. Garbling French at them. His little English useless now as panic crept over him.

More words, pleading words, came babbling from him. At some hushed sound Devlin stopped and listened hard as the soft accent repeated itself.

Devlin's hands clamped against the Frenchman's shoulders. Their eyes locked as he grabbed the Frenchman's shirt, pulling him up, Sam Fletcher flung aside.

The Frenchman met his stare and almost smiled as he knew that this one at least understood his promise. Philippe Ducos nodded desperately to the serious, dark face and swore to God.

Fletcher watched, perplexed, at the two almost embracing in some confidence. His simple grasp of humanity had noted that an oath of some kind had passed between the two, and all Fletcher knew of oaths was that the very next words from the desk would be '...and that will be half a guinea.'

But the babbling Frog was still going on, and Peter had asked for the jacket, and Peter had asked for the death, and that bloody Frog was still going on and on and Patrick was listening to it, for Christ's sake. Enough.

Fletcher stood back just far enough to pull his pistol clear and fire into the side of the Frenchman's skull, all three of them reeling from the shock of fire and blood, but only the Frenchman falling.

The crows took to the air again, laughing over the wicked court of men, as the explosion ripped away Ducos's final pleas.

Fletcher spat at the trembling corpse, the Frenchman still lisping some pointless utterance.

Devlin could taste the bitter blood of the man on his lips from the spatter. Fletcher laughed as the Irishman wiped the blood away with the dead man's linen.

He started to pull off the jacket, still maniacally chuckling at Devlin's bloodied face. Devlin cursed him as he knelt down and started to pull at the Frenchman's brown leather boots. The boots were old, probably the man's father's before him, but they were good.

'What you doing, Pat?'

'This Frog might have feet as big as mine, for a change. My shoes have had it. These'll do.'

'Aye. Perhaps the stench will be better and all. What was all that Frog-talk he was jawing about? You get any of that, Pat?' Fletcher had freed the coat from the limp body and then fingered through the scant effects, not listening for an answer and missing entirely the slow movement Devlin had made to lay his hand to his pistol butt. He touched it, brushed the lock with his palm, then went back to hauling off the boots.

'No. Just thought I might try. Seemed like he had something to say.'

'Aye, well, teaches him for being a Frog, don't it? I'm having the tobacco tin. Peter said we could takes what we wants.' Then he added, 'But don't tell him, mate. You know what he's like. He'll have it himself and leave me the thimble.' Fletcher carried up the tunic and skipped away, burying the tin in his waistcoat.

Sitting down, Devlin had put one boot on, and indeed they were as if made for him, despite the dampness of the blood that his stocking was soaking up.

Pulling the other over his calf, he inched his eyes around the circle of trees. Fletcher had gone. He was alone with the dead.

He felt into the leather. Sure enough, there was a folded parchment inside, just as Philippe Ducos had said there would be. Devlin allowed one finger to brush the paper, then pulled the rest of the boot on. He made a throwing motion, as if tossing a small pebble he had found inside. The only one to watch the act was the dead Philippe Ducos.

Devlin stood and looked down at the Frenchman, who had

sat huddled below deck with them for the past week. His shy separation from the crew had mirrored Devlin's own first days aboard. He thought of old man Kennedy, long dead now, telling him when he had first escaped to London from a foaming-mouthed magistrate in Ireland, never to give away too much about yourself, not for pride's sake: 'But for lest someone finds a reason to hang you for it, Patrick.'

There had never been a reason to tell his new companions that he spoke French like a *corsaire*, after the murder of Kennedy had put him to his feet again and to the forts and coasts of Brittany to barely survive as a fisherman. Forced to learn from his coarse fellows, who laughed at his clumsy Irish vowels, then donning the Marine Royale tunic himself for a short time, before the protective wing of Captain Coxon had swept over him.

Devlin absently checked the flint in his pistol, screwing it tighter, as he turned to take the long walk back to the shore.

Philippe Ducos lay dead, his blood already matting hard on the grass and being inspected by tropical ants. Mosquitoes flew in and out of the crack in his head like escaping dreams.

The book that was his short military life had closed with the snap of a pistol from a man who could not write his own name.

The last of the crew of a French sloop that had delivered a fortune of the king's own gold to a secret island in the Caribbean now grew cold in the afternoon heat. The location of the gold remained nestled roughly in the boots that were now calmly striding away. The only sound in the small glade was from the busily curious insects gathering on the fallen Frenchman.

Chapter One

X

Stepping from the damp closeness of the jungle to the blinding brightness of the beach took a moment of adjustment. Devlin shielded his eyes from the glare of the sand. He had been given no order other than to assure the death of the Frenchman, so he took the time to ponder the significance of the parchment hidden in the dead man's boots.

He moved down to a rocky vantage along the edge of the jungle, every step reminding him of the folded secret rubbing against his calf.

He sat on the volcanic outcrop and squinted out to sea. They had landed on the east of the island, which had provided them the best sounding, and now, as Devlin stared out, he could just make out the coast of Africa herself, stretching like a line of black ink drawn across the horizon, an enormous blanket of thunderous dark clouds threatening to swallow her. The archipelago the Frenchman had led them to was more than thirty leagues distant, yet as far as Devlin's gaze panned, his view was the dark shore of an enormous other world. He had never walked upon the land of nightmarish beasts and black backs that shouldered the wealth of the New World, but had seen the remnants of men who had found disease Africa's only promise. Still, what point a sailor, if home were all he craved?

In the offing, the *Lucy* sat. A black-and-white two-mast brigantine. Square-rigged on the foremast, gaff-rigged on the main, with a full set of jibs and staysails for speed and agility. A young ship, fourteen years out of Chatham, although most of her spars and yards had been cannibalised from older souls. She had the extravagance of both capstan over windlass and wheel over tiller, and a quarterdeck that made every sloop of war look twice upon her.

Eighty feet long with only eight six-pounders, she was a baby compared to the French and English frigates that Devlin was used to, but she could move as swiftly as running your finger across a map.

Stern and bow, the pirates' stanchion mounted three pairs of swivel guns along the rails. These half-pound falconets, loaded with grape, could devastate an opposing crew, peppering the shrouds and decks, pulling at flesh like fish hooks. Two further six-pounders, one placed as a chaser, the other aft, peeped out of the *Lucy*'s hull through crudely cut ports, but by far the pirates' most deadly weapons were the men themselves.

Fully armed, weapons kept immaculately clean and dry through wax and tallow strip, each man was formidable with a musket; even Devlin, a poacher in his youth, an old matchlock his bedside companion, was denied a musket until he came up to their standard.

In a 'surprisal' at sea, groups of them stood in the rigging, firing off rounds, as casually as shelling nuts, down into the prize, and every shot killed or maimed. Two shots could splice a sheet. Four could bring down a yard. Six men aloft were worth more than one twelve-pounder, and each man could fire three to the gun's pitiful one, his only pause to wipe the stinging powder from his red-rimmed eyes.

The *Lucy*. Overmanned fit to bursting. The sheer numbers of men sealed most of their victories, with a merchant often shy to defend his trade against a comparative army of drunken, cursing maniacs bearing down upon him.

To make room amongst the cramped decks, any spare bit of wood that was not necessary to float went overboard. Bulkheads were ripped out, cabins, doors and tables removed. Men slept on the open deck or close together below, often 'matelot' style, sharing hammocks and blankets and eating meals in the open air upon rugs and sailcloth. Such closeness mocked the fourteen inches allotted to a sailor upon a king's ship, and it was for the good of all that you got on with the man you slept, ate and fought beside. Ever since the old Tortuga buccaneers, this notion of brotherhood had marked the pirates' success. The 'Brethren of the Coast' both in name and most certainly in number.

Out of Devlin's long waistcoat came a muslin bag of tobacco. He placed it on the rock, first checking for dampness. Taking his clay pipe from his pocket, he blew out any lint and filled it with the Virginian blend introduced to a drop of port some months before.

Lifting his head to check for eyes upon him, aware that his mates could appear at any moment, Devlin pulled out the possession most prized before Philippe Ducos's gift.

A small, narrow tube. Hardly four inches long. Silver. A laughing devil engraved on the top. At the slip of a thumbnail, the devil could be prised up to reveal a dozen narrow pinewood sticks coated in an awful-smelling substance.

Inside the lid, a roughened glassy surface sparked the wood into life, and before Devlin had shaken out the flame and tossed the wood to the sea, the silver tube was back in his pocket. The tube was a gift from his former master from the *Noble*, John Coxon. At the time, Captain Coxon was dying of dysentery in Cape Coast Castle and was unaware of making the 'gift'.

He sucked on his pipe, drawing it into life, avoiding the urge to study the paper that Ducos's fate had given him. From the Frenchman's final, desperate outburst he had only gathered the promise of a map to a king's fortune, guarded and hidden. A fortune in gold, stored as a stronghold for the French forces in the Antilles.

Until he looked at the paper he would not know what hand it would deal him. But his worst fate would be to be found studying a map taken from a dead prisoner for some unknown personal gain. In his contemplation, his eyes had carried back out to sea. He noticed, reflective, amused, that his exhalations of smoke matched the crashing of the afternoon surf.

'Did you not think that you should declare those boots to your quartermaster, then, Patrick?' He turned with a start to see Peter Sam standing by his side. The others were following across the white sand, William Magnes carrying a lifeless goat across his shoulders.

Devlin cursed himself. He had not heard a distant shot to explain for the goat, and coming across the sand the party should have sounded like carts on cobblestones to his poacher's ears.

Peter Sam, one eye closed against the glare of the sun, spied Devlin's new footwear. 'Pretty nice boots that Frenchman had, eh? Did you not want to share them?'

Devlin's composure returned as five pairs of envious and greedy eyes, including Fletcher's, were turned to his boots.

'Now be fair, Peter: we'd look pretty foolish wearing a boot between us.'

All, apart from the fiery quartermaster, cackled in agreement, Fletcher, in his ignorance, the loudest.

'Get that meat to the boat!' Peter Sam growled with his

Bristol drawl through his red beard, glaring at them all as they grumbled past him. He turned back to Devlin.

He had disliked Devlin from the moment they had relieved him from his duty aboard the *Noble*. Although clearly a servant, he had been unwilling to join his pirate rescuers who had so easily mauled the English sixth-rate. Now, Devlin sat before him, grinning behind his pipe, perched on a rock, blood speckled on his linen shirt, the boots in question similarly dappled.

'Suppose I want those boots for myself, Patrick? And what else did you gets from that Frog?'

'If you go back there' – Devlin indicated to the jungle with his pipe – 'you'll find a thimble, a flint and a broken pipe.' With a flourish he pulled out the handkerchief, also covered in blood. 'But you're welcome to this if you want, Peter.'

Peter Sam leaned towards Devlin's face. 'I wouldn't mind trying those boots, Patrick.'

Devlin dropped off the rock, his face levelled to Peter Sam's, and he passed a look up and down the brute. Unlike most of the crew, who wore the finest linen and waistcoats, albeit tallow- and pitch-stained, motley as harlequins, Peter Sam wore goat-leather breeches and a leather jerkin. Gracing his chest was a deadly bandoleer of cartouche boxes and generations of pistols holstered with leather straps. He was the image of an old-time '*boucanier*'.

'I took these boots off a dead man. You'll have to do the same.' Devlin brushed past and walked to the boat, Peter Sam's eyes at his back.

The row back to the *Lucy* was a quiet one. Thomas Deakins, the young lad whom Peter Sam had led away into the jungle, and never strayed far from, now wore Philippe Ducos's blue tunic.

Devlin had become accustomed to the closeness of some of the pirate brethren to each other, and when Peter took the arm of Thomas on the island, no one had raised a head. In many ways the closeness was of benefit to a ship. Some of the men worked in pairs like twins, and worked gladly. Every man seemed to be a 'bosun' rather than just a mate, running the shrouds and ratlines as smoothly as painting a wall.

Despite the drunken nature of their days, there was no job neglected or position lacking. That which could not be spliced or repaired could soon be stolen or bartered, and every sheet hauled or rope reeved was done for the purpose of filling the coffers of all. Their songs were sung for the joy of the life and not just to bolster the rhythm of the work. They had an envious camaraderie that Devlin had not seen since his days out of the close-knit ports of St Malo. Peter Sam's dark gaze from across the boat, however, suggested there were exceptions.

The boat was belayed to the *Lucy*, left to loll alongside as the lads all clambered up the tumblehome with a rampant thirst.

The lack of the *cochon-marron*, the marooned brown pig that the Frenchman had promised with his drawings and mime, was disappointing, but there were goats, most probably landed by some long-dead Portuguese adventurer as a larder for the world, and an oasis of fruit that might inspire the captain to stay and supply.

Not that food seemed to be a concern in the company that Devlin now kept. On his first day, the afternoon the *Noble* had been lost, Devlin and Alastair Lewis, the only prisoners from the English frigate, ate a pork and mango stew with cobbles of fresh bread and a shilling's worth of butter, whilst being questioned by the charismatic captain, Seth Toombs, who sliced corners of cheese and wedges of apples straight into his mouth off the back of an ivory-hilted blade.

Now, Captain Toombs lay sprawled on the deck in front of his open cabin, all limbs outstretched across a red and gold Indian carpet that, back in London, would have graciously filled any gentleman's hall, but perhaps not in its current frayed and rent condition.

It was hours past noon. No course to go for. Every soul on board had supped a draught or two whilst waiting for the longboat's return. The captain's burgundy tricorne lay across his eyes, and he lifted a corner of it to watch Peter Sam as he approached.

'Ah, Peter,' Toombs yawned, 'I gather there be no pig farm on that there island? Seeing as we are now absent of our French lubber?' Toombs's dialect was as far westbound as Peter's.

'Aye, Cap'n. No pig farm. But there be plenty of goat if we want to stay. Fruit too. Mangoes, plantains.'

'Not plantains, please, Peter. Say not plantains! Mate, my guts will turn blue for another!' He lay back down with a belch.

'Aye, Cap'n.' Peter bent down, swooped up the captain's leather mug and idled over to the half-hog of punch that was permanently on deck.

Devlin watched the party from the longboat dissipate amidships. The dead goat, his sorry head hanging, was carried below. The quartermaster had his back to him and was on his second draught. Toombs appeared to be asleep; then the glint of a catlike eye beneath the cock of his hat betrayed otherwise. A hand beckoned to Devlin.

Devlin came across the wet deck towards Seth Toombs, who was now raised on an elbow and smiling him closer, quite gentrified in his brown twill coat and scarlet brocade waistcoat. He was as young as Devlin maybe – not yet thirty; but rough drink and Newfoundland winds had weathered his face and made coarse his blond hair. Toombs, Peter Sam and old William Magnes were the original three who had stolen a sloop out of Newfoundland two years before.

They were codmen, pressed into freezing their youth away along the harsh North American coast. One winter had been enough, and the three Bristol men slipped away in the night, just after Peter had slipped away the life of the sloop's master. The first man he had killed for Seth Toombs.

A dozen stories later, Toombs was the elected captain of a hundred men, but Devlin had summed him up as all swagger and stagger. A lucky, dirty soul.

'Now, Patrick. Mister Devlin, sir.' Still looking asleep, Toombs spoke on. 'I have had a wonderful conversation with Mister Lewis this fine morning.'

'Captain?'

'Mister Lewis.' He rolled himself up to sit. 'Your former navigator on that burning frigate you frequented? Come closer, man!'

Devlin moved forward to within a step of the captain. All about them, men were laughing in cross-legged groups, sharing mugs of punch: their diet of rum, water and limes stirred with muscovado sugar.

'Who has my mug?' Toombs asked the air about him. 'Never mind. Sit down, Patrick, and listen to me.' He patted his carpet to motion Devlin to him. Devlin shifted his sword and crouched, one knee down, his left hand on the hilt.

'You have performed well, Patrick. I be proud of your

schooling.' Toombs smiled. 'On that French sloop you fought like a true pirate. I'm shining of you, sir, so I am!' He slapped Devlin heartily. 'But,' he whispered, 'did you not think that those few men fought rather hard for what little they had to offer? Would you not be of a mind to think that now?'

'I don't know, Captain.'

'Shush, never mind, sir, never mind.' He patted Devlin's forearm patriarchally. 'However, as I say, Mister Lewis and I have been a-talking.'

Alastair Lewis was the navigator on board the *Noble.* Like Devlin he had resisted capture. But whereas Devlin gave defence to the ship when the dead no longer could or the living had fled to the boats, Lewis and Acting Captain Thorn had locked themselves in the Great Cabin. The pirates had broken through the door just as the blaze got beyond Thorn's control.

They had used Thorn for target, hanging by his arms across the main's yardarm, after they discovered he had burned all the charts, the cause of the fire, and thrown Lewis's tools to the sea. Then the fire had spread, assuring the pirate's half-victory, and the loss of the ship.

When they drank to the tale the day after, the more 'romantic' of them told how they had heard the beams of the old girl scream.

'Come and see what we were talking about.' He had stood up and gently tugged Devlin into the cabin, or rather the shell of one.

The doors were missing and every chair. The customary accoutrements that Devlin was used to were absent. There were no bookshelves, no desk nor cot, no personal effects. Everything that could be ripped out was gone. Only the hanging lanterns, the lockers beneath the windows and the large table remained as furniture. The austerity of the rest of the room made the table seem cluttered and chaotic, piled as it was with navigational instruments and towers of papers.

The three small paned bottle-glass windows were open but, even from this distance, Africa crept in with a dark humidity and Devlin's trailing hair clung to his neck, filtering a trickle of sweat down his back.

Toombs ambled forward, his hat brushing the overhead. He leaned on the far side of the table and waved Devlin closer; on its return his hand strayed over a bottle of Jerez wine and he took a swig.

Devlin stepped to the table. This was the first time he had been in the cabin, despite the truth that, unlike on a regulated ship, the pirate captain's cabin was not sacrosanct, merely a sleeping berth for the captain – a small reverence to title but a room that belonged to the whole.

The captain ate or drank no better than any other soul on board, and God forgive him if he did.

He rarely even fought in boardings but took two shares in all that was taken in deference to the fact that he would most surely hang when the day came to remove his hat and bow his head.

He had one overpowering responsibility that his leadership was based on: 'To where do we sail?' His was the plan. The luck. The path.

For this a good navigator was essential. On a pirate vessel, common sailors made up the ship. What often surprised their victims was not the pirates' interest in their gold and jewels but the ravenous search for medicines, tools and sea charts.

To many the navigator's skills were nothing short of necromancy and his capture mandatory. To this end Alastair Lewis was their prize on seizing the *Noble*, but Thorn's panic in burning everything he was able to had cost them dear.

'I have a problem, Patrick.' Toombs motioned a hand across the objects on the table. 'I have sailors and gentlemen of fortune up to my ears, but no dedicated soul to navigate.'

Devlin looked down at the charts and tools. A wooden Portuguese astrolabe, a Mercator world map, an African coastal chart that took in Madagascar, a map of the Antilles and the Florida coast weighted down by conch and stone, and an enormous French backstaff stretching across the table.

On one side were piles of papers and oilskin wallets holding more charts. The *Lucy*'s original gimbal compass took pride of place in the centre with a couple of wooden dividers hovering near a crock inkwell.

Innocuous objects. The only keys one needed to unlock the heavens, but to the unfamiliar hand and eye they were as unreachable as the stars they divined.

The pirates' world was a small one. The hardest route Toombs had ever sailed was the capricious twelve hundred miles from Newfoundland to Providence on board the *Cricket*, the small sloop that the three old standers originally stole.

Now, with a hundred able men and a larger ship, they cruised the same paths month in, month out.

In summer, they sailed the Newfoundland coast, endeavouring to catch the cod merchants and other traders sailing to the Mediterranean or back home to England.

In winter, they would head southeast, following the trade winds to Africa, hoping to hit the Sixteenth Parallel, close to the Verdes, to pick off the traders who waited to spy the islands before heading west to the Indies.

Eventually the winds would carry them four degrees down to Africa's Guinea coast, where they could catch the fat galley slavers embarking on their second leg of the triangular trade that ruled the world, or the Dutch and English Indiamen on the trawl from the East, sailing low in the water, laden with spices and rich fabrics ripe for plunder.

If their sweet trade gathered too much attention, they would head west to spend the rest of the winter in the Caribbee islands, running as close as they could back up to the Sixteenth Parallel to catch the merchantmen heading back to Europe with their rum, sugar, tobacco, cotton and molasses purchased off the backs of slaves.

Then, as May appeared, they would sail back to Newfoundland or the inlets of the Carolinas, before the hurricanes, which wrecked unwary ships more than all the powder ever lit, came to visit the Caribbean.

So it went on. Months of pirating interspersed with times of careening on deserted spits of land and wild carousing in wicked forsaken holes, and all the while being hunted by all the navies of the world trying to protect the interests of obese investors and mentally affected kings and queens who had made theft, cruelty and exploitation their nations' proudest achievements.

Toombs enlightened Devlin that a pirate ship freed the men from the torturous labour of the navy watch.

A pirate led an idle life. No longer was he expected to turn a sand glass and ring a bell on every half-hour for every four hours of the day and night; thus the calculation of time and one of the aids to accurate longitude was lost. The longitude itself depended on the varied maps acquired from ransacked cabins, for each of the voyaging nations of the old world held their own meridian.

At local noon, the sun at its zenith, they took a latitude and a speed.

'From this I can plot where I'll be by the same time on the morrow. If we travel at five knots I'll gather two degrees of latitude by noon the next day, don't you see?'

Devlin saw. Any weathered salt let out of the waist of a ship could plot a course by dead reckoning, providing he knew where he set off from, his bearing and speed, and tried to maintain a constant.

The mystery, the lost leagues, came with the clouded sky, the starless night. The man before the mast needed a Pole Star reading, where the altitude of the star against the horizon would give the latitude.

For greater accuracy a skilled navigator, an 'artist', could measure the altitude of over fifty other stars and compare that to the astrolabe, the almost magical disc that showed the stars and their latitudes throughout the year. The Portuguese, the magicians of the sea, were its masters.

Without the stars to guide, a navigator would rely on the ship's 'waggoner', the eclectic collection of maps and charts, and his own dead reckoning. Lonely hours spent by tallow light hunched over a chart, a loupe sweeping over reef markers and soundings, making the jump of imagination to connect the scratches of ink, the veiled warnings of dead men, to the pitching and heaving beast outside the cabin door. That was the art. Toombs needed someone to turn the flat paper charts into a globe.

'I can't navigate like that, Patrick. It's not in my soul! I can reckon with the best of 'em, but I needs someone with the mind for the whole manner of it!' His eyes gleamed. 'My thoughts are, Patrick, that if I can navigate well, the whole world could open up to us! The East, the South Seas! Cut away from these lanes! With good longitude, I could save weeks off a voyage and run rings round those navy boys!' He slapped the table passionately and swigged at his wine.

'To what end would this be my concern, Captain?' Devlin squinted as the sun lowered into the window.

Toombs began the account that Lewis had told him. How Devlin was the manservant to Captain John Coxon. How Coxon was a skilled navigator, one who could tell where he was in the world just by fathoms and the samples the soundings brought up, even by the colour of the sea and the yaw of the ship. How, when Coxon went to take his morning readings, Devlin was there with his coffee, and for every reading throughout the day. That Devlin was present whenever Lewis and Coxon compared readings, when courses were plotted and noted.

'I would begin to suspect, mate, that it would be not entirely unreasonable to assume that some of that knowledge might "soak" in, so to speak, you might say.'

Devlin could not disagree. The years with Coxon had been instructive. Coxon had shared his books with Devlin when he discovered with delight that his steward could read and read well. Devlin helped teach the young midshipmen the duty of the traverse board, the peg and wood diagram that kept the course and speed of the ship throughout the watch.

He could 'box' the compass in French, to Coxon's amusement, and Coxon would beam with pride when he slapped the backstaff into Devlin's hands and bade him read the correct latitude, if he would be so kind, after some lieutenant had fuddled his way through an incoherent attempt.

After too much Madeira and flank steak, Coxon would bemoan Devlin's Irish birth and his brief dalliance under the *pavillion-blanc* flag of the Marine Royale that would deny him a fine second or third lieutenant.

'But perhaps a sailing master you could be, Patrick? That could be done. It is only exams, after all, don't you know?' Then Devlin would clear the table, brush Coxon's hat and coat before returning with the last black coffee of the night.

Just how much Lewis had spoken of him, how much of his past, would need careful teasing out of Toombs.

He looked Toombs square in the eye. 'No more than anything else, Captain. But Lewis was Coxon's navigator. His is the skill.'

Toombs turned away to the stern window, which was glowing in the afternoon sun. 'Lewis disapproves of us... gentlemen.'

It was only then that Devlin had noticed Alastair Lewis's absence. Ever since they were both pressed into service, Lewis was either on the quarterdeck with the captain or occupied in the sparse cabin. He looked at Toombs's silhouetted back and watched his head lower.

Lewis was passionate about his loyalties, that had been obvious. He seemed to clash with Toombs every day, and Toombs, Devlin was sure, would ultimately distrust him to occupy such an important position on his quarterdeck.

Behind him, Devlin could hear the songs of the crew calling in the evening, songs of lubrication and bordellos, the friendly creaking of the boards beneath him and the slow lapping of the sea against the hull. He waited for Toombs to speak.

'If you knew him, and had any kinship with him, you may go and see him.' Toombs turned. 'But I'm afraid, Pat, he's been blinded by some of the mates.'

He elaborated that he had wanted Lewis to plot a course to St Nicholas, one of the Verde Islands. The course should be taken away from the coast to avoid patrols, and continue through the night for added safety, especially as it was only weeks since they had left a burning English frigate near the Straits of Gibraltar. Toombs's own weakness with navigation had required Lewis's skill. Lewis had refused and Toombs had taken him below, in the dark and heat, and forced him onto his knees. A thick, knotted oakum rope, coarse as broken glass, had been put round his head, across his eyes, and twisted over and over, tighter and tighter. Some sweet tongue had christened the act 'the rosary of pain'; most just called it 'woollding'.

Usually the victim will have a change of heart as the ears start to rip, the blood starts to run down the neck and the eyes are forced back into the skull. Lewis just screamed on and on, until his eyelids tore and his eyes began to grind against the burning knots. The men had shocked themselves, their torturer's giggles switching to heavy, almost carnal gasps. They let him collapse to the wet, dark deck. Cowering in his own blood. Retching in pain.

'If you don't want to see him, we'll just shoot him and give him to the sharks. The lads could do with the sport.' He placed his knuckles upon the table. 'Then you can join him, or sail my ship with me.' He looked Devlin up and down with a sway of the head. 'Fine boots by the way there, mate.'

Below, Devlin was greeted by the stench of bodies and rotten food fuming in the African heat. He left the final step of the companion, instinctively lowering his head as he walked through the dark.

Sunlight slatted through from the hatches above, thick dust swimming in its rays. The songs of the men pitched just above the incessant moaning of the ship as Devlin weaved his way past swaying lanterns and piles of stores towards a dark lump sitting slumped against sacks of rice.

He knelt before Lewis, pushing his dragging sword behind. Lewis was trembling, sobbing. Across his eyes his own blood-stained linen blindfolded his pain. Devlin spoke Lewis's name softly, and the man jerked.

'Patrick? Is that you, man? Thank the Lord! Have you come to save me?' In the months he had known Alastair Lewis this was the first time he had addressed Devlin as 'man'. It was slightly more reverent than the 'boy' he was used to. He only recalled Lewis barking demands for port and coffees, clean shoes and linen, as Lewis took advantage of his position and knew what Irishmen were for. He pitied Lewis's fate, but only as he might that of a rabid dog.

Since their capture he had never even glanced at Devlin. Lewis had replaced Coxon's quarterdeck with Toombs's and simply argued slightly more on this one. Devlin wanted to see him, to find out what had been said about him in Lewis's torture.

He touched Lewis's shoulder. 'No, Mister Lewis, sir. You're too ill to live.'

Lewis's hand reached out for Devlin and grabbed his arm. 'Surely not, Patrick! My wife! Tell them about my wife!'

Devlin knew nothing about Lewis's wife. He only knew that Lewis was a navigator appointed by the South Sea Company to attend to their interests in the *Noble*'s escorting of one of their slavers. He removed Lewis's hand.

'I need to know what you told them about me, sir.'

'About you?' Lewis turned his head as if listening for other voices. 'What would you have to do with anything, man! Just get me out of here! Help me!'

Devlin's concern was that Lewis knew he could speak French. He had lived for two years in St Malo before rolling into the Marine Royale, and happy they were to enlist an Irishman to hamper the English. He was only a couple of months in service before Coxon had captured their sloop of war.

As a prisoner, Devlin stepped forward to negotiate between

Coxon and the French officers, thinking only of his belly and dislike for chains. Coxon had found an Irishman in the French navy amusing, keeping him as his servant rather than imprisoning him with the rest.

That had been four long years ago, the end of the war, and Coxon had never tired of showing off his Irish Frenchman.

If this were known, if the thought had rattled around inside the most sodden brain that some word had passed between Devlin and the Frenchman, either aboard the *Lucy* or on the loneliness of the island, he was sure he would be standing in his own blood. No secrets on a ship. And dead men do not lie.

It clearly gnawed at Toombs that the ten French marines, without officers, had fought like tigers to protect nothing but a couple of hogsheads of stale water and rancid pork. They had met their deaths for that rat food, all but one, and he could only speak his own damned tongue.

They had gathered slowly from him, if not painfully, that the sloop was voyaging to the island for the marooned pig to gain stores, hence their empty hold. Toombs had decided to fulfil this plan, as fresh meat was always welcome. Now, with the promise of pork exposed as a lie, Toombs would be wondering again why the sloop sailed empty, with only ten common sailors on board.

Devlin's shoulders appeared from below and he looked above at the spreading purple sky. He saw Toombs and Peter Sam at the taffrail with a pipe and a mug each, as idle as any gentleman on his country-house balcony.

Toombs saw Devlin approach and tipped his hat back. Peter Sam turned his head to follow Toombs's gaze and immediately stepped towards Devlin to block him as he came up the length of the short stair.

'Where do you think you're stepping, man?'

Devlin pulled himself to the top of the rail, one foot on the deck, staring straight into Peter Sam's black eyes.

'He's our new "artist",' Toombs yelled. 'Ain't you, Patrick?'

Devlin pushed past Peter without a glance and walked to the rail, standing next to Toombs and looking out to mighty Africa.

'Aye, Captain. If you'll have me.'

'Why was I not told of this?' Peter Sam's broad form squared up to the two of them.

Toombs slammed his fist on the rail, almost smashing his pipe in his hand. 'How dare you question me, sir! I needs an artist, and Patrick knows the art well enough to remove the burden from you or I!'

'You don't know that, Captain. He's just some lickerish ponce's waister!' Peter spat. Devlin said nothing and began the routine of filling his own pipe.

'Then he shall have the moment to prove it, Peter. You can summon the men for me, if it's not too much of a trouble for you, mate.'

Peter ground his jaw and spun round to face the drunken brethren beneath. 'Pay attention, you dogs!' he bellowed.

The heads turned and stopped their singing and gaming. An air of wariness spread around in whispers. 'The captain will address you, lads, so pipes down!'

Toombs snapped his coat, tugged the front cock of his hat down and winked at Devlin as he approached the audience looking up at him from the waist of the ship, his mug held high in his left hand.

'Lads! I have good news!' He spread his arms, looked kindly into the faces he liked. 'I know I promised you that English frigate, but that young quim burned it beneath our feet!' A rousing cheer, raised mugs and laughter.

'And our gentleman artist from the lordly South Sea Company has been most "blinded" to our cause!' The men choked on their drink at this one. 'But our newly acquired Patrick Devlin, from the same frigate, the servant you recall painfully who fought you away from the captain's cabin, has agreed to be our new artist!' A satisfied murmur. 'I have a plan, lads, to sail to old St Nick tomorrow.' He closed his right hand into a fist.

'I aims to capture the Portuguese governor there and hold him to ransom! The plan will be revealed to you on the morn, boys, and Patrick will take us there!'

He raised his empty mug. The men roared and took that as the signal to return to their drink. They cared little for their destiny tomorrow – or next year. They would fight and sail when the sun rose and set. The reason immaterial.

Toombs turned back to Devlin and Peter Sam. 'There. Now, Patrick, make any preparations that you need to sail me to St Nicholas. What happened 'twixt you and Lewis, by and by, mate?'

As if in answer, a crack rang out below deck, and Toombs's eyes shot down to the empty belt where Devlin's left-locked pistol used to be.

'I told him it was best not to be fed to the sharks alive.' Devlin tapped his forehead and stepped down to retrieve his pistol.

Chapter Two

✕

Cape Coast Castle, African Gold Coast, April 1717

John Coxon dragged himself to the top of the West Tower, the wind-vane tower that captured the delicious morning African sun before it began to sear. He hung on to the battlements, breathing deep, trying to stave off the threat of nausea. As he had been every morning for the past three months, he was in his full working clothes, despite the aching heat. There was no uniform officer dress but, like most, Coxon had a rotating wardrobe of white breeches and stockings, white linen shirts and dull waistcoats, all wrapped in a square-cut, dark twill greatcoat with muted black piping and brass buttons, which now, after his illness, sloped from his shoulders; he had been forced as well to splice a new notch on his breeches belt.

He looked up and drew in the sea. By the beat of the sun on his back he knew it to be past ten, but there were still some straggling fishermen skimming up to the shore beneath him. The guns to the left and right of him stared out also, like silent sentinels. Nobody ever manned them, and the salt from the sea and air was eating them away. On the first day that he was able to walk any distance he had found a swallow's nest in one of them, the touch-hole carelessly painted over.

The bleached white castle sat on Africa's Gold Coast. It

was the final door that millions of slaves would walk through before they began the long journey to the Americas. Even now, beneath Coxon's feet in the gaol below, nine hundred men stood naked together, waiting for the slavers to arrive, unable to sit down for lack of space and the hardened excrement that made up the floor, in a dark hell that had originally been made for just one hundred and fifty prisoners.

Coxon had sailed to Cape Coast as captain of the *Noble*, the twenty-four-gun frigate he had captained for almost a decade. He had watched her sail away without him, watched her escutcheon until he could no longer make out her name.

There had been delays in waiting for their slaver to be ready to sail and, whilst enjoying the hospitality of the eccentric General Phipps, Coxon had been struck down with the tropics plague of dysentery, or as it was known rather more colloquially, the 'vacuums'.

He was being paid a handsome twelve-and-a-half per cent commission from the South Sea Company to escort the galley to the colonies, and even with a fifteen per cent death rate on the cargo, he figured he might come away with enough to start an emporium of some kind in Boston or one of the cities of the five major colonies. The ones that at least had paved roads.

In the wars, life was simpler, but ten years of conflict, of politics against the French and Spanish, had taken his prime years. This year, at forty, he found himself in a world of trade and companies, powdered wigs and ebony canes.

There was no rich estate or lordly hearth for him to return to – not for him, a clergyman's son – so he had stayed on, taken his peacetime cut in pay. As the navy halved its numbers, he had seen men who had fought beside him now beg for bread in the streets of Portsmouth, and hang around the

Crown Inn hoping for a chance meeting with an old, generous officer.

In peace he had lost most of his officers to the merchant trade, and in his illness he had been forced to leave his ship to the young 'snotty' who was his first lieutenant. He had ordered Thorn to return to England, against his particular articles and orders, rather than attempt the sail to the Indies without him. Thorn had jumped into a dead officer's cot a week before he had transferred to the *Noble*, a second lieutenant of eager if limited ability, judging by his age and date of commission, almost thirty and still unmade. Coxon had followed with a letter explaining his decision and that General Phipps had requisitioned the very next able sloop to convey the slaver, but a fuming Alastair Lewis, the company's navigator, would reach England before the note. The decision would probably lose Coxon his commission from the South Sea Company, but he would rather that than lose the *Noble* to the pirates who had seethed in the Caribbean waters since the end of the war.

Besides, he had half expected to die.

The Guinea coast was infamous for the toll of death it exacted on the white man. Most of the soldiers who made up the hundred or so garrison were either dying or permanently diseased. Nearly all were convicted men who had chosen service rather than gaol.

No one had ever spoken ill to them of Cape Coast Castle, but only because no one ever returned. As one dying clerk managed to write home to warn those contemplating the offer in the cloisters of their cell: 'Rather run a remote hazard of being hanged at home than choose a transfer hither.'

Coxon had survived. Mostly down to his strength of will and the care bestowed on him by General Phipps's mulatto beauty, who had tended to him with local remedies within decent, clean quarters.

Phipps himself seemed fat and immune compared to the ghosts that haunted the rest of the castle. Coxon had noted that he serviced himself from the traders with fresh meats and other victuals. He had a vast orchard nearby that furnished him with fresh oranges, lemons, limes, paw-paws and bananas, as well as European crops he had cultivated. Meanwhile the soldiers, Coxon noted, subsisted on soups, biscuits and theft.

Coxon had been permitted to use Phipps's private walkway, and part of his convalescence had been this daily walk to the ramparts. Often he joined Phipps here, watching the Royal African and South Sea Company ships come in to take out the seemingly endless march of blacks.

Through Phipps's vellum and sharkskin telescope one could see the Dutch El Mina fort, barely two miles further down the coast, herding their purchases to the waiting cutters for ships bound to the South Americas. The Dutch companies reaping the rewards of the triple alliance against Spain that had granted them the *'asiento'* – contract – to transport slaves to their own colonies.

The innumerable tribes sold to both parties, and it was not uncommon for the tribal chief who sold his wares to the Dutch one week to find himself being shipped out through the door of Cape Coast Castle the next, his noble robes of office torn and burned for fear of lice.

It was often remarked upon, when looking at both these forts, that no gun faced inland, for any threat would come from a European front, not from an African one. Coxon, like many, wasted no pity on a nation that sold its own people; he only held a handkerchief to his face to stop the stench as they passed through the gates beneath him.

A voice straight off the docks at Wapping barked from the parade ground behind him. 'Mister Coxon, sir!'

He turned to see a mockery of a soldier in a sun-bleached, almost pink, tunic, grey breeches and sandals looking up at him.

'You will address me as Captain, boy!' Coxon was well lit in the sun, his brass buttons shining in the soldier's eyes. He was already moving to the steps.

'Yes, sir. Captain, sir.' He stood a little straighter, but not much. Coxon was almost upon him now.

'Don't shout at an officer, man. Approach me and wait for my attention!'

'Yes, sir. Sorry, sir.'

Coxon was right at his poxed nose. 'I'm a posted captain, boy, not a sir! I work for my bread! I'll use you for a hawser if you call me that again!'

'Sorry, sir. I mean, Captain, sir.' The soldier tried to look into the sun rather than at Coxon.

'Better, boy.' He took a step back to avoid the man's fetid breath. 'Be aware that you stink, man, and find yourself a pair of shoes. The king wears that uniform every day and you disgrace it. Now what do you have for me, boy?'

The man's head went empty. His mouth motioned something as he avoided the captain's eyes. Then he remembered the smell of bacon and kidneys.

'General Phipps would like you to join him for breakfast... Captain.'

'Noted.' Good. That meant news. Change. Action. Coxon relaxed. Calmed himself, clasping his hands behind his back. 'Dismiss.'

The soldier saluted badly, and turned and walked as quickly as he could towards his barracks.

Phipps had never invited him for breakfast before, though Coxon had often seen the dried remnants of the two-hour feast that ended in a nap, before an afternoon of fervent letter-writing back to England. Phipps never seemed to cease complaining back to Whitehall; mostly about the quality of the men he received, or the clerks sent to aid his governorship, and always again and again about his pitiful funding, for somewhere in his past Phipps had clearly paid attention when some wise soul had winked to him that the squeaky wheel gets the oil.

As for being invited to breakfast with Phipps, Coxon had learned one thing after numerous dinners: watch your plate.

Coxon, tricorne in hand, let himself into the private chambers that led straight from the chapel. General Phipps sat at the opposing broadside of a long, slightly warped table, ignorant of the man who had entered as he gorged on mashed potatoes mixed with egg, bacon and cabbage. He had fresh grapefruit juice and coffee in front of him, along with plates of bacon, the smell of which made Coxon's mouth draw tight with anticipation. He strode up to the table.

'Very kind of you to ask me to breakfast, General.' Coxon dragged a chair out without consent and placed his hat down. All around the table, Phipps's four brown children played, dressed like English princes but wearing bones and shells around their limbs. His concubine, for they were not officially married, floated up to Coxon with a porcelain cup of coffee. She placed the saucer down silently and smiled with antelope's eyes as she rustled backwards in her silks. Coxon permitted himself a moment to take in her jasmine scent as she backed away; then mentally he chided himself.

'Not at all, sir, not at all,' Phipps answered. 'I have need to speak with you.' A spray of potato as he spoke. Phipps was dressed in a simple white Arabian cotton shirt with the cuffs folded under themselves to prevent them straying into the myriad plates. His shirt was open to his ample, flaccid chest and Coxon spied the leather necklace of charms and bones, one of which also decorated his right wrist. Coxon noticed that, despite the informal attire, Phipps was wearing his powdered wig. He assumed this was a concession to his presence, rather than to hide any baldness.

'I must apologise to you that I have been rather slow in some of my administrative duties, although my clerks are idle sods in bringing these matters to my attention, sir.'

Coxon did not follow, and helped himself to some cold toast with his coffee. 'I'm sure you have nothing to apologise for, General.'

'Nevertheless, sir, I hope you will understand that there was no intention to delay your receipt of any information.'

'Information, General?' Coxon's heart beat faster.

'About your ship, man.'

Coxon pushed a plate of vinegar-soaked bacon away from him. 'Go on, General.'

'Letter for you, sir.' With one hand Phipps drained a crystal glass of grapefruit juice, and with the other tossed a packet of paper at the captain's place.

Coxon recognised the cheap waxen paper of the Admiralty at once and slowly opened the folded outer, the seal of which had been brazenly broken by another's hands. The letter would have arrived in a sailcloth packet, now absent.

Acceptably dated three weeks ago, it would have taken about two weeks to reach the castle. He was expecting orders, and true enough it did contain such, but the main of it had to be re-read, the paper becoming stretched flat, his knuckles whitening with the tension in his hands.

The *Noble* had been lost. The frigate that was his command throughout the war had been set ablaze by Acting Captain Thorn. Somewhere northwest of Africa she had been attacked by pirates. The South Sea Company's navigator and an unnamed servant had been captured. Fifteen men were dead including 'Captain' Thorn. The rest of the crew had escaped in the boats and had been rescued by a Dutch corvette three days later. They were now all in Gibraltar awaiting orders.

The room, the stale air, suddenly seemed more temperate. Coxon stood, scraping his chair roughly, and walked to one of the green-shuttered windows. The narrow window was open but no breeze came through. Like most colonial buildings, its design paid no account to the climate in which it sat. A Queen Anne country house had merely descended onto the edge of the jungle, and it, and all its occupants, sweated in the closeted halls. Coxon could just see the ocean beyond the white rocks. She rolled forever towards him and he longed to be poured back into her.

His ship was gone. Twenty-four twelve-pounders, most of which he had christened himself, their nicknames burned into their trucks, lay somewhere out there, never to fire again. She was his first captaincy. Built in 1670, she had fought in the War of the Grand Alliance and the heat of the Spanish Succession. Only two years ago she had been given almost three acres of new American oak. He turned to face Phipps.

'I'm to leave on the first passage back to England, sir. When would that be?'

'Indeed, sir. Indeed.' Phipps wiped his brow as his concubine fanned him. 'But there are all manner of things to consider.'

Coxon moved back to the table and stood with his left hand touching the letter. 'Such as what, General?'

'Consider this, sir.' He put down his napkin. 'You will return to the Admiralty as a captain without a ship. A ship, commissioned to sail to the Americas as an escort to the South Sea Company. Such commissions are what keep the navy afloat, sir. You, sir, involuntarily or not, have lost the ship and the commission. The company will not be happy with that, sir.'

Coxon knew Phipps was right. Somehow the world had gone mad with greed whilst he had spent nights scraping blood off his coat.

The government and the king relied on the growing spread of companies that were opening up the world for them, plundering lands and enslaving people for a guinea. A coin named after the stolen gold and stolen coast from which it came, a coin that Coxon had never seen but had bundles of promissory notes for. Phipps sat before him swollen and mottled, fattening himself on two thousand pounds a year whilst Coxon, one of the men who had allowed him to sit there, stood before him and had not been paid for two years, his pay-cut deducted in arrears.

'What would you suggest, General?'

'It might have occurred to you, Captain, that I have been burdened with a poor quality of men out here. They are wanton and lazy, sir, and it would be worth two hundred pounds a year to me to have a captain of the guard who could control them.' Coxon sat, picked up his papers, and listened.

'An enquiry may already have been conducted in your absence. Your galley sailed without your escort because you had ordered it home. I myself had to appoint a sloop for her, beyond my duty. Who knows what your situation is back home? But consider that here you could have command, pay, good food and pleasant company.' He smiled at his mistress, standing at his shoulder. 'I could write a commission for you to stay here at my request to fulfil my needs – and believe me, sir, my needs are never questioned in England. Never. What say you, man?'

Phipps did not smile or patronise. He stated facts, undeniable truths. Coxon could stay here. Why not, indeed? Removed and remote, checking over the guns and textiles coming in from England and shackling the slaves that went out in exchange. But there was something that perhaps Phipps could never understand. On a ship the world shrunk to a fingernail of existence. Every part of your day was ordered to a bell. You ate to it, you worked to it, you slept to it, the decision of what to do and when removed. You wore the clothes of your position. You mingled with the same people all year round, and the world ended at the rails. In that life all the exterior, superfluous nature of society was gone. A man was stripped down to what he was, not what society made of him.

Some could not face the introspection of the life, and Coxon himself had come across midshipmen who on land were the lord of the dance and kings of the set yet after a year at sea they could no longer look at themselves in the mirror.

Some, a rare few, he had even found lifeless in their cots, with the blood spilling from their arms.

Phipps could never know what it was like to live inside a bell jar and appreciate it. He attempted another approach.

'Do you know turtles, General?'

Phipps stared back vacantly. Coxon continued, 'A turtle always returns to the place of its birth to mate and to lay its eggs. In the Caymans we deliberately wait on shore before dawn for the harvest. Turtles, as you know, General, are a delicious if slightly repulsive-looking green meat, but are a luxury to a sailor. It takes two men to turn them and we leave them writhing on their backs. After a few hours the sand is almost gone from view, so covered is the beach by these beasts.' Coxon slyly noticed that Phipps's mistress had stopped fanning, beguiled, and the children had lifted their silent heads to stare at him.

'The strange thing is that they don't stop coming. They can see and hear the distress of the others, but still they struggle onto the beach, oblivious to our presence. Do you know why, General?'

'I rejoice to say that I do not, Captain,' Phipps mumbled.

'It's because when he is born and digs his way out of the sand and down to the sea, the turtle carries in his mouth a grain of sand from that beach. He carries it with him for the rest of his days, and returns to that very same spot year in, year out. He has to. Regardless. Regardless of any danger or will to do otherwise.' Coxon stood and bowed his head to the elegant concubine, and then to the general.

Phipps bowed his head, and smiled. 'A dog also returns to its vomit, sir. Against others' better judgement.'

'I should like to return with your outgoing post, General. Please inform me when a ship is available. Good morning, sir.' He bowed again, took up his hat and left.

Fourteen hundred miles and eight degrees of latitude away, Patrick Devlin sat on the floor of Captain Seth Toombs's cabin. He had breakfasted on rice, pork and peas, all fried on a skillet by a man with one hand. On His Majesty's ships the man with one hand would have been cast off and left to fend for himself back home. Here, he would be compensated for his joint: two hundred pieces of eight, and given a less trying position. In Dog-Leg Harry's case, ship's cook.

Devlin had risen with the sun and slung his hammock. Generously he had been given the canvas bag that held Alastair Lewis's few remaining possessions. The only one he cared for this morning was a square shaving mirror. In the twilight he had seen his face clearly for the first time in years. The tanned reflection and dark eyes were still young, but now cynical and hard. His hair seemed lighter than the black he remembered, but the years at sea had probably seen to that. Four years as factotum to John Coxon, sleeping on the floors of cabins and rooms in Portsmouth or London. Two years among the citizens of '*la Cité corsaire*', St Malo, where he lived and laughed with the fishermen and brushed shoulders with the privateers who ruled there. The young Irish butcher boy and poacher had gone, and he wondered if he now looked like his father; his memory of the man who had passed him on to the butcher when he was barely eight had long since dimmed. He could remember his father's arms swinging him along, and the huge, rough, square hands, but the voice and the face were in darkness.

He took the mirror and, with his shaver tucked in his belt, walked to the fo'c'sle, over the bodies of his sleeping comrades. Picking up a swab bucket, he sat on the deck in the violet dawn and shaved away the last two months.

Now he leaned against the cabin wall, warming a pipe and waiting for Toombs to awake. He had not dared look at the folded parchment hidden in his right boot, and in his mind's eye he began to see it fading away, an intangible promise.

They were still anchored and there was no watch on deck. The lack of a watch had seemed strange to Devlin, so familiar had the morose chimes of the bell become, but it was just the assertion of another freedom that normal seamen did not have.

Rather than the four-hour shifts between a starboard and a larboard watch, as the men-of-war dictated, Toombs's pirates generally favoured an 'all hands' approach ordered by Peter Sam for the work that wanted, although there was always a soul aloft on the mainmast looking for sails – a favoured task, for if he spied a prize he would have first choice of pistols from her spoils.

Devlin himself had been spared the labour of the watch on Coxon's ship, being a servant, but if he were to be Toombs's artist he would need its discipline.

'Maybe you should have wakened me, Patrick.' Toombs effortlessly got out of his hammock, awakened presumably by his bladder or an aching head.

His coat and hat were slung across the table and he instinctively put them on with his eyes still closed, Devlin noticing that without these accoutrements Toombs looked like any other seaman, if not thinner than most, but with the same hunched shoulders until the burgundy tricorne tipped his head up like a prince's.

'What time is it?' This was his own question, as Toombs had Lewis's timepiece set for London, and his own watch that he reset at noon each day.

'Almost half past ten. Show us your preparations, Pat.'

He swept towards the deck with a yell. 'Dog-Leg! Coffee!' He kicked the nearest man to him. 'Get up, you lazy dog! Prepare to shift that capstan, and fetch me Peter Sam!'

He pulled his pipe from his pocket and took a few steps forward, loading as he went. Glancing upwards at the crosstrees and the man above, seeing him still awake and silent, he knew they were alone for at least a dozen miles in any direction. Eighty feet in the air, the wind strafing his ears and smarting his eyes red until he was weeping, not even able to light a pipe in the wind, standing more over the sea than the deck, he was the loneliest man on earth.

'Any man who calls himself an officer move himself to the cabin! I want movement and breakfast, you dogs! Hands to braces!' He turned, lighting his pipe from his tinderbox, and walked back to the cabin with a wink to Devlin. 'Now you can officially meet the others.'

In the past, Devlin had been privy to many an officer's meeting in the capacity of servant, tray in hand, but this one had a different edge to it. The room stank of drink. In the mid-morning heat it sweated from the men's pores, although no one showed ill of it.

Devlin knew Peter and Seth; the others he knew of – had even worked with – without names being passed between them. Around the table he nodded greetings to the sailing master, William Vernon, or Black Bill as he was known to all, a dark, broad Scot with a great black beard that covered his neck and face. He stood next to 'Little John' Phillips, bosun, whom Devlin supposed was no more than twenty-five.

William Magnes he fairly knew, the tall, nervous-looking carpenter with the grey sideburns, the only one to offer his hand to Devlin that morning. John Watson was the cooper, and a great bawdy storyteller below deck, who fought constantly with Magnes over tools. Lastly, Gunner Captain Robert Hartley, formerly of His Majesty's ships. A half-deaf drunkard, obsessed with sponges and tallow, who spent all his time drinking, sifting powder and swearing at the damp. Devlin felt he was backstage at a French *cirque*, Toombs the ringmaster to the freaks.

Earlier it had been in his mind to share Philippe Ducos's last will and testament with his captain, for last night a drunken

Toombs joyfully declared that he knew Devlin to be one like him, just by the way he wore his sword all the time he was not at work, 'like a lord'.

In truth Devlin wore the sword and crossbelt with a misplaced sense of duty. It was one of Coxon's that he had liberated in defence of the *Noble*. It would be worth twenty guineas if he ever got it to a civilised shore. By wearing it he felt still a part of that orderly world, Coxon hanging at his side. This morning he held back the thought to share his newly found destiny. Meeting the swaying corps had given him confidence. He would stay his hand.

'Gentlemen, I want you to treat Patrick as kindly as you do each other!' An evil laugh pervaded as Dog-Leg poured coffee into pewter mugs.

'What's our plan, Captain?' Black Bill spoke for all.

'A fine, bold plan, Bill. Bold as brass!' Toombs began the rough detail of his scheme. The attack on the frigate had gone badly. Toombs had taken the chance against the sixth-rate ship, but the fire had ended all that. Then, running west, they had met the French sloop – and that had turned out empty.

A pirate captain's tenure was only as substantial as the goods in his hold. To that end, Toombs had dreamed up the audacious kidnapping of the Portuguese governor of one of the Verde Islands.

They would present themselves as English merchants and ingratiate themselves with the governor. Toombs would then invite him aboard for dinner, whereupon they would place a pistol upon his breast and a ten-thousand-doubloon ransom on his head. The ring of the Spanish coin still the finest in all the world.

Peter Sam felt obliged to express that they were already running late in the year: they should be on their way to the

Newfoundland coast by now to avoid the summer heat which bred disease. Black Bill shouted home that if they were not to 'trade up' – fix themselves to a new ship – then they needed to careen and smoke out the vermin before the season changed. Bill always courted the worst of looks from Toombs.

'All of this we know, gentlemen. But am I sailing with women here? Careen! Smoke the hold! Pitiful swabs. I'm talking of giving the Portos the vapours here! Enough coin for us to suckle for the whole summer in Trepassey! Vane has done it, why not I?'

'Aye.' John Watson, the cooper, sucked on his pipe. 'The scheme's good enough, but how's it to be done, patroon? We don't look like no English coffee boys.'

Toombs laughed and slapped the table. 'That frigate wasn't a total waste, lads. Did we not grab us sackfuls of proper seaman's slops?'

Dog-Leg silently produced a bowl of Italian grapes and each grabbed a handful.

'And are we not flying an English pennant now, sir?' He took a hold of Devlin. 'Sow the seed, Pat! What we be doing?'

Devlin came to the edge of the table, map under his arm. He pushed away the litter of mugs and spread the Mercator chart over the table, dragging the mugs back again to fasten down each corner.

'Pay attention, boys, to the hydrographica tabula.' He sang the words, and enjoyed his audience.

'Bill?' The black eyes looked dolefully upon him. 'I'll need you to get me seven knots at least, against the wind as we are. We'll have a northwest tack for two hours, then a northeast for one, then back again. That way we should stay away from the coast but still keep to this course.' He pointed on the map with a divider to a course he had mapped.

'Beating upwind as we are and as weatherly as the *Lucy* is, the sails are up to you. Close-hauled and no pinching, if you please. I wants and needs no more than seven knots, but I needs them. That should bring us here' – he stabbed with the divider a few points north of St Nicholas – 'by this time in two days, where we can sail downwind and around her eastern cape into Preguica harbour.'

All looked down at the small clump of islands scattered off the coast of Africa like dice on a table.

'The Islands of the Blest', the Portuguese had named them. Almost in the middle of the scattering sat their destination: São Nicolau. St Nicholas.

Long and thin, São Nicolau was pinched almost in the very middle to less than six miles across, its mountain ranges skirted by small colonies of towns, each one full of winding streets and alleyways lined with a colourful collection of terracotta-roofed dwellings.

The capital, Ribeira Brava, nestled below the watch of Monte Cordo, the largest mountain on the island, but the governor had made his home south of Preguica, at a far quieter locale on the south coast, which suited the pirates' needs.

'You're sure you know where we be starting from, then, Patrick?' Peter Sam asked quietly.

'The latitude I took this morning by God Himself don't lie. But we'll take another at noon today before we leave and I'll show you, Peter.'

'You can show me!' Bill bellowed.

'All are welcome, lads.' Devlin smiled as everyone looked upon him with different eyes. 'But there's one thing I have to insist on, boys. That is, if you're not going to shoot me in two days' time when we don't make it else.'

'What be that now, Patrick?' Toombs asked.

In answer, Devlin reached beneath the table and slammed down the old sand-timer that Dog-Leg had found for him.

'I'll need that turned every half-hour. With a bell rung to tell me it's changed, and to tell Bill to change tack.' The officers straightened at the sight of the glass.

'Without it, I can't check myself, and Bill can't change tack. He can check speed, but I need to check time and distance. I'll make my own traverse board.'

'I can keep time,' Toombs offered.

'Not good enough, Captain,' Devlin asserted himself. 'From noon today we're turning this glass.' He looked at Peter Sam. 'I'll not press you to keep a watch. Give me four men, preferably sailors, one of whom will be Sam Fletcher, and I'll sail you within half an hour of St Nicholas.'

All were silent. Toombs cracked the silence with a laugh and a back-slap to Devlin.

'By God, sir! That's a threat! You shall have it! Peter, find him his men. King's own each!' He popped a cork as if from nowhere, and drained a draught of wine. 'Through the night, I take it, an' all, sir?'

'Through the night.'

'Four men? Almost two days on a watch? By God, sir, the navy missed you!'

'They never even saw me, Captain. I'll need your men to keep with me through the night, Bill.'

Bill looked at Devlin like the dog to the hare. 'Don't expect any of 'em to listen to your bells, man. Just shout at 'em to change sails.'

'I'll do that.'

'Would you be wanting for anything else, Patrick?' Toombs asked in a low voice. A slow circle of respectful eyes fell upon him.

'The noonday sun, Captain.'

An hour later, the sun already searing, Devlin stood on the quarterdeck with Toombs, Black Bill and Peter Sam. The starboard-bow anchor was coming up and men hung over the yardarms like pegs on a washline, waiting for orders.

Below stood four men, including Sam Fletcher, arguing about where the half-hour glass should be tied. Fletcher was a deserter the crew had picked up in Providence before Devlin came aboard, and he still wore the calico and wool uniform. Devlin did not care for him, but he hoped he still had enough of the whistle piped into him to keep watch, and he had promised each man a twist of tobacco if they worked through this. Toombs agreed to the tobacco, in his own interests, naturally.

'What time do you have there, Captain?' Devlin asked, the backstaff's sighting to his eye. The instrument itself was longer than a musketoon, the sun was to his back and he prayed for a shadow to fall in the horizon vane to qualify his stance upon the deck as the last crank of the capstan dragging up the anchor rang in his ears.

'That's eleven fifty-six as I believe it to be.'

'That's good enough.' He kissed the backstaff, its numbers gladdening his heart, her wooden degrees his psalms as Coxon had taught him. 'Latitude as it was. Set that watch for noon and give it to me.'

Toombs passed the watch, receiving the backstaff in return.

'I will check it according to the sands, Captain.' His calm countenance broke and he yelled below, 'Fletcher, turn that glass, man!'

And it began.

Devlin approached the deck and yelled forward, 'Keep those sheets out of the wind now, lads! Make sail! Mister Vernon?'

'Aye, sir?' Black Bill heard himself say.

'Chip log, if you please, Bill. Any sail you have to give me seven knots.'

'Aye, aye, Patrick,' and he was away, down the waist of the ship, pushing men out of his path, yelling his strange calls.

'Mister Phillips!' Devlin's eyes caught the bosun staring up at him from below.

'Aye, Pat?'

'Lifts and braces, if you please, Little John. Follow Bill!'

'Aye, sir!' and away he ran.

Devlin turned to face Toombs's querying look, and Peter Sam's dark face.

'Don't be so keen to yell out orders on my ship, Patrick.' Toombs raised his chin. 'These are my men.'

The rattling and luffing of the sails filled the air. A fury of shouts and hauling followed from the fore, and the jib was backed until the *Lucy* slowly began to drift. Peter, at the helm, swung the wheel hard to larboard and the terrible lurch one never got used to pitched the horizon round. The *Lucy* heeled up, showing three more of her starboard staves, the shadows of the masts falling aft, sweeping across the deck.

Toombs stood back to watch his sails fill. For the next quarter-hour the narrow deck was a dance of activity. Lanyards were secured, halyards tied, and all the while the *Lucy* grabbed the wind. Her bow plunged and rose, playfully spraying anyone fore with a light, warm rain.

Beneath her keel a pair of marlins kept chase through the azure sea, and the 'porkers' that had been circling them for days returned to the depths, sated only by Alastair Lewis's corpulence.

Black Bill ascended to the taffrail aft of the ship with the drogue, the wooden board that would carry the log. One of his mates held the heavy reel of rope that would pay out behind the *Lucy*. Without a word between them, the drogue was tossed to the sea.

The progress seemed fast as the spray hit their faces from all sides, but that was only the joy of the *Lucy* letting go under courses and topsails after sitting as she had been for two long days.

A fraction under thirty seconds later and the tiny sand-timer held in Bill's hand emptied. He closed his fist on the line.

'Six knots, Patrick!' Bill shouted over his shoulder. The triangle of Devlin, Toombs and Peter Sam stood at different points on the quarterdeck. Devlin separated himself by walking down the steps, yelling as he came.

'Get your linen out, lads. I want seven before the first bell!' He landed next to Sam Fletcher, and put his hand to his shoulder. 'Ring that bell every turn, Sam. Like you used to. I'll bring you a drink each time.'

'Aye, Patrick.'

From inside his shirt, Devlin pulled out Lewis's log with pencil attached by pitched string. He wrote down the time and the latitude and walked back into the cabin. Laying the watch down on the table, he looked at the world spread out on the map before him. It seemed smaller than before; he could almost see the *Lucy* on its face, tearing across the paper. Above his head, the rudder beams yawned across the overhead, signifying Peter setting the wheel. He watched the compass swing to NNW and marked the bearing alongside the latitude. Toombs danced into the room.

'We're on our way, Pat. And you are now on the sweet account for a share and a half, my man.' He grabbed his bottle and drank to their health. 'Every man's on deck or aloft. 'Tis a grand sight.' He slapped the bottle into Devlin's hand.

Then, with a firmer voice, 'I need this one to come off for the good, Patrick. You get me to that island, else you'll find there's a reason why sharks follow my ship, sir.' He winked, and removed himself, barking insults to anyone in his eye as he strode out.

Alone, Devlin drank a mouthful of the sweet red wine.

He glanced over to the piles of papers at the side of the table. Scribbled notes and small coastal maps showing reefs and soundings gathered from raided ships. Some were tied closed with ribbon; others peered out from oilskin wallets.

Devlin reached for a pile and spread it before him. Their detail and sizes differed, as did their language and age, but Devlin paid little attention. He looked up. He was still alone.

Reaching down into his boot, he pulled out the parchment that Philippe Ducos had bequeathed him. For the first time, despite the nights it kept him awake, against his leg like a manacle, he creased it apart and placed his ace amongst the deck.

It showed the map of a long, small island, marked with deadly soundings and jungle all over, indicated by childlike smatterings of trees. Near the centre of the island, drawn in red ink, sat a crude image of a small fort.

In the bottom-right corner sat a fleur-de-lys compass rose; a swift hand had penned a full latitude and longitude trailing along the relevant point.

The longitude was presumably French, an easy calculation from the English. Even without checking, Devlin could see the island being lapped by cool waves south of Cuba. North of the Cayman Islands.

Taking up Lewis's log, he pencilled the figures into its white pages. A bulky shadow fell across his hand as he wrote. He slid his eyes up to see the figure of Peter Sam in the doorway, his arms stretching across the frame, staring straight at him, straight at the table.

Toombs was at the fo'c'sle, looking out to the horizon with a leisurely eye when the shot and the jeers came winging aft from the cabin. He whipped round and ran across the deck to join the crowd already heaving under the lintel. Toombs barged and cursed his way through, his elbows scuffing skulls, his hat some way behind him on the deck.

Breathless, hardly able to see, having come so quickly from the bright deck into the half-light of the cabin, he could just make out Devlin on the floor, sitting with a bloodied mouth, a shattered window behind him. To his right stood Peter Sam, a smoking pistol in his hand, reversed like a club, being held back by Black Bill.

'What in hell is going on here?' Toombs yelled.

'Ask him!' Peter Sam wrestled in Bill's grip. 'The little shite's too clever for his own good!'

'Patrick?' Toombs walked up to the table where the papers lay strewn about. 'Why are shots being fired in my cabin?'

Devlin stood, wiping the blood from his mouth. 'He fired, Captain, not I.' Devlin's voice was calm, his eyes narrowed.

'He's the one with all the lip,' Peter Sam spat.

'Aye, and a swollen lip at that,' Toombs noted to all. 'But for why, Peter?'

Bill's grip loosened and Peter shrugged himself free. 'I caught him studying the maps. I asked him what he was about. He comes back with: "Peter, you'd have to be able to read to understand!"' Laughter broke out in the gathering. Peter yelled above it, 'I've enough of his damned mouth, Captain! He's up to no good among us!'

'He's the navigator, Peter! He's the one to study the waggoner, is he not? Behold yourself, man.' He turned to Devlin. 'Put these papers away. And hold your tongue!'

'Aye, Cap'n.' Devlin began squaring the charts, hiding his own map amongst them.

Black Bill begged his captain's ear, whispering of articles, of rules and discipline, and 'sport'.

'That's a sure fact, Bill, sure enough. Quartermaster?' Toombs looked back to Peter.

Peter Sam's head was lowered. He scowled upwards at Devlin as he quoted. 'Article Eight. No striking one another on board. Every man's quarrels to be ended on shore. At sword and pistol.'

'Then that shall be done,' Toombs declared. 'As soon as our current business is attended to, lads, one of you shall have first blood.'

Peter Sam quipped, 'I already have first blood!' He licked Devlin's blood off the cap of his pistol to the approving agreement of the crowd. 'And I'll see you on shore!' He wiped the rest off with an open palm and rubbed it across his bald head, his face grinning like a skull. Behind them all, diligent and dogged, their heads turning to the sound, Sam Fletcher rang his bell and turned his glass.

Chapter Three

*P*repare to repel boarders!' Thorn yelled the order
from the quarterdeck. It carried halfway down the
waist of the ship, sparking Mister Carey and Mister Laney,
his young midshipmen, to repeat the order to their respective
parties, just as loudly but unfortunately just as unsure of its
implication.

The freeboards of the two ships began to scrape together.
A teeth-rattling row of wood grating endlessly, deafeningly
accompanied by the unholy noise of the spars and rigging
clasping one another, pulling, wrenching, to snap each other
free from the shackles of the mast.

The last of the cannon smoke had passed. Now faces could
be seen. Fearful and red-rimmed eyes. Monstrous, barbaric
expressions, caused more by the smoke and the clamour than
by justification and enmity.

Thorn had fought battles on paper and blackboard. Over
lamb and mustard, port and rum. In barracks, in taverns,
amongst serving maids and landlords. He had passed pepper
pots amid knives and explained how poundage of guns, range
and elevation won conflicts. Straight at 'em, he would say,
take the wind from their sails, close-hauled, and on the uproll.
'Fire!'

The pirates, however, had not been privy to Thorn's lunch-
eons that stretched into dusk.

They threw their iron crow's feet spikes from the rigging, the raw metal slicing the bare feet of Thorn's crew like cheese wire. Their clay pots, flaming rag-stuffed crock bottles, exploded on the decks, filling the waist of the *Noble* with yellow clouds of sulphur, and showering glass and nails into the faces of his officers.

And all the while, as the ships clashed and clawed at each other, the balls whistled down from the spars and the shrouds. A hail of shot flew from invisible placements, echoed by laughter and howls, and the hot rain left more men on their backs than were standing at the bulwarks, ramming their pikes wildly at the body-filled rigging of the pirate brigantine.

Devlin stood by the Great Cabin. He had pilfered one of Coxon's swords and any easily hidden silver he could find. At the first exploding 'stinkpot', he had run his necktie through a swab bucket, tied it across his lower face, covering his nose and mouth like a footpad.

He grabbed a manrope as the two worlds collided and the ship rocked and the cannons rolled around the deck. He stared up at the marines hanging from the rigging like bats. Blood dripping like the last of the wine. They had still been biting the paper from their cartridges when the lead spun them from their perches.

Devlin watched Thorn leap down the steps from the quarterdeck. His black hair hung damp with sweat under his tricorne. The long sideburns that covered almost half his face and that he cultivated to age him years beyond his twenty looked false and foolish. Now he looked like a schoolboy lost on the wrong side of the Thames.

The noise finally broke him. A noise from the time of the Caesars. Then, ages past, it was the sound of ten thousand spears rattling in formation against a legion's shields. Here and now it was the thumping of a hundred cutlasses against the brigantine's gunwales, again and again and again.

Thorn stared wildly around him. Looking for something. Something unknown. Something he never found. His eyes fell on Devlin, taking a second to recognise him through the necktie wrapped round his face. Then he leaped through the cabin door and bolted it behind him.

It was a fine story. Toombs had been there for the end of it. Under a million stars, spilled like grains of salt across an ebony table, Devlin stood with Toombs at the fo'c'sle.

They smoked contentedly, leaning back beneath the moonless sky, watching the sails glow in the faintest of light from the stars on the water and listening to the weary strains of the jibs above them.

Both men were unable to sleep. The bell had kept ringing, the sails kept changing with Devlin's tack, still maintaining seven knots upon his traverse board, so Toombs and Devlin had found themselves drinking punch and smoking through the night.

Devlin needed to be awake but, despite the rum, Toombs found that the bell outside his cabin was not conducive to sleep. They sailed in darkness, with no sidelights, whispering their talk as if in fear of disturbing the *Lucy*.

Mostly the pair talked about each other: how they came to this point. Holding all the right pieces back, but revealing secrets, as men are apt to do beneath infinity.

Toombs laughed, blackly, about how he had been peeled off the table of a Bristol tavern to be a cod fisherman. How his masters loaned him money in lieu of pay and charged him twenty shillings for a loaf of bread. He told of great storms and shipwrecks, of ghosts born from the long, cold, murderous nights along the Newfoundland coast.

Every few months, pirates would come from the Caribbean to fish for men, and the fear and dread of the governors at their approach, and the reticence of the navy to offer protection, had inspired him to consider that the waters of piracy were maybe less muddy than those of a fisherman.

'But what about you, Patrick?' he asked. 'Why were you on that ship? A servant, no less?'

Devlin shifted uncomfortably. He testified that his life was of little consequence. His father had sold him to a butcher in Kilkenny for four guineas. He had only been eight at the time but he'd been tall and his father had sold him as a twelve-year-old. He had spent his early years, motherless, playing with stones and mice in a one-street, four-horse town near the ever-freezing River Barrow, learning to curse and fight before learning to pray.

He remembered trying to bring living fish home and wondering why they died before he brought them through the door, sharing this memory with Toombs and blushing at the utterance.

He had never known his mother, only the warmth of his father's sister, who looked after him every summer whilst his father picked hops alongside *his* father for the Kilkenny breweries. Dead or living, his mother had gone, and Devlin paid her no mind. He did not blush at that to his captain.

At ten, he was a poacher for the butcher. At first with snares for rabbit, hare and duck, then with a matchlock musket taller than himself, spending days in brush and thicket, under a sailcloth tent, waiting for the deer to sniff out the morning.

Teaching himself to read from books that people stole from their squires to offer as payment to the butcher, the only one that served all the fine houses along the Three Sisters, he read much and ate well. Kilkenny was a plump town in which to be young and vital. Almost a decade went by before destiny caught up with him.

At nineteen, one of his fowl still carried some shot that cracked the rotten teeth of a magistrate's wife, and Devlin was chased down for the crime against her person.

He had run from his punishment to England, with the blue Wicklow Hills shrinking away from the stern of a Deal yawl his last memory of home. He'd worked and tramped his way east, drifting finally to the docks of London. As an Irishman, he sought out others, and found his way to Pelican Stairs, the sailors' district in Wapping. There he was taken in by a father and son named Kennedy, serving in an anchorsmith's with old man Kennedy.

The son, Walter, never took to work, preferring burglary and theft, and father and son fought like dogs. In the summer of 1710, Devlin came back to the small, damp, tumbledown house to find old man Kennedy with a dirk sticking out of his chest, and the young Walter Kennedy gone.

'It is my shame still,' he confessed, stabbing a pipe at Toombs, 'that I ran from the house that night for terror of my own neck.'

'What did you do?'

'There was a war. I gave my oath.' He sipped at his mug, removing the history that he had fled to St Malo and had laid his own eyes on the infamous corsair René Duguay-Trouin, the pirate that loaned even King Louis money.

He had stayed there two years, fishing along the coast before starvation led him into Louis's flotilla and barely a month later into the hands of the English.

'Were you not a servant, though, Pat? Not a signed man?'

Devlin had slipped. It was still in his mind to keep his French past hidden. Toombs was not a fool.

'I began before the mast. A younker furling sail. But not for long. I had a happening along the gangway one day: I was flogged for not tugging my forelock to a snotty. The captain felt that an Irishman on his ship was a lost cause anyways. He enlisted me as his man instead.' He took a drink, swallowing the lie.

Toombs blew out a veil of smoke. 'He taught you well, though. I don't know the man, but I can see his shadow in you for sure.'

'I spent four years by his side.' Devlin's voice was bitter. 'He didn't teach me, Cap'n. I Jewed his clothes and I listened.' He turned and stared across the deck to where Dan Teague, with the only lantern allowed, stood watching the sand-timer dance with the rolling of the ship.

Devlin gave his mug to Toombs, and pulled out the brass pocketwatch. In the glow from his pipe as he drew a little, he saw her arm drag to two o'clock just as Dan chanted out his morbid four bells.

'Curse you, Patrick, for not allowing me to sleep,' Toombs muttered.

The lads were doing well. The watch was working. Devlin made his way to the helm. He took the long walk sparse with men, for they huddled in closer quarters below, away from the bells. Crewmen shuffled past him to the staysails for the change in direction. Devlin unlashed the wheel and set NNW to the spinning binnacle at his knee. He looked down the ship and watched the ropes being belayed by grey spirits in the dark.

For a few minutes he relished the pull of the ship, the water struggling against the wheel in his hands as the earth turned; then he lashed her to her course and went down to relieve Dan.

By dawn the men of the watch were spent. Devlin ducked out of the cabin, spyglass in hand, to find a new face, not one of the allotted four maintaining the sand.

The man nodded at him without a word and Devlin climbed to the quarterdeck. Somewhere in the night the crew had come to their own arrangement. The brethren's spirit for each other continued to stagger Devlin. Extending the three-draw telescope to the northeast, he scanned the horizon.

He had not pushed to take a chip log during the night, leaving the sails to read their speed. Before a noon reading, and by dead reckoning, he was hoping to see the island of Brava in his sights. The misty view through the 'bring me closer' rolled up and down, but Devlin saw nothing. He panned himself right, hoping to be late, perhaps, but there was still no shoulder of land. The spyglass was snapped shut with a curse.

'I'm thinking you won't see Brava, Patrick.' The voice of Black Bill rumbled in his ear.

Devlin turned to the old mariner. 'Is that right, Bill?'

'Aye. Oh, she's there. And we're about thirty miles off of her, I reckon. As do you, lad, by your charts.' Devlin had been plotting through the night and Bill had spent a while mulling over his reckoning. 'Me and the boys will take a sounding. I'll lay you a pound of powder it'll be shell at six fathoms.' He pointed over the rails, scowling into the rising sun. 'See that cloud? That's Brava under that. She's a bairn compared to St Nick, but she's there, and you plotted well, Pat.'

'Well, I thank you, Bill, for being a gentleman.' Devlin smiled.

'Nay, lad. Never a gentleman.' The big man leaned on the

rail, his wiry black beard lifting in the wind as he looked out across the calm sea. 'Tomorrow night we'll arrive at St Nick. Keep an eye north. There's plenty of black rocks that'll mark our passage. Birds too. Clouds of them. We need a good account, Pat. It's been a bad winter. The lads' songs are full of laments. Yet they run the sails without complaint all night. And turn your glass.' Bill elbowed Devlin as he passed to the companion. 'You're pistol-proof, Patrick Devlin,' he told him. Then added, ominously, 'Just keep arm's-length away from Peter if you can, lad.'

That evening the officers stood around a lantern-lit table, mired in each other's smoke. They had dined out on deck with the rest of the crew, on a spiced dish of rice with chicken taken fresh from the small coop next to the mizzen, and washed down with as much small beer as they needed to take away the memory of Dog-Leg's fare. Toombs had called them to discuss the prospects for the following night's adventures.

'The way I see it, lads, we're coming down here.' He stabbed at the chart on the table with his pipe. 'The bay of St George. Patrick will bring us northwards by early tomorrow evening. Then we sail along the shore and around this cape, windward like, to come to Preguica, here.' He stabbed again at the knuckle of the island. 'As if we'd just sailed off the lap of King George himself. And all hands dressed like common blue sailors. Just a few fishermen and the governor's house are all that's there, and I'll bet a portion that he hasn't more than a handful of men.'

'But we don't know that, do we, Cap'n?' Will Magnes asked.

'That's truth talking, so it is, Will, but it don't matter anyhow – we'll be flying the king's colours, remember? And I ain't intending to go ashore and count his men. All we'll be doing is inviting the poor governor for a friendly dinner in the company of his peers!'

'What if he doesn't want to come over?' Peter Sam queried.

Toombs inhaled at the question, closing his eyes briefly. 'This island, mate, is a volcanic rock. The Portos have been there nigh on a hundred years and have grown nothing but tired. We show up with news, wine, coffee and tobacco. We'll have to fight the buggers off.' He tossed down his pipe upon the island with a clatter.

'The governor's probably some nobleman's rapist son hiding out here. His island's naught but a signpost for us civilised squires heading for the Indies.'

'So who's going to pay ten thousand doubloons for him?' Peter again spoke up.

'Don't fret about that, Peter. I know these bastards keep that in tin just to pay for slaves to colonise the bloody hole!'

'What if he asks us over to him, Captain?' Devlin asked.

Toombs's jaw clenched. 'What, pray, is that of a comment, Patrick?'

'Wouldn't we be supposing a boat comes out to meet us, rightly so? They look around the ship, all done and happy, then they invite us to dine with them?'

Everyone watched Toombs.

'No, he dines with us. He comes aboard, we pull our pistols.' Toombs spoke as if the whole event had already happened and they were snug in their hammocks weighted down with gold.

'But should we be asked to the island, we can't refuse, can we now?' Devlin turned to his fellow officers. 'It doesn't matter to the plan: if we sup on the island one night, the governor eats with us the next, but' – he paused, picked up a divider and pointed at the island – 'I suggest we land a boat here on the north shore, at the narrowest point, six miles north to south. Half a dozen men to cover the risk that we find ourselves separated from the ship. We could make our way there should we smell a trap.' He looked straight at Peter Sam. 'Six men to watch our backs.'

Toombs's voice was strained. 'What are you saying, Pat?'

'We're thinking of deeds against this man, ain't we? It's just an insurance that he's not thinking the same about us, Captain.'

John Watson, the cooper, drew long on his pipe. 'That's not a bad plan, Captain. He has a thought sure enough.' The others stood still.

Devlin carried on, 'And when they come aboard to spy us out, we only have enough blues for a quarter of the men. We should put as many men in the hold as possible. The rest are to dress as plain as print. I never saw a merchant yet with a hundred men aboard.' There were murmurs of agreement.

Toombs looked around his table. 'Aye. Maybe so. We don't know what we're sailing into, that's for sure. No harm in safety, ladies, if that's the way you want your cards. Who's to sail the boat?'

Peter Sam raised a hand. 'I'll take that honour, Captain. I'll pick my own cox'n and mates, if you please.'

'Aye, but young Thomas will be with me, Peter. If I'm to go ashore, I want the handsomest lads with me. That carries you with me as well, Patrick, and you, Little John. Black Bill – you'll hold the *Lucy* for me until we return.'

'Aye, Cap'n.' Bill winked.

'Then that plan's a mainstay. That is if you're all happy now with Patrick's suggestion?'

Toombs turned and vanished into the gloom of the corner of the cabin. He carried back a large roll of black cloth and unfurled a portion of it upon the table. The rolled-out piece revealed the cross-stitched eye of a white skull and a crude hourglass.

'Stronger than pistols, boys. Swear on this.' All spat on their hands, Devlin last of all, and slapped the flag.

'We have an accord!' Toombs jeered and rolled back the cloth. 'Dog-Leg! Rum for all!'

He had never seen a morning rain of its kind before. It came down like a wall of water, giving an eerie luminosity to the courtyard below the window. The low, flat roofs of Cape Coast Castle hissed with steam. John Coxon looked up to the beamed ceiling in his quarters, apparently being ridden over by a thousand horses.

Through the small paned window in his room, peeling its green paint, Coxon could see the hazy form of the frigate that would take him home. Back to sea. She lay out in the small bay, her almost skeletal prow grinning at him through the cascading rain.

A fifth-rate frigate of thirty-four guns, no doubt twelve-pounders. Crisp yellow and black paintwork across her strakes. Coincidence or not, Phipps had made his proposal to keep Coxon there, and two days later the *Starling* appeared on her way back from the Indian factories.

Not wishing to take command, he would come on board as commander under the captain. Probably some midshipman would be ousted from his berth for him, or perhaps the political adviser's space would be vacant. Nevertheless, he would be at sea. Twelve days, maybe fourteen, he would be back in England, standing before a table of wigs, ribbons and engorged faces.

As a fighting man, they would punish him by sending him

out to the Caribbean to quell the tide of cut-throats that had swelled since the Peace of Utrecht and the Spanish raids on the colonies of English woodcutters along the Brazilian coast, clawing back what the war had cost them, had pushed hundreds of rovers upon the sea.

That would suit. That would do. Just to get back to the sea. To find the man who deemed himself worthy to attack his ship. To lash the man against his own mast before setting him ablaze and tossing him into the sea.

You could not hang these men. Each time you brought one back to Execution Dock, five more were inspired to take his place. Do not show them off for their crimes, wasting time on trials and hangmen. Whittle them down. Just let them disappear like winds, their voices never heard.

Chapter Four

*I*t's time, Peter.' Toombs gripped the quartermaster's shoulder.

Peter Sam responded, shaking Toombs's forearm. Six men sat below in the boat, its single mast lowered, all men at the oars. It was early evening now. That afternoon the windward island of St Nicholas seemed as if she was powering towards them across the water, her great black volcanic peaks standing directly on the narrow rocky shore.

Each man armed with a musket, two pistols apiece, and with Peter Sam in charge of a special assortment of grenadoes, all safely stowed beneath the sheets of the longboat, they began the slow trawl to shore.

An hour's sail brought the sun falling behind the cracked, speckled hills as the *Lucy* rounded the eastern bay, São Jorge, her pennant flying the colours of the Union Flag and only a handful of widows' sons on deck.

'Hello?' Toombs raised the spyglass. 'There's something there that the Lord hadn't considered.'

Devlin and Black Bill were by his side at the fo'c'sle. Devlin shielded his eyes with his palm as he looked out.

Across the bay from them, a mile away, sat a black and red frigate facing south, out to sea. Toombs, through the glass, laid odds that she was nigh on a hundred feet long. Devlin watched Toombs's mouth counting. 'Twenty guns and a couple aft and fore, no doubt. No less than nine-pounders, I reckon. What say you, Bill?'

'Could be, could be.' Bill leaned on the rail. 'We could be generous, Cap'n, and give them five to a gun. Maybe another thirty more for hands.'

Toombs lowered the shargreen and vellum tube. 'Outgunned for sure. Best keep on his good side. That's a Porto pennant she's flying. Keep that merchant jack up high, Bill.'

Devlin took in the dark sight. At least a hundred feet long for sure, with a jutting rostrum and short, high bowsprit. The gun ports were painted blood red; everything else on the freeboard was black, up to the gunwale, with all three masts rigged to the gallants, her grey sails furled. She was a forbidding sight.

'That's far enough, Cap'n, they've seen us now.' Bill straightened up. He moved to the deck and prepared to haul sail, lower the anchor. Toombs and Devlin moved across to starboard in silence.

Toombs raised the telescope again, but found it near useless in the shrinking light and joined Devlin in straining to see any life in Preguica port. They could just make out the smattering of fishing huts. Even at this distance the smell of smoked fish and pork came drifting in on the wind.

A small wooden jetty poked out into the harbour, the whole of which was necklaced by a low redoubtable stone wall. They could imagine rows of soldiers with cannon elevated over the edge, laughing at them, as the six-pound balls from the *Lucy* died hopelessly on the beach.

The shouts of men hauling away broke them from their thoughts. Minutes later the rattle of the anchor confirmed their position. They settled south of the bay. The soundings had marked this the surest bed, albeit with quite a swell. The anchorage also kept them well out of range of any cannonade.

Together, Toombs and Devlin looked again to the shore with a sharp eye; for now, in the gloom, could be seen the orange dance of three lanterns slowly swinging their way down to the pier from a higher place inland.

'Like moths to a flame, eh, Patrick?' Toombs grinned.

'Aye, Captain.' Devlin heard his own voice as a whisper. 'Aye, indeed.'

Half an hour had passed since they had watched the boat creep its way from the dock. Every man had a job to do to hide the normally languid role of the pirate. Despite the dark, men were mending sails, preparing oakum, holystoning the deck, whilst the bulk of the cut-throats hid in the putrefying hell of the hold, all to give the illusion of a moderately crewed merchantman to the party slowly approaching.

Adorned with a new shirt and breeches, Devlin prepared himself. He stood in the cabin and stuck a small ebony-hilted dagger in his belt behind his back. Next, also tucked behind his back, a small Queen Anne turn-off pistol, patch-loaded, a small wad of linen to keep the ball and powder from falling out. Then his French left-locked pistol. The same one he had been allowed to choose from the weapons locker after he had signed the articles. He had rummaged until he had found a left-locked one. A preference that would matter several times in his life. The fast draw it provided was favoured by the French. It was a brute of a weapon with a hexagonal fourteen-inch iron barrel and iron nose, similarly patch-loaded, and placed on the right-hand side of his belt.

He put on a square-tailed black twill greatcoat that must have belonged to a fine gentleman, so heavy was the cloth and so stout the fit. He pulled out the pleated linen cuffs of his shirt until they reached his knuckles, then picked up his crossbelt. No scabbard, the sword just hanging tight in its baldric, he placed it over his head and right shoulder. Although fashion now frowned on the crossbelt, Devlin welcomed the extra protection that a four-inch leather belt across his heart afforded.

A few shifting adjustments and the hilt of the sword came just to his left wrist. He turned to see Toombs standing in the doorway, dressed almost identically, save for his baldric lying beneath his coat.

'They're here, mate,' Toombs announced.

Both men emerged to receive their guests as the last of the three took the final short step down onto the deck and joined his companions.

Toombs introduced himself to the finest. The first two wore the breastplates and purple caps of guardsmen, sporting too the regulation moustaches. The third, however, wore fine red silk brocade, and had the longest black hair Devlin had ever seen on a man.

Clean-shaven, with a benevolent face, he seemed the picture of a Portuguese gentleman. In his velvet belt he carried a graceful Spanish pistol. On the other side, a filigree hilt and a promise of his skill and wealth, hidden in a golden scabbard.

'My name is Alvaro Contes, Captain. I speak for Valentim Mendes, who is the governor of São Nicolau. May I welcome you and ask what is the nature of your business here?'

'If it should please His Grace, sir, we would like the opportunity to gather fresh water in the morn. And perhaps we could trade a little.' Toombs bowed. 'We have plenty of tobacco on board on its way back to England, and it wouldn't hurt now to miss a few twists for the right price, you see?'

'Where have you sailed from, Captain?' Alvaro asked.

'From Virginia, sir. We are mostly carrying post back to England, but find ourselves short on water and beer for the remainder of our journey, and as a sign of friendship we would like to extend the courtesy of inviting His Grace, the governor, to dine with me and my officers.'

'That is very gracious of you, Captain. Would you also be so gracious as to allow my men to check the validation and worthiness of your vessel?'

'Indeed, sir, and may I say they look like the perfect officers to fulfil such a task. May I introduce you to my men, sir?'

Contes nodded humbly, casting his eyes over Devlin. 'This is Mister Patrick Devlin, our navigator. He has a rather fine lodestone that he would like to present to His Grace should he attend us.' Contes bowed and Devlin did likewise. 'Mister William Vernon, our sailing master and a fine Catholic. He keeps his eye on all of us, don't you, Will?'

'That I do, Cap'n.' Black Bill tugged his prodigious forelock.

'And this is Mister John Phillips, our bosun, and proud to have him we are. He'll gladly show your lads around, sir.' Phillips heartily agreed.

'Thank you, Captain Toombs. You are gracious indeed.' Contes smiled with some constraint, then with a nod dismissed the soldiers to follow Phillips. 'Now, Captain, if it is not too much trouble, I should like to see some of your ship. It is so rare that I get to see life on a working merchant.'

'Not much to see, to be truthful, sir,' Toombs confided. 'We live but humble lives. But we eats well. Which I'd like you to address to His Grace.'

'Really?' Contes moved towards the cabin. 'One would have thought your food to be – how you may say – *terrible*. Is that correct?'

Toombs and Devlin moved with him. Bill stayed by the bulwark, silent and watchful.

'No, no. Not at all, sir.' Toombs walked ahead. 'As much cackle fruit as you could eat – that be eggs and chickens to you, sir. Pork, apples, sauces, dried beef. You see, we don't hold by familiarities you might see on a warship, sir. We have an oven, laid on a hearth here' – he gestured to the galley stove incongruously sitting amidships – 'with cauldrons to feed all the men. I always say you can't run a ship on a cold stomach! Don't I, Patrick?'

'Indeed you do, Captain,' Devlin conceded.

Contes turned towards him as they reached the cabin entrance. 'You are the navigator, Señor…Devlin?'

'I am, sir.'

'My master is most keen on navigation. Your English John Davies is a hero of his.'

'We should have much to talk about. I have a small mounted lodestone that I would like to present to him as an English gift.'

Contes moved into the cabin. 'I myself know nothing of such things.' As he looked around the cabin, his face filled with disdain. 'You have very little…of anything. Captain Toombs?'

'Ah. Indeed, señor. Worms, you see. Rather than let them spread, I chose to throw all the wasted furniture over. Although don't you fret. We have enough left to entertain His Grace. My table should suffice for all the chickens I have planned!'

'Quite. I do not doubt your veracity on that matter, Captain.'

'I'm as veracious as they come, señor!'

'I'm so glad to hear you say it, Captain!' A positive inflection from the Portuguese gentleman. 'Now I would be gladdened to hear you select any officers whom you may choose to join me back at His Grace's home to dine with us. We should like to commence in under an hour.'

Toombs looked at Devlin, then back slowly at Contes. 'I had hoped that His Grace might favour us with his company, señor. What with our "veracity" an' all.'

'No. That will not happen this evening,' Contes stated flatly.

'Whose is that frigate in the bay, señor?' Devlin asked, as much to distract from the tension emanating from Toombs as anything.

Contes's eyes glowed at Devlin. 'That is Governor Mendes's frigate, Mister Devlin. She is French-built, you may perceive. "*A Sombra.*" How you may say? The *Shadow*. A fancy of His Grace's, I feel.'

'She's beautiful.'

'Again, I know very little of such things. Perhaps you may discuss it with Governor Mendes over dinner, señor? Ah, my men return!' Alvaro Contes swept past them. With his back to the pirates, he conferred with his men for only seconds in the doorway. Pleased, he turned and held out an outstretched black-gloved hand to Toombs. 'Come, it is only a sea stroll away to the finest fish you have ever eaten. Bring anyone you wish, Captain.'

'I should stress, señor, that I had hoped that you would dine with us this evening.' Toombs's voice was less adamant than his words. 'As a visitor, that is. To show my own good favour.'

'Oh, most certainly, Captain. But it is late, and you are unprepared, whereas His Grace has a fine meal that we are more than proud to present.' He bowed. 'It is required that you join us.'

In Toombs's mind he saw Alvaro falling backwards into

his men's arms, a quarter-inch hole where his nose should have been, a surprised look on the remainder of his face. Instead, he bowed also.

'Of course. But tomorrow, whilst my men fetch water, you must allow His Grace to partake of my favours.' Toombs found it hard to smile.

'I see no possible objection to that, Captain. However, tonight you are our guests.' Another affectation of a smile, this time aimed at Devlin, who smiled back.

'With that being the case, Señor Contes,' Devlin said, 'allow me to fetch my hat.' He excused himself. Toombs picked up his own burgundy tricorne. His hand trembled as he held it against his thigh, his own plan now awry and following Devlin's lead.

'I would like, señor, if my bosun and his mate could be in my party?'

'Naturally, Captain. The more company, the more conversation. We are so bereft of good conversation.'

Below deck, aft of the ship where he had gained some small private quarter, Devlin pulled out from his belongings Lewis's old pocket compass and the lodestone to present as a gift.

He patted his coat pocket for the reassurance of his cartridge box. It was apparent to him – and presumably Toombs as well – that the evening ahead might be dangerous.

They were leaving the ship. A few hours out of their world and away from the security of their brethren. Seth Toombs's plan delayed. Dangerous or not, with Peter Sam's party already camped ashore there would be ten pirates abroad that night. Pity the governor if he should have designs other than supper.

He picked up his own black tricorne and made his way

back, grateful to leave the stifling heat behind, sparing a thought for the pirates sweltering in the bowels of the ship amongst the ballast and the stench of the well.

Phillips and young Thomas had helped the two silent soldiers row the distance to the shore. Contes had passed pleasantries with an increasingly uncomfortable Toombs, and Devlin watched the *Lucy* shrink away. Her sidelights were lit now, a stark contrast to the black frigate sitting in darkness across from her.

The narrow crescent beach was festooned with a dozen or more small fishing boats and the jetty was perfumed with the sweet kelp smell of lobster cages. Slowly they walked a dirt road upwards, through a cloud of moths and biting winged insects drawn by the soldiers' amber lanterns. Alvaro Contes seemed immune to them. Devlin guessed that he must have some local defence, as he glided along unaffected, whilst they brushed at their faces like fools.

Devlin noticed that Toombs lost his footing for a step or two. It was either the lack of drink or the length of time at sea. He smiled as he recalled a time in Falmouth, after almost a year aboard, when he had stumbled carrying Coxon's bags. It was as if the ground shrank away from his feet and was the strangest sensation.

He was woken from this reminiscence by a whispered swearing from Thomas at his side as they came to the house. He looked up, but saw nothing to curse at. There before them was rough stone wall, no taller than a man, with a single iron gate, behind which stood a narrow, two-storey stucco building.

One large balcony window on the second floor glowed before them. The four windows either side were shuttered in darkness. The ground floor, barren of windows, had two crenels or gunloops, on either side of the arched oak door. Four pillars made up the entrance to the house, topped by the small balcony for the window above.

The wall surrounding the garden was the same style as the redoubt that curved along the harbour, with a jagged top of pointed slate to hinder the curious. The alcove in which the double oak door sat shone orange from recessed oil lamps at its four pillars.

As they walked into the small garden, mostly sand and rocks, Devlin could sense that the house was long, like some London homes he had frequented with Coxon on their rare social outings. This was confirmed as Alvaro guided them into a cold slate hall that was easily as long as the *Lucy*'s deck; a narrow stone staircase spiralling to the floor above stood in the centre.

'Welcome to the home of Valentim Mendes, gentlemen,' Alvaro flourished with a bow. 'Stay, and kindly leave some of the happiness that you bring.'

They were left alone for a moment as Alvaro turned and walked to the stairs and Toombs caught Devlin's eye.

'Keep a weather eye out,' he whispered.

They followed Contes across the hall to the staircase. The guards remained at the closed outer door as the pirates trailed after Alvaro, up the narrow steps to a set of arched oak doors.

Candlelight filled the stairs as he slowly pushed both oak doors open and ushered them in. Toombs never looked back. He strode into the room and removed his hat in the same step. The others followed.

The long dining table and twelve high-backed chairs lay before them. On the table's surface was laid a generous spread of pewter plates, candelabra and silver, and a cornucopia of fruit, cold meats, carafes of wine and piles of seeded bread.

The aroma of poached fish came to Devlin and he spied the array of covered platters on the other side of the room, and also the lithe, white-shirted form of Valentim Mendes looking through a wooden telescope perched between the open balcony windows.

'I congratulate you, Captain,' the voice accentuated every syllable. 'She is a charming little ship.' He straightened up to reveal a dark, handsome face, a head of black, shoulder-length hair and an exuberant smile framed by an elegant beard. He was unarmed save for a glass of brandy. He wore black knee-length riding boots with black breeches and red sash, and cut a dashing silhouette.

'I thank you, sir. We are all fond of her.'

Valentim moved to greet his guests, who introduced them-selves one by one. He bowed, holding his glass out to his side.

'I am Valentim Mendes, the law on São Nicolas, and your servant this night.' He swooped upright. 'Please allow me to get you drinks.' From the right corner of the room came a black, bald giant of a servant, carrying a charger of goblets.

The pirates took the generous glasses of red wine, passing uneasy looks between each other, aware that they were all still standing in front of the door.

'Please come in, gentlemen. We should sit and talk over much food.' Valentim gestured to the table.

'Too generous of you, Your Grace.' Toombs lowered his head politely. 'A noggin of small beer would have done the lads and me without a doubt.' Toombs sauntered to the left side of the table and sat down, choosing a chair that showed him the door, and almost at arm's-length from the table, pushing his hanger so it stuck straight behind him. His hand resting on its hilt.

Valentim moved himself to the head of the table, facing the balcony, and the others followed. Devlin removed his hat, and took a seat at the corner along from Toombs. Little John Phillips and Thomas Deakins sat on Valentim's left. Devlin gave himself as much room as Toombs at the table, conscious of the need to have space to draw weapons if called upon.

In the candlelight from the table, Valentim's face was obscured but Devlin could see his hands resting gently on the table.

'Be welcome to help yourselves, gentlemen. In Portugal we favour eating with a knife' – he held up a delicately tapered blade – 'and our hands. I can bring you "forks" if you prefer?' The pirates declined the offer, each reaching for a jug of wine. Thomas and Little John's hands colliding on the same carafe brought a welcome laugh from them all.

They settled in to eating the cold meats and seasoned potatoes, olives and wine-soaked sausage that Devlin for one had never tasted before. He noticed that Alvaro Contes occupied a comfortable chair beside the telescope, peeling off his velvet gloves and paying no attention to the table. The black servant stood by the lidded platters at the far wall. Devlin observed he held a small pistol in his belt. Even so, between them the pirates had at least five shots, maybe more hidden, and Valentim was clearly without a pistol.

Devlin dragged himself closer to the table as his appetite brought on a more relaxed temperament. It was then that he spied a collection of navigational instruments resting on a merchant chest opposite the table. Standing next to the chest was an eye-level perch, on which sat a motionless white raven.

'Ah, Señor Devlin.' Valentim stood, wiping his mouth as he walked over to the perch. 'You notice my unusual friend. He is a white raven. Rare indeed. And do you know where I found my little companion?'

'In a head of flour no doubt?' Toombs laughed.

Valentim smiled. 'In a cemetery. On this island there are surprisingly many. You see, it is two hundred years since we discovered these islands' – he stroked the bird, which responded with gentle pecks – 'but we soon discovered that others had been here before. There are many strange carvings we have found, markings on the rocks along the coast. We know not what they mean.' He addressed all of them as he spoke. 'Our first settlers soon found out that the islands were well known to pirates, however, and many deaths occurred. Gradually all our peoples moved inland in an attempt to hide from the raiders, but alas we are still prone to many, many assaults.'

'It is a shame' – Toombs shook his head in sympathy – 'that men can be forced to be so cruel sometimes.'

'Quite.' Valentim nodded gratefully. 'Many of our early colonists are buried in premature graves. It was in one of these places, paying my respects, that I found this little fellow. He was almost dead and very young.' The bird walked onto his hand and he placed it on his shoulder. 'You see, the other birds – his own kind, you understand – were attacking him. He was so weak he allowed me to pluck him from the bush from where he cowered. I have fed him from my own hand ever since.'

'There is a storm coming,' Alvaro Contes spoke from his chair, gesturing to the open balcony window. 'I can smell it in the air,' he explained. All eyes were upon him and he continued, almost embarrassed, 'It comes from the African coast, gentlemen. A few hours and it will be upon us.'

A silence followed Alvaro's statement, and he stiffened as Devlin rose. 'I see you have some tools there, Governor? May I see?'

'But of course, Señor Devlin.' Mendes welcomed him to the chest. 'You are interested in navigation?'

'Indeed, Your Grace.' Devlin said, as he looked over the various instruments, not daring to touch. There was a compass set in an ivory housing, a brass Persian astrolabe that must have been twenty inches across, a wooden volvelle, a series of plates that moved to follow the tides and phases of the moon, and an exquisite gold astronomical compendium, a marvellous small, beautiful box that held a compass, a sundial and even a wind vane. The compendium was too small to be practical, the compass probably could not guide one over a hill, but it was a truly delightful object. It reminded Devlin that beautiful things did still exist and were still being made, so long had he been from the world of ordinary men.

'You like, eh, señor?' Mendes eyed him warmly, a gentle play from his hand courting the bird on his shoulder.

'Truly, Your Grace. Which reminds me, I have something for you.' Devlin reached into his wide pocket. Alvaro's head sprang up at the movement. Devlin produced the lodestone with its brass-clasped housing. 'It's not much. Not much at all, sir. Just a lodestone.' He handed it to Valentim.

'No, Señor Devlin' – Mendes was genuinely pleased – 'it is a wonderful gift. Surely one of the most precious things in this world is to know where you are in it, is it not? If all else falls around me, and I have but this one thing, still I will have the means to know where I am in this world. I thank you very much, señor.'

Toombs spoke up, 'And truly, Your Grace, there is rather

a precious thing of beauty sitting out there off your harbour. Is she yours? That frigate, that is?'

'She is ours, Captain. The *Shadow*. I named her myself, for she is very black.'

Devlin watched Mendes place the lodestone down amongst the collection. Both men walked back to the table.

'I had always thought,' Devlin said, sitting, 'that your navy preferred Dutch designs. Fluytes and suchlike.'

'Indeed. But the French is more built for war. I have spent many years trying to get some ship to defend our interests here. This one I crew myself. But she is not ready, still.' Mendes chewed through a piece of roast pork.

Toombs put down his glass. 'Is that so?' His eyes widened. 'In what sense be that, Governor?'

'I have but thirty men upon her, that is all. Good men, but I am having great difficulty now, without a war, to persuade my country to provide me with more.'

'Ah, well,' Toombs sighed. 'That is the problem that we all face, señor.' Then he held up a hand, a look of benefaction on his face. 'I'll tell you what, Your Grace, so I will. Tomorrow evening, you dines with us, and I'll get some of my men over to that ship of yours to teach your boys a thing or two about sailing short-handed. There's nothing them boys don't know about sailing light. Why, I had to sail all the way from Boston to Bristol with only ten men once, didn't I, Little John?'

Devlin closed his eyes at the pirate name. John Phillips, his chin shining with grease, winked at him. 'Aye, Cap'n. That we did.'

'*Little John?*' Mendes queried with a staccato accent. 'What a strange title to give one of your men, Captain, is that not?'

'Ah, well.' Toombs poured himself some more wine. 'I've known some of these lads for so long that I find myself often christening them with little affections, señor!'

'I see.' Valentim looked calmly around his company. 'You talked of dining on your ship, Captain Toombs?'

Alvaro cleared his throat. 'Yes, Your Grace. Captain Toombs was wondering if you might dine with him tomorrow night whilst his men gather water?'

'And perhaps trade a little, señor,' Toombs added. 'I have some fine tobacco on board. Straight from Virginia. Sweat still on it, so it is.'

'That sounds very interesting. But now I am ignorant with my manners.' Mendes sat up tall and spread out his hands in apology. 'I forget the *pez*! The fish! And a special dish for you, Captain.' He closed his eyes and lowered his head. 'In honour of your visiting our humble home. Leandro!' He waved his servant to the table.

Leandro picked up one of the covered dishes and placed it in front of Mendes. He walked back and brought another. Placing it in the centre of the table, it rang like a bell as he swept off the lid. Whatever the fish was, it was lost beneath a white sauce brimming with capers and lemons.

'Too kind, Governor. Too kind.' Toombs raised his palms in protest at the generosity.

'That is for your men, Captain.' Another dish swept in front of Toombs. 'This one is for you especially.' Mendes sat back, his fingers entwined as if in prayer.

Leandro stayed at Toombs's side, his hand on the domed lid. Devlin felt Alvaro Contes moving away from the balcony and towards the table, but his eyes were only watching Thomas pour more wine for himself and John Phillips.

Leandro lifted the lid from Toombs's platter with silent grace, and Toombs found himself staring at candlelight reflecting off the silver surface, the platter empty.

'I am not sure if I understand this, Your Grace. I have an empty dish, I see?' Toombs spoke nervously. The other guests looked at the empty charger and began to lower their wine glasses slowly to the table.

'Oh?' Mendes feigned concern. 'Did I not explain, Captain? That is my manners again, you must forgive me!'

He raised the lid of his own dish, placing it down to reveal two dragoon pistols lying side by side on folded green silk that had silenced their trip to the table.

There was a click as Leandro cocked his pistol, pushing its cold barrel against Toombs's temple before he could move.

'Ah,' was all Toombs said. Quietly.

'That dish, Captain,' Mendes spat, 'is where I will place your pirate *head*!' His arms snapped forward for the pistols as the pirates scraped back their chairs.

The albino bird, panicked by the sudden lurch, sprang from his shoulder, screeching straight into the candelabra, which rattled to the floor, shivering the table into darkness.

Chapter Five

*T*hose who survived would struggle to recall what tran-
spired after the raven sent the candelabra to the floor.
It would be remembered only through a series of flashbacks, a
cold recollection of frizzen sparks and muzzle flash.

There was still faint light in the room as the serene moon
flowed in through the balcony window.

The instant the candles vanished and snapped the table into
darkness the first pistol shot and a catlike wail came from
Toombs's side. In the same moment, Devlin sent his chair
flying backwards and reached across his body to his pistol.
He turned instinctively to Alvaro, mirroring the same action,
as smoke snaked in the moonlight between them.

And *there* was the difference.

Alvaro's pistol was a beautiful Spanish work of art with
an ornate bulb grip, its dog-head and pan on the right-hand
side of the gun.

To avoid the lock digging into his side all day, and catching
his clothes as he drew, he placed the pistol in his velvet belt
with the lock facing out, and hence also upside down to the
left hand now reaching for it. The right hand was naturally
for the sword. For most activities during the shooter's day
this mattered little; however, at this precise moment a pirate
faced him across the room, pulling his left-locked pistol. Surely
it was only one more movement? Alvaro simply had to turn

his wrist to grip the pistol and then again to cock it as it rose. He had done it dozens of times; it took the speed of thought to execute. But Devlin did not have to do it at all.

Before Devlin's barrel had cleared his frayed leather belt, the flint was locked. Alvaro cocked his weapon at about the same time that a small ball of lead thudded into his chest. He felt ribs crack like twigs within him. He fell back, forever, firing uselessly into the ceiling.

Three flashes so far. Three snaps of light that framed the action for a moment. The acrid smell of powder filled the dark. Devlin became aware of a struggle around the table. Now he held his pistol reversed like a club, and reached for the smaller one tucked behind his back.

Another flash and crack of air. He saw Valentim's snarling face lit for that instant. Someone cried out – a child's voice – then another shot followed from the right of the room.

Devlin crouched and fired low at the air where he had seen Valentim's head, then turned to the growl of Leandro bearing down on him like a bull, wielding a hatchet above his head, howling as he crashed into him.

The pair tumbled backwards to the balcony doors like playful lovers, sending the telescope crashing down. Devlin's dagger flew from his belt, scuffing along the floor. They rolled. The scalloped guard of Devlin's sword jabbed against his ribs.

Burdened by the axe, Leandro let it drop, preferring the power of his hands clasped round Devlin's coughing throat as he snarled through bared glowing teeth.

Devlin let go of the small gun and pulled uselessly at the giant's grip with his free hand. Leandro shook his head and giggled at the futile effort, but the grip gave Devlin enough leverage to roll and hammer his massive iron club of a pistol into Leandro's head.

The blow was enough. Leandro yelped off. They stood panting as an English curse and a shot rang out behind them. Leandro shook off the blow in time to see Devlin scrape out his blade with a grin.

In more restful times, Devlin would tell of his surprise as Leandro ignored the sword, put his sweating bald pate down and charged again. Devlin's lungs exploded as the blow took them flying through the doors and into the night.

It was inevitable. It happened in a heartbeat. The two of them went over the balcony. Devlin threw his sword as they fell, twisting Leandro beneath him. The thud of the landing on the stone below winded Devlin. It killed Leandro.

Devlin rolled upwards and left the sleeping giant. Breathing hard, he ran to retrieve his sword, sticking his pistol in his belt. His back ran cold with sweat. He turned and looked up at the dark house. Suddenly the room above was bathed in light and shouts. The guards had mounted the stairs and burst into the fray. More shots. More yelling. It was over then. It had taken seconds.

Devlin spun round and made for the gate, almost pulling it from its hinge; then he was through it and running, off the path and bolting away from the house.

He ran only for a few minutes, wading through waist-tall grass and low trees; then he began to struggle as the land slanted uphill, his chest like a furnace. He had to rest. He glanced behind. The house was no longer visible.

Kneeling down, hidden in the grass, he checked the action on his pistol for damage from the fall. He reloaded methodically, finding comfort in the clicks and snaps from his weapon and its partners, the patch pouch and cartridge box.

The ammo was prepared. A paper-load of powder wrapped round each ball with a twist. Bite, prime, pour, load, ram.

The ramrod refused to find its way home through his trembling hands.

Crouching there, under the moon, brought him back to the Kilkenny fields and his poaching days, years from this place. Killing one thing was as good as another. Blood as a butcher's boy, blood as a poacher, blood as a fisherman, four years of it with Coxon, and Philippe Ducos's blood still staining his boots.

Devlin took out the compass. He would have to head north to find the shore where Peter Sam had landed, having already discounted the bay where *his* party had arrived since – even if he made it to the boat – a lone man rowing out to the *Lucy* would be a grand target. Besides, he was counting on any pursuers making that judgement and granting him escape time. He looked up at the volcanic hills. North, over those hills, avoiding the roads, was a hard passage. His crossbelt and sword now hung over his waistcoat, as he bundled the heavy coat in his arms and pressed on.

Valentim, still holding a French dragoon pistol in his right hand, looked over the balcony at Leandro's broken body. 'I want him found!' he yelled to the guards. 'He will make his way to the boat. Do so yourselves. If you cannot find him, if the boat is still there, return to me.' They bowed and ran from the room.

Valentim moved back inside. His foot kicked against something and his eyes fell to watch Devlin's ebony dagger spinning across the stone floor. As if woken from a dream, he picked it up and admired it before placing it cautiously in the sash round his waist. The white raven alighted on his shoulder and preened. He looked down at the dead Alvaro Contes, his friend, and crossed himself. The only breathing sound in the room was his own.

Slowly he turned back to his fallen telescope. Lying his pistol on the balcony chair, he re-erected the wood and brass instrument. A minute later he had sighted it on the *Lucy*. She sat still, a ship asleep, silhouetted against the moon. He swung left and beheld the *Shadow* on the other side of the bay.

It had not been a lie about the lack of men on board, although within a day he could maybe add thirty more from the townsfolk and slaves. Nevertheless, the *Shadow*'s acting captain, overweight and indolent as he was, would have also recognised the brigantine for the pirate ship described in the recent correspondence from Cape Coast Castle. The captain doubtlessly had watched Alvaro escort the party to shore and surely would have maintained a cautious watch.

He had anticipated capturing the pirates and forcing the ship to surrender. The triumph would make him a legend amongst the islands, possibly gain him enough fame to sail his way off this slave rock and back home to Portugal.

He would have time yet before the crew began to miss their pirate brothers. Enough time to get to the *Shadow* and inform its feckless captain of what had occurred and then, with a single broadside, advise the pirates to kneel or suffer the fate of their brothers and the wrath of his frigate.

But there were plenty of dories around the island to steal. The man Devlin could get back to his ship, inform them that the *Shadow* had only thirty men, that the house had few defences and even fewer guards. The pirate Devlin must be found. Found and silenced.

Returning to the telescope, he could see the lanterns of his men by the shore. The boat was still there. Devlin had run inland. He would not escape. It was fortunate that the horses had not yet been stabled for the night.

*

Devlin made his way to the top of another hill. Covered in grass seeds and sweat, a raging thirst at his throat, he willed the black clouds to break. From up here he could discern a road, maybe some houses, and in the distance what might be the sea, or perhaps just more of the same bloody dirt that his boots were full of.

Six miles at most to reach Peter Sam on the northern shore – not a great distance by any reckoning, and certainly not when being pursued. He fumbled for the compass in his coat, its whalebone face glowing beneath the moon as its dial danced on his palm. NNE would take him away from Ribeira Brava, the largest town and the one best avoided, for if there was any garrison on the island it would be in Ribeira.

Readjusting the boulder that his coat had become, he moved down the hill. He plucked at the shirt, stuck to his back with sweat. He thought of abandoning the heavy woollen twill coat, but not only did its pockets hold all that he had to carry him through this night, it also had other advantages. He had noticed the ordinariness of Seth Toombs without his. A good coat and a fine hat would always mark one as a cut above the rabble. It was like a priest's vestments in as much as it could transform the simple into the sublime. He would hold on to it.

A crack of thunder directly above him made him cower and look to the clouds in awe. The earth seemed to join the sky all around him with the falling of the African rain. Blinded by the sudden wave of water, Devlin shook the coat on gratefully, but mourned the tricorne he had left behind on Valentim Mendes's table as its three corners would now be running the hammering rain away from his back. He trotted on, the warm rain seeming to laugh at him as he stumbled through its walls of water.

*

Black Bill, the rain clinging to his beard, leaned on the starboard gunwale to look to the black frigate across the bay, her shape cut out against the hills by the cascade of rain.

He had spent the last hour sheathing the guns from the downpour, aided by the drunken gunner captain, Robert Hartley, who cursed the mongrels of the gods for the rain they had decided to throw upon him and his guns.

Below him a neverending rum-laden chorus of 'Leave Her, Johnny' hailed up through the deck.

> *It was rotten meat and weevil bread,*
> *Leave her, Johnny, leave her.*
> *'You'll eat or starve,' the old man said,*
> *And it's time for us to leave her.*

Soaked as he was, he remained, watching the whitecaps growing as the harbour seemed to boil. It would be a short rain, for he knew any fall was rare in the Verdes: the dust of the earth and the tinder branches of the dragon trees were testament to that. Nonetheless, it would no doubt delay the return of the men ashore.

He thought of Peter Sam's small encampment. They were probably huddled under their makeshift tents eating cold meats and drinking dry the seven jugs they had taken with them. They had enough supplies for two days, but now were no doubt swearing against the soul of Patrick Devlin for suggesting such a course as they tried to keep their lanterns and, more importantly, their powder dry. He spat over the side and moved down to join his brethren and hoped no fool was trying to light a pipe below.

*

Devlin had found a nook in the black hillside to shelter and watch the forks of lightning rape the sky. He wore his coat over his head and had smothered his pistol inside his waistcoat to try and keep her dry. The slope was perhaps only thirty feet up from the dirt path, but he could see the snaking road from where he came, and to his left the passage that would take him to the rocky shore where Peter Sam lay as his rescuer.

He estimated that in less than an hour he could join them. Every moment of lightning showed him the sea in the distance all around him, the view blocked only by the mountain peaks that echoed the thunder like giants threatening to rise up and walk.

A movement from the path made him snap his head. A lightning flash revealed four crouching dogs lurching along the road to his right. No, not dogs. The blue crash of light was addling his brain, changing the creatures. Horses. They were horses, and upon them black oilskinned wraiths sniffing him out.

He watched as the rider in front wheeled his horse to face the others. The rider swung out his arm to indicate a direction and one of his companions pointed to another path in response. They moved closer together, and even through the rain Devlin could hear raised voices.

He drew his coat around his head, permitting himself a single eye to stare out through a hanging forelock, fearing his face would glow and reveal his presence if they turned towards him. Another flash of light and they vanished with it, riding to the east.

The time he had to make the remaining few miles grew ever shorter. He rose up and stumbled down to the north road, gasping at the rain as if drowning in it, throwing glances behind at every step, looking for the riders.

*

The rocky shore on which the boat had landed gave little comfort to the seven pirates camped there. Peter Sam sat beneath his crude tent of sailcloth tied to a wooden pole and watched the ocean, trying to grapple back their boat from the pebbled beach. They had heard the first rumblings of the squall two hours ago from the south. Hugh Harris had lovingly wrapped his pair of matching duelling pistols in his coat before putting them to bed within his tent to shield them from the coming rain.

Peter Sam drank from a jug of colonial whisky, switching left and right as he did so to check for eyes upon him, for it was a personal thing with him and he loathed sharing his drink. He savoured the warm liquid, knowing that his brothers would not appreciate its smoky, caramel taste.

They camped against a wind-free wall from where a natural passage crept up to coarse bushes that led to the barren countryside. From here they could see any approach; it had proved the best-hidden landing point, if not the most hospitable.

Another flash of lightning and he began to ponder on the night's events. If all had gone well, the fat, wealthy governor would have ferried himself out to the *Lucy* and found his first course to be a leaden one. Under a flag of truce, two of the men would then have rowed back to shore to deliver the ransom threat.

Whatever guard the governor possessed would have trembled in their boots. They would have sent a runner to Ribeira for more men, for that would be the garrison town; then the priest would take command and insist on paying the ransom.

Toombs would barter on the whole account being settled whilst it was still dark, before the light of day brought courage to the foolish. The money would be theirs, and shortly after dawn the *Lucy* would swim in from the west and pick them up to make a mockery of Devlin for his concerns.

Grinning at this, Peter Sam thought of the bond between himself and Toombs. It would never have occurred to him that after getting the doubloons Toombs might cut and leave. He had murdered two men for Toombs in his time, without thought or question. As fishermen together they had shared fur blankets and black bread as the Newfoundland winds sliced at their bones. It was Toombs's plan to go on the account over three years ago and Peter Sam had never regretted it. He ate what he wanted and drank like a priest. For fifteen years he had been a hungry fisherman; now his belly was sated and his heart utterly loyal to Toombs.

Chomping on a pickled egg, combing the flecks of it out of his beard with a black thumbnail, he watched Hugh, weaving his way to the longboat to fetch another bottle, swinging his arms, ape-like, in his own drunken style. Silhouetted against the sea, shrouded in rain, he raised the rum above his head in triumph, generating a low, bovine cheer from the other tents.

His scarecrow-like form suddenly stood stock-still, his eyes wide. The bottle fell from his right hand, almost hitting his streaking cutlass as it flew out.

Without a pause the other six were upright and following Hugh's stare, a flash of lightning dancing off their drawn blades.

They spread out, backing towards the pistol tent, all except Peter Sam, who stared razor-eyed at the figure breaking its way through the bushes before them. The black, headless shape appeared, staggering towards them. With a sweep of its arms, off came the sodden, cape-like coat that concealed the bedraggled form of Patrick Devlin.

The others relaxed in recognition; only Peter kept his apprehensive expression.

'What are you doing here?' Peter asked, moving towards him.

'Water,' Devlin croaked. 'Water, Peter.'

Peter Sam grabbed Devlin and pulled him to his face.

'Where's Seth?' He swallowed hard. 'Where's Thomas Deakins?'

The others put their weapons away and moved to join them.

'Dead, for all I know!' Devlin gasped. 'We were attacked. I got away.'

Peter pushed him away. The rain slowed.

'Oh! And you got aways! Now isn't that a page of the good book I'd like to hear! Who attacked you?'

'A trap.' Devlin bent down, panting. 'Governor trapped us. He's following me now!'

Andrew Morris, a Dorset sailor, a pirate for a year only, spoke with a tremor. 'Following you now?' he asked.

'Aye. Four of them. Behind me somewheres.' Devlin reached for his coat and straightened up.

'He's lying!' Peter snarled. 'He's given them up for his own hide, and led the Portos to us!' He stepped back quickly, his cutlass whirling loosely in his hand. 'What did you sell them for, Patrick? How many pieces?'

Devlin stopped putting on his coat and let it fall. 'Water, Peter. I'll not ask again. I've killed two men this night already.'

Hugh Harris faced Peter Sam and shouted through the rain and thunder: 'Give him quarter, Peter! For all our sakes!'

Peter pushed him aside. 'Article Eight, lads. Quarrel shall be ended,' he yelled. 'On shore by sword or pistol. By first blood!'

'I don't want to shoot you, Peter. I need you,' Devlin said wearily.

'By sword it be, then,' and Peter drew his dagger to partner his cutlass. 'No quarter, dog!' The others moved out in a silent crescent around the two.

Devlin's shoulders sank, then rose again in a forlorn breath. 'We've no time for this!' he shouted against the rain. 'They'll be on us!' But Peter had already drawn back his cutlass and sprang forward, cleaving the air.

Devlin's sword barely cleared in time to cross his body and meet the blow as he leaped backwards, the impact rattling through his arm.

He crept further back, his sword high before his face. He had seen how the pirates fought. There was no interest in a handsome fight or skilfully disarming an opponent. Simply slice off a part of your foe's head and move on to the next man. The victim might catch part of his face as it fell into his hands and would slump to his knees, then suck the air in disbelief as a following pirate ran him through.

Peter hacked again, a blow intent on smashing Devlin's thinner blade. His dagger dived in towards Devlin's liver but stabbed into the walnut grip of his pistol instead, marking it forever. A lightning flash as the steel clashed again, blades sliding down to their hilts as they came together, the two blades running with rain as if made of water. Peter hissed something through the roar of the thunder as Devlin's left hand snatched the wrist that drove the dagger, pulling Peter with it. Peter's body turned with the knife as Devlin's sword arm wrapped itself round his neck. His back was at Devlin's chest. His ear at his mouth. He could smell the brass guard of Devlin's sword at his throat.

'We can't do this!' Devlin spat. 'Stop this now!'

With a boar's roar Peter shot forward, hurling Devlin over his shoulder. Devlin saw the ground spin away from him as he crashed onto his back. His pistol fell from his waistcoat.

He rolled away in instinct and felt Peter's cutlass crack the ground where his head had been. He pushed himself up and back, checking for any of the others joining in. They stood, impassively, as if looking from a carriage window.

He appealed again to Peter, 'Have sense, man! Cool your head! There's danger here!'

Peter's chest heaved. He slung the dagger down and ran his hand across his face in a futile effort to wipe off the rain, then charged again, his sword hand almost behind him as if to hurl the cutlass. Devlin jumped back as the sword cut through the air in front of his eyes.

Missing his mark, Peter unbalanced, stumbling through like a lubber missing the last step of the companion. Devlin caught his fall, pushing him to the ground and holding him there, his forearm over his throat, slamming his sword onto Peter's cutlass.

Peter's body seethed beneath Devlin's, surprised by the strength within the Irishman; then he heard the words whispering from Devlin's mouth. In his rage they made no sense at first, as they had made no sense to Sam Fletcher when he first heard them whimpering from Philippe Ducos upon the island. But this time they were in English and Peter Sam knew the words very well.

'Gold,' Devlin had said. 'Hundreds of thousands of louis in gold and I know where it lies! If I die it never gets found. I *was* up to something, and this is it, Peter. A fortune in gold and I need you to get it and I need you to get the man who's killed Seth. Who's killed Thomas. Now belay this shite for another day and let's kill the Porto bastard together!'

Devlin released his arm and stood up, slow and breathless, his head lowered, a pain across his shoulders all of a sudden. He backed away and sheathed his sword. Peter Sam brought himself up as if struggling against the fall of rain.

The two men glared at each other. Steam wisped off them like smoke from snuffed-out candles. The race of their hearts in their ears drowned out even the rush of the rain.

Peter Sam lifted up his cutlass to the expectant eyes still standing around the two men. He looked once down the length of the blade, as if it had a secret etched into the steel. He turned the blade and ran it home to his belt.

'Show me where the bastard is!' was all that he said.

Chapter Six

*T*he rain had stopped. For almost an hour the riders had searched whilst their oilskin cloaks turned to lead across their backs. The horses' white sweat streaked down their hides, their heads rocking and snorting in protest at their labours.

They trotted northwards through the valleys, having returned spent from the ride to Carrical in search of the Irishman.

Twelve miles east they had ridden on Valentim Mendes's instinct that Devlin would try to hide away from the larger towns and seek a fishing boat to steal with a mind to try and return to the pirate brigantine. The sky had cleared and the moon had already started her path downward as midnight waned. With every hour fewer words passed amongst them, each man conscious of the murder he might commit at any turn in the path.

Mendes had ordered two men to stay at the pirates' longboat; the rest of his personal guard rode with him. He had been confident as he galloped out into the night that he would ride over Devlin stumbling in the dark; now, two hours having passed, he rued not riding straight to Ribeira Brava to at least alert the small garrison of idle soldiers that doubled as choirboys. Now Ribeira was his last hope, and truculently he turned his mount along the path to the town.

His head lifted at the stamping of his black horse and the chattering of his men: before them, in the road, lay the prone form of a man, his black coat spread away from his body like bats' wings.

In a heart murmur Mendes conceived that Devlin had been injured by his own servant, the brave and murdered Leandro, and now here he lay dead or dying, probably all the time they had been searching further east.

Raising his hand, he silenced his men and slid down from his horse. The still body lay some twenty yards in front of him, and by the second step he had drawn his fine Toledo blade as he made his approach. One by one his men followed, rolling their muskets off their backs.

Mendes looked up to the slopes of the valley for any ambush, but saw only the dark vagueness of the dragon trees and bushes that grew amongst the rocks above them.

He was at the body now. His first instinct was to run it through. Pierce down until the ribs grated and the dirt stopped his lunge, then pull back with the body sucking at the blade. But the man might still be alive and, before he became a corpse, he should look at the gentleman who would send him righteously from this world.

Reaching down, Mendes pulled at the coat's left shoulder, which suddenly rolled against his grip. He found his face inches from the eye of the octagonal muzzle of Devlin's pistol, clicking thrice into life from the cover of the coat.

'And how are you doing, Valentim?' Devlin grinned.

A curtain of men rose on either side of the moonlit valley. Peter Sam and three stood up on his left with muskets pointed at Mendes's guard, whilst Hugh Harris and the others levelled their guns direct at the governor.

Mendes's men, mouths agape, shunned their guns like

pitchforks in wintertime. They knew pirates, and they knew they would be fed whether they fought or not.

Mendes rose with Devlin and sent cursed looks to his men. One of them felt Mendes's glare and bent swiftly to take up his musket; in the same movement he fell dead as a crack echoed from the left slope.

'Wise not to move, gentlemen,' Devlin said, edging backwards, his pistol set on Mendes.

'So,' Mendes smiled, 'you were never alone, *pirate*?' He stood aloof from the gathering, his sword resting on his right shoulder like a parasol.

Devlin smiled back. He shouted up to Hugh Harris, 'Hugh, come relieve these men of any duty they have left so as they can sleep peaceful, like, this morning!'

The three pirates came lumbering down the hillside, the buckles rattling on their shoes and crossbelts mimicking their cackling laughter.

One by one they picked up the wheel-lock muskets, and pulled the cheap and pitted hangers from the soldiers' belts, piling it like firewood on the side of the road. All the while, Mendes never stopped grinning, and never took his eyes from Devlin's.

'And what of me, Señor Devlin? Would you like to take *my* sword and pistol?' Mendes sidestepped, cutting his Toledo through the air, pointing to the amused pirates.

'He moves quickly for a lubberly soul, don't he?' Hugh remarked kindly and they leisurely gave him space. Mendes threw off his cloak and balanced himself to face Devlin.

'I am not so afraid of you sea dogs as you may hope to think, señor!'

As his last word hung in the air, a blinding spark flew off his outstretched blade. The bones in his hand hummed and the sword leaped away to quiver on the ground yards away.

'You should be!' Peter Sam's voice boomed from behind the sights of a smoking musket high up on the slope. All eyes gaped at the shot.

Mendes recovered first and pulled his pistol at Devlin, who had followed everyone in staring up at the black shape of the quartermaster.

Devlin turned back in time to hear the dog-head strike the pan with a flat click, then watch Mendes's face as he realised the gun had become nothing but wet driftwood in his hand. He cursed, the pistol still raised; then his eyes blinked shut and he collapsed forward, unconscious from the blow that Hugh Harris had swiped across his nape with his club of a pistol.

'You couldn't have shot him, then, Hugh, no? Before he fired at me and all?' Devlin asked, bending to pick up Mendes's weapon and spying his dagger hiding in Mendes's sash.

'Me powder's probably as wet as his, Pat. I didn't want to risk the fact,' Hugh stated earnestly.

It was the pain within Mendes's shoulder blades and skull that finally hauled him awake. He had no concept of how long had passed, but it was with struggling horror that he realised that he was tied to a broad tree, his chest and arms naked. The pirates had used the straps from his soldiers' muskets to bind his legs and chest.

Curiously his right arm was free, but could not release the leather snares holding him, no matter how he tugged at them. His left arm was outstretched and numb with agony as he tried to move it; then he followed the length and found it to be bound to a neighbouring tree, the hand wrapped entirely in a leather and cloth bundle.

Through the bundle he could feel something cold and hard in his forced fist. He reached over with his free hand but, tied tight as he was across the body, he could hardly even reach his elbow. He struggled to pull against his bonds, feeling his bare back tearing against the bark.

Exasperated, he became vaguely aware of voices in front of him, below the ridge of trees where he was trapped. The group of pirates sat huddled near the road locked in conversation back and forth. Beyond them he glimpsed the strange sight of his guard, naked from the waist up, sitting backwards on their peacefully grazing horses and, close by, his doublet and weapons.

He yelled at the pirates. His voice was unintelligible even to himself, like the rambling panic of a dream, but it brought attention. Slowly Devlin and Peter Sam got up and approached. Mendes recalled the big bald one as the rogue who had shot the sword from his hand. Now he carried a small boarding axe, and Devlin strolled towards him tossing the ebony-handled dagger a few times before placing it again behind his back.

Any modicum of respect and title had fallen from Mendes. Yesterday a man like Devlin held as much importance in his world as his morning stools. Now the former servant would talk to him about death or life. Mendes would not be the first nobleman to have his birthright shaved away by the slash of a pirate's blade.

Devlin smiled his most modest smirk, and spoke plainly. 'We're of a divided opinion, Valentim. Peter Sam and I.' He leaned with a languid arm against the tree close to Mendes's head. 'You can be of some help in the matter.'

Mendes's voice was guttural and distinct. 'You will not use my Christian name, dog. Untie me!'

Devlin continued unabashed, 'I believe, *Valentim*, that the good folks in Ribeira are unaware of us, and that we could make our way back to the ship with no harm to ourselves. However' – he indicated the grim, dark form of Peter Sam – 'Peter here thinks that the *Lucy*'s boat be surrounded by soldiers and we should take the long way round in his. What say you to that point, *Valentim*?'

'I will tell you nothing! Release me at once!'

'I'm telling you, Devlin,' Peter Sam snapped. 'No sense going back to the ship at all! The *Lucy*'s got that frigate staring at her. I counted a hundred men on her myself, man!'

It was only a small reaction from Mendes, a slightly unfocused look, the slow opening of the mouth as if to speak, but it was the very look Devlin was striving to see.

'It was true, then, Valentim?' His eyes shone. 'That beauty has only thirty men aboard? 'Tis all I needed to know, señor. You see, Peter? Easy pickings. I'll also wager a penny that a fine gentleman like Valentim here would keep his purse on that there ship. Nice and safe, like, from servants and pirates. What say you, Valentim?'

Valentim blasphemed and wrestled against his bonds, swinging his free right arm wildly until Peter's grip held it fast. He looked hatefully, furiously, between the two men, but whereas Devlin's face was still very genial, the other pirate hated back.

'Who is this oaf who stares at me so? Why am I tied like this?'

'Ah, now there's a tragic circumstance and no mistake,' Devlin sighed. Taking the time to check that the strange bundle of leather and cloth round Mendes's wrist was tight enough, he set out the position they now found themselves in.

Devlin himself, he explained to Mendes, had persuaded

the pirates that instant retribution was unfair. After all, Mendes was only defending himself against their attitudes towards him. He had behaved exactly as any one of them would have done. Rather more unfortunate was the fact that one of their late companions was close to Peter Sam, but that was as nothing compared to the loss of their captain. Revenge was inevitable: it had always been their way.

'Because of this, Valentim, I must do what I must. Right was on your side: we all agree that and hold no more against you. But this is how it plays for you now.'

Mendes suddenly became aware of the long black fuse that trailed down from his sealed wrist and along the ground.

'What is this madness?' he asked, his voice faltering.

'Our Hugh has been kind enough to make us a fuse. Hopefully, by his arm-lengths, he reckons it to be a ten-minuter.' Devlin carried the black length away with him a few steps backwards. 'The purpose of which is to blow up the grenadoe that you're holding in your left hand.'

Mendes stared. Devlin continued, 'If providence is with you, Valentim, the fuse may burn out before it reaches its mark. But, for your bravery against us, we'll give you a pirate's chance as well.' At his closing words, Peter Sam slapped the short axe into Mendes's open right hand and stood away. Mendes's mind raced but still did not comprehend. 'You can't reach your ankles with it, but it should just afford you enough reach to do whatever you decide is best.'

Mendes felt the weight of the hatchet in his grip and he lifted it to his eyes. It was old but sharp, maybe eighteen inches in all.

'I understand none of this.' He spoke quietly.

'It's plain as print, Your Grace.' Devlin bowed. 'You could wait the whole ten minutes and slap at the fuse with the axe hoping to put it out, or hope it dies itself – although I wouldn't like to count on that personally.' He took his unloaded pistol and placed the charred end of the charge against the pan, drawing back the head with a fateful click. 'Or you could take five minutes to hack at your own wrist. Once your left arm is free – minus your hand, naturally – you'll have more movement to escape. That is, if you're able to concentrate after all that.'

Peter Sam chipped in, 'Don't gamble that the grenadoe would only take your hand anyways, Your Grace. I've seen Robert make them to take down three men. You'll be looking at all sorts of parts whilst you bleed to death tied to a tree.' He strolled away down to his brothers, some satisfaction growing within him.

Devlin cocked his head to the half-naked soldiers on horseback. 'They may offer you some encouragement, Valentim. And the prospect, of course, of chasing us down before we reach the shore and all.'

The other pirates had already started to move along the southern road back to Preguica. 'Goodnight, Your Grace,' Devlin whispered, and fired the gun. The fuse blazed into life, then calmly smoked and smouldered along its deadly path as Devlin let it fall. He turned his back and moved to join the others. He walked down to the road, expecting to hear the curses and pleadings of the man strapped to the tree. He heard nothing and he never looked back.

Adão Mota was the captain of the black frigate in the bay of Preguica. He had come with her from Lisbon, commanding a collection of farmers and soldiers, none of whom had any worth at sea.

For over a month they had stayed here, always waiting for

more men, being inspected twice a week by the governor, with his unnatural bird perched menacingly on his shoulder.

Proudly, *A Sombra* sat on the windward shore, her head to the sea. Immaculate with her new grey sails and freshly blackened rigging, and yet almost daily Adão would poke away cobwebs from between her shrouds.

He was woken by one of his men shouting and rapping on his cabin door.

'Capitão, Capitão! It is I, Estêvão! Awake!'

Adão dragged open his eyes and brushed away a wayward sweaty lock from his brow. He looked to the stern windows at the dark and the moths planted on the glass. He quietened down the rapping with an even louder questioning of Estêvão's parentage before crawling from his cot for his blue coat of rank to accompany his nightshirt, which was also his dayshirt.

Scratching his grey beard, he asked Estêvão abruptly why he had been woken from his dream of schoolgirls at evening song, only to be told in a rapid report that it was the two o'clock watch and that a boat was approaching from the shore.

Cursing, Adão fumbled for his spyglass and stumbled barefoot and without breeches to the weatherdeck, followed by Estêvão. He hurried to the starboard gunwale and stared to the shore.

A small boat was indeed coming across. From the lantern that one of its passengers was holding aloft he counted five soldiers, distinctive in their purple caps and breastplates.

'What is this now?' Adão snapped the glass shut and slapped the chest of the soldier next to him. 'Tell me, Estêvão, has anything happened this evening?'

'No, Capitão. Nothing has happened since the boat rowed to shore hours ago.'

'Nobody else left that merchant ship?'

The soldier shook his head. 'Perhaps they have run out of wine, Capitão?'

'Who is on watch?' Adão moved to the forequarter to study the *Lucy*.

'Just Damião and me, Capitão.'

'You were right to rouse me, Estêvão. Maybe there is trouble. Grab your pike.' Estêvão departed to fetch one of the boarding pikes that stood guard around the mizzen mast.

Adão raised the glass again and weaved it across the deck of the *Lucy*. All was still. Just before nine he had watched the boat carrying Alvaro Contes to the merchant ship, then saw it struggle away again with some foreigners aboard. Nothing unusual in that. Governor Mendes would often entertain visiting merchants and he had paid it no mind. Why was a party approaching his ship so early in the morning? Maybe it *was* for more wine, absurd as that seemed.

Estêvão returned to his captain's side with his fearsome weapon, a ten-foot-long wooden shaft with an iron spike. His only other was his chipped rusty sword.

'I will go and get dressed properly, Estêvão. Bring Damião and watch that boat,' Adão ordered. 'Call me when they are here if I have not returned. Let no one up without me.'

He trotted back to the Great Cabin to clear some of the fog of slumber with a little Jerez wine, then paused as he reached the door and turned his head to Estêvão.

'That ship, Estêvão, how many guns does she have?'

Estêvão had counted them for the last three hours of his watch, apart from the hour of the rain when he had sheltered below.

'Only eight, Capitão: she is a small boat.' Estêvão shrugged.

Adão shrugged in return and ducked into his cabin. Eight

guns were no match for his frigate's twenty-four. If there was trouble afoot he would not be found caught with his breeches down, and with a confident snort he looked about the cabin for where he had tossed them.

From the top of the *Lucy*'s mainmast, Sam Morwell watched the slow progress of the longboat. From almost eighty feet in the air it was like watching a play from the top gallery. He could see the trembling of the sea from the rowing of the oars and even the flickering of the lantern light as moths danced around its glass.

On the deck of the frigate he watched the captain march to and fro, seemingly fretting. He watched him descend below, leaving two soldiers pointing out to each other the approaching boat. With a sigh, Sam Morwell slung himself down the shrouds. His feet gripped like fists, travelling down like a spider across his web.

He jumped the remaining feet rather than slinging off the gunwale, and went to tell Bill what he had seen.

Adão reappeared, a pistol stuck in his belt, a cutlass hanging at his side. He joined the soldiers at the bulwark. The boat was almost upon them, certainly within shouting distance. The only man facing them was the coxswain, holding the lantern on a pole. Adão decided to call first.

'Ahoy! Why so late a visit? What occurs?' he yelled through cupped hands. There was no reply, only the slow waving of the lantern holder's free arm as acknowledgement. 'Well, we will just wait and see,' he said to Estêvão. 'I will have to have a late morning because of this.'

A few minutes later and the narrow gap between the two boats had disappeared with a thump. A rope was thrown up from the dark. Estêvão belayed it to a pin and they watched the first of them climbing up the tumblehome.

'Welcome aboard, soldier!' Adão exclaimed as the face of a common soul emerged over the side, smiling from beneath the purple sloping cap.

'Ho, chum!' Hugh Harris grinned, and unloaded one of his long pistols into Adão's face. He fired his second into Estêvão's stunned mouth.

He let go of his guns as the bodies fell; they swung from his neck on a linen sling. He drew his cutlass to Damião, who leaped backwards with his pike thrust forwards, his whole form quaking with shock. Andrew Morris swept over the side and put Damião at his ease by a shot to the head that showered his blood across the side of the longboat hanging above the deck.

As the others clambered aboard, encumbered with weapons, Hugh and Andrew dashed fore and aft to the companionways to the lower deck, slamming their hatches down and battening them to the coaming. The crew were already shouting and moving below in the hot gloom.

Devlin heard himself laughing as they took off the breastplates and caps of Valentim's guards. The subterfuge had worked well enough to get them to the *Shadow*, whilst the other three pirates laid low in the bottom of the boat beneath the sheets.

The breastplates rattled to the deck, the lantern light from each mast shining off them. Peter Sam approached carrying the satchel of grenadoes across his shoulders.

'That went well,' he said.

'Didn't it, though?' Devlin agreed. 'Now for the rest of it.' He walked calmly to the main hatch and looked down through the grating into the dark, cautious of a possible shot from below. He could see and hear anxious movement in the dark, like the rustling of rats. He spoke loudly and slowly. 'English!' he said. Then, '*Pirata!*'

Panic spread below. Hugh shouted the same word above the closed companion aft, then chuckled wickedly at the response of cursing and prayers.

Devlin carried on, 'It's early morn, gentlemen. If any of you know English you know pirates. That ship yonder: that's no merchant. That's an honest-to-sainthood pirate!' More prayers. 'There's thirty of us up here and another seventy over there and I have something for you.' He beckoned to Peter Sam to remove the battens.

Lifting it a few inches, Peter bowled an unlit grenadoe into the dark, hearing it rolling delightfully below. The response rocked the ship as more than two dozen men ran scrambling through hammocks and each other to escape.

'The next one won't be so still, lads!' Devlin shouted as the hatch slammed down again. Peter Sam took a small clay pot from his bag and dashed aft to Hugh.

Devlin continued, 'I would be after suggesting that you take the trouble to escape as you can.' He signalled two of his men to the swivel guns, stanchion mounted on the quarterdeck rail, and they knuckled their foreheads and ran gleefully to it.

Hugh unbattened the aft companion as Peter Sam lit the fuse of the clay pot from the wick of the mizzen's lantern. He hurled it down the hole; it smashed somewhere below and the 'stinkpot' ignited. It was a foul concoction of brimstone, tar, powder and rags, designed to cause fear and confusion with its noxious fumes and clouds of smoke. The effect was tremendous, as eddies of smoke wafted up through the hatch, and Devlin stepped back along the skidbeams to avoid the stench. The pirates controlled the only means upwards from the lower decks: Hugh and Peter Sam covered the companion below the belfry, Andrew Morris the forward one before the fo'c'sle.

Hands began to poke up through the main hatch, waving like fishtails, voices pleading for saints. They would have to move swiftly now, before a brain began to form a plan below. The sailors could reach the weapon locker; some martyr might run to the magazine. Darkness, confusion and fear were all the pirates had to their advantage against the numbers of the crew. They ran aft, shouting and cursing, stamping their boots and shouting to invisible comrades, raising the 'vapours', banging their steel against anything that rattled back, creating the same clamour that had panicked the otherwise formidable crew of the *Noble.*

They opened the companion aft and by pistol and snarl dragged up the wide-eyed young men five at a time, kicking and beating them to the ship's waist, where the swivel guns from the quarterdeck kept them seated on their hands.

They moved fast, viciously, until all were up and huddled in groups in the gangways on both sides, in order to separate them, whilst still allowing them to take in the bloody sight of their dead captain and comrades, lying like discarded marionettes across the deck. Less than two minutes had passed.

Before the sweat had dried on the crew, three-quarters of them had been taken down to the boat waiting below, almost grateful that seven men had taken the responsibility of the ship from them. They pushed away from the ship, excited to be alive, even saluted their aggressors as they rowed to shore.

'We'll need to flush the decks and hold,' Devlin spoke to Peter Sam. 'Make sure they're all out.'

'Aye.' Peter Sam nodded. 'Time enough.'

'True,' Devlin agreed. He faced the six remaining crewmen, their eyes magnetised by the sword in his hand, which motioned to the capstan aft of the mainmast. 'I'll assume the hawser is still hooked up, gentlemen, so I expects you to move it for me now. Move! Up anchor!'

His actions were clear and they rose. They moved along the starboard gangway as if chained together and were grateful for the familiarity of taking hold of the capstan's shafts as they began to push, their heads down.

Devlin and Peter Sam stood shoulder to shoulder and looked above to the rigging. 'Get a couple of souls aloft. Fore course and main course will get us to the *Lucy*. The new lads can warp us along in the boats or we'll never get out with the wind to us,' Devlin said.

'Aye, Pat.' Peter nodded, then he looked Devlin hard in the eye. 'Once we're back with the others you can tell me about that gold. All of it. And be sure I believe you.'

'That I will, mate, surely.' Devlin slapped the big man's shoulder. 'Now, let me stand to the fo'c'sle and get Bill to take a look at me. Let him know it's us upon him.' He wheeled away, confident about Peter Sam's ability to muster the small crew to make sail.

It had been a long night. Devlin took out his pipe and tobacco, which he had secreted well enough to keep dry. He looked almost mournfully at the silver tube with the devilish face engraved upon it. Once it was empty he would return to tapers and tinderbox or lanterns for lighting his pipe. He remembered how the pinewood sticks dipped in sulphur and phosphorous were a gift, so Coxon had told him, to Coxon's father, from a man of science named Boyle. He could purchase no more. They were a curious but useful tool and now there were only six left.

He was cold now. He had left his coat on the shore when they changed into the soldiers' garments. Drawing on his pipe, he looked back to the deck at the lifeless body of Adão and the fine, heavy dark coat he wore. Before the body went over the side, he would remove it from him: the coat made a difference.

They would search the ship for any treasures she offered, but the greatest treasure was surely the *Shadow* herself. A frigate, no less. A man-of-war. Twenty nine-pounders to bear. Coming to her from the shore, he spied two more at her stern and now, as he stretched himself over the bow, two chasers to match.

As soon as he had laid eyes on the *Shadow* he had craved her, and it was as if the night's events had drawn him irrevocably towards her.

Watching the main course drop and crack against the wind, he thought of the men he had fallen in with. They were brave and resourceful, drunken and dissolute, but he had met men like that before. It had taken months of being with them and this evening to seal his opinion of why they were different, why the ship was different.

All along it was there: in their food, their drink, their work, their loyalty to one another. They were equal. They were free.

For weeks Devlin had wanted to return to the servitude and drudgery that had been his whole life, living from hand to mouth and day to day, like everybody else. Hanging out of the pocket of another man. For what purpose?

Now men who would have ordered or pitied him would lie dead at his feet. His pockets would hang heavy with what they owned or had taken from the sweat of others.

He watched the terrified Portuguese sailors secure the anchor to the cathead under the watchful eyes of Peter Sam, who next pushed them to lower the longboat and the gig in order to warp the ship to the *Lucy*. The morning would have them signed on to the crew, six more men gone from whatever life they had before to wind up their sheet either rich or dead.

The approaching dawn would also bring the prospect of the French gold ever closer. On seeing the *Shadow*, it had rekindled the flame of the idea within him. The folded parchment had provided him with a chance of greatness. The possibility of a wealth he and his kind should never know, only marvel at in tales of Tew and Avery and their fabled riches pirated from sultans and treasure ships. But just like them, he could not gain it alone.

He drew long and hard on the meerschaum pipe, standing alone on the fo'c'sle and listening to the splash of the oars as the six Portos began the effort of warping the behemoth away. He would need these ships. He would need these men.

'Opportunity makes a thief.' He recalled the words from some page somewhere far behind in another world, and he glowed from the sense of it and from the warmth of his pipe.

Come the dawn, nothing could stop him.

Chapter Seven

*L*etter from Father Carlos Barrios, Ribeira Brava, São Nicolau, Nossa Senhora Da Luz to General Phipps, Cape Coast Castle

April 1717

For the great interest of all who hear or read the presents herein, Greeting,

It is with a low heart that I must report attack upon our home by pirata vessel so benevolently warned upon us by your generous self. I must inform you of detail passed on me by the Governor His Grace Valentim Mendes that assault has resulted in theft of ship Sombra of twenty-four cannon by the pirata Devlin and the death of Capitão Mota of Sombra and several crew and guard of Sombra and São Nicolau.

It is with much horror that I must also inform you of the grave injury caused upon His Grace by the pirata Devlin which unable him to write directly to yourself.

By all intervention I request on His Grace behalf to enable all communication between all our ally to require apprehension of the man the pirata Devlin.

I draft letter to Lisbon in companion. I give herein blessed silk thread for your prayers.

Father Carlos Barrios, Ribeira Brava

*

May 1717, Portsmouth. The familiar sounds of hammer against wood, of hauling and singing came wafting across the harbour as the gangs worked away at the veritable garden of ships that nestled around the quay. The two-week sail from Africa to England was ending now with the promise of a beautiful day ahead, with the skies clear enough to make out the green shoulder of the Isle of Wight in the distance. Coxon, from almost a mile away, could observe through the clarity the colourful actions of drays, coaches and stevedores' cranes loading and unloading the gently bobbing barges along the quay.

Without turning to the sound, he heard the patter of Captain William Guinneys' soft, elegant shoes joining him at the starboard bulwark. The young man with the ever-present grin and the long brown queue, without the neatness of a bag, just a single black bow, stepped into Coxon's peripheral vision.

Guinneys breathed in deeply, tapping his knuckles on the rail as if entering his mistress's chambers. Behind them the calls and whistles of the bosun and the subsequent hue and cry of the men forced Guinneys to raise his voice unnaturally.

'Fine day to arrive back home, wouldn't you say, there, Captain?' Then, 'Makes one wonder why we ever leaves.'

'I was not aware that we do *leave*,' Coxon corrected. 'I have always been *sent*, Captain.'

'Quite so, sir. Quite so.' Guinneys grinned the implacable white smile that had ground on Coxon from the moment he had been piped aboard the *Starling*.

He had spent an insufferable fortnight with Guinneys and his young lieutenants, with their crude humour mixed with questionable discipline. He had surmised that months of journeying between England, Guangzhou and the India stations had softened them all. Had bred too much familiarity between decks.

Coxon looked round to the smartly dressed crew running thither like mice in a galley. Two weeks ago he had barely listened to the lieutenants' and the midshipmen's names as he walked the line of introductions, rather he looked for the leather-necked, cracked, ruddy faces and grey sideburns of old hands rough as oakum. Instead he saw sinewy young men, blacks, even Indians, all of them shiny and bright.

He recalled times when he had ruefully accepted invitations to ladies' parties and, before his cloak had been removed by his man, he would be scanning the hall for faces he knew: captains and post-captains, rear admirals, blushing lieutenants. Every year of the war the rooms grew thinner. The faces changed. Now he longed to see an old seaman's face. Just some old man knuckling a lined forehead and rushing past him, someone who might have tasted the same air of powder and smoke. Not these pups, these company men of saddle wax and silk.

'Mister Howard!' Guinneys yelled to the fo'c'sle. 'What see you there?'

Thomas Howard, sixteen, midshipman, a clergyman's son like Coxon, stood on the fo'c'sle deck, with the glass, surveying the port.

'Yellow flag, Captain!' he yelled back. Guinneys and Coxon exchanged looks, broken only by the sudden approach of the dark-suited and somewhat short form of Edward Talton, the designated representative of the East India Company joining the group at the bulwark.

'A yellow flag?' Talton's voice bounced between the two men. 'Yellow flag? What does it mean, gentlemen?' Fidgeting in his pockets, he took out his watch and brushed the moisture from its crystal surface.

'Good morning, Mister Talton.' Guinneys beamed, look-ing down at the diminutive fellow. 'We're very well, thank you, sir.'

'Pardon, Mister Guinneys? No, sir, you misheard me. What does the flag mean, sir?'

Guinneys moved towards the fo'c'sle, stepping effortlessly around coils of ropes and the waisters amidships, his hands behind his back. Coxon and Talton followed.

'Surely any sailor knows the significance of a yellow flag, sir? Or is it perhaps, like myself, that you appreciate the significance of very little before noon?'

'I believe, Captain' – Talton rose almost a third of an inch – 'that it means quarantine. I was merely questioning whether it had some other meaning that I was not aware of.'

'No, Mister Talton.' Guinneys stepped up to the deck. 'There is nothing I am aware of that is quite akin to your unawareness.' And he winked back to Coxon.

Thomas Howard moved aside for the three men to look out over the rails. The telescope was unnecessary; the square yellow flag was ominously evident.

'Does it refer to us, Captain?' Talton asked.

'We shall see, Mister Talton.' Guinneys turned to Thomas Howard. 'Mister Howard, it is your watch. Would you be so kind as to lower the fore topgallant?'

'Aye, Captain.' Thomas Howard ran off to summon the bosun. The lowering signal of the sail would warrant a response from the shore to confirm if the flag referred to the *Starling*, although Coxon and Guinneys were both silently agreed.

Quarantine. Stay where you are. Await further orders.

Five minutes later a single cannon blast from the port responded to the lowered sail, confirming the order related to the *Starling*.

'That's that, then,' Guinneys affirmed. 'We're to wait. Damn shame.'

Coxon looked across to the steely gaze of the crew. They also recognised the significance of the yellow flag and their hands slowed in their duty.

'How long have your men been aboard, Captain Guinneys?' he asked.

'No one's been ashore since Bengal, sir.'

Coxon straightened, placed his hands on the rail and began to almost pull it from its nails. 'Drill your marines. In full view of the men. Loaded muskets.'

'You may have a point there, indeed you may, Post-Captain, sir. What do you suppose the flag's about?'

'It's about us not going ashore. The lads won't be happy. Muskets being rammed will quiet them. An hour or two will tell.'

Guinneys nodded. He screwed his tricorne upon his head and strode down to order the stoic marines to drill and call his company to order. Coxon watched.

'You fear mutiny, Captain Coxon?' Edward Talton asked.

'I would probably not be alive today if I had never, Mister Talton. But mutiny is a little strong for the time of day. I would say nothing more than ... discord,' Coxon said enigmatically, and followed Guinneys, leaving Talton on his own staring to the shore, his glasses misting.

Coxon was not alone in disliking the prevalence of the Honourable John Company on board peacetime ships. Although the company had its own merchantmen, in peace it proved more economical to hire struggling naval vessels to pursue its dominance in the Indian continent. Now that the Mughal emperor had granted the company free trade, with the profitable exemption of any custom duties in Bengal, the sailings had increased, and Guinneys and his lieutenants had benefited from their own personal trade to all ports between China and Africa.

The company turned a blind eye to individual captains' enterprises, as long as the tea, the saltpetre and the silks kept coming home, whilst the Dutch, the Portuguese and the pirates were kept at bay.

Guinneys by his own account, after a third of port of an evening, had attested to his familiarity with the Hongs along the Chinese coast who had made returning to England more a curse than a blessing. An inconvenience to his private enterprises.

Five bells brought Coxon and Guinneys to the quarter-deck, watching the longboat rowing towards them. Sailors at the oars, stern and bow, a selection of white wigs amid. Stiff and uncomfortable, holding on to the sides, weak at the thought that they had no power over the waves lapping at the vulnerable boat, they could be heard taking out their nerves with curses and chidings on the men who rowed them to the *Starling* and kept their eyes down.

Coxon and Guinneys took the time of the approach to brush their salt-soaked coats and hats. Lieutenants Anderson and Scott readied the Great Cabin.

The consensus on board was that they would not be going ashore but straight out again. The grumbling of the crew was audible. Men had families waiting for them, wages to spend, trinkets to sell.

The display of the dozen marines, drilling to the drum of the small boy, resplendent in his toy-soldier perfection, reminded the crew of their position and the consequence of grievance. Yesterday, the officers smiled at the hands, familiar after months at sea. Today, their hats shadowed over their eyes; they barked the men's names.

Before another bell had chimed from the belfry, a long two-tone whistle indicated that the first traverse of the bosun's chair was swinging aboard.

Coxon looked on, amused as much as the whole watch, as the glowing white-stockinged legs of James Whitlock, Member of Parliament, swayed in an undignified arc over the deck.

Coxon stood with Guinneys and his lieutenants. They watched the grey-wigged, red-faced man descend as gracefully as he could.

'Two Whigs, I reckon.' Guinneys nodded to Coxon. 'Rear Admiral Land of the Blue is there as well, and some other fellow. Looks French to me. Bloody wine's going to be short, I know that much.'

Coxon observed the leather satchel Whitlock carried, as the chair descended over the bulwark again. No doubt it held papers fresh from Whitehall. In order for these two Whigs to appear they must have been expecting the *Starling*. They had probably been down here for a few days. Rear Admiral Land was based in Portsmouth. Coxon had only met him once and he seemed a sound enough fellow.

He watched the last of them remove himself from the chair, generalising from the elongated cuffs, the extravagant doublet and enormous plumed hat that he was indeed a French nobleman. At the sharp whistle, dismissing the chair and clearing the deck for space, Guinneys and Coxon stepped forward for the reception.

James Whitlock was joined by his fellow parliamentary member Samuel Taylor-Woode. Both men bowed their heads at the line of officers with tight-lipped severity. Sir Clive Land, tall and gracious, was less solemn, but he seemed to take no pleasure in introducing the pale, brightly dressed French ambassador, Geffroi Cayeux.

Preliminaries undertaken, officers and their mysterious guests withdrew to the comfort of the Great Cabin. Coxon's eyes followed Cayeux's back. This was the first time he had known a Frenchman aboard the same ship as himself who was not a prisoner. His world was getting larger.

Inside the surprisingly spacious cabin, most of Guinneys' extravagances having been squared away, matters moved swiftly. Whilst there was no uniform to distinguish the navy officers from the politicians, they were as farmers to kings in terms of linen and attire. Coxon looked dourly at the wear on his coat, no longer having his own man brushing his clothes nightly and the black fading green in the coat's folds and across his back.

James Whitlock spread out his ledgers and orders from his leather bag, uttering a small affirmation to each one. The lieutenants had prepared inkwells and quills in the centre of the table along with Guinneys' personal glassware, water, wine and some Indian sweets, which added some delicate colour to the white-walled cabin.

Whitlock and Taylor-Woode seated themselves at the head of the table, with Rear Admiral Land at the opposite end. The French ambassador sat next to Taylor-Woode's elbow and cast his eyes over the bundles of yellow paper tied up with red ribbon. Coxon and Guinneys sat together, at Land's portion of the table, separating themselves from the politicians.

Talton positioned himself on Cayeux's breadth of the table and brought out his spectacles, which he cleaned, fulminating against the dew that seemed to adhere to every glass surface he possessed, then Talton, without any knowledge of propriety, spoke first.

'Would it be acceptable to breakfast at all, gentlemen, or am I expected to wait till luncheon?'

Whitlock looked up, expressionless. 'Are you addressing me, sir?' he responded.

'Indeed. Your presence was unexpected, sir, and I have not had time to eat this morning.' In truth he had simply ignored the call to partake at eight bells with the midshipmen and had been unable to find any hand who could bring him so much as an egg afterwards.

'I breakfasted at dawn, Mister Talton.' Whitlock offered this information, as if by some process of osmosis Talton's hunger would be appeased. 'I would like to proceed, as time is an imperative to us all.'

'Undoubtedly,' Guinneys confirmed, his words generating a small cough from Lieutenant Scott, with whom Guinneys had bet a crown that he would speak only in three-syllable words.

Whitlock continued, 'Captain Coxon?'

'Yes, Mister Whitlock?' Coxon rested his right arm on the table and leaned in.

'You were captain of the *Noble*, were you not, sir?' He acknowledged Coxon's confirmation and carried on. 'And you have been made aware that the vessel was attacked by pirates near Gibraltar, have you not?'

'I have been made aware that the *Noble* was subsequently set ablaze by my first lieutenant,' Coxon's voice grieved.

'Catastrophe,' Guinneys sighed.

'Indeed,' Whitlock concurred. 'Although perhaps if Post-Captain Coxon had seen fit to allow the *Noble* to complete her passage, such a calamity would never have come to pass.' He saw Coxon open his mouth and raised a quietening palm to hold his tongue. 'However, we have reason to believe from the description of the pirate brigantine that two weeks ago these same rogues also attacked the governor of one of the Verde Islands, and subsequently made off with a twenty-six-gun frigate belonging to the Portuguese. Twenty-six including the swivels, of course.'

'Good God, sir!' Rear Admiral Land exclaimed. 'Do you say that there's a band of brigands out there with a man-of-war?'

'I do, sir,' Whitlock returned. 'And a brigantine. Over a hundred men according to witnesses from the *Noble*.'

'Horrendous,' Guinneys murmured.

Coxon interjected, 'Are men from the *Noble* still in Gibraltar, Mister Whitlock?'

'The devil I know, sir. That is not my business.'

'Then pray,' Admiral Land asserted his position, 'what exactly is your business, sir?'

Whitlock motioned to Ambassador Cayeux. 'The ambassador of His Most Gracious Majesty, Monsieur Cayeux, has brought a rather important event to Whitehall's attention.'

Cayeux bowed at the mention of his name. 'It is a pleasure to meet you all, gentlemen.' His chin lowered to his chest, his accent subdued.

Whitlock carried on, 'My colleague, the Honourable Mister Samuel Taylor-Woode' – another bow – 'holds many positions in Whitehall. And his coat buttons up over a number of closely guarded secrets, one of which was related to him by Monsieur Cayeux. I will now hand the elaborations over to his good self.'

'Pardon my interruption, Mister Whitlock,' Talton spoke up as the Whig started to rise from his seat. 'But I should like to know if we will be able to unload our cargo? I have duties to the company to perform at our house, don't you know?'

Whitlock glared at him. 'No soul will leave this ship, Mister Talton. I am perfectly capable of dealing with your cargo. And you may pass your tally on to me consequently. What transpires here this morning must never leave this vessel. Do you understand me, sir?'

Coxon feigned surprise. 'Are we to take it, then, Mister Whitlock, that none of your company will leave this ship also?' he asked.

'The king trusts me, Post-Captain, to keep my silence.'

'Indubitably,' Guinneys agreed. Lieutenant Scott sniffed hard, stifling a sneeze.

'And do not hope to forget, Captain, that Whitehall is most well aware you turned the *Noble* home rather than escort a "Blackbirder" of the South Sea Company. The subsequent consequence of which was the loss of a company man and a rather expensive king's frigate.' Whitlock took some water, eyeing Coxon over the glass.

Coxon felt his face flushing as he spoke. 'My report to the board, which I will gladly address directly, indicated quite satisfactorily my concerns, sir, about sending an officer as inexperienced as Lieutenant Thorn to the Indies. A place the fellow had never been to, and certainly no place to send a man jumped up from a midshipman two weeks previous. Especially as my Irish steward could traverse with better reckoning!'

Whitlock placed down his glass. 'I'm sure he could, Captain.'

Land interceded. 'Let us address the matter at hand, Mister Whitlock. I would be most interested to listen to Mister Taylor-Woode's discourse.'

'Your servant, Rear Admiral.' Taylor-Woode bowed to Land as he finally rose.

He was young for a politician, perhaps thirty or so, with an unpleasant red rash above his collar, his face a day short of a shave. He touched some of the bound papers before him as if looking for a lost purpose.

'I am in uncertain terms, gentlemen, as to what we are to achieve today.' He smiled uncomfortably. 'I have orders, but as to their value I am unsure to my utmost.' His ambiguity drew glances across the whole table. 'I will therefore simply put forward our situation and hope that it speaks for itself. I have some papers here...' He began to unravel his scripts, some shadow-marked with candle burns, some smeared with clumsy wax seals. 'Firstly, I must assure you that Monsieur Cayeux has our highest regard. You must take his word as well as I hope you may take my own.'

'Absolutely,' Guinneys stated.

'My gratitude. Without much distraction, I hope, I must establish a series of tragedies that necessitate my presence here today.' Taylor-Woode spoke with all the verbosity of a true politician.

'Late last month, Monsieur Cayeux' – a bow to the ambassador – 'made aware to my council the failure of a certain sloop to arrive back at Calais. This sloop was returning from the Caribbean Sea after transporting a considerable gold fortune to a secret island location. An island unknown except to all but a handful of souls in possession of its map. The map is now believed lost with that sloop.'

Taylor-Woode raised a furled piece of paper in his right hand. 'This paper is the only other map in existence that reveals the location of the island itself.' The paper drew the eyes of the entire table. '*This* ship, gentlemen, will have this map, signed by Philippe the Second, with His Majesty's blessing. This ship will sail to the island with the purpose to hold its secret safe until such time that French forces can arrive.'

Samuel Taylor-Woode paused for the drama to sink in. Coxon and the other sailors, however, were corks in a turbulent sea daily, and simply waited for the Whig to continue, their eyes meeting briefly across the table.

'I am assured by Monsieur Cayeux that the vast majority of French warships are engaged with blockading the Spanish. Ever the enemy. And the only avenue of opportunity to address the vulnerability of this gold is to send an able British ally to safeguard and carry word to the French forces in the Caribbean, whereupon the *Starling* is our apt choice.'

Coxon shifted his seat. 'Why is the *Starling* so apt, Mister Taylor-Woode?'

Taylor-Woode's head craned towards Coxon. 'Why, *you* are on board of course, Captain,' he declared with almost insidious delight.

'I beg your pardon, sir?'

Taylor-Woode looked down to a correspondence in front of him. 'You are aware, no doubt, that in the loss of the *Noble*, Captain, we also lost the ability and personage of one Alastair Lewis. His fate is unknown. Also amongst the sailors in Gibraltar there was one other soul who was absent from their company. His fate was unknown also, until the recent information regarding the theft of the Portuguese frigate from the Verdes. His importance would have passed us until we noticed in our inquiry that he drew rations with yourself, Captain.'

'I do not follow, sir?' Coxon felt the cold, unpleasant creep of his own skin, a tightness around his chest.

'Does the name "Devlin" mean anything to you, Captain Coxon?'

'It does, sir.'

Whitlock interrupted, turning his body to Coxon. 'In what sense, sir?'

'Some years ago, at the end of the war, I liberated a Patrick Devlin' – he looked coldly to the French ambassador – 'from a French sloop. A sloop of war. I took him as my manservant. He served me on the *Noble.*'

'He accompanied you on land, I take it, as well?' Whitlock asked.

'Of course.'

'Your Irishman who could reckon better than Lieutenant Thorn?' Whitlock leaned forward.

'Yes.'

'Taught him yourself, I'll warrant?'

'He was very observant, sir.'

'Catholic too presumably, sir?' Whitlock looked away to the stern windows with a satisfied smirk.

'Not that I noticed. What relevance is all of this, may I ask, sir?'

Taylor-Woode shook his head. 'According to our information, Captain Coxon, your man, Patrick Devlin, is the pirate leader of these ship thieves.'

Coxon's body turned to lead, all but his head, which had begun to swim.

'Would you mind' – he cleared his throat – 'reiterating that point, Mister Taylor-Woode?'

'Our information, Captain, is that Patrick Devlin is the pirate leader of over a hundred men, which affords you, as his former master, a unique opportunity to pull him to heel, as it were.'

'Astounding!' Guinneys gasped.

Coxon sat back. 'Devlin was a servant. It's only been a couple of months since he was shining my shoes. I'd find it remarkable that he could do such a thing.'

'Irishmen!' Whitlock snorted.

'Nevertheless, Captain, it seems he was able to convince the governor of St Nicholas that some other dog was the pirates' captain, whom he willingly sacrificed in order to trap the governor, murder several of his men and sail away with a prize warship. Hardly the abilities of a mere boot-wipe, would you say, Captain?'

Rear Admiral Land rapped the table. 'What has this to do with this gold that you mentioned, Mister Taylor-Woode?'

'Ah, Rear Admiral, what indeed.' Samuel Taylor-Woode sat down and drew more papers towards him, opening the sealed ones carefully. 'Shortly before Post-Captain Coxon left for the Guinea coast in January, he attended a social occasion, accompanied by Devlin, in London. The occasion was without importance other than that the Swedish ambassador was present. That same evening, the ambassador was arrested for conspiring with known Jacobite factions. The *Noble* sailed the next morning.'

There was an uncomfortable movement around the table. The movement was not unnoticed by the Whigs.

Taylor-Woode continued, 'We are in precarious times, gentlemen. It is only two years since Mar and his devils attempted to overthrow our noble king. The "old pretender" has fled to Rome since the death of his patron, Louis the Fourteenth, and we are assured by the regent Philippe, on the young king's behalf, that France has no desire to aid in his unlawful return to our United Kingdom.' Taylor-Woode paused to pour himself some wine, seemingly exhausted from a speech he had long prepared.

'It is the opinion, the comprehensive concern of Ambassador Cayeux, his government and ours that the knowledge of the location of this gold fortune, the passage of the sloop and its no doubt unfortunate brave sailors were revealed by some division of spies to these brigands.' He took a draught of wine. 'Jacobite spies.'

'Jacobites!' Guinneys hissed. Lieutenant Scott choked.

'It would not stretch incredulity, gentlemen,' the Whig continued, 'to presume that this gold may be used to fund some audacious attempt to return the "Stuart" to the throne. To rekindle some Jacobite spark amongst the Catholic peoples and misguided gentry!' Taylor-Woode slammed his fist down with barely enough fervour to rattle the inkwells.

The sound of Coxon laughing disturbed the atmosphere more.

Whitlock's voice raised itself above the laugh. 'You find this amusing, sir?'

'No, sir. Not at all.' Coxon calmed himself.

'Then why the mirth, sir?'

'I find the notion that there may be pirates who are interested in restoring a "Stuart" to the throne absurd, Mister Whitlock.'

'It is a well-known truth, Captain Coxon, that many of these devils do in fact ally themselves with Jacobite ideals as justification for their crimes! The ones we hang every day will attest to that, sir!' he retorted.

Samuel Taylor-Woode ignored the duel across the table. 'It is our belief that some rebellious faction has latched on to this pirate band and is directing their actions. To wit, the seizure of this gold and a warship to take it.'

Coxon listened, his arms crossed. He allowed two ticks of the clock on the writing desk to pass.

'As I have understood, gentlemen, you do not know what the fate of this sloop is. You are assuming this knowledge has fallen into pirate hands. Are you even sure this gold has arrived at this island?'

'That is precisely why we need a man-of-war to sail immediately: to affirm what we do and do not know, Post-Captain!' Whitlock snapped back, his face scarlet. 'And, God willing, give us some hope of keeping one step ahead of this Jacobite terror!'

Coxon bolted up. His chair danced away. 'I've had enough of this wash!'

'I beg your pardon,' Whitlock exhaled. 'Sir?' His eyes widened.

Coxon stood back from the table. 'This wash, sir! This wash! Ever since the war ended, with no common enemy, you slack-jawed philanderers have harped on about rebellion! Pirates! Jacobites! Trying to save your own hides and fortunes lest we question your worth at all!' Bile rose in his throat and he paused to swallow. His eyes were suddenly watering, clouding the table before him.

'How *dare* you, *sir!*' Whitlock hissed. His fists were white upon the table. 'Are you completely unaware of the events of the rebellion? Our *worth*, sir, is the security of this nation!'

'Oh, spare me your servitude,' Coxon mocked. 'Erskine's pitiful folly? I could pull a better attempt out of my arse, sir. And as for this *pirate*? Five years ago you'd be making him governor of his own bloody island for what he's done! I knew men who had chased Morgan for years only to watch your fathers give him the whole of bloody Jamaica at the end of it! And you'd have given *me* an honour for shooting *this* bag of shite!' He shot a finger at Ambassador Cayeux, whose jaw fell, aghast.

'You speak above your station, Captain Coxon!' Whitlock exclaimed.

'With respect, Mister Whitlock' – Coxon's hands were trembling – 'this *is* my station.'

'Steady now, John.' Land's calming voice returned order instantly. The clock ticked twice again. Lieutenant Scott was staring at its face to avoid looking at the table. 'No need for this. We're all together here.'

Coxon looked at Land and felt his face grow hot with blushing. He looked around the table. 'I apologise, gentlemen.'

The clock chimed twelve, a small bell like the gentle tap of a teaspoon on a plate. Coxon waited for it to finish. Talton checked his watch, wiping the surface with a tut.

Coxon continued, 'It has been a trying time these past few months.' He sat down, exhausted from his outburst. 'I must account that I almost died through disease in Africa, and some part of me in truth did die when my ship was lost. Now I hear that my own man has fallen in with pirates. It is all too much to comprehend.' He wiped a clammy hand across his forehead. He felt nauseous.

Taylor-Woode resumed his course. 'Be that as it may, Captain, I will take your irreverent outburst as a post-expression of your malady and the disappointing actions of your recent manservant. Our concern, I assure you, is for us all as a sovereign nation and for our allies. Your orders are contained within these sealed documents. Rear Admiral Land will decide who is to command the *Starling*. Mister Whitlock will discuss with Captain Guinneys and Mister Talton the supplying of the ship and any sale of goods, the processing of which must take no more than one day, gentlemen.'

'Impossible!' Guinneys protested. Lieutenant Scott coughed and begged pardon.

Taylor-Woode carried on. 'These pirates, who we believe are making their way west, have a two-week start on the

Starling. It is possible to catch them if you adopt a twenty-four-hour sail, for our studies indicate that pirates are unlikely to sail for more than fourteen hours at a time.'

'We can only hope that the pirates have studied the same perfect books as you, Mister Taylor-Woode,' Coxon said.

Taylor-Woode ignored the remark. 'The *Starling* will take the Azores route to the Caribbean. From the Verdes, the pirates should take just about thirty days to reach there. Via the Azores, the *Starling* will take under forty, at good speed. With luck the pirates may head for Providence Island for supplies or to careen, that will be your edge. It will be a close thing, gentlemen.'

'Close enough,' Land commented.

'I will leave the peculiar details to your orders, gentlemen. One batch each for Captains Guinneys and Coxon.' He slung the sealed papers to the officers' side of the table. 'Our prayers are that we are all wrong, that the gold is safe and the sloop merely lost. If not, then prepare to eradicate a formidable force that may well threaten the peace of our nation.'

Two hours later found Guinneys and Coxon on the quarter-deck watching a barge carrying some of their cargo to shore under the watchful eyes of Talton and Whitlock. The latter issued the transire, the customs warrant for the company's goods, though Talton palpitated with fury at the undervalued receipts with which Whitlock had furnished him.

The morale of the men improved with the vast assortment of hogsheads that were swung on board. For months they had loaded badly packed Indian goods from the factories along the Bengal coast. Now beer, rum, salted meats, sauerkraut and vegetables were stowed below, taking their minds from the English shore so tantalisingly close.

Guinneys tapped his forehead to Coxon and left the seemingly brooding post-captain, his five-guinea hat disappearing down the aft companion.

Coxon had been given command of the *Starling* for the mission, his rank of post-captain and his experience outweighing that of Guinneys, despite his foul humour in the Great Cabin.

Guinneys declined the quasi-rank of master and commander, and temporarily resigned himself to first lieutenant, immediately shuffling every other officer on board down a peg or two. A situation that made Coxon mildly uncomfortable.

Guinneys had merely smiled at the prospect of being yet another few months away from his creditors. He had even offered Coxon his valet, but Coxon had refused, asking for a volunteer amongst the men. The skinny form of Oscar Hodge had stepped up to the post gladly, although Coxon had found his permanently half-closed right eye, a remnant from a disorder of the nerves apparently, somewhat disconcerting.

The two men had not shared their orders. Coxon was unsure whether Guinneys had even bothered to open his, for he had accepted his demotion with a nod to Rear Admiral Land and a glass of wine to his lips, before removing his effects from the Great Cabin, even leaving the wine rack in the coach untouched.

Coxon's orders repeated the importance of ensuring the safety of the gold. The sloop had sailed with an escort. A French barque that had landed nine marines and one captain to protect the small outpost. She had then sailed on to Massachusetts and the sloop back to Calais. The barque would return to the island in late June, at which time the *Starling*'s duty would cease. Easy words. Easily written and dusted by a fine hand.

The elaborate script confirmed the English interest: His Majesty was only concerned to establish whether the safety of the gold had been compromised by pirate action. If not, wait for the French barque and secure the island. If so, hunt down the pirates without hesitation or mercy.

Coxon scoffed at the idea of a gold depository. He had no doubt that such secret locations existed, the islands of the Caribbean as numerous as fleas on a dog and Europe ready to flare up again at any moment, but he doubted that it held such a noble purpose of wages for the forces of France and her colonial governors.

France was building. Fortifications had sprung up all over her American colonies since the end of the war. He rolled out the map before him and nodded to himself. Aye. The gold was nothing more than scrap metal for cannon, he could be sure of that. They would not be pleased to see an English warship.

All the officers had studied the paper that the island lay detailed on. She sat a few minutes north of the twentieth parallel, above the Caymans, close to the archipelago of the Cuban Jardines.

If the pirates had taken a route through the Bahamas, to make Providence, they could either turn south to Hispaniola and take the Windward Passage or sail west and around the long north coast of Cuba to reach the island, adding a week to their journey. It would be longer. But it would be safer.

Coxon would take the Windward Passage, then creep up through the Cayman Trench. He hoped the pirate captain would take the quieter route west around Cuba's northern shore. A safe pirate drag.

If luck and fate were with him, the two would approach the island from opposite compass points almost to the day.

Coming together like jousting knights across a battlefield, their lances now bowsprits. But the weather gauge would be with the *Starling*, not the pirates, for the trade winds blew from the south.

If the pirates did go through the Bahamas, of course. *If* they went to Providence. Too many unknowns. Too many maybes and second-guesses, and all the while there was the possibility that his own man was their leader.

How could it be Devlin? Coxon found it inconceivable that a man he had known, trusted, could willingly turn pirate.

The lure was there for any common man, no doubt, but surely not Devlin? Coxon himself had beaten many of the unsavoury aspects out of the man. He had shown him attitudes to raise himself from the gutter.

Perhaps he had been too kind. He had taken the magnanimous bearing of his father and shown respect to the Irishman, even taking the time to confer knowledge upon the man.

On discovering that the former butcher's boy could read, Coxon had loaned him his copy of Dampier's memoirs and bestowed him access to the logs on Sundays. Devlin was good company. A bright young man, born wrong.

If the assumption was true, there would come a day when he would stand before him. That day would end with Devlin cowering like an apologetic dog. One that had once slept on the floor of Coxon's own cabin, now biting the hand that had given him a semblance of dignity beyond his birthright.

The unloading and loading would carry on into the night by lantern and sidelights. The *Starling* was a fine ship. A fifth-rate with thirty-four guns, going against, according to his orders, a twenty-six-gun frigate and a ten-gun brigantine. By the time he reached the Azores, his blond young men would be black with powder and firing three rounds per minute in their sleep. Her lines were weatherly enough to sail five and a half knots; laying five points from the wind, she would fairly fly to the Antilles. Aye, a good ship.

The whole Jacobite nonsense had incensed him. Whatever the politicians' true motives were, he had been given the opportunity to have some portion of revenge against at least some of the men who had attacked the *Noble*, attacked his ship.

And as for Devlin? A man who had stood behind Coxon for years, lurking in his shadow? Coxon stifled the thought and moved slowly down to the deck, watching all turn their heads away from his step. His world *was* getting larger.

Chapter Eight

✗

Twenty-First Parallel, North Atlantic Ocean,
May 1717

To the captain of *Ter Meer* it was the only course of action. They had come across the black smoked mirage of the two ships locked in combat shortly after one o'clock, two points off the starboard bow, two miles ESE.

At first the Dutch fluyte believed it to be a ship ablaze and intended to seek some 'waveson', the floating goods of a sinking ship – along with any survivors, naturally.

As they drew closer, Captain Claes Aarland perceived two ships crawling through a floating fog of battle, sailing abreast of one another, their sterns facing his spyglass. The escutcheon of one read *Lucy*, the rather innocent name besmirched by the black and white flag she clearly flew. The other, to his horror, nobly displayed the tricolour of his countrymen, her name plainly shot away, her sails in disarray, although his sailing master had insisted that the flag had not been visible moments before.

Nevertheless, Captain Aarland had given the order to close: to aid the black Dutch frigate, assured that there was no pirate who would stand against two allied ships. With their odds out of favour they would flee like the cowards they were.

Ter Meer boasted only ten six-pounders and eighty souls,

a merchant sailing home from Curaçao, but to the frigate she would be an angel, and the brigantine that through some lucky happenstance had surprised her would surely show her heels. Aarland pictured the celebratory meal that the two gallant captains would share and the gratitude that would be bestowed upon him.

It was somewhat disappointing to Aarland, then, that he found himself now chained to his own foremast with the fearful cackling of the pirates ringing throughout his deck like the black pleasure of a crowd around a gallows.

At first all had gone well. As *Ter Meer* approached, the brigantine had lowered her sails; the cannon stopped; she veered away. Cheers echoed across the *Ter Meer* as her anxious crew realised they would not fight this day and they could forget about their wages being lost along with their blood amongst the scuppers.

There had been some mild concern that as they reached the frigate, the gun-crew still seemed engaged in frantic action, but this had been dismissed as wise caution as the pirate brigantine was still close by.

On drawing level with the stationary frigate, Aarland scanned the ship for her captain and waved above his head, slow and high, to signal his presence.

Instead of the salutations of a beholden compatriot, a deafening broadside of chainshot cracked from the deck and quivered over Aarland's head. There was a strange sensation of air being sucked away, of an alien heat against his face. Rigging and spars flew from their place. Men seemed to shrink, returned to wailing children as black smoke crept over the gunwale.

The shouts of Baernt Corniel, his sailing master, spat into his face, and Aarland turned to see the travelling masts of the brigantine above their bow. She had turned, a formidable show of speed, heeling against the wind. Now her larboard guns faced *Ter Meer*, and on the up-roll released a broadside of chain into the foremast, tearing the course like paper.

His wife would weep at an empty grave now, he was sure, no doubt baring her shoulders in a black dress to his brother. Such thoughts at such a time. Focus on the now. Concentrate on the black-haired pirate now wearing Aarland's tricorne, moving amongst the quelled crew, who sat with lowered heads and crowded the deck. He dared, audaciously, to make a speech to the men. *His* men. Some insistence that they would not be relieved of their personal belongings, that they were safe as long as they obeyed, for only the cargo held the pirates' interest, and the officers' wares of course.

Now the pirate turned his attention to Aarland. He stepped carefully over the legs of the crew towards him, the deck mercifully free from blood due to their immediate surrender.

Aarland was lashed uncomfortably to the mast, his coat long stolen and being worn by a scarlet-faced brigand, his grey wig slanted almost over one eye, sweat sticking his shirt to his narrow back. He was in this state, far removed from the one he awoke in, when a pirate spoke to him.

'Captain Aarland.' The man's voice was soft, even cultured almost. 'The deception of the cannon was my own thought, designed to bring you gallantly to our rescue. My apologies if I have humiliated you, but you must admit that my plan caused the least harm to us both.'

'Damn you, English! I will not have words with you! How dare you speak to me!' Aarland's Dutch accent was proud and Devlin let him have his moment of bravado.

'My men will remove whatever you have in your hold that's of use to us. I myself require more trivial goods, namely your logs and any news you may have carried from the Indies of what goes on lately. If you'd be so kind.'

'I will be kind enough to tell you to go to hell, dog!' Aarland's voice was shrill. His anger had grown from the moment that the man with the bald head and red beard lashed him to his own ship. He had watched helplessly as men ran from his cabin carrying his medicine chest, personal goods and sea charts. Now he was raging.

Devlin winced. 'Now that attitude won't help any of us settle this matter quickly, will it, Captain?'

'It is my dignity that forbids me from helping you, *sir*, not my humour!'

'Ah! Is that it? I understand.' Devlin wheeled round to the Dutch sailors. He watched their curious faces staring at the two captains. He half turned back to Aarland. 'I can remove that obstacle from you, Captain, if it helps our discussion.'

A few minutes standing naked in front of his crew and Claes Aarland found a new voice. With some encouragement, Devlin learned of the blizzards that had paralysed trade all along the northeast coast of the colonies at the end of February. Of the death of the infamous Sam Bellamy, former consort of Benjamin Hornigold, whose ship *Whydah* went down with all but two of its crew in a storm off Wellfleet, Massachusetts, barely a fortnight ago, the sinking of which had brought treasure hunters from all nations to drag the area. The world was rid of a notorious cut-throat.

There was little news of consequence to cause any consternation in Devlin. He thanked the captain for the access to his logs as he leafed casually through the tome that Sam Fletcher had brought him.

Devlin walked the waist of the ship as he tried to read the Dutch scrawl. Deciphering most of the words was strangely simple but he found himself hovering over the cargo list, until the scrawl became meaningless again. He was broken from his thoughts by the unfortunate sound of Hugh Harris singing drunkenly from the quarterdeck, a bottle of brandy in each hand, Aarland's wig now adorning his head, his pistols hanging from a red sling round his neck.

Most of the rather frugal goods had been craned aloft or shouldered by the crew to the *Lucy*, now designated consort to the *Shadow*, the name he had properly christened the frigate.

Molasses, rum, hogsheads of pork and indigo were all the hold of the *Ter Meer* seemed to have, but Devlin's eyes returned to the log.

There were pages of figures. Scribblings, often written in double figures, that from their dimensions made no sense until it dawned that they could only be ages, and that the repetition of three words over and over were the Dutch words for woman, boy, girl, alongside the obvious '*man*'.

It was as the words on the page began to cohere that something else also fell into place: the smell.

On coming aboard after the first few exciting minutes were over and the Dutch had been corralled, there had been amongst the customary scent of damp wood, pitch and oakum, an echo of something almost effluent, akin to all the obnoxious discharges that flow down London's streets and mingle with the vomit of the starving drunks outside the gin houses.

Peter Sam appeared before him and Devlin looked up at the severe face and closed the book. Peter Sam held a small chest, the timbers of which were held together by black iron-work, the lock smashed.

'I'd say there were about ten guineas' worth of Dutch tin in here. A poor haul by accounts.' He sighed his disappointment. 'Nothing but these notes is all else there is.' He passed a crumpled batch of papers into Devlin's left hand. Each slip was no larger than a note of credit.

Devlin had not been below. Peter Sam had.

'What's it like in the hold, Peter?' he asked.

'Stinks like they swab with chamber lye, Cap'n.' He grinned.

'Chamber lye?'

'Piss, Cap'n. It stinks like they swab with piss. They got more irons down there than Newgate, I wouldn't doubt and all.'

Devlin looked to the notes in his hand, then turned and walked back to Captain Aarland.

Aarland's grey body was still lashed to the foremast. He was holding his gaze above the heads of his crew and watching his goods being swung over to the pirate vessel by pulleys rigged over the yardarms as makeshift derricks.

'Aarland.' Devlin pushed Aarland's shoulder to force his attention. 'There were slaves aboard this ship. Where's the gold for them?'

'I have no gold for them,' he sneered. 'What I have are those papers in your hand.'

'What are these?'

'Worthless to you, *piraat*.' Aarland spoke confidently, as if it did not matter about his exposed extremities. 'I had sixty Negroes from El Mina. They were diseased; over half died. Those papers are my insurance I must take back to reclaim my monies.'

Devlin glanced at the notes. 'These chits are for all the Negroes. You said half died?'

'Ignorant fool! I don't get insurance for half a cargo! They all go over the side! They are all chained together, it is easier, they fall like rosary beads!'

Devlin had only ever met one slave. It had been outside a

house in Chatham one freezing February night. Devlin had stood, tramping his feet, clenching his fists and hunching against the cold, waiting for Coxon to appear from the warmth within.

Standing at one of the pillars of the house had been a black man, smartly dressed with fine buckled shoes and white stockings, but quite absurd in a white wig above his ebony face. Devlin had offered him some tobacco, which he had politely refused. Devlin had asked him his name.

'Adam,' he had replied. Then, in a second breath, 'But my real name is Ehioze Omolara.' His eyes had glowed wistfully. 'It means "Born at the right time above the envy of others". May I ask what is your name, sir?'

'Patrick Devlin.'

'And what does that mean, "Patrick Devlin"?'

'It means I'm stuck out here with you, Adam.'

'We should leave, Cap'n,' Peter Sam stated. 'We should take some men with us.' This was true. The real motive when Sam Morwell had first spied the Dutch fluyte was to gain more hands. Splitting forces between the two ships, twenty-five on the *Lucy*, eighty on the *Shadow*, with Black Bill commanding the *Lucy*, left the pirates shorter-handed than they liked it. Devlin, however, was reluctant to press men into his service, but the Dutch sailors looked neither hungry nor desperate.

'I'll ask the question of them, Sam.' He looked over Peter's shoulder as he watched Dan Teague carrying a sack. A light load considering he held it away from him like a dead thing.

'Take a look at this, Cap'n.' Dan presented the bag at the foot of the mast before Aarland. Devlin and Peter Sam both peered into its mouth at what appeared to be black clumps of coarse, wiry wool.

'Hair.' Aarland nodded to the sack. 'For *kussen*, you know? Cushions. Cheaper than feather. Very good.'

Devlin straightened himself. 'I'm confident of that, Aarland. I'm beginning to think that your mother raised you from afar.' His speech was muted. He felt a rising in his stomach and the smell of the ship became almost palpable. 'You say these sixty notes are for your insurance, then, Aarland?'

'*Ja*. No monies you will have from me, *piraat*.'

'We'd best be putting them somewheres safe, then, eh?' He winked at Aarland, then shouted to Hugh Harris. 'Hugh! Be bringing me a bottle of that brandy fore!'

'Time's a-wasting, Pat,' Peter Sam reminded him.

'Long summer, Peter. Get back to the *Shadow*. I'll be along.' Peter Sam nodded and moved to ascend the boards that joined the ships.

Hugh came up and slapped a bottle into Devlin's hand. 'Now, Kapitein' – he faced Aarland – 'I would be happy to see you eat the fruits of your labours.' He stuffed the first of the notes into Aarland's shocked mouth, then poured a swig of brandy into his face. Aarland sputtered a stream of soaked obscenities. Devlin answered by shoving more paper into his hole.

He kicked Aarland's legs from under him and pushed him down the mast to sit awkwardly upon the deck. Aarland choked as the paper went down. Devlin poured more brandy down his throat, then passed the paper and brandy to Hugh.

'Finish it, Hugh,' he said to the pirate. 'Make him eat them all.' He looked to Aarland, making sure he heard his words. 'Else stick a dagger in his ear and keep pushing till he dies.' From somewhere the dagger was already in Hugh's right hand.

'Aye, Cap'n.' Hugh knelt down to Aarland and went merrily to his task.

Devlin turned to the Dutch crew. 'I'll make this short,' he said, his hands on his broad belt. 'If you can understand me, I invite you to join us.' He looked at the blue eyes before him not knowing if they could read his intentions. 'I have only four rules.' He held up four fingers. 'Eat well, drink well, fight well and swear to leave me when you have a thousand pounds tc your own account.' He cocked his head back to the naked, retching Aarland. 'Or stay and go home with this paper-eating dog who gave you up like a hand of cards.' He paused. There was little movement from the huddled crew.

Then one stood up. Tall and white-haired. Young and broad-shouldered. Devlin guessed that he had some sway in the crew, for as he rose four others followed after him, each one in bold contrast to the skinny, liver-wrecked crew he had inherited. The remainder of the crew sunk their heads into their chests, forlorn but loyal. Devlin pointed to the *Shadow*.

'Go ahead. Make yourself known by any name that you will. A doubloon greets your signing hand.' He bowed and motioned to his ship. A few men but honestly taken. It would do.

An hour later and the *Ter Meer* was a memory to drink to. It was testimony to the fear the brotherhood could create that at the end only Hugh and Devlin remained on the ship, surrounded by almost eighty men and masters, who did nothing to oppose the will of two men.

They hardly glanced when the body of their captain slumped awkwardly sideways, tied as he was, unconscious and drooling.

They watched with half-lifted eyes as the boots tramped like giants past them, not one of them daring to look up. There was the solemn moment when the planks and hooks scraped off the gunwale at the fo'c'sle and the shadow of the

144

frigate began to pass along the deck, its masts shrinking away across the boards like the fingers of a withdrawing hand.

No one could remember hearing the sounds of a ship under-way, the shouts, the chains, the reeving of ropes through blocks accompanied by the heaving calls of sailors.

They were only awakened from their numbness by the flapping of their broken sails and yards and the dryness of their throats. Still sitting, talking in hushed voices, below the protection of the bulwarks, they tended to their captain, try-ing vainly to salvage some of the smeared notes that littered the deck. It was a considerable time before the bosun pulled himself up and raised his head above the side.

The ocean was calm, as blue as the sky, empty, save for what appeared to be a white tablecloth floating slowly towards the hull. The bosun stood, safe now in their loneliness, and trained his eyes upon it. Obligingly, the ocean pulled the cloth tight. The sailor turned away, his eyes welling with anger or shame, and he brushed past his sailing master, who stepped up to the bulwark to see for himself the fallen flag of the red, the white and the blue that danced along beside them.

The remnants of a boiled fowl lay pitifully across a silver platter in the *Shadow*'s Great Cabin, surrounded by several green bottles in varying states of emptiness. Devlin had kept the luxury of the cabin that occupied the rear of the upper deck, so he and Peter Sam sat pleasantly enough in the room, ruminating on plans afoot.

Miles behind them, strewn across the ocean, were all the useless officers' quarters and bulkheads from the upper deck. Torn from place to afford more space. More space for men. More space to cut out gun ports. More space to fight.

The two pirates sat smoking upon the window lockers,

staring over the sea through the open slanting stern windows. The once-secret map lay stretched out, its corners weighted down with pistols upon the table.

Peter Sam spoke through a blue cloud of smoke. 'If those peaks be accurate on that paper, there'll be no landing on the north side: that'll be sheer cliffs all the way round.'

'Aye. The only landable shore is the windward one, which would not be our wisest.' Devlin sighed.

The windward shore would not be hospitable to either ship. One could come in too fast and run aground on some hidden reef and, should any hostile action occur, the *Shadow*, for all her bluff lines, would be against the wind like a boot in mud. The *Lucy* would fare better with her fore-and-aft rigging, and Devlin suggested such to Peter Sam.

'Proposition sure enough. Still risky getting her in.'

The two men stood, walked to the table and looked down at their future. The island stretched out like a miniature Cuba, probably no more than five miles across by three wide, but the simple diagram was littered with peaks and troughs; both men envisioned the black volcanic rock rising straight out of the bright blue sea, forbidding any landing from almost all sides. Only the southern side, the windward one, provided any sort of beach.

'We could sit the *Shadow* two miles west' – Devlin placed his finger offshore – 'boat the men across to the *Lucy* and sail her into the beach.'

'Aye. The problem I have' – Peter Sam picked up Devlin's hand and placed his finger on the west coast – 'is that if I were a small garrison I would have a lookout on either coast. I could see a ship from maybe twenty or thirty miles approaching me. You're clever, Devlin. But you can't make a ship invisible.'

'I can try.' He took his hand away and reached for a bottle. Peter Sam smiled his rare grin. Devlin had grown on him sure enough.

The men had voted Devlin captain unanimously, the day after leaving the Verdes. Peter Sam had no wish to be captain, and Devlin had a glamour about him without a doubt. He could navigate, he had a humour, and somehow his plans worked with no loss of life. Their lives at least.

Toombs's plans had been desperate of late and the purse had been growing thin. With ease, Devlin had turned calamity into prospect. The wine stores of the *Shadow* had granted the men a heady passage, and Valentim Mendes's own personal fortune, luckily kept in the captain's cabin, had added almost a thousand doubloons to their coffers.

Peter Sam still harboured one shred of misgiving: the abiding thought that if Devlin had brought the map to everyone's attention before São Nicolau, Seth might have forsaken his drunken plan. And Thomas Deakins would still be alive and not with his bones strewn amongst the dragon and marmulan trees of some godforsaken island spat out from Africa.

Peter Sam had accepted, when they had broken bread and bottlenecks together, that Devlin feared a choking if he had revealed the map to them too soon. He believed him when he said he had planned to enlighten them as soon as Toombs's plan had come to fruition.

All that was fair. All that was understandable. But a ship was a small place to hide a secret. And Thomas Deakins would still be alive.

'We'll need more men,' Peter Sam said. 'Providence is where we'll find them. We can divvy up and all.' He left no room for disagreement. 'It's required.'

'Fair enough,' Devlin agreed. 'I take it we could careen the *Lucy* there. She drags so.'

'Aye. And the men need a few days of raping and loosing.'

'Coin is weighing me down too.' Devlin smiled rakishly. 'After which we'll plot a course.' He looked down at the paper. 'Of which there are but two. Either north around Cuba or through the Windward Passage of Hispaniola.'

'If this gold is still sitting there. With only this little fort protecting it.'

'Its strength is in its weakness. To secure it would be obvious.'

'Ha!' Peter Sam chinked a bottle against Devlin's. 'I hope the French aren't half as bold as you, Captain!'

'*Fortes fortuna adiuvat*, mate.' He smirked to his confused quartermaster. 'Fortune helps the brave. Trust me.'

'*Quot homines, tot sententiae*: so many men, so many opinions,' Coxon attested. He took his coffee in a gulp.

'I am merely suggesting, Captain' – Guinneys' voice was almost seductive – 'that perhaps we should sail to Providence and attempt to catch the pirates napping.'

The two men stood around Coxon's table, in his cabin, flanked by Lieutenants Scott and Anderson. The polished surface of the table was obscured by charts and Coxon's scribbled calculations. Edward Talton of the Honourable East India Trading Company did not attend, and apart from a few breathers on deck had mostly chosen to spend his days scratching a complaining quill across sheets of paper, which nobody had raised objection to.

They had passed the Azores yesterday forenoon, ahead of schedule, and Coxon was now discussing his plans for their second stage. He would listen to suggestions, even adapt good ones to his own plan, but he would not waver from the course in his resolute mind. He picked up his log from where it lay across the map's face.

'We are here, gentlemen. Bearing west-so' west.' He pointed west of the Azores following a pencilled line from Portsmouth, the white cuff of his shirt covering the string of islands of the Caribbean to the west. 'The pirate vessel is approximately ten days ahead of us if, I hasten to add, they sleep at night and anchor until noon before sailing. If their captain—'

'Your man Devlin,' Guinneys felt obliged to remind the assembly.

'Indeed. If their captain is sailing to the Bahamas, from the Verdes, he is currently on a west-by-north bearing.' Coxon drew a fingernail across a second line that ended at the neat little island of Providence. 'Even if we gave him the generosity of two days to careen, he would still be a week ahead of us.' He looked charitably to Guinneys. 'There is no point in chasing him. We should continue on to this French island and either find him there or long gone.'

'Is it not possible, Captain,' Anderson theorised, 'that they may, from Providence, take the Windward Passage also, cutting through the islands? We could meet them if they chose that route.'

Coxon sank more coffee, then carried on. 'When you were a schoolboy at Eton, Mister Anderson, and you walked back to your rooms, did you not avoid the main corridors in the hope of not bumping into some of the prefects, else they razed you?'

'Everyone tries to avoid the older lads, sir.' The corners of Anderson's mouth twitched.

'So you took the quieter route, did you not?' Coxon tossed down a letter from his coat.

Guinneys picked up the proclamation, written in the elaborate hand of Whitehall. It had come as part of Coxon's orders. The letter was dated 15 September 1716.

Complaint having been made to His Majesty, by great Numbers of Merchants, Masters of Ships and others, as well as by several Governors of His Majesty's Islands & Plantations in the West Indies, that the Pyrates are grown so numerous, that they infest not only the Seas near Jamaica, but even those of the North Continent of America; and that, unless some effectual Means be used, the whole Trade from Great Britain to those Parts, will not be only obstructed, but in imminent Danger of being lost: His Majesty has, upon mature Deliberation in Council, been pleased, in the first Place, to order a proper force to be employ'd for the suppressing of the said Pyrates, which Force to be employed, is as follows.

There on the paper was a list of rates, fourteen ships in total, sailing from all points from New York to Barbados. Some names – *Pearl, Squirrel, Adventure* and *Scarborough* – Guinneys knew; the others not. But only two out of the fourteen were sloops; the rest were fifth- and sixth-rate frigates.

'Impressive.' He nodded.

'Those ships are there now.' Coxon began to feel himself perspire. 'All over the Caribbean. If I were a pirate wishing to avoid patrols and trying to get amid the Caymans, I would travel around Cuba's shore rather than risk sailing through the Windward Passage.' Coxon sat down, compelled by exhaustion. His head was light. Sometimes before lunch the nausea and the sweat that he had carried with him from Africa still resurfaced to remind him how close he had come to death.

He was the only man sitting and was dwarfed by the young, stiff men. For a moment he could not raise his eyes above their silken waistcoats. Uncomfortably they exchanged lowered looks before Guinneys spoke.

'I concur, Captain.' He pulled out a chair and sat, his knee touching Coxon's. 'If I were also a brigand, I would go west from Providence to the Caymans rather than sail south past this lot. We will gain ground on them as a result.'

'Maintain the sail, William.' Coxon mopped his brow. 'Pork pie for lunch, don't you know.'

Chapter Nine

✖

*L*etter from Claes Aarland to the Dutch West India
Company

12 May 1717
To all who will see these presents, Greeting,

*It is with regret and sorrow of heart that I must inform upon the
unsatisfactory nature of our voyage under the most prominent order
of the offices of the Dutch West India Company. On the day of the
eleventh of May at the watch of noon His Honourable Majesty's
ship Ter Meer was attacked and abused by a collection of two pyrate
vessels under the command of one Patrick Devlin. A frigate of
unknown name and twenty-four main guns of unknown poundage
beset upon us joined in conspiration with a brigantine under the title
Lucy of eight main guns and unknown poundage. Complement of one
hundred men at approximation.*

*It is with honour that I report no loss of life due to the competent
action of my officers and command. It is with regret that I must report
the theft of all stock relevant to our voyage and the theft of five crew
to be named and counted as stock for insurance to be claimed.*

40 Negro men
12 Negro women, two with child
8 Negro male child
29 bottle of wine

15 bottle of rum
7 bottle of brandy
2 hog of pork
1 barrel of peas
3 barrel of salted cabbage
6 barrel of molasses
2 barrel of indigo
2 hundredweight sailcloth
400 yards of running rigging
1 hog of beer
2 barrel of gunpowder

It is with honour that I report my return safely of the ship from pyrate hands and of my gallant crew and officers to their homes and service. With this letter I wish to express our united concern for the apprehension of the pyrate Devlin with the utmost expedience and wish his actions to be reported with much affront to our allies who have fathered such a man.

Captain Claes Aarland.
His Majesty's ship Ter Meer.

Providence. Twenty-eight miles long. Eleven miles across at its widest breadth. A million miles from heaven, a footstep into damnation.

In 1700, the combined efforts of the French and Spanish pushed the neglected English governor and his fort off the map. Settlements were burned, properties plundered, Englishmen forced to serve as slaves to Spanish masters.

Those who could escape ran northwards to the Carolinas, spreading the word that the isle was lost.

Some lords with foresight beseeched the queen in 1705 that Providence could be an important stronghold. She had a harbour that could hold up to five hundred ships, with a small island lying off her north shore that provided a sand bar to the harbour, through which no large man-of-war could pass.

For whatever eventual reason, no English force came to reclaim Providence. At least not through the front door.

Slowly, as slowly as the sea laps at Providence's long white beaches, pirates began to descend on the island. They were prompted at first by Spanish gold in return for English and French goods, for as long as the raiding of a ship happened within five leagues of the island, it was a legitimate act of privateering.

Many simply forgot that it was the Spanish raids on Campeche that had forced them onto their dread path, and the rest remembered that it was the English who had abandoned them when peace came.

Through the next ten years, the English colonial buildings sang with English voices again, and when Spain became the common enemy against all the earth, the pirates ruled Providence. In 1717, England turned her eyes towards it again.

Many of those who carved their names on the island were former English privateers. They served Anne. They would turn to George if granted amnesty. They would turn if given land to colonise, if their crimes were pardoned. Naturally their memory would be short after years of rotting with rum. England would gain Providence again without a shot being fired.

For now, Devlin and Peter Sam walked the winding dirt streets with impunity. With all the English-style taverns of broad, stone facings, American oak beams and two-storey houses mingling with small fishermen's cottages, they could be in a Cornish village if it were not for the palm and dragon trees swaying over the yellow sand.

The *Shadow* sat a mile east of the harbour, due to the shallows. The *Lucy*, however, could sail straight in and was beached for careening. There were plenty of black gangs along the shore to carry out the slow process of scraping and caulking her keel, experts at the task for a price.

All of the *Lucy*'s crew were ashore whilst she lay on her side. Forty men today from the *Shadow*, the rest tomorrow. Eagerly they were rowed to shore, overspilling the two boats that the ship possessed – rampant men, bulging with coin, desire shining across their faces.

William Magnes, the old carpenter, had acted as purser to the two ships, and Devlin took his tally to gain a fair price for the excess goods they carried: chiefly the surplus from the *Ter Meer* that they could not eat or drink.

Peter Sam, as quartermaster, took Devlin to the largest tavern on the island, Devlin bowing to Peter Sam's far better knowledge of such dealings.

They came to a stone, two-storey building at the top of the twisting town. A wooden porch skirted the building, the upper storey overhanging the lower. White silken promises hung out of the windows above, drying in the sun.

Despite the early hour of the day and the rising heat, the windows were shuttered below; still Devlin could hear the rising of songs and laughter as they approached.

Peter Sam's long arm reached the wooden handle almost at the same time as his foot fell upon the decked porch. He paused and grinned at Devlin through his red beard.

'No doubt you've met a lot of good men in your life, I'd say, Cap'n.' He nodded inward to the door. 'Prepare to meet a damn bad one.'

The door resisted Peter's arm as if trying to protect the outside world from the horrors within. A wall of noise and smoke greeted them as they stepped over the threshold and across the sawdust-covered stone floor.

Devlin's senses were bewildered by the cacophony of songs and the pressure of bodies almost locked together in a perpetual rolling tune. The room was surprisingly cool, the result of the large slabs of stone that made up its walls and floor, coupled with the high, tobacco-stained ceiling.

Sunlight strained through the shuttered windows, bounced off the hilts of cutlasses and green bottles stuffed with sweating candles that sat on almost every level surface. A long table ran down the centre of the tavern, with benches along its sides, on which sat or lolled men seemingly from every nation of the earth, united in their love of ale and rum.

Other smaller, square tables littered the room, similarly packed, whilst half a dozen smiling black maids weaved skilfully amongst them, pouring crock jugs of wine into leather mugs.

As Devlin followed Peter Sam through the maze of tables and stools, he rested his left hand on the hilt of his sword, passing sailors gaming at dice at one table, cards at the next. The familiar chink of coin was everywhere, almost beating a rhythm along with the quartet of musicians. They sat above everyone's heads, urgently fifing a jig or scraping fiddles, seemingly producing a different tune for every table.

Through the smoky gloom Devlin and Sam reached a short stair in the right corner of the tavern, which led to a raised area like a quarterdeck complete with rails, just large enough for the single round table that sat there.

In the corner of this stage was a clean-shaven man with a grey frock coat, white bob wig laced with black ribbons, and an oversized black tricorne that had once been trimmed with white plume but now showed patchy and grey across its wax-stained felt. He sat alone against the wall, with probably the only backed chair in the place, dealing cards to himself for some intricate purpose. A pistol lay to his right hand, whilst a red sash around his collar ended tied to the fingerguard of another, larger flintlock, the brass cap of which peered up from the edge of the table.

As they mounted the stair, Devlin noticed that the tip of the man's unsheathed sword poked innocently out of the rails, ready to score the ear of an unwary passer-by. As the shadow of the two men fell across him, he raised his head angrily, relaxing with a growling grin as he recalled some previous meeting.

'Peter!' he exclaimed almost gleefully. His voice gave no accent to his birth. 'Well met, sir!'

'Cap'n Vane.' Peter Sam nodded coolly. 'Good to see you're still breathing.'

'Aye. And you and all.' He turned his eyes searchingly to Devlin. 'Who be this, then, you've brought to meet me?'

Devlin stepped forward and tipped his hat. 'Patrick Devlin. Captain Devlin of *Shadow* and *Lucy*. Warmest greetings, Captain Vane.'

'Aye. Indeed. I am Captain Charles Vane. Many happy days to you, sir.' He kicked out a stool from under the table. 'Take a sit, lads.' He beckoned with square, stubby hands. 'Let's drink to old friends.'

Devlin pulled out the stool and sat opposite whilst Vane raised his hand to catch the eye of a serving maid. Peter Sam pulled out another stool and sat at Vane's right hand, which surreptitiously moved the pistol to below the table.

Moments later, mugs were set and wine was brought for his company. Vane poured an amber liquid from his own crock bottle into one of the 'blackjack' leather mugs preferred by establishments for less breakages. Vane offered a small snuffbox to Devlin and Peter Sam, which they pinched from politely, after which Vane turned his head to Peter Sam.

'And, of old friends, where be Seth, then, Peter?'

'Gone. Dead,' Peter Sam said flatly.

'Ah. 'Tis a shame. How'd it happen, lad?'

Peter Sam recounted the yarn that brought them to Providence, even managing to bestow a solemn admiration for Devlin.

'I'm of believing he could polish mud,' he offered to Vane, who nodded respectfully at Devlin.

'Seth was always overestimating himself. But a good soul, nonetheless.' Vane raised his mug and the three drained their drinks. 'May the Lord and saints preserve us!' he cried. 'Now, gentlemen, what brings you to my table?'

'We have goods to sell, Captain,' Devlin said. 'Peter says you'll get us the best prices. For a tribute of course.'

'Aye. I can manage that. Least I can manage that your goods will make it to Stockdale's store.'

'You be law on this island, then, Captain Vane?' Devlin asked.

'Hush, lad. Kind words, quietly spoken. Jennings be the true lord around here. But in his absence, myself or Hornigold will act as lords to the bar, so to speak.' He leaned forward conspiratorially. 'You're lucky to catch even me. I be heading to the Carolinas in a week or two. Mark my words, gentlemen, the hurricanes start in June, but the waters south of here be swarming with English warships to take you down before then. It be the shallows that keeps them away from us and the islands, and sure enough the narrows in the Carolinas be fine for me and the *Ranger*.'

Devlin and Peter Sam swapped looks at word of the warships.

'Ah. I knows that countenance!' Vane laughed. 'There were schemes in thy brains, lads!'

'We'll be grateful if you could appraise our tally, Captain Vane.' Devlin closed the conversation.

'That I can, Captain Devlin. *Rackham!*' He called over the rails, and like a genie a young man dressed in a short white linen jacket appeared below them, wiping a greasy chin across his wide sleeve.

'Aye, Cap'n?'

Taking no time to introduce the man clad exclusively in calico and linen, Vane handed the tally to him.

'Take this to Stockdale. Tin to be delivered to Captain Devlin here by noon tomorrow, John.'

'Aye, Cap'n.' He swaggered off, pulling his hat down purposefully and weaving through the crowd. Vane took a long drink.

'Tell me, Captain Devlin, do you still sail under Toombs's black flag?'

'For want of another, Captain Vane.'

'Well, that ends today, sir!' He slapped the table. 'Peter! Take him to the widow, man! Do you have no sense of honour, you rake?'

'That was my very next visitation, Cap'n,' Peter Sam confirmed.

Devlin stood, bringing the meeting to an end. 'Hope I find you well again, Captain Vane.'

Vane did not stand. He merely proffered his left hand, palm down, keeping his right below the table. They took his hand in turn.

'Honestly glad to have met you, Captain Vane.' Devlin smiled and bowed slightly.

'Aye, lad. Take care. Don't bow to no pardon now. They just wants to own everybody.'

'I'll be my own keeper, Captain Vane.'

They left the tavern leaving no remark or following stare. As if no one cared that they had ever entered.

The word 'crone' could have been created for her. She stooped as if perpetuity had condemned her to forever look for her food from the droppings of others.

She groped her way around the dark wooden shack, her black, shapeless gown hanging from hollow shoulders dappled with stains and flour, her head half hidden by a black bonnet tied under her chin so tight that the skin of her wizened neck draped over the once elegant bow like a bulldog's jowls.

Devlin sat on a spindly chair older than himself that complained every time he breathed in the stale tobacco air. He tried to smile each time the old lady flashed a grey, watery glance towards him. At his smile she giggled breathlessly, scurrying away, her lungs gurgling with glee and pleurisy.

Peter Sam stood leaning against the sloping door frame, picking his fingernails with a small piece of silver cutlery that he could find no other purpose for. He spoke impatiently.

'Come on, old woman!' he growled. 'We have no time for this!'

'Oh, is that so, Peter Sam?' She stopped in her crablike scuttling. 'And much do you know about time, I shouldn't wonder.' She resumed her search amongst the candles and the bottles muttering about Peter Sam's red beard and alluding to her own, unseen particulars.

'Ah, this be a good one!' she exclaimed, producing a yard or so of calico from a shelf low enough for her reach and slapping it down in front of Devlin with surprising alacrity.

'Won't go grey for many a year. Though you be dead by then, of course!' Again her gasping laugh filled the room. 'Now what do you want from this white pattern, "Captain"

Devlin? Don't worry about the black, I got plenty of black, just tell me what you wants on it.'

Devlin had thought a little on the subject. Peter Sam had suggested the importance of a new standard, as it was naturally bad luck to sail under the flag of a dead man.

'I should like a skull, madam. A grinning skull. Planted in the middle of a compass rose. Crude as you like, but quite apparent as to what it is.' He paused and looked behind him to Peter Sam, who continued to pick at his nails, his gaze lowered. 'And two crossed pistols beneath. Bone pistols. Crossed, mind, not on top of each other. That'll do, madam.'

'Oh, that'll do, will it, Captain Devlin? That'll do?' She tried to smile, the soot-lined face cracked like tree bark. 'Compass rose, he says. How many points do you want? says I. How many hands do you think I have? says I.'

'Just the semblance of a compass will do, madam. And crossed pistols, please. If you'd be so kind.' Devlin smiled warmly and touched her cold, bony hand. He stood as he spoke. 'Two flags by the morrow. Two bottles of brandy.'

She scuttled away again. 'One flag. Two bottles. Find a Jew on board to make your other. Now leave me, Peter Sam and Patrick Devlin. You'll have your flag. Much good it'll do you!' She cackled away, a needle already appearing in her twig-like grasp, her back turned, their audience over.

'Tomorrow, then, widow.' Devlin bowed and retreated, rapping Peter Sam's chest as he stepped out through the door and into the afternoon sun. He was glad to be free of the rank air of the dilapidated hut.

''Tis strange that,' mused Peter Sam. He joined Devlin's side as they strolled back down into the town from the high wooded hill where the old woman lived.

'What be that, then, Peter?' Devlin asked. For the first time in months, he felt like a young man rather than a weather-beaten sailor, the Caribbean sun warming his damp Irish bones.

'She called you "Patrick Devlin".'

'Well, so now, what be the harm in that?'

'I never called you Patrick. And I'm sure you never did, Cap'n.'

Devlin looked back to the shack, half expecting it to have vanished magically.

'I think you be right, Peter. She *knew* me.'

'Aye. Don't be too enamoured by that, Patrick. Fame is the beginning of the end.'

Devlin stopped and faced the big man. 'You still have issues with me, Peter?' His words gentle.

Peter Sam looked away as he spoke. 'I have a fair wealth, Cap'n. If I comes across a man with luck and a plan to make me more so, I have no bones against accounting with him awhile.' He looked back at his captain. 'And hell help the man who gets in his way.'

The dust grew around them as they paced down the hill, Devlin's rakish grin growing ever wider.

'The Porker's End' was the most salubrious of the brothels on Providence. Several of the *Lucy*'s crew sat at the two round tables, their insides warmed with rum and their laps warm with the closeness of dark, thin, flowing-haired ladies.

A stool flew back with a crash, shattering the happy mood and silencing the hands of the jolly fiddlers. Dan Teague had sprung from his brethren's table and slammed a yellow-coated, sniggering stranger to the wall, his dirk pressing to the man's throat as he spoke.

'And what,' Dan snarled to the goatee-bearded, finely dressed young man, 'is so amusing about my choice of whore?'

Dan had singled out one of the few white women in the place who had seemingly spent most of her formative years singling out the cream and jam from whatever house she had run from.

The choice had amused the young man in the plumed yellow hat, for Dan was a scrawny man; still, the fellow had been surprised by his alarming vigour, and to find himself against the grimy stone wall, only imagining what its slime was doing to his gold silk justaucorps.

'It's not sport, my friend, I assure you.' The young man squirmed, grinning through dirty teeth, his two front ones capped with dull gold, his breath reeking of rum. 'I am Annie's doctor, so to speak. That is to say, I am indeed her physician. And as such I was picturing the conjoining of your rapturous forms and was wondering which one of your fine friends would volunteer to fish you out' – pause – 'mate.'

His voice was Virginian, but infected by the slang and diction of a thousand travellers. Dan's eyes moved back and forth across the man's face, trying to read a threat, finding nothing but amusement behind the eyes. Dan broke into a wicked laugh, removing the blade. The tables returned to their previous jovial form.

'You may have a thought there, mate, sure enough!' He slapped the fellow's shoulder and resumed his seat. 'A doctor, you say? What type of doctor?' He gestured for the man to join them at their table. The young man straightened his clothes with a tug and a brush of his palm, and sat down, leaving enough space between the edge of the table and himself, which he judged to be a sword-thrust away from his companions.

'A physician who has lost his way, sir.' He poured himself a watery rum into a pewter mug. 'I apply my time here' – he indicated their surroundings with a wave of his hand and a roll of his eyes – 'scraping and bursting my way through the greasy capons that frequent this establishment. Present company excluded, gentlemen.' He sipped at his rum, his eyes closed. Placing the mug down with a satisfied sigh, he wiped the amber liquid from his moustache and continued, 'For the reward of a straw mattress and a noggin of rum, I attend to all the ladies of this palace.'

This remark brought admiring leers and growls from his company. 'Oh, indeed, believe me, gentlemen, there is nothing that you will see tonight that I have not, a thousand times over. And all the putrid colours of the rainbow.'

'So you be a pox doctor, then, mate?' Sam Morwell asked.

'Aye. I am at the centre of the mark of civilisation. There are colleagues of mine who would sell their souls for such a wealth of subject and project that befalls me. So I must be truly blessed.' He drank again.

'Ho!' Dan laughed. 'You be touched for a doctor, that's for sure! What be you called, mate?'

'What so, indeed?' he said, leaning his head on his fist and staring into the candle flame dancing from the neck of a green bottle in the centre of the table. As if speaking to himself, his gaze became cloudy and he muttered, 'You may call me Dandon, gentlemen. That will do.'

At first appraisal, Dandon was a fine figure in his golden brocade coat and yellow wide-brimmed feathered hat. Closer inspection in the candlelight showed the worn pattern and frayed hem of the coat, the dust and grime upon the brim of his hat. His buckled shoes were torn and thin, his stockings and breeches far from white, the breeches particularly unpleasantly stained.

His dark face had tight, handsome features with charming eyes that had however become sallow with the drink that had claimed his future.

'*Dandon?*' Dan Teague was curious. 'Where be that from, then?'

'It is not my original name, to be sure, sir.' He stretched his neck towards a half-eaten chicken on a pewter charger. 'If you were to avail me some use of that small hen, I would be willing to share the peculiarities of its origins, sir. By that I mean my name, not the hen.'

Dan pushed the charger accompanied by a bone-handled gully towards the young man. Dandon happily began to relate the story that had brought him to the pirate haven.

Three years previously, he had been subsisting, barely, as an apothecary's assistant in Bath Towne, North Carolina. He spent his quiet days mixing remedies and poring over second-hand medical journals fooling himself that such a practice would substitute for real medical training and would catapult him into the comparatively wealthy world of medicine.

Amongst the jars of leeches and mercury compounds he noticed the growing popularity of sea-salt pills and powders, particularly those salts originating from the Bahamas. Like most young men at some time or another, a scheme to profit quickly for minimum effort infects their otherwise noble and straightforward plans. As with most of these schemes, small harm occurs. The young man realises the error of his ways and returns to honest effort instead, thanking his saints that the venture cost him and those around him little.

The young apothecary's assistant was not so fortunate, however. After a scrimption of research, he saw how easily one could set up a small salt-refining concern, right on the very beach of Providence Island. This saltern would actually cost only a pocketful of coin to build; all he had to do was undersell all the other unscrupulous pill-peddlers and his fortune would be secure.

The plan was promising but the realisation that he barely earned enough money to eat and sleep warm in the back room of the apothecary, let alone to afford such an enterprise, meant that his dreams would only ever be that.

Bitterness began to crawl within him. He felt exploited by his bloated master, who only appeared in the shop to remove the coin from the premises, deduct the rent for his assistant's lodgings from his wage, and on a Monday bestow upon him the cold and fatty remains of his Sunday beef by way of charity.

Almost without thought and certainly without guilt, he slowly found himself depositing less and less of the cash in the wooden box beneath the counter.

He knew it would only be a few months before his master noticed a fall in stock with a diminishing return, but some ironic providence favoured the assistant and his master became ill and bedridden. All trust of the business fell to his loyal assistant whilst his master recuperated.

Three weeks of tireless embezzlement later and the man who would become Dandon sailed to the island of Providence with one hundred and twenty guineas and a new golden silk justaucorps coat and matching feathered hat, with dreams of building a saltern business in the Bahamas, perhaps an empire of them, and why not?

In his mind he considered the stolen money merely a secret loan. He would repay it, anonymously of course, as soon as he began to reap the rewards of his vision.

'But alas and alack, gentlemen' – Dandon sipped his rum – 'I found myself a fly in a spider's world. The saltern business was a – shall we say? – *competitive* one. My attempts even to find tools to build were met with violence and theft. I was not fortunate enough to have the backing of a band of brothers such as yourselves. You, my friends, are all protected by the companionship of each other. You may find it is a hard world for the lonely.'

Dandon managed to insert a whole chicken leg into his mouth; a moment later, he pulled it out again, naked of meat, his gold front teeth glistening with grease.

'With time I found myself frequenting the hostelries of my new home, offering my medical knowledge. My fellow islanders took amusement from my yellow attire and christened me "Dandelion". Over the years, those more familiar have come to call me Dandon. Which is how I present myself to you, my friends.'

'Then it is a pleasure to acquaint with you, Dandon.' Dan Teague raised his mug in appreciation of the tale.

The evening descended into the fumbling of petticoats, the rolling of rum bottles across the stone floor, and the endless yaw of sailors' songs, merrily married to the wail of bouncing, jigging fiddles.

Outside, the familiar sounds drew the tall man in like a siren's song. His square-tailed crimson coat was smeared with pitch. Across his chest he wore braces of pistols, six in all, two of which hung at the end of a sling of red silk round his neck.

The black matted beard began just above his waistcoat and covered half his dark, narrow face, mingling with the coarse black hair that cascaded down his back, all topped with a broad black tricorne.

In one movement he downed the dregs of a green bottle and sent it smashing to the ground. He grinned up at the sign, crudely depicting a sailor in a cutter boat harpooning a great white that had leaped half out of the water, and then ducked beneath it and through the door.

Edward Teach had returned to Providence.

Chapter Ten

✗

*A*bove the revelry, in one of the gaudy sweating rooms of the Porker's End, Patrick Devlin, dressed in shirt and breeches, lay languidly on his side across a tousled bed, toying with a doubloon, spinning it repeatedly upon the dusty surface of a short cabinet beside the bed.

The room was dark. A small oil lamp at the window lit barely half the room, and threw fluttering shadows upon the naked shoulders of the young woman putting up her tawny hair in front of a speckled mirror.

She hummed an unrecognisable melody to herself, seemingly unaware of the man on the bed behind her, or the dancing of the coin as it fell again and again.

Without turning she spoke, quietly, in a soft Carolina accent. 'Where you be going after Providence, Patrick Devlin?' she asked.

'I have an island I have to pay homage to, Sarah.' He spoke absently, never removing his concentration from the spinning coin.

'For more doubloons, no wonder. Don't suppose I'll be getting one of those at all?' She turned to look lovingly at him, revealing her small bruised breasts.

'Three pieces of eight, my girl, and be thankful. It used to take me six months to earn that in shillings.'

'Lucky me.' She turned back to her mirror. 'Why do you

rovers need so much money, anyways? None of you ever lives to spend it all, from what I see.'

Devlin paused the coin for a moment. 'Oh, I intend to stop, Sarah. I'll take my fill and I'll part my ways. And as to why? The coin is the most of it, that's true, but there's more. We don't take money from the likes of you.' He stretched out, his hand high in the air, admiring the coin between his fingers. 'We take only that which people think belongs to them. The monies they take from the hearts and backs of men. Piracy is not theft. I understand that much. I could spend my life breaking into the homes of the poor and stealing all I need to live on and nobody would raise a sniff. But take a hogshead of sugar from the interests of a gentleman, that's a different matter. That's interfering with the grease of the world. That's a degradation in the ledger of the mighty. That's half the bloody navy on your arse protecting the greed of a handful of men.' He went back to spinning his coin.

'Aye, you're all bloody heroes. Shame, then, that nobody's ever pleased to see you. Now me? Wherever I go, everybody's pleased to see me and the girls. Light up the world, we do.'

She was startled by the violent slapping of the coin on the wood, and crossed her arms across her breasts in alarm, whipping her neck to him, cursing.

'You bloody fool! You nearly gave me a failure banging the table like that!'

'Say that again, Sarah!' He sat up urgently.

'Say what again?'

'You're true as they come, Sarah my girl! Every man is always glad to see a whore! Every sailor and every soldier! You've earned this doubloon, my girl, and another if you come sailing with me!'

'Do what now?'

'Tell me, girl, do you have any French ladies here?'

Through the sudden tension in the small room, amid the sounds of laughter and music below, the muffled shot of a pistol cracked. The music stopped.

Devlin grabbed his sword belt and pistol before stumbling, bootless, through the door. Sarah opened her mouth to protest at the suddenness of his departure, but closed it when she saw the shining gold coin still lighting up the room.

For the second time that evening, Dandon found himself pinned unceremoniously to the filthy wall, this time by a powerful right forearm; the left hand was pointing a pistol mouth at his sweating temple.

'I beseech you, Captain Teach,' Dandon spoke calmly, despite choking on the arm at his neck. 'I was not of suggesting that the odour was related to your personage entering the tavern, merely if anyone could inform me of its source, that is all!'

Teach's pupils were needle-holes, the whites of his eyes growing every sweating second.

'Dandelion! Every time I see you I wants to kill you more!'

'We are agreed, then, that absence is our preferred situation. We should follow on such a notion, surely, so as not to displease the nature of the world.' Dandon grinned his most effacing gold-capped smile. Teach could see his own savage, skeletal rack reflected in their sheen.

'You're not worthy of pistol shot, you wretch!' Teach pushed the dragoon pistol into his belt and released his arm from Dandon's throat, only to replace it a breath later with the tapered tip of his cutlass. 'I'll run you through likes I been promising since I first saw you!'

Sam Morwell was standing, along with his brethren, all of

them half reaching for their own weapons, unsure of the proper tack to take against the man about whom even pirates spoke only in whispers.

'He's no weapons, Teach! Leave him be!' he pleaded.

'Bide your steel, boys!' Teach glared back at them with a sweep of his head. 'Else you'll all follow his judgement!'

'Come now! Judgement, is it?' Devlin's voice rang from the flight of stairs at the back of the tavern. 'Leave the devil some work!'

Teach had to swing round to see the owner of the voice. All eyes in the room watched Devlin, sans stockings and boots, levelling his pistol at the tall, black-framed pirate, his sword belt in his left hand.

'Did I disturb you, sir?' Teach queried. All the heads in the room, sensing a contest, sidled back to Teach, whose beard lifted up as he grinned. 'But I'd put that pistol away. Before I do. My business is none of yours.'

The expectant faces weaved back to Devlin, who took a soft step down the stairs.

'As you notice – "*Teach*", was it? – I have nowheres to secrete my pistol. So I must either drop it or have it dropped for me. And I'm loath to risk a dent to my pistol by my own hand. Which is it to be, Teach?'

Dandon felt his breath return to him in relief that Teach's attention was distracted.

'Do you not know me, man?' Teach asked, lowering his sword almost in disbelief.

'I am new to Providence. I got the name. Other than that I have responded with drawn pistol as I heard a shot and those two tables are full of my men. It's in their interest that I stand before you.' Devlin took the final step to the slab floor, fifteen feet from the towering pirate.

'*Your* men?' Teach took in the tables either side of him. 'I reckon some of these to be Seth Toombs's lads.'

'Aye,' Dan Teague spoke up. 'Toombs be dead, Captain Teach.' He was almost apologetic. 'Captain Devlin be the lord now.' Dan twisted his head to Devlin and almost bowed as he spoke. 'This be Captain Teach, Devlin. Have you not heard the name Blackbeard in your life before?'

'Devlin? That be you, then?' Teach's Bristol accent came to the fore. Unknown to Devlin, Edward Teach had joined on the account with Benjamin Hornigold late the previous year and had swiftly courted a bloody reputation that grew as fast as his hirsute jowls. A vagrant privateer from the war. Intelligent and astute. Violent and drunken. Blackbeard.

Devlin showed no recognition and gave his own introduction. 'Aye. Captain Patrick Devlin. Captain of the brigantine *Lucy* and the frigate *Shadow*. And I'm sure it is only my ignorance that stops my arm from quivering with fear, Captain Teach.' Devlin bowed.

Teach took a step forward; Dandon began to slip along the wall like a shadow.

'Not knowing me is no crime. But know me as consort captain to Ben Hornigold. One who may be lord in this republic. It be a wrong man to go against me. And a short life for him.'

Teach's eyes never wavered from Devlin's, and he paid no attention to the pointing pistol. 'I'm no threat to your men, Captain Devlin. My humour is for Dandelion here. He be nothing to you.'

Sam Morwell broached his tongue. 'He's a doctor, Captain. He has powders and all sorts.' Sam presented this information as if he had just found the infant Jesus in his arms, but lowered his eyes as his brothers glared at him.

'Is this true, Mister Teague?' Devlin enquired of Dan Teague, the only one of his men who had committed his right hand to the hilt of his cutlass, his eyes watchful on Teach.

'Aye, Captain,' he sighed. 'A doctor, to be sure.' Dan could feel the evening going badly. Sam Morwell had proposed a reason to defend the man Dandon and he would stand by his brother. He only regretted the absence of Peter Sam at such a decision. 'We needs a doctor.'

'Seems this man may have some meaning to me, Captain Teach. I may ask you to forgo your humour, sir.'

Devlin raised his voice to the fellow creeping along the wall. 'You, sir! Dandelion! Are you in need of proper employment?'

Dandon stopped and straightened himself. 'I prefer the sobriquet "Dandon" this year, Captain, if you please.' He tipped his hat. 'But a coin or two and a noggin of rumbustion I would welcome, sir.'

'Then we shall talk terms, when I am properly attired.'

Devlin returned his study to Teach. 'Now, Captain, I am afraid that I would have to take offence if you caused any harm to a member of my crew, as I would expect you to also. Would you not say?' He lowered the pistol, keeping it cocked.

Teach could feel his very spleen engorge with blood, but he was no fool. He stood alone in a tavern full of Devlin's brethren.

No Black Caesar behind him. No Israel Hands by his side. He had come ashore alone from the six-gun sloop he commanded, leaving all seventy souls aboard. Hornigold's orders were to wait for him if Teach's sloop arrived at Providence before him. Teach was a day ahead after their latest cruise, and fancied himself a little dallying ashore. He feared no man or devil, but to die alone and far from his brethren was against his own plan.

The long, matted black beard rose again in amusement.

Slowly, with an awful scraping, he put up and drove home to his belt the grey blade of his cutlass; at the same time a large clasp knife appeared in his left hand from his fustian overcoat. He stepped purposefully to the table where Dan Teague still stood, ready to draw his blade, not unnoticed by Teach.

The dark blade of the clasp knife sighed open, clicking like a pistol. Teach's black eyes swayed across Devlin's men; they all struggled to meet his rolling stare.

Devlin felt uneasy as he watched the mysterious actions of the tall pirate, and widened his stance for a sudden defence.

Teach picked up the bottle that held the candle. His face glowed eerily in its yellow light for an instant; then he blew it out softly.

As the smoke danced around his beard, he slammed the bottle down on its side, shaking awake everyone who had been mesmerised by his movements. He began to saw at the candle with the knife; moments later a quarter of it was in his hand. The blade snapped shut and disappeared within the confines of his coat.

Carefully, Teach studied the small white stump of wax. Satisfied, he buried it beneath his coat, seemingly in a pocket close to his heart. He swelled to his full height and returned his undivided attention to Devlin.

''Till we meet again, Captain.' And then Blackbeard swept out of the tavern in three swift silent steps, the slamming of the door behind him jarring the walls.

With the closing of the door, Devlin's composure returned, and he joined Dan Teague at the table. The green bottle still rocked on its side, the candle naked and short.

'What was that about, Mister Teague?' Devlin asked, carelessly dropping his long pistol to the table with a clatter and hanging his sword belt on a chair.

Dan Teague smiled nervously at his captain as they both sat down together, reaching for mugs and crock bottles simultaneously.

'That be an old buccaneer habit, Cap'n,' Dan spoke, lowering his voice as he continued, spying that Dandon was joining their table with a smile to the bottles of rum.

'In what manner, Mister Teague?' Devlin asked, gulping a draught of rum, trying to drown the drama of Teach's presence away with every swallow.

'Well, Cap'n, by cutting the candle he's taking time away from you. Keeping it for himself, like. It's the mark of your days and he keeps it in his pocket.'

'For what?'

Dan seemed incredulous at his captain's ignorance. 'For when he meets you again, of course!' Dan continued with a belch, 'He'll aim to kill you. Then, when you're dead, he'll light the candle, removing the last of your life from this world. The last days of your life belong to him now, Cap'n … If you believe such things, that is.'

Devlin raked his fingers through the carcass of the fowl, now cold and skeletal. With some success he found one of the bird's oysters still intact and popped it in his mouth with satisfaction.

'To hell with Teach, then, Mister Teague.'

'Aye, most probably, Cap'n.'

'Now, Mister Teague' – Devlin leaned forward – 'do you have any French speech in that broken old head of yours?'

'No, Cap'n.' Dan sounded bemused. 'Reckon I don't.'

'No bother. Drag out Peter Sam from wherever he be and tell him I need boulting cloth, coloured silks and such. Enough to festoon the *Lucy*. That old widow will be the place.'

'What for, Cap'n?'

'*Lucy*'s going to open her legs to the French and I needs

her to look pretty, like.' He picked up the pistol and waved it loosely to Dandon. 'And you, sir? Doctor Dandon? Can you speak French?'

'*Non*, monsieur.' Dandon raised his hands against the pistol, perceiving it to be still cocked. 'At least the threat of arms diminishes my ability to do so. If you'd be so kind as to remove the teeth from your hound, I may be inclined to extend my tale to the intimacy that my former master was a Fort Louis de la Louisiane man before the floods. I can pray and curse with the worst of them, if you would only lower your weapon, Captain Devlin.'

'This?' Devlin raised the weapon to the ceiling with a flourish and pulled the trigger. The empty pistol fired into the air with a flat snap and silent spark. He slapped it down again upon the table, shaking his head to the young doctor. 'You don't takes a loaded pistol into a whore's chamber, Dandon. I'd have thought you'd have known that.'

From behind them, the fiddlers began again, slower this time. A long, whining dirge. One of them started out with a low hum until he found his tone. When the pitch was his, he began in a high, Scottish drone:

Oh me name is Captain Kidd as I sailed, as I sailed.
Oh me name is Captain Kidd as I sailed.
Oh me name is Captain Kidd and God's laws I did
  forbid.
And most wickedly I did
As I sailed.

'Why do we have shortened sail, Mister Guinneys?' Coxon's head and shoulders appeared, rising to the quarterdeck. 'I thought we were to carry on?' His manner was polite, querying, with deference to his officer as former captain. Coxon had broken from a rare nap before dinner during Guinneys' evening watch. It was after seven, the sun had set and the sky was a duck-egg blue.

'Standard setting, Captain, for unknown reef waters.' Guinneys smiled back. 'Soundings by mark three. Leather, sir.' He referred to the lead sounding of rope that fathomed the depth of the waters.

They were passing through the Windward Passage of the Greater Antilles. Off the larboard quarter, the island of Hispaniola veered away from them, smothered in mist. To starboard, to the northwest, there was the white outline across the horizon of Cuba, and before dawn the pleasing blue mountains of Jamaica would come towards them, signalling them to change course NNW to the Caymans.

'Make sail, Mister Guinneys,' Coxon ordered. 'I could sail our gallant king's mistress through these waters. They are not unknown to me.'

'Aye, aye, sir,' Guinneys rapped.

'Remember, Mister Guinneys, that we are trying to reach this island before the gold is lost. If sail is shortened we will delay our passage. I have sailed these waters for many years. The course is good.'

'Was that with your pirate acquaintance, Captain?' Guinneys' eyes broadened.

Coxon allowed the smirk that flashed upon Guinneys' face and just as rapidly vanished. He had not seen it, or at least he had not seen it enough to bother him.

'Carry on, Mister Guinneys. You will not leave your watch till the sails are set.'

'Aye, aye, Captain.' Guinneys bowed, turned to the deck, shouting for a midshipman of the watch to carry out his orders.

Coxon looked up to the early stars breaking through the firmament, which suddenly began to sway before his eyes. Silently, he stepped backwards, putting a hand behind to the rail to steady himself. He stared anxiously across the ship. Guinneys' back was turned. No one had seen. He swallowed the lake of saliva that had suddenly filled his mouth. His eyes swung up to a bearded fellow in a Monmouth cap standing in the crosstrees of the mainmast. The man studied his captain for a moment, then turned his back and disappeared down the ratlines like an ape.

Coxon watched the unsteady form of Oscar Hodge, his new valet, coming up the stair with a small pewter tray, a single cup of coffee sitting nervously upon it. Thanking Hodge for the coffee, he sipped slowly, the bitter roast sharpening his mind almost instantly. He politely asked Hodge to prepare fresh clothes for the morning, to brush his hat and coat before he retired. Hodge murmured agreement and removed himself, leaving Coxon to dwell on the new career of his previous servant.

Rightly or wrongly, he knew that the young gentlemen who were his officers felt that he was partly to blame for the creation of the pirate, that without his presence on board they would be swanning around parties in London by now, writing secret messages on the fans of blushing ladies and buying new horses for the season.

Once, a few days past, a dizzy spell had caused him to miss a step on the companion to the quarterdeck, whereupon Guinneys and Scott had bitten laughs with the backs of their hands. He had recovered his footing and they had tugged their forelocks as if nothing had happened.

Still, Coxon felt that they merely tolerated their new captain, that there was almost something temporary about him, and in truth when it was all over this would not be his ship, not be his men. But it could all be in his own doubtful mind.

Perhaps it was merely a nostrum of his own, built out of his weakened state. These men were half his age. They were indestructible.

Conflict would settle it. Finding Devlin, his hands dipped in gold, bedecked in jewels, then watching him quake before his guns and submit to his master.

Aye, he thought, that was it. They all blamed him for Devlin. All of them. Whitehall and his officers. His redemption could only come from Devlin's destruction. If his actions had lost the *Noble*, then this was his olive branch, and it would come sticking out of the bloodied chest of his butcher's boy.

Three days. That was all it would take. Three days to reach him. To reach him and break him. Three more morning watches. He drained his coffee, his thoughts now passing to the slow weatherly progress of the *Starling* amongst the shouts and calls of the crew. The certainty of Patrick Devlin's death ebbed its way towards him.

He tossed the small porcelain cup over the taffrail and watched it boil in the effervescence of the *Starling*'s wake for a moment before it disappeared forever. One porcelain coffee cup from Guinneys' own tableware. Worth at least three guineas. He snapped his hat and returned below, nodding admiringly to the man at the helm.

Chapter Eleven

✗

The Island

Favre Callier enjoyed the time alone on the cliff top. From the small calico tent that was his sentry post on the west of the island he could see for twenty miles all around him. The wind whipped at the sides of the tent but it was warm and always dry under the blue skies. He spent the hours of his watch with charcoal and paper, refining the multitude of sketches that he kept in his leather satchel.

He had painstakingly drawn, over the last few weeks, all the foliage that the small world outside the tent offered; now he drafted portraits of his comrades, their barracks and any ships that appeared in the offing.

For occasional inspiration and relief from the monotony of his forenoon watch, he walked the short distance to the edge of the cliff and cautiously watched the breakers and white catspaws licking the rocks below, silent and gentle from this height.

From his vantage, two hundred feet high, he could see the crescent sand bar spreading for miles around, only broken by the savage dagger-points of black volcanic rock, threatening to rip the hull of any ship foolish enough to approach.

He sat cross-legged on the sandy, straw-like grass in the mouth of his tent and perused his sketches.

He disliked his rendition of the *Cressy*, the sloop that had brought them to the island. It was lifeless, dark and morose, yet he recalled it as a happy ship. The nineteen men on board had enjoyed an easy passage to the island. Nine had remained on the island under Captain Bessette; the remainder sailed the little sloop back home.

Three months ago the responsibility had seemed immense. Now they had fallen into a dull routine of watches and manual labour. Soldiering had been replaced by gardening and land-scaping the area around the fort. Men planted individual veg-etable patches, cleared rocks and trees to give a wide field of defence should any lucky soul stumble upon their outpost.

The small fort he had caught well. Once home, when their duty would be relieved next month, he would try to paint it, as a memory for his children yet-to-be, as a testament to the duty that he had done for his king.

Two L-shaped buildings, large enough for twenty men. One was their barracks, a log cabin with six single shuttered windows with gunloops crossed upon them. The other housed Captain Bessette's quarters and their mess room. Ah, and there was the scowling portrait of Bessette himself. Strange how he scowled all those months ago as well. Now it seemed impossible to imagine him any other way, for it was almost a month since his jaw had begun to fester and pulse, sending him into spasms of agony. It would be June before any relief would come. Bessette would probably shoot himself before then. Callier was content at the thought. A *cochon* of a man turned into a *sanglier*.

Only one reminder of the solemnity of their purpose met them every morning as they crossed from their barracks to the mess, and in Callier's sketch the small nine-pounder behind a sand redoubt could barely be seen. It aimed directly at the wooden gates, straight down the middle of the two buildings, sited to decimate an assault breaking through the gates.

Callier riffled through his rough papers with familiarity, finally resting his eyes on the elegant features of Lieutenant Philippe Ducos. Ducos was staring out at him from beneath the corner of the great chest of gold, borne on the shoulders of five other marines stepping out of the sea.

The likeness pleased Favre, and he held it out in admiration until something pricked his attention from the blanket of sea and he looked over the top of the paper with an artist's eye.

The endless line of the horizon was broken by the hint of a grey shape, miles distant. Calmly he placed down his sketches and picked up his two-draw telescope and brought the vessel closer to him. Through the smoky, rippled lens he saw the three masts under full sail moving south. South and safely past the island towards the Caymans or Jamaica.

His study was broken by the crunch of urgent footsteps on the shingle behind him. He turned to the sweating approach of Dominic Duphot, his messmate, pounding up the cliff towards him, the brim of his wide hat bouncing as he ran.

Callier called out, 'Ho, Duphot! Why so happy to relieve me?' He slammed the tube closed and moved towards his comrade, who had eased his pace and was adjusting his cross-belt and dragging a sleeve across his brow. 'What occurs, brother?' Callier asked.

Gasping, swallowing the air like water, Dominic Duphot steadied himself. 'Whores, Favre… A ship of whores is in the bay… Everyone is on the beach. Come!'

Favre Callier swept into his small tent, grabbed his hat, satchel and cutlass, and trotted down the steep path riven through the cliff, jostling his laughing comrade.

Behind them, over the sea, the dark ship crept silently along, seemingly smaller now, in fact only two masts visible, as the *Shadow*'s bow pointed towards the island.

The trip had taken the *Lucy* just over six days. Devlin passed command of the *Shadow* to Peter Sam and they parted company ten miles west of Cabo San Antonio, off Cuba's west coast. The *Shadow* was to sail SSE until she hit the Twenty-First Parallel, then head due east until the water became almost white and the devilfish swam in the cream of the *Shadow*'s wake.

Lucy traversed ESE directly for almost four hundred miles on a close reach. It was a difficult sail for Devlin and the nine others he had chosen to man her. But they were all old hands, the winds were fair and Dandon kept the songs French and bawdy.

A watch had been maintained since noon on the third day as they passed San Antonio, and – almost to the hour that the black cross had been marked by Devlin on the map – at six, in the morning watch of the sixth day, Sam Morwell gave the cry of 'Land ho!' from the topsail.

Men who were sleeping dragged themselves to the main deck where a spontaneous jig erupted. The beat of the men's feet on the oak did little, however, to stir the five ladies swinging and snoring in the hammocks below.

Dandon and Devlin stood at the starboard quarter outside the doorless cabin, Devlin, with the scope to his eye, was barely able to discern the black shape rising through the mist off the bow. Dandon tucked his frayed cuffs into his sleeves and heartily slapped Devlin's back, bringing the sea crashing into Devlin's scope like a cloak as he pitched forward.

'Although I have the notion, mate, that I have come into this play in the final act, I feel that even I should offer my homage to your indubitable success!'

Dandon grinned his gold-capped smile. Devlin nodded, looking up at the fore stays and main braces, trimmed with square flags of red and white bunting, the mainmast limply displaying a gold and white French pennant. He looked around at the *Lucy*, surveying her absently.

There, along the gunwale, were axe marks, like the smiting of a giant cat. Looking aft were gaps in the rails along the quarterdeck; at his feet there was the faint smearing of blood along the scuppers. All signs of a weary ship of adventure and risk. A pirate ship.

'It ain't over yet there, Dandon. Ways to go. And the hardest part. You may well regret signing on.' He clapped the telescope into Dandon's hands and moved to the head to join his men. It was the first morning of the rest of his life and he would spend the opening hours of it in the company of happy men.

Dandon watched him attempt a jig, linking shoulders with Hugh Harris and Sam Fletcher. The pirate captain danced a few steps, then excused himself to the gunwale with an exaggerated shyness to pull out his pipe and look out to the island. It was the first time Dandon had seen him truly alone. An unusual guilt came across him as he watched the man enjoying a moment of solitude staring out over the dawn sea.

Dandon knew nothing about him. He had two ships and a hundred men; Dandon had seen dozens of men who could claim such wealth, but not one who had set out that way. At twenty-five, Dandon had felt his life over, his days dwindling down to the measure of each bottle. Now he had met a man not much older than himself who seemed to have a purpose and who even valued him as well, for whatever little he was worth.

He found the sharp eyes of the pirate Devlin looking back at him and he tipped his hat. Aye, Devlin had a purpose to be sure, and even a damned purpose was better than none at all.

A little over six hours later and the *Lucy* sat becalmed, her port side a quarter of a mile from the shallow waters of the crescent white beach. As expected, they had been spotted approaching from the east hours ago, and now a small party of five musketeers and a fine gentleman in a short blue jacket with matching breeches and stockings stared at them through a silver spyglass.

Devlin took the time to muster up a fine shirt, black necktie and brown waistcoat whilst the men adopted a more subdued dress of white shirts, blue breeches and Monmouth woollen hats. No stockings or shoes, just sailor slops, their filthy and ragged finery stowed with the hammock nettings along the bulwarks.

For those exchanging the spyglass on the beach it was the rumbustious ladies, now waving handkerchiefs and blowing kisses from the fo'c'sle, who were the focus of the most attention.

The five of them – Alice, Sarah, Bernadette, Josephine and Annie – were now five doubloons richer apiece. Devlin selected Bernadette to accompany him and Dandon to the shore. Being French, she provided the greatest smoke screen for the task.

Devlin's Brittany background would help him now, and Dandon seemed to be able to bluff his way through most conversations with a smattering of colloquialisms, thanks to years of slapped wrists from his Louisiana master.

On board were Sam Morwell, Dan Teague, Hugh Harris, the five broad Dutchmen eased from *Ter Meer* and Sam Fletcher, the guttersnipe whom Devlin singled out for a special duty.

Sam was able. Not bright, but keen, and Devlin closed his hand around his, pushing into Fletcher's palm the only lifeline Devlin could think of should all go awry.

'You understand, Sam?' He winked at the scrawny young wastrel, who looked into his hand at the small silver tube with the laughing devil engraved upon it. 'Not a moment's hesitation if it's all gone from me. And Peter Sam will need it. You understand that? It's the only way now, Sam.'

'Aye, Cap'n. Never fear.' And he knuckled his forehead, backing away respectfully. Devlin slapped the boy's shoulder and turned to his small band of brothers.

'Now to it, boys! Anchor stern and bow for she's a shoal bed on a lee shore. Remember, though, we may have to cut and run!' Devlin yelled.

'Give me a white flag upon the longboat, Dan.' He swept to the lady closest to him. 'Bernadette?' The rouged cheeks and blue-painted eyelids turned to face him. 'Your carriage awaits.' He whisked his hat to his thighs, bowing courteously.

Six hundred and thirty-five pounds. Peter Sam looked over his account. A fortune, bloodied and guilt-stained sure enough, but which fortune was not? Twenty guineas' worth of tin on him, the rest stowed away in his sea chest.

They had divvied up whilst at Providence, each man at least fifty guineas richer than he was the day before, Devlin twice as much again. Most of the crew spent as soon as they could. Drink and women. Drink to forget and women to remember. But Peter preferred the feel of money, the weight of it, the knowledge of it. When a man has money he can be more dangerous than one without; the fear of the absence of it can devour him.

He and Black Bill Vernon were the old standers. They had been Seth Toombs's brethren from Trepassey. And were they not setting the sails on a fine frigate to the course of an upstart Irishman? A bog-trotting lubber. But there was the jangle of the purse. And there was the promise of a shovelful of the jangle if he kept his course.

A short tap on the cabin door broke his dark thoughts. The ungodly form of Robert Hartley, the gunner captain, came wheeling in a moment later, lowering his head as if shamed by his own presence in the world.

'Pardon me, Mister Sam, sir.' His coarse voice slurring, despite the early hour of the day.

'Aye, Robert, what occurs?' Peter Sam stood, never wanting his to be the shortest stature in any room.

''Tis about the *Lucy*, sir. There's a guilt about her that I thinks you should know.'

'What about her?'

''Tis the powder, sir.'

Hartley explained hastily that none of it was his fault, but that the *Lucy* had a very poor quality of powder indeed. He had sifted and refined the stuff but it was mostly grain and dust.

'Good for grape and chain. Nought much else. I'd have been happiest if I could have transferred some of this Porto lot over to her, but I'm afraid the rum got the better of me.'

'Kind of you, Robert. Not much good for the captain now.'

'No, sir. She's got barrels of the stuff and enough shot for a two-hour standoff, but no reach, you see?'

'I don't think the captain has a fight in his plans, Robert.'

Peter Sam's voice was grim. 'Just make sure *I* have enough to blow that island out of the water, or I'll give you your last bottle.'

Robert tugged his hair, bowing, his side scraping the door frame as he dragged himself out. 'Aye, aye, sir.'

Peter Sam turned to the slanting windows hanging over the sea. The sun was up now, the sea just beginning to become clear as he looked out west, the *Shadow*'s bow screwing its way towards the island to the east.

'Something ails you, Peter?' Black Bill's husky voice swung the big man round.

'Bill!' Peter Sam clutched his bag of coin in his fist. 'Taken to surprising a man in his cabin now? A proper failure you nearly had upon me!'

Bill ducked into the room without a word and slowly lit his pipe from the solitary lamp on the table.

'Ain't your cabin, Peter,' he drawled through the pipe, his lips smacking against the meerschaum through his beard. 'Is it?'

'Aye. You knows what I mean.' He shuffled around the table, tossing the bag lightly. 'What can I do for you, Bill, before breakfast and all? Ain't lost your way to the head, I hope?'

'No. Just wondering what old Hartley wanted. And, as I said, what ails you, Peter Sam?'

'Nothing ails me, Bill Vernon. Why would it?'

Bill exhaled a curtain of smoke between him and Peter.

'I've known you for over three years now, Peter Sam. Lived a shaving of wood away from you in that time. I know when you're going to fart before you do. You're juggling your purse like you're looking for your first whore.' He drew in deeply, crackling the pipe like firewood. 'So I says again, what ails you, Peter?'

Peter looked hard at his old friend. He trusted Bill as much as he had trusted Seth, but the words came hard.

'I think we should turn south,' he said at last, and watched Bill close his eyes. 'This is nothing but a fool's path! We have the ship and the men! What do we owe that Irish pup?'

Bill nodded. 'Nothing. Don't owe him anything at all, that's the truth. Could leave him and the lads to it. They may work out fine on their own. Hugh Harris wouldn't blame us. Probably do the same himself if he had the chance.'

'Aye,' Sam sniffed, 'he would at that!'

''Course, we wouldn't have the ship if it hadn't been for the captain. Wouldn't have the map neither. Then we wouldn't have to leave them behind on the island at all. Then there's all that gold...I tell you what, Peter Sam? I'll go out and finish my tobacco and shorten sail. You come and tell me what you want me to set. Devlin left you in command, after all.'

He trod softly out, leaving the brooding Peter Sam passing the leather purse back and forth between his giant hands.

'Ah! It is good to touch the earth again.' Devlin had crouched upon the sands and run the white gentleness of it through his fingers, his informal French receiving no reaction from the crowd who had helped them drag the boat from the surf.

'What is your purpose here, monsieur?' Captain Bessette was a tall, bearded man, dark-haired, but bald where his hat would lie. His eyebrows were overgrown and brushed upwards as if to compensate, crowning fierce black eyes. He resembled a priest Devlin had once known back home who had turned out to be a child murderer. 'This is a private island belonging to His Majesty. There is nothing for you here.' The wide eyes of his men had not gone unnoticed by Bessette as

Bernadette curtsied to them all, and he was pressing his authority to the first new people he had seen for over five months since he left Calais.

'We require nothing, monsieur, save water. Surely you would not deny a fellow countryman the chance to fill his heads with water?'

'I can deny you everything, monsieur. I am Capitaine Bessette and I am governor here.'

Devlin moved forward, his arms open. He beckoned behind him to Dandon. 'This is Doctor Dandon. This mademoiselle is Bernadette Caron, and I am Capitaine Jean Coqsan.' He swept off his hat and placed it over his heart.

'You perceive, Capitaine, that we are unarmed. We are making our way to Saint-Domingue from Providence, hoping that the "Pearl of the Antilles" will be a safer place for my ladies to ply their trade, by which I profit only for their health and wellbeing. I only ask that my ladies may come ashore for some walking and air. Only I and Dandon will chaperone them; my crew will remain aboard. I ask you, Capitaine, I plead with you, what harm is there in two unarmed men and five beautiful ladies?'

At that moment Favre Callier and Dominic Duphot trundled from the path onto the beach, but Bessette turned and barked at them, ordering them back to their posts. They slunk away like curtailed dogs.

Eight, Devlin noted. Eight so far.

Bessette swivelled back to Devlin and Dandon. 'Why this course to Saint-Domingue?' He reached to his jaw with a damp cloth, pressing hard against a swollen cheek. 'The Bahamas are more customary.'

'And full of pirates, Capitaine. You may find that this route will be the custom from now on.'

'That's as may be, monsieur, but I am afraid I cannot allow whores upon an island annexed by... *Mon Dieu!*' Bessette cried out, wincing in agony. He howled like a cat in heat and doubled over in pain as the root of his tooth threatened to pierce his brain for the third time that morning.

His men remained still, their gazes crawling over the blushing Bernadette.

'*Merde!*' he cried, raising his head again, his eyes full of fury and pain.

Dandon lifted a finger in the air and almost danced forward. 'Ah, Capitaine, it may be most prudent of myself to make your governorship aware that I was once stationed at Mobile, where I availed myself to study Faulchard's methods and texts for service to the dental needs of a whole garrison.' Then added, to clarify to the weeping Bessette, 'Surgical dentist.'

Bessette gripped his jaw, his knuckles whitening as he took in the dirty golden-coated man before him.

'Perhaps I might be permitted a glance into your oral cavity, Capitaine? No fee.'

'You are skilled, monsieur?' Bessette wiped tears from his eyes.

'You see these?' Dandon wiped a black finger across his gold front teeth. 'All my own work. Never felt a thing. Didn't even need a mirror.'

Bessette felt the faintest shaft of hope glimmering in the dark world of pain that had been his life for the past three weeks. No brandy eased the nagging pulsing in his jaw, food gave nothing but torment, and the odour that seeped from his mouth turned his very soul. Could it be that this ridiculous yellow-garbed beacon offered release from his torture?

He straightened himself, some dignity returning to his face, mopping the drool from the side of his mouth with the sodden cloth. 'You may approach, monsieur.' And he beckoned Dandon to him.

Dandon stepped across the warm sand with trepidation, unsure of his feet upon the soft white powder. Ten paces later, winking as he passed Devlin's gaze, he stood by the chin of Capitaine Bessette.

'Would you be so kind as to lower yourself somewhat, Capitaine.'

Bessette dropped to his knees, his sword ploughing its way behind him through the sand, his eyes and mouth open and expectant, as if awaiting the miracle of transformation from his first communion.

Dandon's lips drew back as he caught the decaying stench that issued from the yellow and angry lump that occupied a wide portion of Bessette's inside right jaw. He caught Bessette's nervous eyes and smiled warmly.

'I've had worse.'

'You can help me?' Bessette rose, wiping his mouth.

'Immeasurably.' He grinned kindly.

Bessette smiled back, then raised himself to shout to Devlin, 'Capitaine, you may stay. Only yourself and this man, you understand.'

'I do, Capitaine.' Devlin walked slowly forward. 'But what of some water, I beseech you?'

'In good time. For now you will refresh yourselves as my guests. Come.'

'Ah.' Dandon raised an enquiring hand. 'I will need to return to the ship for my requisites and accoutrements.'

'Of course,' Bessette concurred willingly.

'And an assistant. One of the girls naturally.'

'Yes, yes. Go now.' Bessette's right cheek grew redder.

'And naturally if I bring one girl, it would be impossible to leave the others.'

'No,' Bessette was firm. 'Only one more.'

The head of his lieutenant, Abelard Xavier, identifiable by his lace collar and red sash, slyly leaned into his captain's shoulder. Whispers were exchanged. Sentiments quietly voiced. Devlin could only imagine that the verse Abelard suggested was of an appeal to the Gallic nature of them all.

'Very well.' Bessette was irritable, imagining the ten minutes of pain he would have to endure whilst he waited for Dandon's case to be rowed back to him, his dark walnut box with its little green baize alcoves of bottles and folded papers of powders, which now Bessette held in the same regard as the Ark of the Covenant. 'Bring all the women. But leave all the men aboard. Leave me some semblance of order to my king.'

'Of course, Capitaine.' Devlin bowed again. 'Your generosity will not go unrewarded.'

Dandon clapped his hands and began his clumsy-footed return to the boat.

'To my things! Capitaine Coqsan, if you please?'

'With your permission, Capitaine Bessette?' Devlin smiled.

'Yes, yes! Go now!' Then he added, 'Mademoiselle Bernadette may stay with us.'

'By your leave, Capitaine.' And he joined Dandon back in the surf. Then in confidence, in low English, he queried Dandon's actions. 'Have you done this before, Dandon?'

'I have done everything at least once, Captain,' he muttered into his chest as they dragged the boat from the shore. The sea sucked back the longboat to her realm and they leaped aboard.

Devlin spat the spray from his mouth as he picked up the

oars. 'Do you always play at life, Dandon?' he asked, his limbs taking the strain of the sea.

'You have to play at something, Captain.' Dandon smiled, forgetting to pick up his own share of wood.

On returning to the shore with their colourful companions, the party, after brief blushing introductions and curtsies, began the ungraceful trudge up the steep incline from the beach. The early afternoon sun beat mercilessly at the necks and backs of the men, the quintet of ladies protected by elegant flimsy parasols that they twirled as often as they giggled at the leers of the five soldiers.

Devlin and Dandon struggled with the mahogany and walnut case with the brass fittings, barely two foot square, which the soldiers had opened and inspected. They carried and dragged it up the path between them, grateful for the half-logs embedded in the shingle for purchase, but were still exhausted when they reached the crest, only to be told that there was now a downhill walk of another half-mile east.

Abelard Xavier, Bessette's lieutenant, was amused by the two sweating men. At first their appearance had caused apprehension amongst the men and the captain, but now they represented pleasure and relief from the dull days of gardening and watches. They were unarmed, not so much as a clasp knife between them, and had brought with them such lovely, warm, blushing women, perspiring like flowers in the dew.

Mindful of his duty, Abelard stopped at a gap in the path that tumbled down to the beach and gave a clear view of the brigantine in the bay. He ordered one of his men to remain to observe the ship. From this point they were halfway to the barracks, more than enough time for a warning should any party leave the ship.

Reluctantly the man took up the post, permitting his hand to brush briefly across the lavender taffeta dress of Annie as she passed.

Devlin and Dandon exchanged glances over the top of the chest between struggles for air, their eyes conveying as much as words.

A new wave of enthusiasm flowed over the pair when they came to a corner and looked down into a dusty clearing almost a hundred feet below. In the clearing sat a small square stockade, barely large enough for the two L-shaped barracks housed within its log walls.

In the right-hand corner, closest to them, a simple platform with a sailcloth shade rose above the perimeter, serving as a watchtower. A soldier sat beneath the shade, cross-legged, and looked up at their approach.

Nine, thought Devlin. Nine men. Nine shots. His eye fell upon the familiar sight between the barracks, behind a redoubt, of a single small gun, a field gun on iron-spoked wheels – perhaps a nine-pounder or less. One gun. They carried on along the path, moving downwards now, the burning sun almost fanned away by the uplifting fluttering of his heart.

Coxon sipped at his Bordeaux. He sat at his open stern windows, clad in only his shirt, breeches and stockings. That morning he had washed his hair, which had been rank with the smell of salt water and smoke from the small hearth in the galley. An amber carbolic soap that he had picked up in Chatham and was now worn to a sliver had provided the much-needed distraction from his concerns and the perfect companion to his morning ablutions.

His senses absorbed the morning beauty of the Caymans through the open windows. It had always been peaceful in the Caymans. Even the wildlife and sea creatures were otherworldly; he recalled letters he had written suggesting that naturalists should be as prominent as parsons on naval ships above fifth-rate.

The sound of his door swinging open pulled his head from the windows. He passed a taciturn look not at the hulking form of a marine announcing a visitor, but at the black-suited frame of Edward Talton of the Honourable East India Company standing uninvited in his doorway.

'Pardon my interruption, Captain.' Talton was vexed, his glasses steamed. 'But I would like to enquire whether you may have a more efficient pen I could borrow, rather than these apparent chickens' quills I have acquired that break so.'

Coxon ignored his question. 'Mister Talton, did you perceive a lighted lantern outside my cabin?'

'I did, sir, but—'

'And perhaps a stout fellow in clay piping and red?'

'Ah, but—'

'If you did perceive these things, then you should understand that' – his voice rose now to a bellow that caused the surface of his wine to tremble – 'you are to knock before entering my chambers, *sir!*'

'My apologies, Captain Coxon.' Talton almost cracked his spine resigning himself to a bow. 'I am unfamiliar with your naval customs.'

'I collect it has always been customary to knock before one enters private rooms.'

'Quite.' Talton conceded the point, as if they were agreeing on the rudeness of a third party.

Coxon rose to pull on his white waistcoat draped over the back of a chair, placing down his goblet of wine, his taste for it gone. 'Furthermore,' he lowered his voice as he focused on buttoning half of the seventeen plate buttons, noting with pleasure that some weight had returned to him, 'I expect that whilst you are on board you are to obey me and my officers absolutely. As one day, sir, it may save your life.'

He saw Talton's fishlike mouth droop open, about to protest, but lifted an indignant finger, anticipating his voice. 'Despite the fact that this ship sails by grant of the investment of the company. Do you understand, Mister Talton?'

Talton agreed, anxiously removing his spectacles and cleaning them furiously, sending dazzling reflections of sunlight dancing around the small cabin.

'Please do not blame your man by the door, Captain. My intrusion was too swift for him to question.' He carefully entwined the thin golden arms of his spectacles behind his ears. 'Now, would it be possible to avail myself of a writing instrument?' He held up between his thumb and forefinger the fletchless, ink-stained quill that was the cause of his distress.

Coxon approached and inspected the pen. 'Crow, I perceive.' He took it from Talton and flexed it in his hand. 'Not hardened enough, I'll wager.'

'It is the third of such a type that I have had ruin on me.' Talton sighed.

'I imagine it is part of my duty to ensure that the company's secretary and observer be furnished with appropriate tools...' Coxon's voice trailed off, diplomatic and polite again, noting the pride that he saw rising in Talton's thin mouth.

Coxon moved over to his writing desk with its pewter wells and green leather surface. From a narrow drawer he picked out a quill, the fletch removed save for a few feathers at the very end for dusting the paper. With some ceremony he presented the expensive pen that had once belonged to the left wing of a Suffolk spring swan.

Talton, visibly pleased, gratefully acknowledged the loan. He declined the volunteering of ink, bowed and reversed out of the cabin. Coxon had no objection to the loss of the quill, the whole desk and its contents being originally Guinneys' official bureau, and he smiled accordingly.

Moving to pick up his wine again, he casually passed his eye across the chart laid out upon the table. A solid black line reaching from the Caymans plotted them to the island in less than five hours' time. Luncheon. Designating boarding parties, gunner captains, checking shot garlands – and then head to *him* with all malice.

Coxon knew Devlin was already there. A few short weeks ago the whole scenario seemed merely the fancy of Whitehall, but there had been times when pacing on the quarterdeck alone, the feeling of a heaviness in the air seemed to drift off the still waters. A tight feeling across the chest born of expectation. The same feeling he felt moments before the cry 'Sail ho!' brought a line of French frigates across the horizon.

How strangely his fate had shifted. By now he had imagined himself closeted in a few rented rooms in Portsmouth on half-pay, brought down to master and commander or, worse, paid off altogether; unable to recover from the loss of the *Noble*, ending up as an old sot bestowing wisdom on young officers in exchange for noggins of rum.

Now he was watching the sea rise and fall from the stern windows as the *Starling* ploughed along at five knots running off the wind. Post-captain still. Honour would be restored; position retained. Life in the bell jar he loved.

Luncheon. A side of dried beef, soaked in salt water for two days until it became almost palatable, sauerkraut, carrots and shelled peas. All wasted on Guinneys, who nibbled at shavings of beef upon ship's biscuit, but drained enough wine for three courses seemingly without effect.

Coxon asked his first lieutenant to dine with him as this would probably be the last meal they ate this day, now they were but three hours from the island.

Coxon maintained his old habit of cutting off a slice of beef to keep in his coat pocket along with his own compass, a precaution against the unknown of tomorrow, and he shared this with Guinneys.

'Amusing so,' Guinneys said. 'I have often seen common seamen hiding tack upon themselves before a fleet action. You reveal your background too much, Captain!' He smiled kindly.

'Why do you dislike me so, William?' Coxon stared straight at him, masticating violently against the almost wooden beef. The question was meant to shock, a shot across Guinneys' bows to aggravate and draw out an honest response. He had expected Guinneys to reply with a denial, a simpering, snorting retort. Instead Guinneys placed down his glass with a chime of crystal.

'I suppose it may be because you are not a gentleman, Captain,' he said.

'Explain?' Coxon spoke through his beef, strangely satisfied by the answer.

'Well, you have the rolling gait of a sailor, not the strut of an officer born. You do not hunt, which I'm afraid I do not understand at all. But mostly it is because you are a post-captain. And since you are not a gentleman, that means you must have done some great deed of war whilst I must now rot in peacetime whoring myself to these damned company men waiting for you, or someone like you, to die off.'

His glass fairly flew to his mouth; he closed his eyes as he drained it, putting it down with a grimace. 'Damn! St James, my arse! Where do they dredge this stuff from?'

'Thank you, William. I hope you do not get your wish.'

'What wish is that, sir?' Guinneys wiped his mouth, genuinely enquiring with wide eyes, as if he had missed something.

For the second time that day, Coxon's door swept open unannounced and, without apology or doffing of hat, the sixteen-year-old midshipman Thomas Howard scuffed into the room skidding like a dog on a marble floor.

'Surgeon sent me, sir!' he squealed and, not waiting for reproach from the two angry faces, bravely dropped his tone to declare, 'It's Mister Talton, Captain. He's dead, sir!'

Coxon had spent almost a fortnight in the rear quarters of the lower deck on the way from Cape Coast Castle with Edward Talton. They shared a common narrow corridor, divided by wooden and hemp walls. Doors almost as thin as gaming cards separated him from Talton and Midshipman Howard. Coxon welcomed the closeness of the windowless cubbyholes, the flimsy folds. Here was solitude.

Talton had now found his own solitude.

Surgeon Richard Wood sat on the narrow cot that doubled as a locker, mopping his brow fervently. The heat was stifling, the air like sawdust. Coxon filled the door frame, Guinneys' head strained a view over his shoulder. Midshipman Howard fidgeted behind them, both wanting to see and afraid to do so again.

Talton sat in his shirt at the fold-down desk that clipped out of the wall, his cuffs tucked under, pen still in his right hand, his head hanging to his chest.

The tortoiseshell lamp was swinging with the sea, giving

his shadow an eerie animation in the gloom, back and forth across the paper.

'Who found him?' Coxon asked in a whisper.

'Midshipman Howard. Not ten minutes ago, Captain.'

Surgeon Wood sighed the words in his lowland, melancholy Scots. He was the archetypal image of a navy surgeon too old to be at sea, too old to be successful on land. With a shiny bald pate above a distinguished set of gold pince-nez, he dressed like a farmer going to church and cut men like a tailor getting paid by the yard.

Coxon had turned round to look at Howard, and spoke softly to him. The boy was visibly shaken. His hat was slanted, his freckled face red and swollen.

'How did you come to find him, Thomas?'

Thomas Howard gathered himself instantly at his captain's voice. He explained that he had been late on watch, that Lieutenant Anderson had punished him by having him pick oakum all morning. His hands and wrists cramped like hell and, begging your pardon, sir, he had gone to his cabin to pity himself somewhat.

Talton's door had been ajar but the noise of the pen that filled his days was absent and Howard had cadged a peek, to his horror. No more keyholes for Thomas Howard after that lesson, Captain. No, sir.

Lieutenant Scott stumbled into the corridor; news had swabbed the deck faster than forty hands. Coxon shifted back to the door and almost stepped through Guinneys, who stayed silent and watchful.

'What killed him, Mister Wood?' Coxon asked.

'He wasn't killed, Captain. He just died.' Wood rose with tired difficulty.

'Of what, would you say?'

'I don't know.' He sighed mournfully, removing his half-framed spectacles and pinching his bridge. 'A failure of some kind. He's not marked. No injury. He just died.'

Guinneys shook his head. 'To think I heard him scribbling away not more than an hour ago. Before lunch. I was taking of some water from the scuttle-butt for that poxed vegetation in my hole that I'm damned if I can get to do anything but wilt.' He tutted at his lack of horticultural ability. 'It must be the lack of light. Perhaps I should cloister it next to the coop. Out of the way.'

Coxon looked around the room absently. Guinneys' prattling was barely audible, or worth attention. He had not liked Talton. No one had. And damn him now. Hours away from retribution and a company man dies in his lap.

'No burial until tomorrow, Doctor. Too much to do today.'

'Aye, Captain.'

Surveying the cramped room, he looked over Talton's shoulder. A pile of letters by his left hand. His large effeminate hand plainly readable. A letter to a Mrs Williams.

Was Bath still as nice as he remembered? Were her daughters married yet? And were there any new dogs that he did not know about? And on and on, and then Coxon froze.

His eyes had travelled from the papers on the left to the hand that wrote them on the right, lying pale upon a fresh blank page. The blood ran cold to his feet. Without hesitation he swung round to the scant hook that held Talton's short black velvet coat.

'Best rule out if Mister Howard's hands are as wandering as his eyes.' His arm had reached the coat before he had finished speaking. 'Purse present. Tobacco present...' He tentatively picked his way through the pockets. 'No offence, Mister Howard. Back to your watch.'

'Thank you, Captain.' Howard gratefully walked out of the corridor, shuffling past Scott and Guinneys; then the sound of his feet went rattling up the companion ladder as fast as hail.

Coxon smiled at Guinneys and Scott. 'We were all sixteen once, eh, lads? Doctor, would you like to attend to some men to remove this body, if you please?'

'Aye, Captain.' The two men stepped into the corridor.

'William' – Coxon laid his palm on Guinneys' shoulder – 'would you secure this room once Mister Talton has been sequestered below?'

'Of course, Captain.' Guinneys tapped his head.

'I will be in my cabin, sorrowfully recording this event. Gentlemen, if you please.' Coxon was already climbing to the upper deck before he had finished speaking. He was greeted with the traditional flurry of activity whenever the captain's head appeared, but instead of continuing to his coach he stayed by the companion hatch and looked about him.

He had felt the instinctive swell of the water, the keel rising a little more than previously, and he tramped up to the quarterdeck, nodding to the timoneer at the helm, saluting the midshipmen and Sailing Master Dawson before expectantly looking up to the topmast with a shielded hand at the man aloft. No cry came, and he hoped the distraction would ease the thought that was rising uncomfortably in his mind. He leaned over the rail and looked fore to the bow, carving through the waves like a carpenter's plane, curling out spirals of sea along the strakes like wood shavings. He stared until his eyes could no longer take the peppering of salt-spray spitting up from below and the thought could no longer be ignored.

He moved amidships, ignoring the salutes that greeted almost every step, the bodies making themselves both busy and invisible before him. He clasped his hands behind him to hide the tremble that rattled through them.

'*The door had been ajar.*' Thomas Howard's words had flown past him at first, only returning when he spied the broken crow quill that Talton had shown him not an hour earlier perched in his dead right hand.

The exclusive swan pen was still nestling in Talton's coat. Coxon had felt the tip of the fletch and glimpsed a flash of white. *Yet Guinneys had heard him writing.*

He tried to imagine the act of Talton removing his coat and ignoring the elegant pen his captain had bestowed upon him and then sitting at his writing place and picking up a broken nib and musing on the variety of ink blots he was about to create. *Yet Guinneys had heard him writing.*

The *Starling* hit a rogue wave. His thoughts were broken by the sudden rise of the deck, the clutching of lifelines by bare-footed men, the sway of the horizon as the *Starling* regained her hold upon the water like a horse on turf after the gate.

All ears filled with the cries of the bosun hailing out to the watch to regain their point of wind as the leeway shifted through everyone's feet; then came a cry from the topsail reverberating through the caller's speaking trumpet, the cry Coxon knew was imminent when he'd felt the keel rise beneath him as tides met.

'Land ho! Two points to larboard bow!'

Coxon sprinted back to the quarterdeck. Drawing the telescope from its becket at the binnacle, he trained it in the direction of the arm of the man aloft, instantly lowering it with a curse to wipe the condensation from the front before slapping it to his eye again.

There she was. A grey growth swelling out of the sea, a white trim marking her on the horizon. Fifteen miles. Slow now to four knots. Less than three hours, for sure. He had long given up celebrating the accuracy of his sail, but afforded the men their cheers.

He passed on the order to shorten sail to Mister Anderson and stepped down to the deck, his eye falling on the closed conversation between Guinneys and Scott by the foremast stays.

No time now. No time at all. Too much to do. Have to ignore that bristling on the back of the neck; all hands would be needed. Keep Guinneys close. Wear him like a coat. Keep him, at hand and dependable. There would be time enough after the island was secured. Time enough to question why he had murdered Edward Talton.

Chapter Twelve

✖

*T*he plan *had* been bolder. Devlin, Dandon and the women would disembark and bring themselves into favour with the island's inhabitants. A few hours later the *Shadow* would arrive, raining furious anger down on the poor *Lucy*. The frigate could not come in due to the shallows, but she could lay warmly to the *Lucy* with hot iron from almost a mile away.

After which, with much pleading and exemplification of the hearts of his small crew, Devlin's men would be allowed to row ashore to escape the black flag bearing down on them. The same ploy that had worked against *Ter Meer* would work again. Without a blow, without a shot, Devlin's band of cut-throats would be almost welcomed into overthrowing the marines.

Now, Devlin followed Dandon's lead. A man come amongst them less than a week before. A man who gave up nothing, whose only path was upwards from the gutter. A man like them all. It did not seem particularly surprising to trust a man who had nothing to lose. From a finer place, one day, it might seem unwise, but for now these were the only men whom Devlin did trust.

They had walked through the stockade, each with a handle between them, swinging the chest now. Devlin cast an eye to the wooden tower in the corner where a musketeer sat, otiose and sullen, although he brightened when the parasols were tipped and the painted faces smiled up at him.

Two L-shaped barracks. Open-shuttered windows facing the gate. A frontal assault on the stockade would be met with muskets jutting from those facing windows, echoed by the nine-pounder with its deadly eye trained on the gate; the same gate that now closed wearily behind them, bringing up a cloud of dust from the dry earth.

Men now followed the women like sheep. They did not need to speak. They smiled as if from a painting and they strolled as if in a park.

Only Bessette remained aloof to the women, his hand pressed permanently against his jaw, looking for all the world like a housemaid striving to remember a list of chores.

Xavier borrowed his captain's ear again as they reached the well-trodden dust between the barracks. Bernadette and Annie stayed close to Devlin and Dandon; the others, with the soft pad of silken shoes and giggles into their chests, were cajoled into the soldiers' mess, the longest part of the left-hand wooden building.

With no words, Devlin, Dandon and the two women were led by Bessette and Xavier to the lower half of the same building, turning a corner past the gun, and passing through Bessette's private door.

Inside was a comfortable drawing room, far removed from the crude exterior. A good-sized dining table dominated the room, a green velvet brocade tablecloth draped across it running to the floor, its drop obscuring even the legs.

To the right of the door as they entered, along the wooden wall hidden by tapestries and unpainted plaster, were the matching green high-backed fauteuils, eight in all. The far wall displayed a superb bow-fronted tiger-maple commode, sporting lozenge-framed portraits of the goddess Diana on its front. A Bible box sat on top of the commode. Devlin eliminated both as the place to secure a hundred thousand louis of gold. A small carriage clock upon the commode brought the room alive with its pleasing movement.

'If you will excuse me, gentlemen.' Xavier bowed, his right hand resting on his holstered pistol. 'I shall wait in the corridor.' He bowed again, this time directly to Bernadette. 'If Mademoiselle would care to accompany me for some refreshment?'

Bernadette shifted an eye to Devlin. He nodded compliantly and she hooked her arm into Xavier's. They crossed the room unnoticed by Bessette, who had already pulled one of the chairs to the table, and they left through a simple adjoining door, giving Devlin the glimpse of a passage he presumed led to the mess.

'Monsieur?' Bessette mumbled to Dandon, who stood absorbed by the weft of the hunting scenes galloping through the tapestries. 'My pain?'

'Of course, Capitaine.' Together the pirates swung the chest onto the velvet tablecloth.

Devlin removed his tricorne and drew linen across his brow. 'My thirst devours me, sir. May I implore you for a drink to ease it?'

'Forgive me. My error, Capitaine Coqsan.' He threw a thumb behind him to a closed door. 'My quarters. You may bring us all some wine.' He winced as he tried to smile.

'Perhaps not for you, Capitaine,' Dandon said, opening the chest like a hallowed tome, revealing handwritten vellum labels on stained bottles; thin, bone-handled drawers beneath them waning beeswax into the room. 'I have some treatment for you that will not mix.'

Devlin circled the room in a heartbeat. A washstand and basin. A cot, with a pair of demi-lune tables either side. A cabinet, by all appearances stripped from the galley of a ship, held a cheap decanter and a set of tall glasses. A narrow, paned window brought the Caribbean sun into the room and looked out on the north wall of the stockade.

There had been no windows in the anteroom, and for a moment Devlin had forgotten the day was only past noon.

With the instinct of an imbiber, he opened the tallest front of the cabinet and discovered two shelves of wax-sealed wine. Using the excuse of riffling the cutlery box for a corkscrew, he tooled himself with a small meat knife, which he tucked under his waistcoat behind his back.

Where was the gold? Eight marines. One gentleman. Perhaps one more sentry on the eastern cliff. Ten men. And just himself and Dandon waiting for the *Shadow* to arrive. Two buildings. Unlikely to be in the mess or the barracks. Perhaps underground? Outside in the jungle? No, definitely within the stockade, that was the whole point.

Breathe deep. Take a drink. There will be violence soon.

Returning to the dining room, Devlin found Dandon, with his coat and hat removed, engrossed in the contents of a small stone mortar. Annie stood behind Bessette, her soft hands placed gently to his temples.

'Now, Capitaine, if you have forgotten what your mother's milk was like, prepare for solace.' Dandon took a small piece of raw cotton wadding and, having drawn some of his strange liquid to it, gestured to Bessette's mouth. 'Open wide now.'

'What is it, Doctor?' Bessette was not suspicious, except of the prospect of more pain.

'Relief. Manna. Vinum Opii.' Dandon looked angelic. Bessette opened his mouth. There was a blinding blaze of pain, the aroma of wine, cinnamon and cloves, and then, a sweet second later, nothing. No pain. No feeling in the right side of his jaw at all. He almost wept. Then he did weep.

'Oh, monsieur! Monsieur!'

'Lo! It is a gift, Capitaine.' Dandon placed the mortar down and slid open one of the drawers. Inside, the cutaways held a line of evil-looking implements. Dandon selected the least offensive, a thin steel probe, curved and rounded. 'Allow me, Capitaine.'

Obediently Bessette dropped open his mouth and Dandon peered inside. Devlin cut and opened the wine, pouring a generous glass for himself and Dandon. The wine was encouraging. He drained his glass and poured another, standing behind Dandon, exchanging nervous glances with Annie.

Moments passed uncomfortably for all. Dandon, his examination complete, leaned back, his lips drawn. 'I will need to administer a little surgery, Capitaine. I must have that poison removed from your jaw.'

'It will hurt, monsieur?' Bessette asked.

'No. You will only feel pressure, that is all, Capitaine.' Dandon went back to his chest and popped the cork on a small frosted-glass bottle. Reversing the contents onto some more wadding, he placed it promptly onto Bessette's tongue.

'Hold that there, Capitaine. And think of France.'

Bessette looked confused then ecstatic as the ethereal spirits began to engulf him and his eyes fell shut. His head lolled back. Annie squealed, her hands clutched to her lips.

Dandon nipped out the ball of wadding with a swift pinch of his finger and tossed it to the floor.

Devlin grabbed Dandon's arm. 'What have you done?' Horror crept over him. The thought of death was ever present in his mind, the violence, the blood; but now was too soon.

Dandon shrugged off his captain's grasp and reached for

the glass of wine. 'Oil of vitriol, Patrick,' Dandon sighed. 'He will sleep for at least an hour. Do not fear, Captain. All is well.' He drank with the gusto of relief.

Devlin looked at the clock on the commode. An hour and a half had passed since they had returned to the island with the chest. The *Shadow* would arrive soon, and still no gold. Now the one man who would most certainly be aware of its place sat drooling and comatose before him.

'Damn you, Dandon! What of the gold? He would know where it lies! Now what, man?' As he spoke he moved to Bessette's sleeping form and retrieved Bessette's pistol and sword, weighing the sword deftly in his hand before stuffing them both into the sash round his waist.

'Captain, I am surprised by you. I had marked you as a calm soul. The lieutenant outside in the corridor is more pressing.'

Without invitation he stepped to Annie and whipped up her petticoat to her waist, revealing the white silk stockings that crept up her legs and the lightly frilled creamy undergarments that had cost her two weeks of lying on her back.

His interest, however, lay in the overcoat pistol she had strapped to her milky thigh.

'*Pardon*, mademoiselle.' Removing the black ribbon that held it there, he checked the lock and primer and placed it in his belt.

'We must secure him first, do you not agree?'

'I disagree!' Devlin snapped. 'The *Shadow* will be here soon causing uproar on the beach. Men will rush in here to tell the captain, and he lies passed out before us! And us armed and alone!'

'Exactly, Patrick. We must gain more control. Is there more wine?'

'Can you not finish one draught before you begin on another!'

'Patrick' – Dandon lowered his head – 'I do not *want* the wine. If there are more bottles, bring them to me. And if you are worried about the gold, then please worry no longer. Have you never hidden anything, man?' And with that he reached for the tasselled hem of the tablecloth and flourished it up to reveal the long black chest that rested beneath it, secured with heavy iron locks and straps.

'There is your gold, sir! And if you do not bring me more wine, you shall never have a day's luck with it! You may lay to that!'

Devlin crouched, tilting his head and taking in the full sight of the long black chest sleeping innocently beneath the table. His face rose in a sparkle-eyed grin. Then his mind began to click back into action.

As if to defend the chest and mark it as his own, he withdrew the knife from behind his back and slammed its point into the underside of the table, leaving it hanging there. Just in case.

He stood; taller now, it seemed to Dandon. The pair of them, in shirt and waistcoat, shook hands and emptied their glasses. Then Devlin poured one for the trembling Annie, who gulped gratefully, swearing through her swallows.

'I'll get the wine.' He nodded to Dandon. 'We'll need ammo and powder. Bessette must have some in his room.'

'No,' Dandon said, removing a brown bottle from his chest. 'I'll get the wine.' He poured some brown fluid into his glass, then filled it with wine.

'You take this to Lieutenant Xavier,' he said, adding unnecessarily, 'Do not drink it, Captain.'

*

Devlin opened the corridor door as quietly as he could manage. A small crack, just enough to see the length of the corridor stretching away to his right. The passage, like the anteroom, was roughly plastered over its wooden walls. A barrel stood halfway down the opposite wall, a ship's lamp glowing upon it.

Devlin pushed upon the door some more, at the same time aware of a giggling along the passage. He saw half of Abelard Xavier seated on a bench along the wall to his right, some white flesh entwined around his blue worsted jacket.

At the far end of the passage, a relief of the Madonna signalled the end of the corridor. The Mother of God leaned her head to the right, indicating to Devlin the second door that led to the mess, where the sound of a flute and a rolling fiddle belonged to another world.

It was eight steps to Xavier. Devlin could run at him, crown him with the butt of Bessette's pistol. Two blows and the brass cap would be bloody and caked in hair. Eight steps. Two blows.

He stepped into the passage, leaving the pistol in his sash, and carried the glass towards Xavier. Two steps in and he noticed the lieutenant's brown leather crossbelt and hanger leaning against the wall.

At a distance he deemed polite enough, Devlin cleared his throat.

'Lieutenant Xavier?' He smiled warmly. 'Capitaine Bessette is happier now and I bring you a small cordial at his request.'

Devlin stepped closer as Abelard Xavier turned his head away from Bernadette's bosom and glared at him.

Xavier was not for fooling. Devlin watched Xavier's eyes fall to the pistol and sword stuck in his sash. Recognising them or not, he sprang up and drew his right arm across to his pistol.

No moment for a bluff. The game had changed. Devlin flashed to his sword as he slung the glass at Xavier's head, sending a scrawl of liquid across the walls.

Bernadette held her palm to her mouth, stifling a scream as Devlin finished drawing the blade, ending the motion with an upswing across the bones of Xavier's right hand.

Xavier's fist sprang open, dropping the pistol as the glass crashed into the Madonna over his shoulder.

Nature made him stare at the back of his hand, glistening with blood; then Devlin grabbed his left shoulder and sent a cold fist through his centre, pulling him towards him like a brother.

Xavier opened his mouth in a gasp, the sound gurgling out of his back along the length of the blade, for his mouth had filled with blood.

Gently, Devlin eased him down the wall and Xavier gave a grateful sigh as the sword was dragged slowly free.

Devlin glanced at the blade as he returned it to his sash. It dripped a watery substance like raw egg white, small freckles of blood across its steel.

Abelard Xavier was the first man he had ever killed with a sword. He paid it no more mind and turned to Bernadette. She had picked up the pistol and now handed it to Devlin. He looked at it in the amber glow of the passage.

A French *pistolet de cavalerie.* Its plain iron barrel marked and dented. Weightless, weak wood. The lock loose and rusted, the trigger missing. The only indication of craftsman-ship was the engraved '*Anno* 1680' on the lock plate. He let it fall back to its owner's body. Dead together.

The pressure of blood eased from Devlin's ears, the sound of his heart dissipated, and he could hear again the high-pitched fiddle and flute song. Good. Peace reigned again.

Bernadette was now chasing through Xavier's garments, swearing at every empty pocket she encountered. Devlin swept to the far door. It was bolted from his side. Excellent. He pulled up the protesting Bernadette and half dragged her back to the anteroom.

Dandon had six opened bottles of red wine standing like soldiers along the table. To each one he was carefully administering the contents of a steel syringe. He looked up as Devlin came through the door.

'I heard a tinkle of glass, Captain. Not unlike a serving bell. All is well, I trust, with Lieutenant Xavier?'

'He wasn't thirsty.' Devlin's face was a white mask. 'What goes on here, Dandon?' He softly clicked the door shut behind him. Bernadette ran to Annie's side, tugging her garments across her modesty.

'Laudanum,' Dandon stated. 'Vinum Opii. I can take down all three men in the mess faster than you can kill them, my capitaine.' Although both men now spoke in English, Dandon was relishing his French accent. 'I have found a flask of powder and a box of ball. You may have the pleasure of carrying them.'

Devlin moved to the table, picked up the hard leather flask with the brass spout and the suede box, placing both in his waistcoat's deep pockets beneath his sash.

Dandon took his penknife and fully removed the wax from the top of one bottle. 'Ladies' – he turned to Bernadette and Annie – 'pay close if not absolute attention. The wine without the red wax is for your consumption. The others are for the guards in the mess. Compliments of their captain in celebration of his new-found health.'

Bessette snored in agreement.

'I'm hungry,' Annie declared.

'You can eat the five doubloons in your purse if you're hungry, my girl, but for now you will sway your hips into that mess with this wine and join your colleagues.'

'Bloody pirates,' Annie murmured, picking up three bottles with ease between her fingers, leaving Bernadette to smile sweetly and pick up the other three, her dress hanging off her left shoulder to reveal the curve of her breast.

Dandon led them to the passage. 'They must all drink swiftly. Pour it down their throats if you have to.' The women passed through into the corridor, their mouths exhibiting a definite downward turn.

Devlin and Dandon followed, simultaneously checking the action on their pistols. 'I have never shot a man, Captain.' Dandon smiled meekly, his eyes lingering on Xavier's body as they stepped past.

'It will not come to that. In a few hours we will be dining on the *Shadow*, laughing about this day.'

They settled against the wall, sharing a breath for a moment. Devlin waved to the women to open the door to the mess.

'Aye,' Dandon whispered, 'or we'll be dining in hell. Either way, we're sure to be eating.'

Annie pulled back the bolt with just the crook of her little finger and shouldered the door. The corridor filled with the sweet song of the flute and fiddle, jeers and the scraping of chairs. There was a roar of approval as the new pair danced into the room, and Annie kicked the door shut behind her, leaving Devlin and Dandon with nothing but a faint waft of sweat and perfume.

They stood silent, listening like elderly chaperones outside a drawing room for any new sound. The jolly music continued. No raised voices. No mistrust. Devlin was almost envious as he shifted to the door and gently locked the bolt again. Three men would live a while longer; Devlin and Dandon's pistols would remain cold.

'And what of him?' Dandon indicated Abelard Xavier.

'We'll lock Bessette's door behind us. He is well hidden in a locked corridor.' Together they hurried back to the anteroom, bolting the adjoining door behind them.

Sanctuary. Devlin could no longer think more than five minutes ahead. He absorbed the peace of the room. Here everything was fine. Here was control. Bessette was dozing. Nobody knew more than them. Everybody knew less. If he could just hold on to this room, hold on to the chest, all would be well.

Devlin moved to the outer door, opening it just enough to view the unmanned cannon, and sidled out, edging his way to the first corner. Daring to inch his head out, he saw the mess door pulled half open, obscuring his view of the gate at the far end. He could spy the watchtower in the far left corner, the marine still sitting there, his back to the rest of the stockade. The only sense of life was the small eddy of smoke that occasionally billowed out from the drawing of his pipe.

If the drink flowed and the laudanum mellowed, the three soldiers would be asleep in minutes. But what then? The *Shadow* should be approaching by now. Her grey sails spotted by either the guard staring straight down to the *Lucy*, or by the watch on the west coast. The thought of a hundred comrades within shooting distance gave Devlin some comfort.

As if in answer, he suddenly saw the gate swing slowly open. He fought the instinct to withdraw his head as he watched two men come through and hail the watchtower.

One of them he recognised as the man stationed to watch the *Lucy* from the path. The other carried a leather satchel over his shoulder; Devlin vaguely recalled him as one of the men barked away from the beach by Bessette.

His cautious eye watched the pantomime of the two gesticulating to the guard in the tower, who rose awkwardly to his feet. Then, and for the first time, Devlin saw the hanging ship's bell under the canopy of the watchtower.

His mind magnified the size of the bell tenfold. He watched the hand reaching for the rope and he clutched at the pistol in his sash, waiting for the terrible moment. Then, out of the door of the mess, just yards in front of him, staggered one of the marines, grasping the lintel to stop himself from falling. The marine timed his incoherent bellow exactly as the first peal of the bell rang out across the air.

A second peal, and the drugged marine fell against the door, slamming it fully open against the mess wall as he succumbed to the comfort of the dirt.

Three pairs of eyes turned to the sound of the crashing door.

They took in the sight of their fellow prone in the dust, then followed through to the man in shirt and waistcoat standing between the two buildings. A pistol already in his left hand. Their captain's distinguished sword in his right.

Devlin could not recall stepping out into view. He could not recall pulling his weapons. He only remembered the echo of the second peal and the sight of the marine from the path slinging the musket from his back.

Devlin ran to the slumbering soldier and briefly glanced into the mess at another world of colour and laughter, oblivious to the bell. He crouched in the door frame and checked his pistol, then glanced up at the three marines bolting at him from the gate.

Devlin raked his eyes over the man at his feet, then kicked

him over, cursing at the lack of a second pistol that would have given him half a chance. The sound of a chair falling to the floor behind him jerked him up, just as a ball sang past, splintering the frame where he had crouched.

Devlin backed away from the men charging towards him, their cutlasses drawn. He edged back to Bessette's quarters, part of him wanting to draw the guards away from the vulnerable ladies in the mess, and part of him wanting to get back to the room where he had control, where he could savour the gold at least once before he died.

At twenty yards, his shot would be worth something. One shot and only one more second to choose a target, then it would be a matter of hacking and hacking with the fine sword until he lived or died.

Oh, for Peter Sam or Dan Teague. They would be laughing as they killed as easily as wiping mud from their shoes. Faces now, fearful and savage, filling the space between the barracks and the mess. One shot. The oldest one. That would be fair. Now.

'*Down*, Captain, if you please!'

Devlin flashed an eye behind, then flung himself to the ground. The marines stared at the man holding a smoking linstock in his hand. He was standing beside the nine-pounder, which now roared and spat a venomous spray of grape.

Their tunics flew apart as if torn by a hundred fish-hooks. They danced up into the air, pirouetting round in a grotesque ballet that left them on their backs, writhing and stunned.

Smoke trailed over Devlin's head as he raised it to peer over his forearm. The silence that followed the cannon blast was gratifying. The sight of the corpses more so.

Standing, again waiting for his heart and his head to run together, he turned to face Dandon, whose normal placid composure was slightly affected by the unfamiliar blast of the cannon. The gun now stood twice its length behind him, smoking passively. Dandon staggered from the redoubt and raised a smile to his captain.

'My apologies, Patrick.' He joined Devlin, who stood brushing the dirt from his clothes. 'I came as soon as I heard the bell, but that blast will surely bring the remainder upon us.'

'I fear there may be only two to concern us.' He did not smile, but raised his pistol again and stepped towards the mess.

Coming over the threshold, he gathered the recent history of the room. Cutlasses lay across the tables. A couple of chairs had their backs to the floor. Two marines lay sprawled amongst a debris of bottles, clay mugs and scraps of food. Dandon's drugged wine had worked well.

The women had run to the rear wall at the sound of the cannon, silhouetted now against the window. At the sight of Devlin, they once again became the animated, swearing vixens they had been since they were fourteen, and set about jostling each other for the scavenger rights to the sleeping marines.

'These men will have to be restrained, Captain,' Dandon's voice came wafting over Devlin's shoulder. 'They are good for an hour perhaps.'

'No mind. That bell the others rang will be on sighting the *Shadow*.' He smiled. 'Our day has come. Let us lay eyes on our gold.'

Chapter Thirteen

✗

*T*he cry of 'Sail ho!' had come an hour ago. Coxon stood with Guinneys at the *Starling*'s fo'c'sle, surveying the black and white brigantine through their respective telescopes.

There were four scopes aboard the *Starling*. Guinneys had his own fine brass, a London-made three-draw with a luscious shargreen finish. Coxon had grabbed the smoky glassed ship's tube from the helm becket. The other vellum tubes were in the lubber hole with the lookout at the topsail, and at the taffrail with Mister William Dawson, the *Starling*'s able sailing master. Only Coxon and Guinneys spied on the *Lucy*. The others had instruction to study the horizon for the fateful showing of the pirate frigate.

'She would appear,' Guinneys reported through clenched lips, 'to be decorated in her rigging with all manner of bunting cloth, Captain.' He lowered his glass. 'Trifle late for May Day, is it not?'

'A deception of some kind,' Coxon wondered aloud. 'See how she flies a French flag as well? That's our man.'

'Well, *your* man certainly, Captain.' Guinneys fashioned a smirk across his tanned features.

Coxon actually smiled at the witticism and let it ride.

'Maintain a three-thousand-yard vantage, Mister Guinneys, half a league.' He pitched his voice for all the hands straining their necks to the brigantine, and swept his scope across her bows. 'Easy sail. Top gallants only. Any reach you fancy.'

He removed the scope from his eye, and let the bright emerald island behind the brigantine map his perspective, her crescent beach welcoming, virgin and white, barely a mile away.

'Three thousand yards, sir?' Guinneys made a small protest by snapping down his waistcoat sharply with a fervent tug. 'Respectfully, Captain, those are no more than nine-pounders on that slut. We have over two hundred pounds to bear against her forty-eight. I could make toothpicks out of her in three rounds.'

'And a fine use you'll have for those toothpicks whilst you rest our keel upon these sands. Have a mind, man! Can you not see the sand? Nor the scrawny wretch hanging out of the shrouds watching us? The ship is empty. A few souls peeping over the gunwale at us. Anchored bow and stern. Out here she is no match for us and they know it well enough. If we venture in' – he gestured to the island – 'we never get out. We draw too much water, William.'

Guinneys looked back to the ship and sniffed in some personal agitation. 'Aye. There may be something in that. Not about power, eh? Position and all that.'

'Blood soon enough, William. I would lay to that. 'Tis the frigate we must worry about. Half a league and we are out of range. And those are four six-pounders she has on us, not niners, so worry not about them, just about yourself. I'm sure you can manage that, Lieutenant.'

He turned to the deck, not waiting for a cynical reply, his eye seeking the keen form of Midshipman Howard. He yelled to the boy.

Howard weaved nimbly through the crowd to attend the rail beneath his captain.

'Aye, Captain?'

'Prepare for your first command, Mister Howard.'

'Sir?'

'Gain the attention of Mister Anderson. Make your boarding parties, and ready your gun-crews.' He spun back to Guinneys. 'Party of eight, Mister Guinneys. Yourself and Lieutenant Scott with me. We're going ashore.'

Guinneys sniffed again; he stiffened as if pulled from the yards above. 'May I be enlightened as to the order of the day, Captain?'

Coxon paused, took the *Lucy* in his sight once more. 'That ship stays there for two reasons only: she is left for unknown purpose whilst the frigate carrying the gold is long gone; or else there are misdeeds afoot on that island and she awaits instruction. Either way we will investigate as per our orders. Will that suffice, Mister Guinneys?'

Guinneys doffed his hat mildly. 'Aye, Captain. That will do.'

'Very well, then. Arm yourself and make ready.' He turned, momentarily freeing himself from the heavy, cold sensation that the sight of Guinneys now invoked within him, and made his way to his cabin, catching the troubled gaze of Midshipman Howard again.

'Mister Howard? You still hover here?'

'Begging your pardon, Captain.' The young man tugged a ginger forelock and walked amidships with Coxon, struggling to keep pace as Coxon headed for his quarters. 'May I make a note of these events, for myself? It won't take long.'

'You may do whatever you wish, Mister Howard, as long as the men on your quarter bill are ready on my return.'

'On your return from the island, Captain?' Howard skipped past a coil of rope, bringing himself in line with his captain.

'On my return from loading my pistols, sir.' He smiled at Howard; then Coxon stopped, halting Howard with a backhand to the chest and looked down into the boy's face. Quietly, he spoke, his voice lowered beneath the cracking of sails and cries of hauling. 'Mind me, Thomas. There is more to fear here than pirates. To your duty and keep a sharp eye, lad. This day may be hard.'

Howard felt the elbow of his captain offering a gentle nudge of conspiracy, and then he was left in the waist of the ship, his eyes following Coxon's back, his mouth taut and dry.

Sam Fletcher slung himself down from the shrouds, his bare feet slapping the wet deck with a thud. 'Still no guns run out on the bastard.'

'We should warn the captain, Sam.' Dan Teague was squatting by the starboard bulwark, switching his gaze tentatively between the *Starling* and his crewmates.

'What say you, Hugh?' Sam Fletcher asked Hugh Harris, the calmest soul amongst them, all the small crew feeling the lack of Peter Sam and Devlin.

Hugh moved to the bulwark, placing a foot on the trucks of a gun, his left hand resting on the guard of his cutlass, and looked over to the *Starling*.

Nine gun ports on the weatherdeck. Two more apiece on the quarterdeck and fo'c'sle. Thirteen guns to bear against them. Could not be less than twelve-pounders. Nine-pound chasers, too, no doubt. Even in peace they had to sail with at least ninety souls.

The *Lucy* was parallel to the shore, rolling slightly in her anchor as they sat against the wind just over four hundred yards from the beach.

They were safe in the shallows. The frigate could not come

in to get them without floundering, but a little closer and she could blow them out of the sea.

The shallows were the pirates' domain. Again and again the governments sent powerful warships to negate the pirate threat, and all misunderstood that the pirates hugged the islands and rarely took to the sea, fishing the trade channels from their sloops and pinnaces. It was too bold to have a frigate. Too open. Hugh shrugged within himself. That frigate would be Devlin's downfall.

But for now a British frigate stood off half a league from their starboard quarter, heading close-hauled to the east of the island. On this reach they would have their larboard guns to the *Lucy*'s bow within minutes, but no range to reach her. The sands would keep them out.

He watched the sails being furled as she prepared to close, slow, under topsails. He could even see the dark black shapes of men moving about the shrouds and the flash of a telescope as it swept across his eyes.

'She could pound us to twigs if she but wished, lads.' He glanced round to his mates, ragged and greasy, all but the five Dutchmen, who still appeared as clean as the day they had come aboard. 'That's a fact not denying. But she may be a-thinking that the gold be on us already. And she wouldn't want to be sending that anywheres now.'

'How'd they know about the gold?' Dan queried, seeing his dreams of fortune seeping away.

'They're here, ain't they?' Hugh snapped. 'English ship turning up within hours of us? 'Course they know, you fool!'

'Where's Peter Sam? Where the bloody hell has he got to?' Sam Morwell cried.

'Gone no doubt, I say!' Dan sniped. 'Gone with what's left of our account, that's what!' A fly of sorts landed on the back of his hand, its eyes jewelled red, and he swatted it to paste. Even the flies could be traitors now.

'No. Not Peter.' Hugh shook his head. 'And if so, not whilst Black Bill still lived.'

Sam Morwell agreed, 'Aye, Bill for sure wouldn't let Peter leave us.' He looked over to the menacing frigate. 'Anyways, we're under a French flag, ain't we? All allies now, ain't we? King George and the boy are proper bedfellows. Why should they go for us, eh?'

'Fair enough.' Hugh nodded. 'No pipes now, lads. Fletcher? We'll carry on with the captain's plan. Lads, check the breeches. Load the swivel guns. Get some powder and bar up. Look alive. If we are allies, they may send a gig over to chat. If we ain't, no harm in loading what we got.'

'Aye, Hugh.'

Fletcher, Dan and Sam Morwell loped away, instinctively keeping their heads low. Hugh turned to the Dutchmen.

'Now, Dutchy.' Hugh had tried to learn their names, but the effort to recall seemed pointless, for they could all be dead in an hour or so. 'Double-check the bulwark nettings. Stuff them deep. Get an axe ready to the hawser. I don't want to be calling for one if we have to slip cable.'

'*Ja*, Mister Hugh!' His name was Eduard Decker, and he slapped his fellows into movement. Hugh looked back to the *Starling*. The ship had not fired a signal-gun to greet an ally, and neither had the *Lucy*. Hugh untied the knot of the brown linen cravat round his neck, freed the ends from inside his shirt and then with care began to tie them to the finger-guards of his matched pair of pistols.

Philippe Ducos had exaggerated. Perhaps in order to value his life more, for which Devlin did not curse him. And, after dragging the chest from beneath the table, inch by inch, which must have weighed twice as much as himself and Dandon together, he was relieved that he had.

Gold has not the lustre one always believes it has. The fortune they had lusted after was a dull muted yellow, pitted black in the minting and the milled edges, yet in its enormity the mound seemed to boil over the more they gaped at it.

They sat back on their haunches, enraptured, forgetting the cursing and banging that had preceded as they had cut at and prised off the hinges rather than attempt a worthless assault on the forbidding padlocks.

Together they suggested a wealth of near ten thousand louis d'ors. Over six thousand pounds, at a time when King George himself drew from his endeavours twenty-five thousand pounds a year.

'"*Weren't not for gold and women there would be no damnation*," ' Dandon quoted, finding no tiring in slapping Devlin's back.

Devlin leaned forward and cupped a year's wage in his dirty palm. He let the coin run through his fingers like the voluminous tresses of some divine first love, and he laughed at the symphony of it falling.

Bessette was tied now to his chair, with the ropes from his own bedroom curtains and a foolish grin sloped up his face as he slept royally. Their troupe of ladies remained in the mess, lapping wine and counting the escudos they had lifted from the pockets of the soldiers. The moment had come for Devlin to possess his own life rather than borrow it from others. But it was not done yet.

'Enough,' Devlin said at last. 'To it. We'll fetch that soul's musket and check the barracks for any fair weapons.'

He stood and tried to concentrate, his eyes still drawn to the chest of gold.

'That bell will bring the guards from the cliffs if they are not here already. The *Shadow* will be presenting her feint attack on *Lucy*. No need for that now. Things have gone better than I had planned, Dandon. We need just get to the beach and tell our mates.'

'And dispatch the remainder of the guards, of course. Assuming there is at least one on either cliff?'

'We saw two men ordered off the beach. One I'm sure lies out there with the soul from the path. That leaves one, for sure. I would lay to it that there is another on the opposite side.'

'May all your assumptions be correct, Captain: I prefer the odds.'

'A handful of coin may persuade them to be less aggressive.' He straightened his waistcoat, tightened his sash, and checked the action on his pistol yet again. The musket outside would be welcome and there might be more pistols in the barracks.

'Come.' He prised Dandon from the mesmerising sight of the gold, and pulled the outer door inwards.

The door had opened less than halfway when a shot raked and whistled through the gap, its path actually visible to them through the dust in its wake; Bessette's body jerked as the ball struck him in the eye and exploded out the back of his head.

Devlin slammed shut the door, his back upon it, holding back the world from his gold.

Dandon bared his gold teeth, repulsed by the bloody end of Captain Bessette. 'So that's how long it takes to walk from the cliffs. I *had* wondered.'

*

Dominic Duphot and Landri Fauche had met and hailed each other almost at the stockade's gate. Landri had been on his winding way from his watch on the eastern cliff when he had heard the bell, followed moments later by the fort's cannon, which had prompted him into a run.

He had paused at the edge of the trees along the path to load his musket. It had taken two attempts; at first he only succeeded in pouring powder over his hand rather than down the barrel as his nerves rattled.

Waiting there, lost as to what had occurred, he felt his heart leap on seeing Duphot running to the gate on the opposite path.

Together they had pushed open the gate, each inch revealing more and more of the lifeless bodies of their comrades in the distance. They exchanged bold looks, drew back the locks on their muskets and stepped over the threshold.

Duphot was drawn to the leather satchel of Favre Callier, abandoned, some of his sketches littering the ground, lifting weakly in the mild breeze. As they passed the fallen musket they began to hunch down, searching for an attack.

They could see the door to their mess open and another of their men lying on his back, cutlass still in hand. Then they reached the bodies sprawled before the cannon, their peppered tunics testament to their fate.

They ducked together and ran behind the barracks on their right, their backs to the wall, their muskets like shields across their chests.

They whispered fearing enemy ears and eyes upon them, and began to creep along the rear of the barracks, between that and the stockade wall, to the bottom corner. Once there, down on one knee, Duphot could edge his head out and see the door to their captain's quarters past the cannon and, to his left, halfway up the wooden wall, the open mess door. For a moment Duphot imagined he could hear the lilt of a woman's voice; then he was distracted by the sound of Landri's weapon discharging next to his right ear.

'I got one, Dominic!' Landri yelled. 'The door opened. Did you see?'

'No, I did not see! *Merde*, and now I cannot hear, you fool!' Duphot readied his gun and trained it on the mess.

'Ugly bastard sitting at the capitaine's table. Smiling, by God! I got him right in the head!'

'Quiet! Look!'

A woman had run to the doorway of the mess, a bottle of wine in her hand, her skirt removed, showing her undergarments, which did not distract Duphot as much as he might have thought it would. Her face was panicked, startled by the shot. Duphot took aim to her belly.

'Halt! Do not move!'

She screamed and vanished instantly stage right.

'*Merde!*' Duphot lowered his musket. 'Did you see any others, Landri?'

'*Non*. Only that bastard, but someone shut the door.'

'They could be in the mess by now. Looking right at us, plotting against us. Those poor women.'

'Cover me whilst I reload, Dominic.' Landri dropped back to the wall of the barracks, standing to begin the long fifteen seconds it would take to prime his musket.

Duphot spied carefully on the gaping door of the mess. The doorway revealed nothing but darkness within. He remained kneeling in a ready pose, the butt of his weapon in the sand, its barrel skyward, the musket nestling into his body as he rested upon it. Nothing moved. The living sounds of the forest came gently over the stockade walls, mocking the tension Duphot felt within; he could not recall the relentless chorus of cicadas ever sounding so urgent and overpowering.

Landri's heart beat once against his ribs as he slid the rod of his musket back into place, empowered again by the solid feeling of a loaded gun.

'What shall we do, Dominic?' he asked, instantly promoting Duphot to his immediate commander.

Dominic wiped the back of his hand across his forehead, momentarily taking his eyes off the doorway of the mess. 'I do not know,' he hissed. 'I am confused. Who is dead? Who is alive?' He returned his fixed stare to the door. 'I only know that I will kill whoever comes from that door.'

'One is dead. How many are there?' Landri's voice was calmer than he felt.

Dominic leafed through the short narrative in his head of what he did know. Two men had come to the island. Two men and one whore stood on the beach. An hour or so later he had heard the faint peal of the bell and the flat, sharp report of the nine-pounder.

He had been lying flat outside the tent on the western post, his afternoon watch under way, idly tracking the sail moving slowly SSE towards them, his telescope constantly fogging, his thumb swiftly wiping it under cursed breath, turning the sail into a greasy smear as he re-sighted it. Somewhere inside the vellum tube, an aphid had found a home, and occasionally it leaped into view, appearing to devour the little ship creeping over the horizon. Favre had shown him the ship when they had slunk back to the cliff, when the women had arrived, when the afternoon had such possibilities. Together they had watched the ship as they sat ripping up tufts of grass like petulant schoolboys, slapping the insects on their faces, moaning how they were having none of the fun, and every now and then glancing up at the grey sail on the horizon.

Favre's watch was over, anyhow. He would take lunch. Make sure there was plenty of stew left for Duphot, and they had bid *au revoir* to one another.

Now Favre was dead. As Duphot trundled down the dusty path, summoned by the bell, he saw the brigantine and the other ship, in the offing, cruising past the breakers, the bluff lines and tight rigging of a man-of-war, a British pennant above. Two ships. Five months of nothing but gardening and drill, and then within hours a fleet descends on their little stronghold.

He did not pause, or dwell on what he saw, but carried on wheeling downhill to the fort, when he saw Landri lurking by the edge of the trees holding his musket, as if surprised that it was in his hands at all.

He related all this to Landri, ignoring the itching in his eyes from Landri's shot and keeping them fixed on the mess.

'But the English, they will help, *non*? We are all allies now, *oui*?' Landri's politics were simple.

'Ah, that is why those men have killed our comrades, *non*? Because we are all friends now, *oui*?' He sniffed derisively at Landri. 'Tell me, Landri, if I pissed down your back would you think that it was raining?'

'Maybe there is only one left? You said there were two, Dominic. I have killed one. Bessette and Lieutenant Xavier would never let anyone else ashore: they would not take such a risk.'

He was right, Duphot thought. No one else would have come ashore. Ah, but Bessette's mind was addled by his abscess, his rotten jaw; he was not as he was. Then again,

Lieutenant Xavier was as sharp as a shard of flint, was he not? Irrepressible. Constant.

Yes. Two men. Some argument had occurred. Perhaps the gold discovered. Women coerced. Tempers unhinged.

'Landri, I think there is only one man. You are right. We will hold out here. That English frigate will be—'

Behind his head there came a click. Duphot knew the sound. He did not know the soft voice that followed it, laced with a layer of menace.

'What English frigate?' Devlin asked.

Dominic Duphot turned slowly, his fingers finding their grasp on the musket weakening. He saw the tall man from the beach standing a spit away from him, his pistol loosely aimed at Duphot's guts. Beside him, the sallow-eyed one in a yellow damask vest held a smaller gun to Landri's trembling neck and relieved him of his musket.

'Carry on,' Devlin encouraged with a beckoning from his pistol. 'What English frigate?'

Duphot stood, his knee cracking awkwardly as he did so, and gently, without request, let his musket rest against the wall of the barracks.

'I will say no more, monsieur.' He spoke in English. Again he thumbed the pages of his mind back through all that must have happened, back to the point after Landri's shot. The two must have run from Bessette's anteroom to his bedchamber and out through the window, making their way up to the gate and around to come up behind them, probably actually following their footsteps.

Duphot spoke dejectedly to his comrade, 'By any chance, Landri, did the soul that you shot have a short beard and a shiny bald head?'

'*Oui.* Bald. Some black hair? But it was just a glimpse.'

Landri looked nervously between the two brigands.

'It was for the best, mate.' Dandon allayed Landri's fears. 'His mouth was worse than a king's, I assure you.'

Duphot continued, speaking slowly to Devlin, for all English were ignorant with gin, 'So there *was* only two of you, eh?' He smiled, almost chuckling. 'Do you have any idea what you have done, monsieur? What you have achieved this day?'

'Some. And you do not have to die because of it. You can help us carry the chest to shore.' At word of the chest, Duphot's shoulders sank, his head became limp almost to his heart and he sighed deeply, shaking his head as Devlin spoke on. 'Those are my ships that look to the beach. Your position here has gone. But I'll grant you safe passage off this island. Or you can stay here with your three countrymen who still live.'

Duphot raised his head. 'You are not a complete devil, then, monsieur, *non*? And these women that are all hiding in the mess are truly with you?'

'They are. Now, what'll it be?' Devlin took a step back, squarely facing Duphot.

He had not expected Duphot to laugh.

'What sails does your ship have, monsieur?'

'Why?'

'And she would fly a British pennant, *non*? Her paint, yellow and black?'

Devlin looked to Dandon. One small look away from Duphot.

All Duphot required.

In the same moment he went from a sluggish Breton to a Parisian lion, and Devlin was on his back, the blue sky framing Duphot's snarling, slavering head as he wrestled the pistol from Devlin's grasp. Prayers of hate spat out through Duphot's teeth. He was heavy, strong, his breath hot and foul. Devlin felt the pistol being dragged effortlessly from him. Then there was the crack of the small overcoat pistol and a look of surprise on Duphot's sagging face as he rolled off Devlin like a spent lover.

Devlin pulled himself up to see Dandon's smoking gun in one hand, Landri flapping like a captured hen in the other.

'Do I have to spend my entire life, Patrick, shooting men for you?' Dandon cursed, slapping Landri across the head to be still.

Duphot was smiling, mumbling, the pistol in his right hand. Devlin stood over him, his left foot on his wrist, and bent to gain back the weapon, catching Duphot's final triumphant words.

'Pity, Capitaine...you almost had it,' he coughed, choking on his own last breath. 'I have seen your ship...I have seen those grey sails. Far away...travelling south. These...this ship are Englishmen...come to kill you, *non*? Your own kind. Heh!' Then his head drifted back, with his last gasp mouthing reverently, 'Those poor, poor women...women.'

Chapter Fourteen

✗

*L*etter from Edward Talton to the East India Trading
Company

To the Officers of Administration
Leadenhall Street
London

14 May 1717
To all who sees these presents, Greetings,

    *I wish notice to be drawn to this letter so dated as displeasure as
to the treatment of the Company concerns regarding our return from
the Company factory placements in our allotted interest. Unsatisfactory relations have developed as direct interference of Whitehall concerns. Sir, our stock has been undervalued beyond our investment in
the Board and my own personal involvement has increased beyond
my role and reasonable fortitude.*

    *When this letter finds you I shall be in the Antilles as partner to
a Board and Parliamentary mission that has no Company require-
ments as consequence of which I suggest removal of percentage of
success from officers related to His Majesty's ship Starling. It has
not been given outside my powers of office to mention most reluctantly that we pursue the adventurous nature of one known now to
me as the pyrate Devlin.*

On my return, some months hence, I will gladly represent the Company interest in complaints and seizures of percentages.

I note with concern the interest that has developed in my position since the appointment of Captain John Coxon has come to the fore.

Several of the officers have visited of late in my own private quarters and shown unwarranted interest in my correspondence.

Whether this is a consequence of the Board is not to my knowledge and I inform the Company in my own interest naturally.

I find the ship to be in good order to the best of my scrutiny and query and suggest any funding to repairs and fitting to be denied.

Your obedient servant,

> *Edward James Talton.*
> *His Majesty's ship Starling.*
> *Captain John Coxon.*

'Tell me, Doctor, is there any means of testing for arsenic poisoning? Immediately, I mean?' Coxon had summoned Surgeon Wood to his cabin as he readied himself for shore, and was silently gratified that the Scotsman was the first person for quite some time to actually knock on his door for permission to enter.

He had partially turned to face Doctor Wood, as he changed into a woollen shirt and a cambric steinkerke, and at such position kept the rising and falling anchorage of the *Lucy* constant through the larboard window of his cabin, never far from his eye.

'Arsenic? Why do you ask, Captain?' Doctor Wood bowed under one of the overhead beams as he stepped into the room and closed the door.

'Before we dispense with Mister Talton, I wondered if it would not be prudent to eliminate any foul play, 'tis all.' He flapped on his dark brown vest, ignoring the slightly damp odour it gave off, and began buttoning.

'You suspect a murder?'

Coxon took a small personal delight in the rolling resonance the Scotsman gave to the word 'murder'. He made the concept almost seductive.

'I should eliminate the prospect. I find such a sudden death unusual at the very least.'

'Aye, well, you could probably discard your arsenic concept, then, Captain.' Wood removed his pince-nez, habitually closing his eyes and squeezing the bridge of his nose. 'It's a painful way to go. Not half as romantic as history may have led you to believe.'

'How so?' Coxon, his vest secured, crossed the cabin to select a sword from the three draped upon the sloping wall.

'It would take almost an hour to actually kill, supposing you had ingested, say, a small ink-bottle's worth. And in that hour you'd be in such agony and all manner of sickness... you would not go quietly.'

'I see.' Coxon decided on a short cutlass and narrow black crossbelt. Once adorned, he made for his cot between the bulkheads, his private partition folded back. 'Is there any test you may be able to perform on Mister Talton to check for poison?'

'I could gut him. Take a look at his organs. Most poisons rely on suffocation of the organs themselves... Are we actually contemplating this, Captain?'

Coxon opened the baize-lined box that contained two simple, brassed English pistols. Not his own. His own commissioned pistols had gone down with the *Noble*, he hoped, rather than survive to be in the hands of some contemptible soul on the ship abreast of them.

'Hmm?' He had been distracted by the implication of

personal arms. 'Oh, not really. Not to concern yourself. But perhaps tomorrow, when this is over, I would appreciate a trip to the cockpit with you, before we commend Talton's body. Just for the sake of my log, you understand.'

Wood nodded compliantly. 'If you wish, Captain. Aye.' He made a note to check his supply of sawdust, and begged if that was all that Coxon required of him.

'Dismissed, Doctor Wood. But,' he added solemnly, 'do not tell anyone of what we have spoken, if you please, sir.'

Wood grunted an accord, knuckled his head and removed himself quietly, silently affirming that all seamen were mad by nature.

Coxon began unfolding from the baize inserts of the pistol box the small waxen folds of paper that held five prepared cartridges apiece. Each cartridge a small packet of powder and ball. Methodically, he patch-loaded and primed each pistol; his mind was elsewhere, however. Guangzhou, to be precise.

Thoughts of China, Bombay, the delicate, deadly, strange Far East. Guinneys had spent three years back and forth throughout the factories and markets of those unholy lands. Guinneys had even attempted to entertain Coxon with tales of how poisoning was a capital punishment – reserved for nobility, no less. It would not take much for a curious man like Guinneys to be persuaded to purchase or even receive as a gift a small, elegant bottle of some substance.

It was a possibility. Although for why, Coxon was at a loss. He stood, aware of how long he had left Guinneys alone, aware that Mister Howard would be counting his quarter bill for the umpteenth time. He picked his hat up off the cot, looked inside, ran a finger round the band, musing on the day ahead.

He would address Guinneys on the island. Informally. Off the ship. Implication now would cause a confusion of loyalties. He needed all behind him to secure the gold. There was one pirate ship. There might be another.

And why not just suppose that Devlin is with the pirates, not as their leader, but a conspirator. Once he reaches the island, he immediately joins the French troops – he can speak French; he would be convincing. A battle occurs. The pirates are beaten. The ship remains, too drunk to sail, more likely than not, and Devlin and the brave troops savour their victory. He and Guinneys would walk into the stockade; Guinneys would be forced to admit that Devlin had learned honour and decency from his master, that he had ideals he was not born to possess but had demonstrated them nonetheless. Virtue by proxy.

He planted his hat firmly in place. And if Devlin had turned to the damned, then his death would be just as redeeming. The island would settle all.

There is a moment, a fleeting moment, that occurs rarely for some, consistently for others, when rowing from a ship. It is a sense of limbo, of being not in one place or another.

You watch the ship from the confines of the longboat, the enormity of her stretching above your head. There are not enough bones in your neck to glance to the top of the mainmast. And then you glance over your shoulder to your destination, small, dwarfed by the sea and sky.

A few minutes later and your ship is smaller now, rising and falling almost urgently. You can no longer hear the wind strumming the shrouds, the flap of the courses against their buntlines, the lazy yawn of the oak all around. And then, just as you notice the absence of these sounds, you see the ship is nothing more than a large painting at the end of a great hall. You turn to the land behind. It seems no larger, only brighter.

And *there* is the moment.

At some point on your journey, the land gets no closer, the ship gets no smaller. You hang in a world that only exists on the sea. It goes on and on.

Nothing gets smaller. Nothing gets larger.

John Coxon was experiencing the moment profoundly. Too profoundly. He began to contemplate staying at this point. Here, he had responsibility for the eight others, and coxswain, in the longboat with him. Nothing else beyond the sides of the boat. Back there, to the *Starling*, was England. Duty. Taxes. Orders. A hundred mouths to feed and water. And forward there, a whole new world of different responsibilities again, as well as bringing all the old ones along for the tour.

But stay here, with just these few stoic souls to worry about, a canvas sack at your feet with two paltry days' worth of food and water. Two days just sitting here. I can hear no one from the ship. I can hear no one from the land. They can ask nothing of me. I would have all the peace of the dead, whilst still holding all the potential of the living. Belonging to neither, mocking them both.

'Are you feeling unwell, Captain?' Lieutenant Scott snatched him from his disembodied thoughts.

'Certainly not, Mister Scott.' Coxon sat up, shielding his eyes from the glare of the afternoon sun. The moment had passed. The island crawled towards them, the longboat slamming through the breakers at each pass of the oars.

Coxon sat at the bow facing Guinneys and Scott, both wearing their boatcloaks, despite the warmth of the day, and both with two pistols and a cutlass apiece.

Behind them, two marines tried to keep pace with the four sailors at the oars, and the coxswain sat with the double honour of maintaining the tiller and keeping the weapons dry beneath the sheets.

They had set off from the starboard side of the *Starling*, away from the eyes of the *Lucy*, as far to the eastern side of the beach as they could, scudding over the pink coral reefs. The *Starling* lay anchored now, with furled sails, hammocks stowed along the bulwark netting, her larboard guns still not run out.

The scant wind came so'west yet, even so, the *Starling's* prow ducked and rose against her anchor. To bring her closer would be the end of Mister Howard's and Mister Anderson's command. Her ship-rigged courses would be fatal against the windward shore, her staysails turning her like a herd of cattle, whilst the pirate brigantine would spin like a coin on a table with her jibs and lateen-rigged mainmast and spanker.

'Look, Captain,' Scott sang out, a grey-gloved hand pointing to the shore over Coxon's shoulder, 'a jolly-boat. The pirates, I'll be damned.'

True enough, as they closed the last thirty yards, Coxon followed Scott's hand to the small boat dragged up on the beach.

The boat was not secured – no land anchor, no proper beaching – suggesting some urgency or an imminent return.

Moments later, coral replaced by silver sand, Guinneys leaped over the gunwale into the warm, soft spume, his Cordova leather riding boots shrugging off the water as he sprinted for the jolly-boat.

Traditionally Coxon would be carried the few yards through the water, still seated on the bench he rode in on, and the rest of the planks would be brought ashore to wedge under the longboat's sides to hold her to the sands. He forsook the honour, soaking his stockings and shoes in the champagne-like effervescence, the hem of his black silk coat dipping in and out of the water as he ran to join Guinneys.

'Empty, sir.' Guinneys sounded disappointed. He glanced up at the brigantine, surprisingly close; he could almost make out the grimy faces peering over her fo'c'sle.

'What were you expecting, William? The gold in the boat?' Coxon joined him in the study of the pirate ship, seeing the men on board ducking away at his stare, like cockroaches away from a lamp. Just his presence had brought fear into them – or, if not fear, then a reminder. A reminder of the discipline. The orders. The bell. The red bag that held the cat with nine tails. Eat when told. Sleep little and sleep sober. Go hungry on my command. And now you had gone too far. Now you would choke for your freedom. Tyburn or Wapping will be the last place for you, my lads.

'She could hit us from here, Captain. Why don't she try?' Guinneys looked warily at the four six-pounders coming from the cutaways on the leeward side facing them.

'We are all friends, William. I may even affect a wave. She holds that *pavillon-blanc* rag: thus we are allies. Neither of us has signalled. If she tries to ply us, the game will be up and the *Starling* will grind her to sawdust. Come. Let's see what goes on at the fort.'

He dragged Guinneys by the arm, wheeling him away. An hour at best, and he could dispense with the pleasant regard. Secure the island. Gain back lost pride. Although Guinneys may well be innocent, Talton's broken pen had written the guilt of someone, of some presence in the small cabin other than of death.

An hour, then. Leave the coxswain at the boat, a pistol for a companion.

The eight of them, armed and justified, strode gallantly up the sandy path, the sound of the surf fading behind, and all noticed silently the army of footsteps that had gone before them.

Landri Fauche had adapted to his situation. He bowed when he presented the pirates with muskets from the barracks, no pistols, and helped Devlin reload the nine-pounder with grape. They all joined the women and the two sleeping guards in the mess. Devlin sat on the edge of a table, Bessette's sword in his hand tapping a rhythm on the floor, his head lowered.

An English ship. By appointment or by chance, it mattered little. No *Shadow.* No Peter Sam. Think. A chest of gold that weighs as much as three men. Perhaps a mile and a half to the shore. A short-handed crew on the *Lucy.* The navy about to make a show.

A party would come to shore first. Probably no more than ten, a fair assumption based on the size of a longboat.

A fleeting image of cannon fire and the clash of cutlasses through the saltpetre smoke of muskets filled his vision, but the spectacle, inspiring as it was, ended in his own inevitable death. He slid from the table and looked for a drink to ease his mind.

'Which one of these is good to drink, Dandon?'

Dandon wore again his elegant, frayed justaucorps and tricorne. He sighed despondently. 'Any of them now, Captain. Who knows? We may be fortunate enough to still be asleep when they hang us.'

Annie chirped up, 'So what are we to do, then? I think our part's been enough, don't you?' All the ladies now adopted the same defiant pose, their hands on their hips, their heads cocked to a sneer.

'I ask no more of you, Annie. You have what monies you were promised. My only regret is that it may not be with us that you are escorted back to Providence.'

'Which is to our own detriment, ladies.' Dandon bowed. 'Now that we are all members of the *demi-monde*.'

'So we're to go down to this English ship, are we? That's it, then?' Annie snapped, her chin jutting to the pair of them.

'I can ask only one thing,' Devlin beseeched, his mind clutching at straws. 'Tell anyone you may see that all is well here. You have done your duty to the barracks and are returning to your ship.'

Annie rasped some kind of agreement through her lips, before swaying her way into the sunlight, the others following like ducklings.

Dandon trotted with them to open the gate. 'I have known most of you ladies, quite intimately, for quite some time.' He sounded almost apologetic for his company. 'And you know that I am not a brave man. I would be most grateful if you could find a good word to say about me to any official who may ask as to my nature.'

'You could come with us, Dandon. You owe that pirate nothing.'

'Ah, *Deus misereatur.* If I felt that I could leave such a fortune for one man to carry to his grave...' He opened the gate, grabbing a look at the jungle outside and the empty path beyond. 'And if you do return to Providence, be sure to tell Mrs Haggins to keep my eminent position open for me.'

'It'll be the first words I say, Dandelion old mate.' Annie grinned, and waved as they departed.

'Goodbye, sweet ladies.' He shut and barred the gate; for why, he was not sure. It seemed the thing to do.

He returned to find Landri and Devlin conversing politely

on the situation. Landri confirmed there was no other shore on the island, not without traversing through several miles of thick jungle to reach a sheer drop straight to jagged rocks. The path ran from the east coast lookout to the west coast, with a break to reach the shore and that was all.

'No underground stores? Hidden landings?'

'*Non*, monsieur. If you wish I will gladly accept your parole. If you are willing to surrender?'

'It may come to that indeed.' Devlin turned away. He had dressed himself with a soldier's cutlass to partner Bessette's elegant scallop-guarded hanger, and now he drew it to have both in his hands as he paced the room. Dandon, a sword alien to him, stood by the door, a shoulder and an eye facing the gate of the stockade, leaning on the barrel of a musket.

'Think, Dandon.' Devlin gritted his teeth. 'What do we know? We have the gold. We have four men alive here' – he nodded to the Frenchman – 'including yourself, Monsieur Fauche. They will wake soon…'

'I can alleviate that distraction, Captain,' Dandon volunteered.

'Get to it. One less problem.'

Dandon gently leaned his musket to the wall and dashed to fetch his ethereal spirits. Devlin continued, now only talking to a bemused Landri.

'He could have lied. Your comrade. The bell *was* for a ship. My ship. There's no English ship at all.' He stopped pacing. 'Were you expecting a ship?'

Landri nodded in affirmation. 'But not until June, monsieur.'

'Then there's hope. It could be the *Shadow*. I need to lay eyes on that ship.' He resumed his anxious pacing.

'We'll know soon enough, Captain.' Dandon came back into the room, a small brown bottle in one hand, a large green carafe in the other, from which he took a draught. 'If the ladies are at the beach, our own mates will come and get us and all will be well.'

Devlin's mind twisted options over and over. The grand ones, the foolish ones, the bold ones. Disguise, deception, bluff, and all for a chest of gold that, for its damnable weight, might as well have been shining from the moon. A ship. If not the *Shadow*, then where was she? Where was Peter Sam? How far off? If at all.

He slashed the cutlass deep into the edge of a table with an alarming fury.

'I'm still here, you *bastards*!' He snapped the cutlass free again, dragging the protesting table a few inches. His eyes closed for a moment. Landri and Dandon shared a glance.

Sam Fletcher appeared before Devlin's lidded eyes. No other choice. If Fletcher and Hugh Harris were willing, if they were still able to follow through, if the *Shadow* was nearby...

'Right,' he said at last, and pointed a blade to Landri. 'How rich do you want to be, Fauche?'

They were coming down the path now, the stockade silent before them, the surprising party of women they had met traipsing up to meet them still a leering subject of conversation amongst the chortling tars.

With gentlemanly goodwill, Coxon had ordered the marines to stay with the women, find shade if possible, whilst he, Guinneys, Scott and the four hands ventured on, somewhat confused by the ladies' claims of compliance with the fort.

Coxon had questioned three of them. The one called Annie had appeared to be their hostess and she assured him that they had arrived from the ship for one purpose, and now attended to and handsomely paid they were returning, for repose, naturally. Everything was fine in the fort. They knew nothing of pirates or of one called Devlin. Their ship was crewed by modest men who had sailed them from Hispaniola for an equal share. The two others had giggled the same story. They were alone, and only as innocent as they were yesterday, no less so.

As they walked on, Guinneys could not help but cast aspersions. 'Surely they belong to the ship, Captain? They're with *them*, are they not? The pirates?'

Coxon removed his tricorne, ran a sleeve across his forehead. 'I have no doubt. A whores' ship the same colour as the pirate brigantine? Unlikely.' A conflict he could not quite grasp kept surfacing within Coxon. Devlin, a pirate captain. Devlin, loyal servant. Devlin, lording over all with bloodied sword and smoking pistol. Devlin, biding his time to overthrow his pirate masters and show his true colours.

'All that bunting, though. It's a possibility,' Guinneys theorised.

'It's a deception. That's how he got in here. Using bloody whores like a Trojan horse. Now hold, William, look alive.' He waved them all down to crouch along the path and observe the fort.

Nothing stirred. No sound from beyond the austere gate. No lookout in the tower.

'Seems quiet, sir,' Guinneys pointed out needlessly.

Coxon ignored him and pulled two of the sailors out to the front. 'You two,' he whispered. 'Go around the walls. See if it's clear. Look sharp now.'

Without hesitation, the two men in slop-hose loped down to the gate. Finding themselves still alive, they sidled round the far wall and disappeared.

Guinneys jostled Scott as he pulled one of his pistols clear of his belt.

'What say you, Scott? Fool's errand? Pirates ahoy, ho-yo, ho-yo, eh?'

'Quiet, old boy,' Scott hissed.

Coxon looked back at his two officers harshly, then back to the fort, waiting for a shot or a yell to break the tension standing on his skin.

Moments later the two sailors popped out from the opposite wall, indicated all was well and waited, stuck fast to the wall.

Guinneys shuffled up to Coxon's side. 'What now, sir? All clear around, it seems?'

'We need to know what goes on in there. Whose party this is.'

'How do we do that, sir?'

'Well, for one thing I've had enough of waiting for something to be done to me.' Coxon dragged Guinneys up and waved the others to follow. 'I'm going through that bloody door. I'm not about to be afraid of a man who used to wipe my shoes.'

They were all against the wall now. The sailors were armed with musketoons, cutlasses and their own gullies, each gentleman with a brace of pistols, hanger or cutlass.

'The door is barred,' Coxon reported from the front.

Guinneys threw off his boatcloak, dashed up the path, then looked back to the fort. 'There is a bell,' he shouted. 'Want me to hit it, Captain?'

'Your shot would draw more attention, William.'

'Yes, of course. Silly of me. Damn nerves, I suspect!' He cocked his pistol.

'No, William.' Coxon raised a palm to him. 'One of the

musketoons will do better.' He gestured to Adam Cole, a burly soul striped in blue. Cole rose out of his crouch and away from the wall. Instinctively he looked upwards for a target; then, aware of all eyes upon him, he snapped back the dog-head and nestled the musketoon into his shoulder, firing, a breath later, over the stockade wall, the explosion reverberating off the walls. He looked to his captain like a child for praise, then lowered his mind to his cartouche, reloading as he walked back to the small group.

'Good, Cole.' Coxon nodded. As if to reinforce the gunfire, he kicked out at the door again and again with his buckled shoes, simulating the impatient knocking of a giant.

Coxon stepped away, perspiring coldly from the heat and the effort of his rapping at the gate.

Guinneys' voice wafted up to his ear. 'Someone locked those ladies out, Captain, not ten minutes ago.'

In response to Guinneys' words, barely uttered, the solid sound of a wooden bar drawing back scraped through them.

The gate dragged slowly inwards, revealing a bright world beyond the shade of the stockade wall, the small, griefstricken form of Landri Fauche stepping into the gap, musket in hand.

'*Bonjour, mes amis.*' He smiled weakly. 'You are English, no? You have come to my aid, monsieur?'

Devlin checked his bonds. His arms were tied behind his back as he sat at the feet of the dead Bessette, the tablecloth again concealing the hiding place of the black chest. Dandon stood at the intersecting door to the corridor, Bessette's pistol in one hand covering Devlin, the other nervously sleeking through his hair beneath his wide yellow hat.

'Did I tell you how I became the captain of these men, Dandon?' Devlin almost sang.

'You did not, sir.' Dandon smiled back.

'It was a day out of the Verdes,' Devlin began. 'We had taken the *Shadow* from the Portuguese. Like an apple from a tree. All hands were to the punch, mourning the loss of Seth Toombs.'

'This Seth Toombs was the previous commander. I have gathered this of late,' Dandon stated.

'Aye. Fellow not much missed, save by Peter Sam I reckon.' He shuffled to have his back to the table and the chest. 'The call went round for a vote, you see. And I was just as drunk as anyone else and on the *Shadow* meself. They launched one of the gigs on a cable from *Lucy*. Then a round robin came aboard. You know what that is?' Dandon shook his head. 'It's a message, a decision of the crew, with all names signed in a circle round the plan. In a circle, so you can't tell who started it. Anyways, Hugh brings the round robin aboard with my name in the centre and all the principal officers signed round it. Then Hugh was staggering in front of me, telling me I was captain. *Told* me I was captain.' He arched his head round to Dandon and grinned as rakishly as he could given he was half beneath a table, his wrists tied. 'Seemed like a fine notion on the day.'

The deafening sound of Guinneys' leather sole stoving in the door made even Bessette's corpse jump. The room filled with sunlight, the dust swirling in it as thick as ash.

Guinneys, pistols drawn, sidestepped into the room and backed to the left wall, darting his eyes between Dandon and Devlin. A weapon on each. Lieutenant Scott followed and took a cautious pose to the right of the door, making way for John Coxon to enter with Landri Fauche at his shoulder.

Coxon's feet echoed twice on the rough wooden floor as he stepped towards the man looking up at him. Coxon's face was impassive, unmoved, as he took in the sight of Devlin at his feet.

'Hello, Patrick.' Coxon heard his voice crack with drought, and he swallowed hard. 'Tell me all about this pirate business now then, eh?'

Chapter Fifteen

'I believed you dead, Captain,' was all Devlin could say. He sighed a laugh of genuine irony.

'I was having doubts myself, Patrick.' Coxon chose to avoid looking at his man, now tanned and bedraggled and far from the shining pale valet he had cultivated. He surveyed the room. The dead Bessette dominated, his head lolled back, dry blood smeared over his face, a peppering of red on the wall some feet behind him.

'Your handiwork, Patrick?' he asked, his head darting around the room like a bird of prey's.

'An accident, Captain Coxon. Not of my doing.' Devlin smiled, his eyes taking in Guinneys and Scott in turn. Landri Fauche had crept into the suddenly crowded room to stand between the open door and the group of sailors inching their heads into the room.

'Cole!' Coxon turned to the door. 'Secure the gate. Get one man into that tower.'

'Aye, Captain!' Cole knuckled his forehead and vanished.

Coxon spoke to Landri as he walked round Bessette, casually examining the black gap in the back of his skull. 'This man' – he flapped a hand to Dandon – 'he is the doctor you spoke of, monsieur?'

Landri's understanding was poor but he gathered enough. '*Oui*, Capitaine.'

'Sir' – he looked straight at the nervous Dandon – 'put your pistol away; this is a place for accidents. I am in charge here now.' Then, with more candour, 'Do you understand?'

'*Oui.*' Dandon smiled and tucked away the pistol, his accent impeccable over his anxiety. 'My English is good, Capitaine. I will help as much as I can. Now you have rescued us.' He nodded nervously to Guinneys, whose pistol still stared at Dandon's chest. Guinneys scowled back, his second pistol barrel trembling slightly as it covered Devlin.

Coxon put his hands behind him, revealing the brassed pommels of his pistols and the cutlass at his side. 'Good. Although you seem to have all in hand, Doctor. Reveal to me what has occurred here today.'

'I should like, Capitaine, to be assured that your presence here is honourable. Under our circumstance, you understand?'

Coxon's jaw tightened. 'I have orders, sir, to secure this post on behalf of the French court. There is the matter of a gold deposit that is my chief concern, but I will repeat that I wish to know what has occurred here this day.'

Dandon did not flinch at the mention of the gold. He removed his hat, slowly, as if it might waken, then stepped out of his corner and to the back of the table. Guinneys' pistol followed his steps as Dandon laid his hat upon the green velvet tablecloth.

'*Pirates*, Capitaine.' His voice wavered as if he might break into tears. 'We were beset by pirates. They duped the soldiers with whores. I was forced to drug them! Although they wished me to kill them, I succeeded in only dosing them gently. They will wake shortly.' He paused to wipe some linen across his forehead.

'Capitaine Bessette was killed, truthfully in accident, when the soldiers discovered the pirates' true motives. A fight ensued.

Deaths, as you see, have happened. Gunfire was everywhere. It was a miracle that myself and the brave Caporal-Chef Fauche endured. That was all this morning. Once they had the gold, their guard relaxed and—'

Coxon interjected, 'They have the gold? Where? When?'

'They took it from Capitaine Bessette's bedchamber.' He indicated the room behind Coxon. 'It took four of them to carry it, Capitaine.' He pointed to the back of Devlin's head. 'This one and two others remained. But his pirate fellows fled when we...Landri and myself...managed to overcome him. It has been that way for two hours now. We kept him alive for our own safe need, waiting for the rest of them to return. And then, mercy of Mary, you and your gallant officers appeared. Praise you, Capitaine! Praise be, your mercies!'

Coxon had stopped listening as Dandon collapsed onto one of the green fauteuils, head in hands. He passed a casual hand and eye over the chest that held Dandon's plethora of bottles and curious paper parcels as he stepped within earshot of Guinneys, who had lowered his pistols. Scott still covered the room nervously.

'The gold must be on that brigantine,' he whispered to Guinneys.

'Then why do they wait?' Guinneys hissed.

Devlin laughed.

Coxon's head pivoted round to glare at the man on the floor. 'What is so amusing, Patrick?'

'Ah, come now, Captain.' Devlin looked to the white-washed ceiling. 'Do we not have more absorbing matters to talk on?'

Captain Coxon bent on a knee to face Devlin, his sword scraping behind him and almost touching Lieutenant Scott's buckled shoe.

'You and I will talk, Patrick. Of many things, be assured. I have come here a long way from where I left you and it is a compulsion within to shoot you where you sit. I am betrayed by you, Patrick Devlin. How little you realise the finality of your acts.'

'Oh, spare me, Captain,' Devlin spat. 'All I have done is my own will. I'll listen to none of your damnings! My soul's my own!'

Coxon lowered his eyes. 'You own nothing, Patrick. And soon you will own even less. Mark me now, lad.'

Guinneys' voice barked, drawing all eyes to him. 'Enough, Captain! What of the gold? How many men aboard that slut, *peasant*? Tell us *now*!' His gun wavered at the end of his grip.

'There are only eight sons of mine on that there ship, pup.' Devlin grinned back. 'And drunk or sober, they'd hang your guts around your neck. You may lay to that!' He met Coxon's steadfast stare. 'I'm for most times scared of them myself.'

'Are they waiting for you, Patrick?' Coxon asked. 'Has the frigate left you?'

The room breathed in.

'They wait for me. I have not seen that frigate for weeks, Captain. And that be the truth of the Lord. But I have that gold.'

'Not for long, Patrick.' Coxon stood and courted the assembly once more, his hands swept behind his back again.

Dandon raised a tearful head in despair. 'Will someone, *please*, for all the saints, remove this horror from my presence!'

'Quiet, dog!' Guinneys' voice cracked, almost panicked, as his gun stabbed towards Dandon's head.

'*Guinneys!*'

Coxon's voice could have carried from the crosstrees to the cockpit. 'Behold yourself, man!'

He swung round to Scott. 'Hold this room with Corporal Fauche. Do not take your pistol off this pirate. Guinneys? Come outside with me, Lieutenant.'

Guinneys lowered his guns and truculently followed his captain out into the scorched yard, leaving the door wide open behind them. Both stepped to the redoubt, eyeing the gun in its small carriage. Puny in comparison to the *Starling*'s twelve-pounders.

Coxon's eye swept along the iron barrel to where his small band of men were guarding the gate. He looked above to the sapphire sky as he spoke.

'William? Losing your temper will serve no good.'

'My apologies, Captain. My blood has been rising since we landed. It will not happen again.'

Coxon nodded. 'Now, what to do.' He walked between the huts, stepping past the drugged and the dead. Guinneys followed as if tethered.

'The gold is with that brigantine. Now we are here, those men will no doubt sail despite their captain.'

'They are pirates after all, sir.'

'And they will run from English guns. Our best approach is to let them sail and to cut them off.'

'She can outrun us, sir.'

Coxon turned and they walked back. 'She can't outrun our guns. We'll tear her rigging apart. A shell of a crew. They'll fold at our first cannon, mark me.'

'Undoubtedly, sir.'

'We shall take Devlin back to the ship. Under their gaze.'

'They may be landing now. They saw us come ashore.'

'And we are in a fort, are we not? Armed to the braces.' Coxon sighed, rapping his hand against the coarse wooden wall of the mess hall.

'There are only a few things that I cannot answer for which I beg your opinion, William.'

'What would they be, Captain?'

Coxon stopped at the mess door, idly looking in to the slumbering soldiers. 'There was a boat on the shore. If the gold is on the ship, hauled up, who rowed back to shore to fetch Devlin?'

'I do not follow, Captain.' Guinneys uncocked his pistols with expert ease and placed them smoothly in his belt beneath his coat.

'Picture it, William: men rowed to the ship with the gold whilst Devlin and a couple of others stayed here.' He added gently, 'If we are to believe *that* corporal and that French doctor, supposedly the others fled when Devlin was captured. Why is there still a boat on the shore? Would they not be aboard by now? If not, then they are hiding somewhere.'

'Perhaps two boats came in? One is left for Devlin?'

'Perhaps. I'll give you the gig may have been used to ferry the gold, although why when there is the larger one ready on the beach? And, if so, what boat did the pirates who fled use? Do you not see, William?' Coxon was pleased with the confused look on Guinneys' face.

'I have to admit that I do not, sir.' Guinneys removed his hat and began to fan himself.

'They are still *here*! In numbers. Watching us even now. Waiting to free Devlin.'

Guinneys could not help but look around the walls of the stockade, his head swivelling slowly.

'Don't look, you *fool*!' Coxon's whisper bristled. 'We are protected by ignorance only. Besides there is one other matter that nags at me.'

'And what is that, Captain?' Guinneys placed his hat back squarely, and snapped his vest tight. A habit now.

'I cannot discuss it even with you, William, until I know one thing more.'

Guinneys paid no attention to Coxon drawing one of his pistols as innocently as pulling out a handkerchief.

'To what is that, sir?'

'Edward Talton was murdered, William. To what extent and why was your hand involved?' Cards down. Play or fold. No bluff to play. Point or play.

'Sir?' Guinneys smirked, his eyes drawn to the neat hole of the muzzle pointed at his chest from Coxon's hip.

'Answer how you may. I will not judge you, lad.' Coxon smiled as a warmth of control swept through him, again generous in his patronage.

'I did not *kill* Talton, Captain. Why would I? Have you gone mad, sir?' Guinneys giggled slightly. Nervous and surprised.

'We will go forward from this point on your honour, William. I ask *only* that. Why did Talton die?'

Guinneys' face lost the good humour that had been its customary setting for the weeks that Coxon had known him. From somewhere else came the look Coxon suspected appeared at the end of the hunt, flecked with mud and blood.

'If you must know, Captain, it was not in my interests to allow an employee of John Company to have any knowledge of my intentions for that gold. I also believed that he would not be a willing party to your undoing. *Sir.*'

Coxon did not move, nor did his face alter from its stoicism, as if he heard such notions every day. 'My undoing?' he calmly asked.

'I am sorry, Captain. In truth I genuinely am. More goes on here than you may be permitted to know.'

'*Permitted?* You *dog*! I have orders from Whitehall! You dare allude to a mutiny while I stand behind them? The very gall of you, sir!'

'Oh, hush now, John, 'tis not a mutiny. I have my own orders, don't you know.' Guinneys' smiling face returned and he stepped back and crowed to the sailors, 'Cole! Williams! To me, now!'

Clay pipes disappeared as if they were never in the mouths at the gate. Straw hats were held tight to their heads with one hand, their musketoons in the other as the two sailors rushed to Guinneys.

Coxon felt the unsettling nausea run through him once more. His face cold in the heat. The pistol heavy in his hand.

'Yes, sir?' Cole spoke to Guinneys, yet nodded to Coxon.

'Cole,' Guinneys said, pulling out a tight wrap of papers from his vest. 'I have orders here that I wish you to witness that relieve Captain Coxon of his position under certain articles of deposition. Will you confirm them for me, Cole?'

Cole looked to both men in confusion. 'Sir?'

'Cole!' Coxon ordered. 'Relieve Lieutenant Guinneys of his weapons, if you please, and place him under arrest without parole at once. By my command, Cole.'

Cole and Williams passed a slow, curious glance to each other. The honourable pair took in the pistol of their new captain and the yellow parchment tied with black ribbon in the hand of their former master, the man who had travelled with them back and forth from Guangzhou and the Indian factories for the last two years. Both men rested their weapons' stocks upon the ground, the barrels between their legs.

Cole held a polite hand for the square wad of paper with soft words to Coxon. 'Begging your pardon, Cap'n.' He pulled off the ribbon at the corners rather than untying the neat bow and moved his head as he painfully began to read.

Guinneys' left hand, now empty of the papers, lowered for Coxon's pistol to be proffered voluntarily. 'Your weapon, Captain. If you please.'

'Cole!' Coxon's voice commanded. 'Those papers to me, now!'

Again, Cole spoke gently with his rumbling voice, 'Begging your pardon, Cap'n,' and returned to his page.

'You may read them, John,' Guinneys deigned magnanimously. 'After you offer me freely your arms.'

Coxon switched his focus from Guinneys to the labours of Cole deciphering the language of commissioners, then back again to the smiling Guinneys. He begged inwardly for a deck beneath his feet, not this French dust with its uncertainty dragging him down like quicksand.

'Whatever you have forged, young man, I have my orders to secure this island and this gold. This madness ends now. You will be detained under my instruction.' Even so, Coxon put away his pistol.

'The ship is mine, John.' And he repeated mockingly the words Coxon had said gallantly to him moments before: 'Understand that much, on *your* honour, and we will move forward from *this* point.' His hand came out more forcibly. 'Your arms, please, John.'

The sound of Cole closing the paper in its fold filled the air between them. He began to pass it back to Guinneys, who fanned his open hand graciously to Coxon. Cole moved the paper to Coxon.

'Seems in order, Captain,' he said, his head bowing swiftly, then rising with a grimace as Coxon took the paper.

Coxon swept his eyes to the bottom of the page. The names, scratched with pride, were unfamiliar. Aylmer and the

Third Earl of Berkeley were named elaborately as commissioners for exercising the office of Lord High Admiral of the Kingdom of Great Britain.

Coxon recalled the second earl. The father. But he had been away so long. These men would only know him as a name on a list, and a short name at that, with a dead clergyman as parent.

He reverted to the order itself. A jigsaw of compliments and phrases that made no sense.

On reaching and securing the island, command was to revert to Guinneys. The arrest of Count Gyllenborg, the Swedish ambassador who had attended a function at which Coxon and Devlin had been present, had cast doubt on Coxon's loyalty to the new king. The Jacobite threat was too powerful. The gold, for its own security, needed to be safeguarded by the British Crown, in the interests of the French, naturally. Coxon's undoubted knowledge of the Indies and his knowledge of the pirate Devlin were invaluable to the endeavour.

Once achieved, however, '*his value is unclear and must be assumed threatening and disadvantageous, the value and unknown extent of which to be determined by Captain William Guinneys to whom the Board grants full warrant.*'

'I am suspected of some Jacobite tendency? From what insanity does this notion spring?' Coxon asked.

'Oh, John.' Guinneys took back the paper. 'From nothing, most probably. Gold is gold. George loves horses, don't you know? Don't take it personally.' Guinneys secreted the paper back in his vest. 'More important is the stink this will make in that confounded Parliament. Jacobite pirates have a vast gold investment to fund a restoration through Spain. Do you want to remain on half-pay forever, for I don't!'

Coxon half turned, removing Cole and Williams from his

vision, his thoughts racking up like bridge pegs. Guinneys' orders were different from his own, their significance beyond his reasoning. The gold was to be taken. Taken for English coffers and blamed on the pirates. And Guinneys to help himself to a slice of it, no doubt.

The Jacobite dross was convenient. Convenient enough to remove the embarrassment that Coxon had obviously become.

Gold. Gilded blood-red. And Guinneys? What was his part? What promise had he been given? Why was Talton dead? Coxon pressed the point, for Cole and Williams to hear.

'And Talton? What does his death achieve?' Coxon turned back, noting the quizzical looks of the two sailors at the mention of the death that had no doubt been the after-watch talk below deck that very morning.

Guinneys smiled once more. 'Your pistols, please, John. You may keep the cutlass, on your honour.'

Coxon peaceably released his pistols to Cole and Williams in turn. 'When I am back aboard, Guinneys, the other officers may dispute your actions. Take care with me, William.'

'Quite. You are referring to the men who have sailed with me as captain for the last few years, are you not? I am sure your men on the *Noble* were just as loyal. You should ask your pirate man about them, perhaps.'

He faced Cole again. 'Back to the gate. Captain Coxon will accompany me as master. I will notify Lieutenant Scott. Keep a weather eye out for the rest of the scum. We will return to the ship with our new entourage and prepare to board that brigantine.'

'Aye, Cap'n.' Cole tapped his forehead, Williams likewise, and they beat their feet.

'Do not feel too bad, John.' Guinneys began to walk back

to Bessette's rooms; Coxon stepped beside him looking straight ahead. 'It is thanks to you that we arrived here in time. I most probably could not have done it with such vigour. But then I had no honour to restore. And, as for the gold, well, I will be posted captain for my part and you will not have to face the ignominy of a council inquiry.'

'And when do you kill me, William?' he asked calmly.

Guinneys laughed, softly. 'I have no wish to kill you, John.'

'But you will,' Coxon clarified.

Guinneys slowed. 'My orders are to ensure that as few souls as possible know the true fate of this gold. And, if I stumble upon a Jacobite plot, my duty will always be to my king. Talton's mishap was purely to remove any involvement of the company in all this. I have known those sods for a long time: their greed is only matched by their power. Although I am impressed that you were able to discern his fate out of the ordinary.'

'I am older than you are, William, but even so you should know there is no such thing as ordinary death on a man-of-war. Only wood, iron and blood. Everything else is suspect.'

'Then I will bow to your more common knowledge.' They had reached the threshold. 'Now let's see what this pirate really knows.'

The room was the same. Dandon still sat at the table, raising his head to the two officers as they entered, Guinneys stepping in first. Fauche still stood close to the wall, his eyes darting between everybody.

'Gentlemen,' Guinneys addressed the assembly grandly, 'we will return to the *Starling*. Your rescue has come.' He drew his Thuraine pistols with the silver plate locks. 'There has been a change of command and circumstance, however, that requires some minor adjustments.'

He fired his left-hand pistol, almost by accident, it seemed, into Fauche's side. All stared at the snaking smoke billowing from the black hole in Fauche's tunic, Fauche looking almost tenderly at the hole as he slid down the wall. His old leather hat became a pillow for his dying head as he lay awkwardly on his side, gurgling his surprise, wide-eyed to the whole room, his musket clattering to the floor a moment later.

The fury of the pistol broke the somnolent atmosphere that the heat of the afternoon had created like an iceberg crashing through the wall.

Coxon, as fast as thought, grabbed Guinneys' smoking left arm.

'Scott,' he cried, 'hold him with me, man! He's mad!'

Guinneys looked at Coxon as if he had merely been disturbed in a daydream.

'Unhand me, John!' He elbowed Coxon off.

Only then did Coxon notice that Scott had never moved. His pistol still pointed at Devlin, and he cocked it with a snap as the pirate's look changed to anger and menace.

'William,' Scott whispered calmly, 'was that completely necessary, old boy?'

Guinneys ignored the comment, pushing Coxon to the wall, his powder-stained hand clicking his second pistol into life and pointing it threateningly to Coxon's chest.

'Hold there, John, if you please.' He smiled.

'What in hell is this, Guinneys?' Coxon yelled.

'Change of plan, 'tis all.' He turned to Lieutenant Scott. 'If the others heard that, Richard, Coxon grabbed my pistol from me and shot the dog, understand?'

'Aye, William.' Scott nodded.

Guinneys eyed Dandon, who still sat, his mouth agape, then smiling as he caught Guinneys' stern gaze, his gold teeth glinting with charm. Both hands were flat on the tablecloth, innocent and still.

Guinneys moved on to Devlin and shoved a boot into his ribs. 'You! *Pirate!* Tell me about the gold.'

Devlin rocked slightly as the boot scraped between his ribs. 'I see the board still picks fine officers, Captain. These two do you proud.' He winked to Coxon.

Guinneys rapped his pistol across Devlin's temple, the small silver bead of the sight drawing pink above his brow. 'Talk to *me*, filth, not him.'

Devlin looked up at Guinneys, and slowly spoke. 'And what do you want to know, *Captain* Guinneys?' His voice low with hate.

'That boat on shore? That waits for you, I take it?'

Devlin's face never moved. 'No. That boat was there when we landed, Captain. I'll gladly swear on your life to that matter, Captain.'

'And what of your men? Are there any hiding around?'

'If there be, it is not to my mind. You say my ship is there. Then that's where my men be. Waiting for my frigate. I am abandoned, I don't doubt. As is the way. They wait, as your ship can't get in past the sand bar. So they wait for the frigate to escort them, I shouldn't wonder. They are short-handed. They would not fare well escaping from you alone.'

'And what of the frigate?' Guinneys shoved his boot again into Devlin's side.

'She was behind us. A day, I reckon. Nigh on a hundred souls. If she was coming, she'd be here.' Devlin looked at Scott and Guinneys in turn. 'I believe I am abandoned twofold.'

Guinneys seemed satisfied. He turned back to Coxon. 'You see, John? Boat was there all along. But I hold to the idea indeed that we are not alone.' He faced the room again. A small frosted bottle had appeared magically in his left hand, stopped with a square jade top, a similarly coloured liquid within the glass.

'Doctor,' he addressed the startled Dandon, 'I request you to administer some drops of this to the remaining guards in the mess.' He levelled his pistol at the startled Dandon. 'Unwillingly, naturally.'

Coxon was transfixed by the bottle. A scenario unfolded before his eyes where the same had been forced upon the unfortunate Edward Talton. A horrible play of struggle and panic in the cramped berth where Talton wrote his letters of disgust.

'Is that the same concoction you killed Talton with, William?' he asked coldly.

'The very same, John.' Guinneys bowed slightly. 'Sayak. An arsenic solidus brimstone mixture. Quite regal, in fact.'

Coxon had hoped that the insinuation of murder would provoke a query from Lieutenant Scott. None was forthcoming. Scott remained steadfastly focused on Devlin, his pistol dutifully aimed at his chest.

Coxon had never felt so powerless. The ship would change things. Bide your time. Get to the ship, back to Howard and Anderson, Surgeon Wood, Sailing Master Dawson. This madness would soon end. His thoughts trailed away, ending abruptly at the realisation that he was sharing a look with Devlin, who immediately lowered his gaze, feeling the same lack of control.

Dandon stood, his chair scraping, disturbing the flies that had begun to settle around Bessette's mottling face. Two dead men, quite strangely being ignored by all, as if they were merely sleeping cats, part of the elegant furniture.

'I do not wish to kill, monsieur,' Dandon said meekly.

'Put your pistol to the table, Doctor,' Guinneys ordered. 'You will go with Lieutenant Scott to the mess. Kill them all.'

Dandon slowly took out the small overcoat pistol and did as he was told. 'I must get some accoutrements from my chest, monsieur. May I?'

'Of course.' Guinneys smiled gracefully. 'Now, we shall retire outside, gentlemen.' He pulled Devlin up like baggage, showing mild surprise as Devlin stood a couple of inches above him. 'To the door, Richard.' Lieutenant Scott obeyed. 'Master Coxon, sir,' Guinneys said, 'if you would join us, please.'

Coxon bowed his head and followed Scott through the door outside into the golden day. Guinneys waited for Dandon to collect some cotton wadding and a thin glass tube. Then, his arm linked with the pirate Devlin, he pushed Dandon to follow Coxon and Scott to the next stage of his performance. They left the silent Bessette and Landri Fauche to stare ever vacant, diligently sitting watch over the ignored and lonely black chest, still waiting for more death, beneath the table.

Chapter Sixteen

*F*ortunately there were only three of the men left alive. By the time Dandon had reached the third, however, his soul had been swallowed irretrievably beneath his feet. He found a shard of consolation, of self-forgiveness, in that Scott's pistol watched every movement of his trembling hands.

As he drew yet another sample through the glass tube from the bottle, transferring it to a cup of wine, a sickness overcame him, a loathing for the gold and the travesty that his life had become.

Once, he had convinced his heart that he would have been a doctor in Bath Towne had it not been for the status of his birth, for the want of money. Now, as he passed the liquid over the pale lips of the last of the young Frenchmen, he knew what others had always known: it had been a slack and wanton nature, a lust for wine, for easy sleep and lazy days in the Caribbee sun. And it brought him here, watching the glassy-eyed wonder in a youth's eyes fade as he lowered the young man's head gently to the floor again.

Dandon stood and placed the cup down amongst the dead bottles. He felt weak, heavy. Wiping the glass tube with some wadding, he turned to face Scott shadowed in the doorway.

'I hope this matter has ended now, Lieutenant.' Dandon's French accent was subdued but never lost as he handed back the deadly bottle. 'I am going back to the room now to collect my chest. I will also be requiring a drink. You may shoot me, if you wish to refuse my request, and I may be thankful if you choose to do so, but I will die with a bottle in my hand. It is a promise I have made myself this day.'

He brushed past Scott, who passed one lingering look across the floor of the mess before closing the door and following Dandon.

In the glare of the sun by the gate, the assembly took on the air of a courtroom. By tradition, and by habit of living in fourteen inches to a man, the group took up a small area. The four men in slops and straw hats stood shoulder to shoulder, whilst Guinneys strutted up and down before them. Coxon stood with his back to the gate, the dust from Guinneys' turn pasting his stockings.

The pirate Devlin stood in pistol range before the sailors, his hands still tied behind him with the soft dainty cord from Bessette's bedchamber curtain. All the while Guinneys spoke, almost chanting a plan of action.

'We will retire to the shore with the pirate and his whores. We will take it that the ship will not fire on him or the women, but even so we will not tarry in reaching our own longboat. On rejoining the marines along the path, close order and loaded weapons are to be maintained. The women will walk outside of us on the premise that some pirates may remain in an attempt to rescue their captain. Our objective is to secure the gold from the pirate vessel. Once they perceive that their captain is lost, they will attempt to leave, at which we should give chase in the *Starling*.' He stopped, his Cordova boots white with dust.

'There is still the threat of the second vessel to contend with. Although you are no doubt as sure as I am that while our ship is made of three hundred acres of colonial oak, our hearts were cut from English trees. Is this not correct?'

A loud, stout affirmation from the men in checked blue wool.

'As ever it shall be.' Guinneys smiled. He watched the approach of Dandon and Lieutenant Scott. Dandon was struggling with his medicine cabinet and a bottle in his hand. 'Mister Scott,' Guinneys called, 'what situation do you have, ho?'

Scott saluted. 'Corporal Fauche will stay and bury the unfortunate, Captain. He will wait for the barque to come and relieve him.'

'Good,' Guinneys approved. 'Very well. We shall move from here to the shore.' He spun to Coxon. 'Master Coxon, you will take the pirate Devlin to the shore.' He turned swiftly round to the swaying Dandon, eyeing him up and down, noting he was still bald of weapons. 'Doctor, you should leave this place of death.'

Dandon had little doubt that his own death was forthcoming, but he bowed all the same before his gibbet.

'Do you feed your prisoners, Captain Guinneys?' Devlin asked as Coxon grabbed his elbow. 'I starve like an Irishman here.'

'Have no fear, pirate.' Guinneys moved towards the gate. 'You'll hang heavy.'

The lumbering walk up the path was hot and hard. The party had not truly noticed that the walk to the stockade meandered downhill. Now, the afternoon drew on the hunt of the evening insects, and the mournful cries of the slumbering birds began to fill the slow creep of the day as the strange troupe trekked across the island.

A collection of knees and gaily coloured dresses greeted

them at the turn of a corner. The women of Providence lay languidly amongst the fronds fringing the path, the pair of red-faced marines suddenly popping up like corks at the sight of the group that rounded the dusty bend.

They marched on, the women on the outside, should an attack occur. Every common man was cradling a musketoon or musket, his head eyeing the trees for shadows, the stock of his weapon slippery with sweat.

Coxon released his arm from Devlin to wipe a cuff down his sweating face. Devlin took the moment to talk.

'Captain, we find ourselves in a fine situation, do we not?'

Coxon left his hand free as they walked on. 'Had you not heard, Patrick? I be master now behind that fine young fellow.'

'Aye. Just a rumour, I'm sure.'

'What has become of you, Patrick?' Coxon shook his head. 'This life does not sort with how I raised you.'

'Come now, Captain. I was a man when we met. Blame yourself little. When I sailed off with Thorn and the *Noble* you were dying and I had more toes than coin. If I told you that I hold enough coin now to buy a horse to shy the king, what would you say?'

'Patrick, anyone can steal. Anyone. The pirate has always been. Always will. Sometimes they hide beneath the coats of gentlemen, but it all ends the same.' Solidly he met his servant's eyes. 'This will end the same. I know that. It's a small world for evil men.'

'Spoken like the son of a clergyman, Captain.' Devlin smirked.

'Your familiarity displeases me, Patrick,' Coxon snapped.

'No, Captain. I would call you John to displease you. I have belittled governors more.'

They had reached the break in the path that looked down to the *Lucy* in the bay.

'Your ship, Patrick. Where you left it. Where your frigate left you all. A pity. I had hoped to lay eyes on her.'

Almost a mile away to the east, the *Starling* sat glowing in the lowering sun, breathing on the swell like a sleeping infant, her sails furled like hammocks. No other ship filled the sea. No *Shadow* in the offing.

'As we were,' Coxon said. 'I hope you at least felt that gold, Patrick.'

'I may feel it still, Captain.' Devlin's face was oddly placid. 'The moon's a long way off.'

Guinneys turned with a shout. 'Master Coxon! Move that dog. Lively now, sir.'

'You're too old to dream, Patrick.' Coxon resumed the hand at Devlin's elbow and dragged him back to the group, now once again moving downhill. Devlin threw a single look to Dandon, who bowed his head from the gaze and busied himself with the encumbrance of his case.

'Tell me, Captain,' Devlin resumed his patter, 'why all this interest in a little of the devil's work?'

Coxon looked to Guinneys' back, noting the fine cut of his black silken coat that had not faded green across the shoulders like his own old cloth.

'It is of an opinion that you have been tempted to stray on a Jacobite path. That some intelligence, possibly Spanish, has guided you to this island to steal the gold.' He coughed a little. 'The purpose of which I am led to believe is to harm relations with our French allies and to fund a Stuart restoration, perhaps. And I myself may have some knowledge on the matter.' Coxon's voice rose higher, as if by changing tone he could wipe the unpleasant thought from his mind. He changed course. 'Pray, what happened on the *Noble*, Patrick? What of young Thorn?'

'Now, as I recall, the last time I saw Mister Thorn, he was swaying from a yardarm trying to catch as much shot as possible. Having decided to dispose of many of Mister Lewis's accoutrements.' Devlin briefly smiled at the thought.

'Ah, Mister Lewis. I had almost forgotten the pompous arse. How fares he? He was taken, I was told. A precious commodity, no doubt.'

'Aye. He had his eyes squeezed from his skull. Then we fed him to the porkers. Not very diplomatic, Mister Lewis, we found.'

Coxon stopped, staring at the stranger beside him. Devlin caught the interlude with a light smile. 'I took it upon myself to be navigator. With your own expertise as my guide, naturally.'

'Aye. That would be so. And what of any of my belongings? Did you hold on to any of them?' They were at the path to the beach now, the pace brisker as they moved down.

'I managed a sword, and some silver, Captain. And that silver tube of lighting sticks you were fond of.'

'Ho! The "Lucifers". Splendid. Good man. Where be they?'

Devlin nodded his chin towards the *Lucy*.

'Damn your eyes, Patrick!' Coxon snarled. 'My father's gift to me. You left them there?'

'I'm after hoping that I'll be bloody glad I did, Captain.' Devlin's look was serious and cold.

Guinneys raised a hand and the walking stopped. The sound of the sea kissing the sands wafted pleasantly to their ears. The same sound the world over.

They were between the two boats on the shore: the longboat from the *Starling*, the coxswain rising from his lump of cheese and hard tack, brushing the crumbs from his worsted jacket and the beer from his lips; and the small craft from the *Lucy*, innocent and serene.

Guinneys beckoned to one of the sailors. A canvas bag was opened and a spyglass passed silently to him. He swept it across the *Lucy* until the blinding glare of another dazzled back into his eye, causing him to curse.

Almost at the same moment, the white and gold pennant began to fall, and the ship became naked of colour save for the boulting cloth amongst the rigging.

'They have given up the pretence,' Guinneys acknowledged proudly. He passed back the brass instrument and strode across the sand to Devlin and Coxon, close enough to smell the wine on Devlin and the damp from Coxon's clothes.

'Master Coxon?' He grinned. 'I hold you to mark this pirate.' Without waiting for a response he turned to Devlin. 'Pirate, I intend to board your vessel. To retrieve the gold. Your men have no doubt seen you as our prisoner. I wish to know if they would resist now all is lost?'

'See for your own mind, Captain.' Devlin looked over Guinneys' head to the *Lucy*, and Guinneys looked in turn to see the gig being lowered hurriedly over the larboard side.

Guinneys' joy was almost holy. 'They flee! How very so! My, they fulfil my expectations of dogs!' He swung back to Devlin. 'What souls you gather around you, pirate.' He abandoned them both and ran to the larger group, shouting as he pounded over the sand. 'Scott! See they are not taking the chest! Cole! The women and the doctor to the longboat. Back to the ship. All to me and to the boat! *Marines!*'

Coxon watched the two marines gather like brides-maids at Guinneys' shoulders. Cole bustled the women to the coxswain, avoiding Coxon's eye, every whore winking, whistling or curtsying to a bowing Devlin as they skipped past.

'They run, Patrick,' he said. 'They always run.' More solemnly he added, 'I cannot save you, you know? You will hang.'

Devlin gave no answer other than the clenching of his jaw as he watched the boat descend and his crew scrambling into her.

Guinneys was next to Scott now, the excitement of near victory running through him, his hands nervously toying with one of his fine pistols.

'They are running, Richard!' he declared. 'Escaping on the gig! Can you believe such folly?'

'Perhaps they know something we do not, William,' Scott replied ambiguously.

'They know the *Starling* will run them down otherwise, man. I have an admiration for a man knowing he is whipped!' He slapped Scott's shoulder. 'We have the gold, Richard! To the boat. We'll board and run them down with their own guns.'

He turned to weigh up his band. The marines would board with him and Scott. Williams would return a pistol to Coxon to guard the pirate Devlin, then return to the ship with the women, the French doctor and Cole. The two remaining sailors, his company of old, Davies and Gregory, he recalled, would remain with Coxon.

'There's no chest with them anyways,' Scott observed with a shading palm to his brow. 'They have probably filled their pockets with what they can, William.'

'As will I, Richard, have no fear. To it, man! They are lowering the gig!'

The two of them flew to the quarterboat, dogged by the two lumbering marines.

Coxon and Devlin watched silently. They were some distance from the rest of the crowd. Williams appeared in front of them, handing Coxon his pistol and repeating Guinneys' orders that he was to stay along with Gregory and Davies as guard to the pirate.

'What's to happen when Captain Guinneys secures the ship, Williams?'

'Don't know, sir. We're returning to the ship with that French doctor and those…ladies. Guessing the captain will come back after. Once the ship and gold be ours.' He smiled uncomfortably. 'Excuse I, sir. I best get that doctor aboard.' With that he turned and went humbly to Dandon.

Dandon bowed at Williams, who obliged him by picking up his chest. Dandon passed by Devlin and Coxon and bowed again, returning upright without spilling a drop of wine or breaking his stride as he ambled to the longboat, now full of cackling women.

Devlin could not read him. He accepted that he might be lost to him, but without blame. Somehow Dandon was close to saving his own skin, and Devlin imagined this was how it had always been with the yellow-coated scoundrel.

'Filthy brute that one' – Coxon watched Dandon's back recede – 'even for a Frog.'

The sound of the quarterboat running into the surf with a bounding of legs brought them back to the matter of the *Lucy*. Devlin and Coxon watched for a moment as the two officers rowed, whilst the marines half crouched with their muskets high, ready to lower and fire in a moment if need be.

'Tell me now, Patrick,' Coxon said, checking the pan on his pistol. 'Out of the merest nod to our history. Are there any more of your men on this island?'

Devlin watched Dandon and the longboat creep slowly away.

'I am the only pirate here, Captain. And you'll live if you want to.'

Coxon could contain himself no longer. The sanctimony of Guinneys; the impudence of his former man turned brigand, shaming his patronage. He stopped the examination of his pistol to bring its brass cap up like the kick of a horse under Devlin's jaw. His right foot then adopted his finest shooting stance, before he cocked the pistol and levelled it at Devlin's writhing form upon the sands.

'How dare you! How dare you, dog! To speak to me! To speak of death to me!' He felt himself being pulled backwards by the rough hands of Davies and Gregory, who had come up silently to wrestle him away.

'Easy now, sir,' Davies begged in his hollow Welsh tones. 'Don't be denying a man a living by shooting him now.'

Devlin rolled up, his head reeling. His eyes were fixed on the *Lucy*, and on the quarterboat, a cable-length from her now. He spat onto the sand a small wad of blood and smiled wickedly.

'*Row*, you swabs!' Hugh Harris yelled at the four Dutchmen. '*Row!*' His yells were unnecessary, the broad blond men could row up a mountain, and already the *Lucy* had begun to shrink. They aimed for the rocks, to get round the corner of the island where the mangrove trees hung over the waters, away from any guns, away from everything.

Sam Fletcher sat giggling, clutching the bundles of maps and oilskins from the cabin. Dan Teague had two pistols in his hands, his eyes watchful on the *Lucy*'s deck. Rattling around the pirates' feet beneath the sheets were as many swords and firearms as they could throw into the gig, a man's-weight worth, and more stashed around every fold of clothing.

'Ho!' Sam Morwell cried with a pointing hand. 'They're aboard!'

All looked to their ship wistfully, at the sight of strangers upon her; then all yelled at the Dutchmen to row faster.

The quarterboat, pushed by the tide, and pulled like a magnet to the *Lucy*'s hull, had banged home. There was the usual ungraceful fumbling of pushing and heaving, until Scott scampered up the freeboard and belayed the boat and one by one each man clambered through the entrance port.

They spread out, the four of them, weapons drawn, moving slowly across the deck, expecting some form of trap. Scott looked scornfully at the unkempt nature of the ship, the swab buckets rolling empty, the mess of broken ropes and untidy sheets. The only sounds were the living creak of the rigging, the faint rattle of chain and the anxious chattering of the hens in the coop behind the mainmast.

'The ship is ours, gentlemen!' Guinneys grinned. He ran to the larboard gunwale, to spy the gig rolling away, already out of pistol shot. 'The cowards! Scott, let's give them a taste.' His eyes fell to the six-pounders either side of him, the gig perfectly framed between them. Scott joined him, then gave him the bad news.

'They've spiked them all, William. Tompions in every one. The starboard guns also.'

Guinneys swore inwardly, then yelled behind, 'Musket! Marine to me!'

'They be out of range, sir!' Fellowes, a Guildford man, now regretting his move to Portsmouth, carried his gun forward.

'I did not ask for your opinion, man!' Guinneys snorted,

and grabbed the weapon, instantly, expertly, familiarising himself with its length and weight, and brought it to his shoulder.

He sighted through the narrow V and brought the bead down on the mass of bodies in the gig. His breathing stopped. The gig rocked up and down before him, bobbing like a reef marker, and on the down roll he fired.

His eyes smarted as the saltpetre smoked. His reward being only the small splash of water more than fifty yards short of the gig. Cursing, he threw the gun back at Fellowes's chest.

'Never mind, lads.' He stepped back and turned his gaze to the open, inviting cabin. All with the same thought, to a man, they rushed to its dark interior, skidding into the open cabin.

It did not take long to surmise the cabin that had belonged to Seth Toombs. It was bare, scattered with papers and broken ship's lamps. The air hung with the smell of cordite, damp and a mist of smoke, as if a spirit with a pipe had stepped past them and onto the deck.

Only one object remained: the table, which in the dim light had taken on the form of an altar.

A black cloth lay upon it, almost to the floor, in much the same way as the green velvet cloth covered the dining table in the quarters of the unfortunate Captain Bessette.

Unsettled by the black sight, Guinneys and Scott cocked their pistols, and all moved to look down at the grinning white skull almost filling the table. Vaguely they realised that the skull sat in a compass rose, the cardinal points spiking viciously outwards and a pair of bone-like pistols crossed beneath.

'Their flag, I presume?' Scott asked the room.

'Undoubtedly,' Guinneys agreed, his eyes now drawn to

the silver tube that lay on the side of the table, the only other object upon it.

Cautiously, as if it might bite, he picked it up. 'What the devil is this?' Not acknowledging the humour in his words, he noticed the smiling horned engraving staring back at him. He opened it, revealing nothing within. An empty, pointless cylinder. 'How odd,' he said. 'Wonder what it's for?'

Guinneys looked up to Scott, who looked around the room as if following the path of a fly. 'What do you suppose this is, Richard?'

'Sorry, William?' Scott's face was perturbed; then he looked at the silver tube. 'I don't know, William. Can you hear that noise?'

The two marines also looked anxiously about them, as the crackling hiss slowly began to fill the room.

Guinneys noticed it then, directly around the table, at his very feet. His fist closed on the tube and he bent to the floor as the source of the sound most definitely emanated from beneath the table.

As one might lift the linen from the face of the deceased in a parlour to pay final respects, Guinneys raised the black cloth from the floor, then swept it up as the horror came upon him.

He stood back, his eyes widening. The others stared in cold mortification at the six white oak barrels of powder that were slowly sucking in the coiled fuse, the one that Hugh Harris had wrapped around his elbow and hand for fifty counts. Fifty lengths, to time for one quarter-hour, or five hundred yards of distance between himself and the kegs.

Thomas Howard stood by the larboard gunwale, watching the longboat on its almost painful crawl back to her home. The boy was dwarfed by Midshipmen Granger and Davison, two years his senior but two years beneath his commission; and so although at table they tweaked his ears and put salt in his tea, on deck they stood out of his shadow and followed Midshipman Howard's word, after that of Lieutenant Anderson, who stood with the glass to his eye at the fo'c'sle, watching all that occurred on the beach almost a mile distant.

Once, some years ago now, before the sea, Anderson had been at a party, in Woolhampton, at the vile home of some wildly successful cheesemonger, the daughter of whom had had a very vivacious chaperone that Anderson had chosen to attend to.

He recalled how there had been a show by some local chap, in which a large black cylinder placed upon a gaming table had been rotated by crude handle and with great enthusiasm. Somehow, when a lighted candle was placed inside the cylinder, and all were seated in fascination before the spinning drum, one could see the form of a horse running as fast as life before one's eyes, flickering in motion, through narrow vents cut in the cylinder's sides.

Anderson had applauded, along with everyone else, and participated in the exchange of smiles, but between himself and the chaperone he confessed that he had found the flickering motion detracting from the miracle. The horse had jerked before his eyes, moving in rapid stages rather than flowing like a rippling beast in nature.

The explosion of the *Lucy* before his isolated eye behind the scope reminded him of the movement of the horse. As if a hand were ripping it away, the quarterdeck flew skywards from the small ship, almost intact before his eye, sawing the mizzen in two, followed by a cloud of black smoke and spiralling wood cascading through the air like straw.

Anderson's left eye opened in awe; he lowered the scope,

and was instantly removed from the scene that he had momentarily been a part of.

The sound hit then. A distant thunder roll, hastily chased by a momentous crack that tore the air of the bay and pulled all the sound from his ears, so he stood in a world of stillness and calm.

The little ship ducked almost beneath the water as another explosion ripped through the main deck, accompanied by the terrifying sight of the cannons imploding, for they had only been spiked after being double-shotted and crammed with powder, sending a golden bloom of fireworks into the air.

A third tremor ripped through the bowels of her keel, the updraught of which kept the *Lucy*'s sails billowing around the whole spectacle, held tight by the stubborn mainmast that had always forbidden itself to let go even through the hardiest storms. The bowsprit catapulted free, only to be snapped back like a whip by the elderly mainstay, for that had also learned long ago from the mainmast never to give in.

But now the decks were full of the crushing sea, and barrels had already begun to bubble upon the surface of the boiling water, covered by the gay flotsam of clothes and hammocks.

With an awful drawing howl like the moaning of a whale, the brigantine that had sailed new from Bristol to all the ports of Africa's slave coast, to unnamed islands of the Antilles, the archipelagos of the Americas and the frozen haunts of Nova Scotia, laid herself in pieces on the shallow shore of an unknown island somewhere north of the Caymans, south of Cuba.

The wave hit the *Starling*, sending water up to the gun ports, the splash of which awoke the young officers from the mournful sight that they did not understand.

It was Thomas Howard who spoke first. 'Did we not see Guinneys go aboard there, Mister Anderson?' He lifted his head fore.

'Aye,' Anderson agreed. 'We did indeed, Mister Howard.'

Anderson shivered, then gathered himself to look to the longboat still bobbing, oars motionless, frozen in time as her crew watched the mainmast of the *Lucy* hovering above the white, sandy water. 'Boat there! Row, and get those passengers aboard!' His first thought was to get back to the island. Coxon was there. Officers were dead. A ship had exploded before his eyes and he was sure Coxon had seen such terrors before.

There was a cold, unfamiliar feeling crawling over Mister Anderson's back and, in an unwelcome recollection, his father, Vice Admiral Anderson, grinned at him over his porter before a crackling peat fire and whispered about such a feeling, hoping his son would know it someday.

'Move, man! To me!' he shouted to Cole in the boat, who instantly put his back to work.

Dandon had been sitting quietly until the *Lucy* had shattered his solemnity. He watched now as the ocean calmed itself again and small blazing rafts of deck began to drift away from the wreck and the black smoke already wafted above the peaks of the island.

He turned to gaze behind him, away from the horrified ladies, to watch the play of tiny figures on the beach. A smile crept to his lips from behind his gold teeth as he looked up again to the almost volcanic cloud hovering over the island, climbing higher and higher.

He laughed, slapping his thigh. 'Aye, that'd do it! Sure enough, that'd do, God damn you, sir!' He suddenly felt like a dog locked in the butcher's shop to stop him eating the bread from the baker's next door. He cocked a wink at Cole, who had screwed up his brow at the colonial accent coming from the French doctor's mouth.

Devlin still sat. He had watched the explosion and the backs of the three men with him fold up in instinct. With a foul slap, something landed at his feet that resembled the poor man's delicacy of a dried, baked sow's ear.

He looked closer to see the row of white teeth grinning along its side, and he took that as the moment to stand and peel free the pretence of the knot that tied his wrists.

Chapter Seventeen

*D*evlin sang. He moved whilst the others still ducked as the black smoke trailed over the beach carried by the so'west breeze and they stared at him as at a madman.

> *Oh I have a house.*
> *And I have some land,*
> *And I have a daughter that shall be at your command,*
> *If you sink her in that lonely lonesome water,*
> *If you sink her in that lonesome sea . . .*

His hands were outstretched, demonstrating their freedom. He had walked free of Coxon's side and crossed back to stand directly in front of him.

'I told you, John. You could live if you want to,' and he grabbed Coxon's pistol hand, tickling the weapon loose as swiftly as he used to tickle the salmon in days of old.

Gregory and Davies half watched the dying ship, half watched Devlin weave behind Coxon and stab the muzzle into his spine before they remembered they had weapons of their own.

'Have you completely gone, Patrick?' Coxon exclaimed. 'You have no ship! No men! Nothing! Unhand me!'

'Come, John, is this not how it's always been? Myself standing behind you?'

Coxon felt Devlin's hand grip his collar, his knuckles brush tense against his neck as he held him fast. 'Davies! Shoot him, man!' he ordered.

Davies and Gregory held their weapons waist high, their barrels pointed to the body of the two men, the dog-heads still resting against the pan, modestly threatening.

'Let the captain go now, lad,' Gregory growled, sure now that Coxon had been reappointed. 'There's nowt else left to do.'

Devlin ignored them. They were sailors. Hands and backs. He had never been one of them. If they killed him, they would tell everyone they would ever meet; their children would tell their children. If he killed them, it would simply be two more to his tally for his day at Execution Dock.

Instead he chose to stand fast, to take a moment of pride in telling Coxon's ear that he had that very morning handed the silver tube of lighting sticks, which unfortunately had shrunk to one, to the bastard son of a bastard, to blow the ship if he arrived on the beach in chains, to blow the ship if she were approached, to blow the ship and send the gold in pieces to the sands.

'And then what, you fool?' Coxon snarled. 'I have almost a hundred men on that ship! Release me and I promise you'll hang in England. You'll have weeks to live instead of hours.'

'Typical of an Englishman to give an Irishman the honour of some English rope. How fine you are to me, John.' He looked up to Davies and Gregory. 'Now, gentlemen, you have done grand today. If you go for me, I will kill your captain, be most assured. Then you will have the honour of dropping me, and the double honour of justifying to your officers why, when it be plain to all that a boat of men will be over shortly to end my desperation and remove your position and ease your present troubles.'

Davies and Gregory's minds took in the soft words. They looked for confirmation or command between the pirate and their captain.

'Throw the arms away,' Devlin soothed. 'As close to the sea as you can, and wait for your officers, and this'll all be done soon enough.'

'Davies!' Coxon boomed. 'I'll see you hanged if you loose your weapon! Mark me, man! Gregory! Shoot Davies if he drops his gun!'

'He has a point, Captain.' Gregory's voice faltered. 'The boat's already at the *Starling*. The others will be here soon.'

True enough, the longboat had reached the ladder home. The women clambered up first, being helped through the entrance port by the hand of Thomas Howard, who reminded them all of some young man or another, or so they told him as they curtsied and he blushed.

The crew were occupied with reeving ropes to lower the captain's gig from its resting place above the hatch between the masts. Aft, the jolly-boat was already being lowered from the stern, with fifteen of the toughest young 'uns Anderson could find.

'Mister Howard!' Anderson yelled from the fo'c'sle. 'See those women are removed to the comfort of the Great Cabin, if you please, sir! No lolling now!'

Howard saluted, and guided the throng aft, just as Dandon pulled himself through the port, amused at the thought of an English deck beneath his feet.

'And who are you, sir?' Anderson called below. Dandon turned and removed his hat. Enthralled by the activity and noise all around, so different from the languid, laughing times of the pirate vessels, he returned to his French attitude.

'Forgive me, monsieur. I am *médecin* for the island. I

have been rescued by the mercy of your great Capitaine Coxon.'

Anderson tipped his hat. 'Lieutenant Anderson. Monsieur, avail yourself of our hospitality by removing yourself from my deck. Mister Granger, kindly take this man to Doctor Wood's quarters, if you will.'

Dandon lifted a suggesting finger. 'Ah, if I may, Lieutenant, your good capitaine has distinguished me with an appointment to chaperone the affairs of the ladies.'

'Very well. Mister Granger, take this fellow where he may do least damage.'

'And my case, Lieutenant? The chest of my trade?'

Anderson bellowed to Cole and Williams to bring the chest aboard, then return to the boat to accompany him and as many souls as the longboat could carry back to the island.

Davies and Gregory's weapons lay idly on the shore, their muzzles staring out to sea. The men themselves sat, covered in shame, eyes also seaward, watching the three boats drawing slowly towards them from the *Starling*. Their arms rested on their knees, straw hats pulled low on their heads, a head-turn and several feet away from the pirate and their captain.

'You may have half an hour remaining to you, Patrick,' Coxon stated. 'I will probably try you on the shore, if I mind to.'

'You have no horse and cart to hang me from, Captain. No derrick.' Devlin sighed.

'I need a tree and some rope. I have acres of both.'

They rested opposite each other. Coxon in white shirt and waistcoat sat upon his coat. Devlin posed on one knee, gun in hand at Coxon's chest, aware of and constantly passing a glance to the packed boats, inching like the dawn to break his peace.

'Tell me, John.' Devlin grinned. 'Why do you not suppose that I have fifty men behind me in those jungles, waiting for your gallant lads? Why so sure that I have lost?'

Coxon calmly lifted the crossbelt over his head and set the cutlass down beside him, far enough away to cause no alarm in the pirate. There was a relief of cool sweat where the belt had been hanging across his shoulder. 'I was of a notion to tell Guinneys my thoughts. That there was one situation that vexed me, that did not ring.'

'And what was that, John? Do tell.'

'You were *still* here,' he said. 'There was a boat on the shore. You had taken the gold upon your ship, and had stayed to be captured by that yellow buffoon and a Frog corporal. No sense in that, Patrick. To my mind.'

'I stayed with a couple of my men to gather arms and belly timber. That is all.'

'Nonsense,' Coxon snorted. 'I am also of the mind that you have no men on this island else we would be with them now. But' – he paused, speaking slower now – 'you are not desperate, and that intrigues too much. A desperate man would have dragged me back to the fort where he has a loaded cannon, food, arms. Time even. Time to forestall the beating of drums…' Coxon was looking to the trees high up behind them, stretching out of the jungle, their waving heads being caressed by the smoke from the wreck. 'But you don't go back to the fort. Why not, Patrick?'

Devlin kept his eyes to the sea, turning his back to Coxon. 'My time cometh. I'm prepared for that. I have one shot. I have all I need.'

Coxon spoke his words as if counting coins. 'One boat on

the shore. You still in the fort. Your brigantine blown to hell.'

'You have become undone, Captain. Hush now.' Devlin sounded as confident as he could now that he could hear the shouts of the coxswain.

Coxon gleamed with satisfaction as the inevitable clicked within him. 'The gold is still *there*! That's what jiggered in my head! Tell me I'm right, Patrick.' Coxon even laughed. 'Ho! You poor, fool boy! You don't even have the gold!' He rocked on his haunches, powered by his mirth. 'And all your men have run!' He laughed harder, hoping to make Devlin turn his head from the boats and show him his crestfallen face.

Devlin did not turn. He had not moved as Coxon laughed at his back. Coxon breathed deep, sated from his laughter, and watched the last of the fires die out on the water. 'You could have left with the gold, Patrick. You had the fort. Yet you did not. Why? Why would you stay?'

Devlin still did not turn round. Coxon could make out Anderson's face amongst the throng in the longboat.

'Ah! Of course!' Coxon snarled. 'We had you, did we not? We came before you had a chance to remove the blessed fortune. Cornered you like a mouse. That is it! Am I not right, Patrick? Trapped you before you had a chance to signal for help. Before events and the Lord got the best of you, my boy!'

Devlin turned then. There was a look of beatitude, an air of calm about him as if he had come to the beach merely for the beauty of the afternoon.

'Aye,' he said as if to a child, 'I had no manner at all, John, of telling a soul that events had gone astray. If only I had prepared for such calamity, as you yourself might have done.'

He stood up, using the pistol to beckon Coxon back and up away from the beach, out of musket range from the longboat.

Coxon's mind raced ahead; a panic chilled his blood as he looked to the black smoke, the only cloud in the sky hanging morbidly above their heads and he realised the other reason why Devlin had blown the ship.

Without a thought of the pistol and its bearer, he sprinted to the shore, stamping on his coat and cutlass, racing past Gregory and Davies, who stood, pulled up by Coxon's breeze as he hurtled past. He splashed into the crystal spume, his hands cupped to his mouth, aiming his bellow to Anderson.

'Get back to the *ship!*' he yelled. 'Get back! Get back *now!*' He watched Anderson's face mouth something in return. They were still a few hundred yards out and Coxon hurled his voice like a spear. '*Pirates!* The *pirates*! Get back to the ship! Get back to the bloody *ship!*'

Dandon reclined on the cushioned lockers by the stern window, savouring a glass of Coxon's Bordeaux. Idly he brushed the white powdery sand from his crossed left-leg stocking and worn-out shoe.

Either side of him women lolled, peacefully, merrily emptying Coxon's decanters down their necks. Others sat around the table, wolfing bread and cheese, awaiting the sausage and sauerkraut that Midshipman Howard had trotted off to fetch.

'So, Dandon.' Annie belched from the captain's table, blowing crumbs from her bread-filled cheeks. 'What happens now? We be prisoners or what?'

'I think not, Annie.' He smiled. 'We are guests. Although it may be a temporal circumstance. I would keep your shoes on. For once.'

Annie resumed her feast, discovering the delight of grapes and cheese in the same mouthful. Dandon leaned back with warm contentment.

He admired the women greatly. They bent like trees in the storm, accepted everything and expected nothing. Their history was always a day old and they asked only for a full belly by twilight's end.

If he could do one good endeavour this day, to charm his soul back to peace, it would be to treat them like a handful of eggs and return them safely to their nest.

He cast an eye out of the starboard window. The comfort and warmth of the cabin, the flowing wine, took him back for a moment to a time he waited in a tavern, just as comforting, back on a Virginian road, for a carriage to take him to the port and to the Bahamas with dreams of salterns and riches. The day he waited, wearing the same coat, but with the stolen purse of his master swelling his pocket. A similar pane of lead-rimmed glass between him and destiny, waiting for the sound of hooves rocketing into the courtyard, or for the next fellow to enter the inn and lay a hand on his shoulder and ask him to come along.

Today the waiting was the same. The comfort came from not having control of which came first. Just drink, eat a little, and wait for the hand on the shoulder or the carriage to take you away.

He found himself straining to see the eastern edge of the island, his cheek almost against the pane to see as wide an area as he could, only to find the imperfections of the glass breaking up the ocean as if it were built of bricks.

'How long will that bloody boy be with my sausage?' Annie squealed, breaking Dandon's gaze.

'I'm sure he will be here soon, my dear Annie. And, please,

all of you, eat well. And stay in this room. I may leave, for a moment only, but I will return. Promise your friend, and doctor, that you will only open the door to myself after I am gone.'

'Why?' Sarah asked.

'It will prompt and encourage me to return. I may need such a vow.' He returned to his watch upon the window.

'You are touched, Dandon. You know that?' Annie jerked her chin upwards.

'Never to mind, my lady: I have an elixir for your touch, I shouldn't wonder.' He grinned at them all in a sweep of the room, just as Midshipman Howard came in with a box brimming with gastronomic delights, struggling to place it down under the swarm of kisses that hammered his flushing cheeks.

'Mister Howard,' Dandon pipped. 'May I enquire as to what occurs above?'

'Strangest matter, sir,' Howard exclaimed. 'The boats are swimming back! Everyone is in an eel of a flap!' He looked about at the disarray of the cabin, his eyes drawn to the captain's cot and the three pairs of white legs dangling there.

'Ah,' Dandon sighed. 'I had heard tell of another ship of pirates attached to this Devlin. Perhaps it has been seen?'

'Oh, no, sir.' Howard's voice was shrill. 'But here's to hoping. I am gunner captain no less, after all, and I am acting lieutenant with Mister Davison!'

'You have fought before, then?' Dandon asked.

'No, sir. Practice all. But Captain Coxon has drilled us fine. Two barrels of powder-worth. I should return to welcome Lieutenant Anderson and beg your leave.'

Dandon stood and looked around for his hat. 'Captain Coxon is returning also? And the pirate Devlin?'

'Not to my eye, sir.' Howard backed out of the cabin. 'You must excuse me for my duty, sir.'

'Mister Howard?' Dandon stepped a pace forward. Howard cocked an eyebrow. 'I will be on deck shortly.' He smiled to the boy. 'Join me if you find a moment, won't you? Perhaps allay my nerves a little with a small tour?'

Howard awkwardly raised the corner of his mouth. 'Aye sir, if I can,' and clicked the door softly closed.

Devlin watched the yells and confusion as the three boats reversed their rowing. He had moved down to Coxon's coat and picked up the crossbelt and sword with one hand, passing it with ease over his head.

Coxon and his two sailors still paid him no mind. He contemplated running for the comparative safety of the stockade. No, he was master here, still the lion amongst the lambs.

He bent down and travelled his hands through Coxon's coat, finding a pouch of prepared cartridges and a generous lump of dried beef, smiling at the remembrance of Coxon's old habit.

Sucking and chewing on the leathery hide, eyeing the world about him like a twelve-point stag stepping out at dawn, daring the hunt, he laboured his mind once more towards that which he knew, and that which he did not.

Peter Sam was to come to the island, attack the *Lucy*, encourage the French to rescue his gallant, motley-dressed crew. Upon which moment, his pirates would seize the island, reinforced by the threat of a heavily crewed frigate yonder.

That had not happened.

An English frigate had happened, captained by his former master. An unfortunate hand of cards that he had lost.

He swallowed a mouthful of the salty meat, the weight of which rang in his empty stomach. Then there was the other plan. The one that he had hidden from all who did not need to know, '*lest someone tries to hang you for it*', or, worse to the hearts of men, betrays you for its worth.

Over narrow flame, the candlelight shivering in the lack of air in the *Shadow*'s hot Great Cabin weeks before, an accord was reached between Black Bill, Peter and their captain, before they parted ways past Cabo San Antonio.

Should the island be 'with company' they were to hold back and wait for a signal that all was well, or all was hell, and act as their own code required.

Hands were shook, pistols sworn upon. But weeks at sea with nothing but the horizon to remind one of the future can change men's ideals, promises just words now and, as Guinneys had remarked, '*What souls you gather around you, pirate.*'

Wait, then. He looked at the pistol. One pistol. One shot. Devlin would not hang. He resumed his bold stance, his shield of confidence.

'Ho, John!' A rampant holler. 'I am glad you still keep the end of the beef before a battle!'

Coxon twisted slowly round, Davies and Gregory following like sheep. Coxon was satisfied that the boats had turned, although the frustration of still being prisoner on Devlin's island swelled bitterly within him.

He became aware of the soaking of his shoes, envying the bare feet of his fellows; a small thing, but it sharpened his hate.

He walked out of the surf, stockinged feet heavy, and he cast an eye to the musketoons resting in the sand.

'Davies, Gregory,' he said calmly, 'run for your guns. Cut him down.'

Silently, Davies and Gregory calculated the drop Devlin had on them, with the black eye of his pistol steadfastly and faithfully readied against their tomorrow.

'Best not, Captain,' Gregory mumbled. Then, 'He would fire upon you first, I'm sure.' Honour retained.

Coxon held out his right hand. 'Your cutlass, Gregory,' he commanded.

'Sir?'

'Hand it to me.' Coxon's eyes fixed on the silhouette of the pirate.

Gregory protested, reminding all to draw attention to the pistol opposing them.

'Your cutlass,' Coxon continued. 'I have the measure of this man. Naught else but a coxcomb. He will not shoot me.' The crude wooden hilt slid into his fist. 'For then you would go for him. He would have no ransom.'

He weighed the cutlass with a dip and rise of his wrist. No balance. Blade heavy. A butcher's cleaver. 'He needs me alive far more than I can stand to look at him living.' Already Coxon had left their side, stepping up the beach towards the pirate.

Devlin's palm tightened around the pistol, then grew looser as Coxon's steps came near.

'Hold, John,' he voiced. 'I will drop you yet.'

'Face me now, Patrick!' Coxon yelled. 'If your men come, I'll show them your head!' His blood was in his temples now, his skull a boiling cauldron.

Devlin's belt took the pistol, its bulk pressing into his gut. His hand passed to the French-made cutlass, its lighter blade almost flying free.

He stepped back, arms open, cutlass almost behind him, inviting Coxon to dance. He lowered his head, part crouched, keeping his weight low and spread wide. He did not speak. He saved his air as if about to dive from a sinking deck. The two began to pace a circle in the sand, measuring out their area of quarter.

'This is folly, John.' Devlin smiled. 'We have no bones against each other.'

Coxon felt peace now, as if decision, the realisation of imminent death, brought tranquillity. He stopped. A body's length from Devlin.

'You will find, Patrick' – he checked his blade, the sun dull upon its grey metal – 'that men have very little against one another. Yet they kill.' He dived towards Devlin's left side, a feint attack to bring the pirate's sword arm into a defence.

Devlin edged back from the thrust, keeping his sword aside. Coxon raised his, stepping closer, sideways to Devlin's blade as he spoke.

'That is *my* cutlass, Patrick. I will take it from you.'

''Tis not the first of yours that I have taken. Although that one be with my ship upon the bed there.'

Before the end of Devlin's words, Coxon sprang forward, sword swinging.

The chime of steel sang across the beach as Devlin met the blow. They pushed each other back silently, shared one sharp breath and clashed again and again, faster now, spinning across the beach, etching their brawl with the sliding and dancing of their feet into its white powdery sand.

Gregory and Davies stood and watched the display, inched together, whispering as if gossiping behind fans at the edge of some ballroom.

Gregory looked idly to the musketoons, being kissed slightly by the lazy Caribbean tide. 'We could get the guns. That'd settle it, don't you think?'

Davies threw a fleeting eye to the weapons and tipped back his straw headpiece. 'Best not confuse the thing, Mister Gregory. A gentleman like Captain Coxon would most likely settle us for disturbing a matter of honour. Or whatever it is he's doing.'

Both men looked up as a thud and a curse indicated that blows from legs and fists had now come into the battle. A scuffle ensued, then broke, clumsily, reluctantly, as if unseen arms had heaved them apart.

Swiftly, in the heat, in the hunger and the thirst, the fury began to seep away. Coxon and Devlin circled, their nostrils flared, their chests heaving, swords dragging them down.

'Surrender to me now, Patrick,' Coxon gasped, 'and I'll let you be drunk when they hang you. There is no ship. You have put your trust in pirates.'

'I have no wish to kill you, John.' Devlin straightened, reversed his stride, his sword arm furthest from Coxon. 'We are fighting over nothing. French gold that your own precious board wanted to steal. If you lay down now to me, I'll grant you safety from my men. Drop your sword, John.'

'I have a great deal to fight about, *pirate*!' Coxon spat. 'The very least of which is that you *will* stop calling me by my bloody Christian *name*!' And he dived again for Devlin's side.

Devlin's left arm snapped out and latched on to the billowing sleeve of Coxon's thrusting arm, pulling the surprised captain through the air as he spun, Coxon's own momentum sending him rolling ungracefully into the sand, where he lay sputtering and cursing as Devlin walked slowly over.

'What is it about the gentlemen I meet of late and the powerful desire they have that I will not use their lawful name?'

His shadow fell on Coxon, who brought his left hand to his brow, half to shade his eyes, half to rub away the salty sand and silica. Devlin let his sword fall to the sand.

'This ends now,' he said. His words were followed by the drawing of his pistol. Coxon began to rise, his progress halted by the weight of a boot pushing him down; his eyes were gripped by the gaping barrel staring back at him. He opened his mouth to speak as Devlin pulled the trigger.

Gregory and Davies darted forward at the sound of the shot, then froze as they heard their captain cry out, more in anger than submission. They watched Devlin turn to face them with the smoking gun. Already his teeth were biting the paper off a cartridge. Coxon rolled up to his knees. His right forearm now sported a crushed red rose. He slapped his left hand to the rose, which suddenly grew a scarlet glove as the blood poured.

Gregory and Davies turned to the musketoons at the shore and scrambled to them, almost on all fours, their heads running away before their legs.

Their hands landed on the comforting wooden stocks a second later but pulled away just as fast, as both laid sight of the small boat rowing into shore, bristling with raised swords and muskets, hauled effortlessly along by the four giant Dutchmen.

Devlin looked up to the boat as he rammed the wad home upon the powder and ball. He turned to Coxon, who had dragged off his cambric necktie, placed one end between gritted teeth, and was tying it tight round his arm to staunch the blood.

'This ends now, John. I hold that you can live if you want to. Mark me.' Devlin's ears were deaf to the cursing and bile howling forth from Coxon's mouth as he calmly picked up both swords and walked to his men.

On the quarterdeck of the *Starling*, Sailing Master Dawson was the only soul still maintaining a sweep of the horizon. His head and eye ached from the bright light and the slight deviation of shade between the blue sky and the endless line of the earth. He looked out westward.

Below his gaze, he had missed the tiny boat of pirates creeping back to the island, looking only for the telltale triangle of white that might mark a sail miles distant.

In the darkness around his concentration and closed eye came the sounds of men hauling, wet feet slapping up and down the decks, the banging of wooden hammers that never seemed to stop as some soul spent forever repairing something, and amidst the sleepy creak of the rigging some fool had found the time to be piping a tune and, yes, of all things, there was the happy wail of a fiddle also.

Aware that somewhere near him Midshipman Granger would be standing erect and stiff, he spoke, never dropping his vigil.

'Mister Granger, is it apt that there be time for the men to be fifing at this hour?'

Granger swung round from his watch. 'I beg your pardon, sir?'

Dawson sighed and lowered the glass. 'A tune, man. Can you not hear that awful drone?'

Granger cocked an ear around the ship. 'I hasten to say I can hear nothing, Mister Dawson. What sort of tune?'

In truth, now his focus had shifted, Dawson could no longer hear the noise. He looked to the island in the distance. The bulk of it like a giant fortress rising out of the sea, sound could echo from it, to be sure, but the music was not from the island.

He passed his gaze over the busy deck, the heads of the crew, the furled sails, trying to filter out the annoying sounds of work, until the pitch carried back to him again.

'There!' he said. 'Plain as day, a pipe and a fiddle. A dancing tune, hear it now, man!'

Granger shook his head. 'I do not, sir. But I shall check below.'

'No...' Dawson moved in front of Granger, dreamlike in concentration. 'It's not on the ship...' He raised his glass to the eastern cape of the island. His vision was swamped by luscious green at first, until he drew it over to the seascape.

The din became magnified by the scope by some magical anomaly, and it was all Dawson could hear now. Then, as if it had always been there, a black bowsprit swam before his eye followed by the jibs. His eye filled with the rush of rigging and bodies and the scope fell and he stared in horror at the masts and full grey sails speeding from behind the island, swathed in hideous green smoke, the row of cannon peering at him like the black eyes of some monstrous sea-creature.

'Oh, my God!' Dawson ran, as his space was taken by Granger, who gawked at the black ship that had come from out of the sea itself to be within a thousand yards of the *Starling.*

She was fully revealed now, billowing supernatural smoke that shielded the spirits on board, a devil's dirge drifting across the gap between them, mocking them.

Granger bellowed, 'Sail *there!*' He spun to the deck, where others joined in the cry as they all saw the black ship at once. Dawson flew to Acting Lieutenant Davison at the fo'c'sle as the cries followed him.

Breathless, he panted the very late news to Davison. 'A ship...the pirate frigate...she is on us!'

Davison was not listening. He stared at the ship that smoked as if ablaze. He had seen pirate ships before. Always skulking on the horizon as the *Starling* sailed home from the East. Schooners and sloops hanging back. Luffing peacefully, waiting for a gap between them and their fat East India consort. Never daring to come close on the English guns.

He had heard too of the 'vapours', the noise and show the

pirates put on to instil fear in their victims, to break the will to fight before a touch-hole had been lit. They must have ovens on deck, he thought, burning something, boiling something, to make that green cloud. My God, if they can fight through that smoke? And music? A jolly tune even! Are they mad?

'Mister Davison!' Dawson snapped him out of his slumber. 'This morning you were a midshipman. This afternoon the ship is yours. Orders, if you please, *sir*?'

Davison came back with a start, then gathered himself in a heartbeat. 'We will beat to quarters!' he yelled, and somewhere the drum rattled and men ran. He looked to Anderson's and the other boats, less than fifty yards away. Good, they had heard the drum, or they could see the ship; either way they were rowing pell-mell back to the ship.

Davison's instinct was to turn larboard, away from the pirates. The *Starling*'s bow faced the island, but he risked two dire events: drowning Anderson and the others in his turn, and giving his stern to the pirates' starboard guns.

No. It would have to be starboard and turn their bow towards them, before the pirates crossed their stern. He barked now at the impatient William Dawson, 'Topsails and gallants, Mister Dawson. Spanker and all jib. Hard to starboard.'

'Aye, aye, sir.' Dawson trotted off to his ropes, his order blasting across the decks. 'Hands to braces! Hard to starboard! Bosun! Slip cable!'

On a good day, when not beset, it took eight minutes to beat to quarters. Marines went into the fighting tops. Cartridges were brought from the magazine. Tables cleared and away, hammock nettings piled along the gunwale, guns cleared for action. Earlier Coxon had prepared as much as possible. Shot garlands were brought up, water to dowse the barrels, weapon lockers readied, and the boats were already free to save them being shattered by shot and spearing all in their path. Not too shabby; Davison thanked himself and spared an eye to the pirate ship.

By God, it moved fast! Already it had passed their starboard quarter, the viridescent smoke trailing behind and off the water like a rolling fog.

Granger joined him now, pointing out that in turning they would delay Anderson coming aboard. Rather that, Davison asserted, than do nothing and show their arse to the pirate guns. How many men to a gun did the *Starling* have? Four would make a two-minute reload. Two men to haul the nine-foot lump of iron, two to load. Six men was a luxury for war-time. Four would do.

Sail fell, throwing darkness and a cool breeze across their heads. Granger and Davison were suddenly swamped by a rush of brown-skinned, bare-backed men running to the jibs.

In the same thought they ran for the command of the higher quarterdeck as the helm lurched the ship beneath their feet and the *Starling* became alive again, bucking up out of her slumber like a slapped horse.

The deck was clear as they ran. Above their heads the men were bracing the yards round, some leaning off the larboard gunwale, their feet glowing white with tension, their arms as tight as the ropes they hauled on.

Marines were taking their dread climb to the wooden platform of the mainmast fighting top. Muskets slung, they climbed gingerly, getting heavier with each leg up, dismissing the lubber hole around the mast. For speed they had to climb outwards, over the shrouds, almost over the sea, before the relief of clambering to the safety of the platform and the eerie sensation of being able to hear every voice at once, from the deck far below, clear as a bell.

Davison and Granger hit the quarterdeck running, joining Mister Dawson and the helmsman.

'Bringing her about, Mister Davison.' Dawson nodded. He had two decades on the young faces, two decades whilst they had been wet-nursing. All he could do was his duty. It would not be his fault if he died this day.

Below deck, in the cockpit afore the manger, Surgeon Wood scattered a burlap bag of sawdust around his table. He unrolled his canvas bag of knives and probes and called for water as he watched his lantern swing and the rattle of bottles chinked all around him.

Dandon stepped cautiously out of the Great Cabin and peered into the half-light. The outer coach had gone, the partitions removed to reveal the clean embrasure of the last two of the twelve-pounders. He moved past the companion-way that led to the quarterdeck and touched the capstan for luck.

The ports were still closed and the guns strained against their tackles as the turn was almost complete. There was a calm about the ship, a rare silence, broken only by the rat-tling of the swaying lanterns.

Nine nine-foot guns either side. Dandon stood where the first four guns patiently stayed beneath the dark of the quarter-deck. Men stood on the larboard side, most with a strange tool as tall as themselves in their hands, waiting. The others were swiftly brushing shot clean of any debris or imperfec-tions in the surface, making sure that their first shots were as fine as they could be.

Thomas Howard saw Dandon and placed down by guns six and seven the serge canisters of powder he was holding, and joined him by the capstan.

'You should not be here, Doctor. It won't be safe.' He

placed a small hand upon Dandon's arm. 'You should go back with the women.'

Dandon ignored him gently. 'Tell me, Lieutenant,' he enquired, 'why are the men only on the one side?'

'That is the side we are bringing to bear on the ship.' He pitied the ignorance of the land-locked. 'You have seen the ship? The pirate ship?'

'Briefly. From the windows. A terrible sight. Then we began this strange turn. Are we in danger of a deadly occurrence?'

'Not at all. We outgun her by any count. This is how it will play.' He proudly walked Dandon into the light of the open deck, like a boy showing his toys to a visiting cousin.

'They will play the old game and so will we. These guns will fire on her hull. We will fire two to her one without a doubt and more iron to bear.'

'Is that the true happening of the circumstance?' Dandon was genuinely curious.

'Aye, she has nine-pounders to our twelves and they are but drunken pirates. No match for honed men.' He carried Dandon along the row of guns. 'See, in a few moments we will run out the guns, on order, and the linstocks will be lit, the quoins lifting the guns to fire below the waterline. Our aim will be to sink the beast.'

'And what will be the pirates' aim?'

'Oh, they will play their book, which is always to go for the rigging, disable the sail, for they will want the ship, you see?'

'Will they?'

'Of course. They will wish to board. They are pirates naturally.'

'Naturally.'

'Most likely it will take three rounds and they'll be off. Do not worry.'

'I will not worry if I can be near you, Mister Howard. I do not carry arms myself, and I would fear for the poor women.'

Howard smiled. 'It will not come to small arms, Mister Dandon. Three rounds, I swear. See how I have only brought up powder for such. Think of it! That's twenty-seven shots! Over three hundred pounds of iron! I could sink a forest with such a barrage!'

'How is it you know so much about the ways of the pirates, Mister Howard, may I enquire? How they will fight and such?'

'From accounts of course. It is well known, sir.'

Dandon hummed thoughtfully as he looked to the sails high above, still at a tight right-angle. 'But surely such accounts come only from failed attempts? Pardon my ignorance on such matters, Lieutenant Howard, but it would occur to me that no one reports on the successful pirate methods, if I can be so bold.' He smiled softly. 'At least not from this world.'

'Hah!' Howard slapped Dandon's arm. 'Be off, sir. Back to the women. I will protect you if it comes to it, I swear.'

Dandon bowed just as a yell from Granger above begged Howard's attendance. The boy excused himself and scurried away. Dandon wheeled his way back to the cabin. He took off his coat as he entered the room and slung it on the back of the captain's chair.

'Make sure all those windows are open, my girls. Take them out if you have to.' He picked up a decanter of golden ambience. 'We are playing the "old game", apparently.'

Chapter Eighteen

At the Hour of Our Death, Amen…

Letter from Thomas Howard to his father, the Hon. Rev. John Howard

May 1717

Dearest Father,

I know this letter will arrive the same instance beside my previous correspondence but I hope you will permit such indulgence. You are aware I have not returned from the foreign factories, but currently upon the Caribbee waters hunting a pyrate no less. We are commanded by a Captain John Coxon, an old salt it seems, for he drills us every day and has me reading Seller's book of instruction every evening and makes every soul wear a hat Sundays.

Today has been most delightful. I am to be Acting Lieutenant whilst Captain Coxon and Lieutenants Guinneys and Scott are embarking upon a most exciting mission to apprehend the pyrate Devlin upon the island of the French which we have landed towards. William Guinneys as you will recall has been Captain for the two years I have been in service. Captain Coxon commands for this endeavour bowing to his more common experience and mature nature no doubt.

I feel Captain Coxon favours me to the good as he has taken the time to talk to me privately and by my name.

I will ask you to remember the name of Mister Edward Talton in

your prayers, Father, as his life was extinguished today. He was purser to the Company's interest on board our ship but I fear the crossing of latitudes may have done for him as Mother feared it may of me.

Please inform Mother that I am well and hearty and keep my head on a swivel at all times. I do not swim, and I have eaten no fruit save apples as she instructed.

If I see the pyrate Devlin I shall not catch his eye and I will pray for his immortal soul. This day will, with all hope and good fortune, end with my permanent commission as Lieutenant Thomas Howard.

I hope you are well, Father, and I anticipate a return to home by mid-August.

Most Gracious Lord save and preserve us.

Your obedient son,

Thomas Howard.
Acting Lieutenant His Majesty's ship Starling.
Captain John Coxon.

On the beach, Hugh Harris looked to the bloody arm of Coxon and the sorrowful faces of Gregory and Davies and cocked his head to Devlin.

'Now, Cap'n,' he scolded, 'can we not leave you for the sixtieth of an hour without you getting yourself into some scrape?'

''Tis good to see you, Hugh.' Devlin passed the spare sword to Dan Teague with a nod and a wink. 'And you, Sam Morwell.' He shook the skinny, flaccid hand and passed on to Sam Fletcher. 'Thank you, Sam. You did well.'

'Pleasure, Cap'n. Though sorrowful for the *Lucy*.' He passed Devlin the left-locked pistol that he favoured, which he had kept dry and loaded.

Devlin sheathed the weapon in his belt with gratitude. He

gripped Sam's shoulder and shook the bones of him. 'Aye. We'll drink to the *Lucy*. Have no thought otherwise.'

'What of these swabs?' Hugh waved a pistol to Gregory and Davies.

'Pay them no mind,' Devlin said. 'They have no teeth and have harmed me none.'

Dan Teague stepped toward Coxon, seeing his bloodied sleeve and drawn lips of seething hate.

'And what of this dog? Stockings an' all? What of him?'

Devlin set out a welcoming arm. 'This, my brothers, be Captain John Coxon, though don't call him John, for it makes him bleed so.'

Dan Teague nodded with recognition, 'John Coxon?' He eyed Coxon up and down. 'Good pirate name, sir,' referring to the famous buccaneer. 'You should be proud to bear it.'

Coxon showed no feeling. He had spied the sorrowful sight of his London duelling pistols nestling in the belt of the pirate called Harris. He squeezed his wounded arm to punish himself and remained silent and hate-filled.

'Glad you came back all,' Devlin breathed relief. 'Although it may be a short victory.'

'We was all of a mind to come back, Cap'n.' Hugh grinned. 'The less time I spends in a boat, the better.' He cast an eye to the slowly moving *Starling*. 'Besides, something goes on there.'

Devlin and Coxon turned to the sea. Both had seen the ship begin her slow turn, without knowing why. They watched the three boats still languishing, struggling to rejoin her as the sails fell. Now the *Starling*'s bow faced out to sea, and she began to move, painfully close-hauled against the so'west breath of wind. They watched the sails flap back as she lay in irons, then continued to heel over, trying to grab the slightest reach.

A heart-wrenching sail. The helm pushed hard over, almost

half her starboard strakes dipping in the waves, yards braced to breaking. And then a Dutchman wailed as he saw the reason from his six-foot vantage.

'Kapitein!' Eduard Decker pointed east to the black ship slowly creeping into view in front of the yellow and black frigate. '*Shadow, ja?*'

The pirates scattered, each straining to get a glimpse of the black ship through the cloud of greenish smoke from the boiling cauldrons; they howled and fired pistol shot into the air in jubilation, causing Davies and Gregory to flinch and crouch, offering nervous smiles in compliance.

Coxon studied his arm, flexed his fingers, looked to his ship, and thought of the boys who commanded her.

'Well done, Mister Howard.' Davison congratulated Howard on the task he had been given. With pencil and paper the boy had drafted the black flag, for permanence; its colours now marked for the log.

The pirate ship paraded her colours from the backstay; the flag wafted through the trail of smoke, the skull appearing to laugh as the wind buffeted the grave cloth. High above, atop the mainmast of the *Shadow*, there was the red flag grabbed taut by the so'west wind. Long before any man in the field of play was born, before any man alive on the earth that day, it had chilled sailors to the marrow.

No mercy. No quarter.

'Mister Davison!' Dawson's voice grated through pinched, impatient lips. 'We have the range, sir, and that sound above us is the luffing of our sails in irons. Our head is in the wind.'

Davison looked up to the cracking sails, the deck still leaning to starboard. It would be too many moments before a beam reach could give them some momentum.

'What might you suggest, Mister Dawson?' he stammered.

Dawson commented that, in similar events, the tackles would be released and all cannon and all hands moved to starboard, to literally weight the ship round on her keel. At other times, dropping a stern quarter anchor at full sail would indubitably bring her about. Some, he pointed out, even held to firing the aft guns to gain momentum, but he did not hold with that personally.

'And for my ears and concerns, what do *you* suggest, Mister Dawson?' snapped Davison.

Dawson looked over the rail to the pirates. He could make out black shapes crowding the decks and shrouds.

'Run out the guns. At the very least a broadside may bring us round a little. They have the reach; they are coming across. Two minutes more and they will have the range and our port bow to their starboard guns.' He wiped his suddenly feverish brow. 'That is what I suggest. Good luck, sir.'

'Run out the guns!' Granger yelled to the main deck, and the port lids yawned open. The two quarterdeck nine-pounders were always out. They would be loaded after the first broadside, in anticipation of closer fire.

Howard sped from the quarterdeck to his gun-crew. He flashed a glance over the gunwale as he dropped down the stair for the boats. Anderson was calling for ropes to drag them in. Good. Another thirty hands and the real lieutenant. All was well. Anderson and the rest.

He reached the tobacco gloom beneath the quarterdeck in time to hear the long roll of the iron heaving into place. Richards, the bosun's mate, could have the bright light of the five guns in the open; the close confines outside the cabin seemed a more intense quarter for a young man.

He swept to number one, lowering his head to look out

the small square gap now filled by the gun, following its line to the *Shadow*. His heart pumped against his ribs as the image rolled down, and the ship rose out of view. Only the roll of the sea was in the window now.

A wall of water, seemingly about to pour through the port at any moment, then the black ship fell again, slowly, a feather floating before his eyes.

Howard jerked back upright. *'Fire!'*

The slow-match of the linstock tickled the touch-hole before the cry had finished. Three young Indian men to light three guns apiece and every soul jumped two steps clear.

The deck shook. The shrouds above them shivered. Hands clasped to ears as the guns came alive one after the other, flying back, laughing thunder, threatening to break any legs and arms left straying near the trucks and breeches. Then, spent and smoking, the tackles pulled short by, shivering dust from their twists of hemp as they tensed and the bulwarks strained to hold them. They hissed angrily as the fourth man rammed the wet sponge down their throats and, amid the clouds of smoke and smarting eyes, the loading began again.

On the quarterdeck, Davison and Granger swept and coughed the cloud away as it travelled on the wind. They could no longer see the *Shadow* through the drifting curtain but, deep in the fog, a succession of orange lights blinked at them silently from afar, nine of them, one by one, followed by the soft rumble of thunder.

Then the whistle came on the wind, and the whistle became a howl. Even the loading men stilled, as all eyes looked to the sky, slowly clearing back to blue, just in time to show the trio of topsails being punched through by three lucky shots. The rest of the whining barrage steamed harmlessly into the sea, far to leeward like tossed pebbles.

'Back to your guns!' Howard yelled. The last blanket of smoke ghosted away. Davison raised his glass once more to the pirate vessel, praying for damage. He swept the freeboard of the ship, his ears ringing. No holes.

The gunwale shattered on the starboard quarter, a rail missing on the quarterdeck. Good. Some satisfaction. His head suddenly became filled with the bellow of Lieutenant Anderson, who hurried upon the deck.

'*Double-shot!* You…' Anderson swallowed his final word. 'You're firing high! Double-shot the guns. Double the quoins and get her below the waterline.' He lowered his voice respectfully to Mister Dawson. 'Courses, Mister Dawson, if you please. We have a close reach, enough to get us three knots at least.'

'Aye, sir,' Mister Dawson sighed, 'but the pirates would love to see us make sail.'

'We'll risk it for the speed; they have courses and are on the same reach, we'll match 'em.'

Anderson turned to the main deck, in time to see the guns being heaved back into the ports for their next broadside.

'Double-shot now, Mister Howard!' he ordered. 'I want to see firewood! Wait for the order!'

'Aye, sir!' Howard wiped the black sweat from his face and handed the Indians their linstocks from the tub amid the skid beams.

Davison and Granger shared a sigh, their signatures for the day now relieved by the actual lieutenant. They would share success, but as long as they stayed alive they would not know blame.

Anderson had left the three boats to be pulled along as the fresh hands busied themselves to the shrouds to clamber up and release the courses. The *Starling* had her reach now, and the jibs along the bowsprit filled and pulled with pride.

Anderson turned to the ship, now within three hundred yards, her cloud of green smoke dissipating, but still arrogantly playing a dancing jig.

They were almost parallel now, broadside to broadside, beam to beam, the pirates slightly ahead, in danger of crossing the *Starling*'s bow where only her two fo'c'sle guns at angle might lay at her.

Anderson had moments to make a choice. He could see the make of it, of the next quarter-hour: stay on this reach, outsail and outfight, side to side until the pirates broke off under superior poundage and rate of fire. Or, boldly, swing about to larboard, bring the *Starling*'s bow in front of the enemy guns, a narrower target but heading straight at them. Then close and head for the stern or hope for surrender. These were undisciplined men; they would surely panic at such a daring direct assault.

Perhaps one more broadside and then decide. Perhaps even one more broadside might make them turn, as they no doubt fumbled drunkenly with their cracked shot and dusty powder.

'Mister Howard!' Anderson raised his right arm as the young man stared up at him. He would flag it down, to snap neatly by his side, before giving the order to fire, but he was distracted by the crack of cannon that came too soon from across the gap of water.

The noise was unfamiliar. The men, strung out across the yards, hastening the furled sails from high above, shared anxious final looks with the marines on the platform as they watched the ball and chain hurtling toward their heads with an unnatural scything cry.

The yards beneath their arms snapped like cobwebs and fell from the mast as the whirling dervish of chain cleaved through the ropes.

A bundle of men fell, wrapped and swathed like discarded fishing tackle into the sea. A marine's head flew from his shoulders, and he staggered for a moment, his fingers splayed out in horror, grasping out to his cowering comrades, who shrank back, screaming to the mast away from his headless bulk until he fell to his knees and tumbled to the deck, pinwheeling all the way.

Silence wept over the deck after the marine's body cracked upon the starboard gunwale and slumped to the gangway. Blood pulsed from the thick gristle in two great, slow waves, then pulsed no more.

The whole ship held a breath. Anderson looked to the missing yards. The courses were still hanging on. He glanced down to the odd sight of the marine, the snow-white spine staring from the neck like an ungodly eye.

Anderson's hand was still raised, but hung in the air as he turned from the corpse to the music playing on and on from the ship across the way.

Peter Sam brought the glass down from his eye with a rare smile. He ran a hand through his red beard, tugging at the final hairs thoughtfully. He turned to the deck.

'Same again, lads. Barshot all!' he bellowed. 'Bring me that mast!'

The small band of musicians stood at the larboard quarter beneath the quarterdeck, fiddling with glee, piping the guncrews to movement.

Black Bill kicked any slow hand to move faster, especially the men clearing the guns with the lambswool sponges, for that would be the end of them all if a gunner loaded powder into a hot barrel.

The first tirade from the *Starling* had skimmed the bulwark and the quarterdeck. It had smashed four pins from the helm wheel and shattered the starboard-quarter gunwale. No men were lost, but that would change.

Peter Sam raised the glass again and caught the black-coated form of his opponent doing the same. He grinned beneath the telescope and then passed his eye to the stern of the ship.

Peter Sam had launched two boats under the cover of the smoke from the cauldrons. Twenty-two of his most vicious brothers, gambling that no soul would be looking to the sea when a smoking, vapouring pirate hung before them. He had held that trick in his pocket, handed down from the *flibustiers* of Tortuga when they first began to creep off the island and sneak aboard passing merchants, which had stopped to trade for the barbecued meat from the *boucaniers*. Even Devlin would be surprised at his brains.

He heard the cannon fire again from the *Starling* at last. A bad one, no doubt; he would take the next second to duck beneath the fo'c'sle bulwark, but for the moment, whilst the iron whined towards them, he could not pull away from the distinct sight of the yellow justaucorps coat hanging out of the open stern windows, bodiless, suspended from a borrowed sword, beckoning the boats towards it.

'I'll be damned,' he whispered, then dropped to the deck in time to feel the pounding hail rattle his spine and rock the ship almost out of the water.

The tirade was brief. Peter Sam pulled himself unsteadily up to the rail afore the helm. Looking over the deck, all seemed well. A few men thrown to their backs, now grasping for handholds, shaking the fog from their heads. He leaned down and dragged the helmsman to his feet, pushing the wheel into his trembling hands.

'*Bill!*' His shout echoed over the heads of all and drew the face to appear behind the foremast. 'What damage?'

Black Bill ran to the gunwale, heaving men out of his way like so many bags of wheat.

'Fine, Peter!' he yelled back through cupped hands. 'Holed but worthy. She'll stand yet!'

'Get five men to the well!' Sam yelled. 'Pump as wants!'

'Aye!' Black Bill looked to the slow-match of his linstock, then to his guns ready to fire, loaded with langridge to tear and rip limb and sail, wood and chain. He raised his head over to the *Starling*, the smoke from her last anger drifting south over her stern and clouding the two boats even more. He lumbered to stand behind numbers one and two before the foremast.

'Stand clear!' and eight men jumped back. 'Hail Mary, full of grace,' and he laid the linstock to the touch-hole of number one and reverently passed his arm to do the same to number two. 'The Lord is with thee.' The guns blazed and rocketed past him to struggle in their tackles, men leaping on them instantly with sponge and ladle ready.

Bill dodged around them to the next two guns, the most open view, clear of shrouds and rigging. 'Blessed art thou amongst women,' the fuse sparked, 'and blessed is the fruit of thy womb, Jesus,' and three and four fired free.

He stilled slightly to watch the first bars hit home and split the fore topmast and gallant like a sword stroke.

'Holy Mary, Mother of God, pray for us sinners.' He stroked the touch-hole of five and six, crowded beneath the main-mast rigging, sparing a look to witness the platform, where the marines stood in the tops of the mainmast, shower into tinder. The sails began to ripple as the tentacles of the stays buckled and writhed.

He winked to the lads beneath the quarterdeck and passed

the linstock on for the final flurry of the last three guns that would rake the mizzen and stern.

'Now and at the hour of our death. Amen.' His final eloquence was drowned out by the three sudden punches of the guns.

'Do you never tire of such foolishness, Bill?' A face, once tanned and young, now black and ancient, crouched breathless beside him.

'You'll thank me one day, lad, mark me.' Bill shoved the man to reload and yelled to Hartley for more of the fine Portuguese red-letter powder that reported so well.

Captain John Coxon stood beside Captain Patrick Devlin, shoulder to shoulder. Through narrowed vision they surveyed the stirring sight before them. The vast colourful panorama, the majesty of the *Starling* ploughing steadily so'west, her shining beauty marred viciously by the faint hacking of the ship's axe to the ropes of the fore topgallant, wildly bucking alongside the starboard bow.

They had watched the tarred, black wooden platform burst apart, smashing the marines like glass, and the fore gallant slowly tumble, yards and all, sail still furled. The sound of deadeyes and tackle plummeting to the deck echoed even to the beach.

Coxon could remember the chaos that was no doubt occurring on deck. The smoke and confusion. Almost a hundred men and officers aware now of only the five men nearest to them, holding on to a small quarter of order within the remnant of their vision that was not crowded by smoke and noise. He winced, pained more from helplessness than the ache in his right arm.

Devlin shared Coxon's tension. He could see the *Shadow*'s fore quarter beyond the *Starling*'s, her masts and sails just visible through the courses and shrouds of the other. Distant. Unreachable.

Devlin had sent his men to the stockade, to the chest, along with Gregory and Davies, leaving the two captains alone on the shore, staring hopelessly at the drama before them. Two captains, commanding nothing.

Coxon suddenly stiffened, broke from Devlin's side and dashed along the beach, staring wildly at the *Starling*.

Devlin followed his gaze to the *Starling*'s stern. At first he could not see the origin of Coxon's apparent panic. The stern glowed in the afternoon light. All seven of the arched windows were up and, from the furthest, strung out like a golden pennant, billowed Dandon's coat.

Coxon's concern was not for the justaucorps, more for the two laden boats crawling towards the hanging ropes of the davit that previously secured the stern gig below the escutcheon.

'Ah,' Devlin crowed, 'that's a shame to have such an avenue of entrance open to all.'

Coxon's voice sang out, to ease the cramped feeling in his chest, 'What, by God, does that Frog fool do!'

'Well' – Devlin stepped easy, closer to his old master – 'I am thankful to discover that he is no fool. You may be shamed to know, however, John, that he not be French either.'

Coxon turned. His face drained, lips ashen, but he would give Devlin no more satisfaction. 'So, he is one of yours, then?' He shook his head. 'Fool me for trusting an Irishman. If you open the front door to one of you, another goes in the back.' He straightened. 'No matter, pirate. They will not catch the ship. She wears too well. I am sure of that much at least.'

'For now, John.' Devlin spoke with charming reverence.

*

'Keep her away, boys!' Anderson yelled from the quarterdeck to the bosun's gangs, making best work of quartering the errant sails. 'Mister Dawson! Very well thus and no higher!'

Dawson's affirmation was lost amid the double-shotted blast from Howard's guns hammering along the deck.

Anderson checked the flight of the balls, glimpsed the surface of the sea tremble as they shot free, then jumped the steps to the main deck. Skidding a foot on water or blood, he shouted back to Granger to angle the pair of quarterdeck guns.

'Aim to the deck!' He almost jumped at the startling hiss of steam that erupted behind him as the sponges rammed home.

The men around him were glowing with torrents of sweat, their faces black, hair melting down their necks, but paused to cheer as they heard at least half of their broadside hit home.

He slapped the back of the nearest man without looking at his face, his eyes seeking Davison. He spied him at the foremast, trying to tidy the mess of clew lines and sheets that were hanging amid the disarray. Anderson moved past the mainmast as he barked to Davison to man the fo'c'sle niners and aim for the deck.

He glanced up briefly to the peculiarly peaceful blue sky above the mainsail, now flecked with the blood of the marines; then his vision flashed red, then black, and something deafening rushed upon him.

His mind floated awake. A lock of his wet hair lay in his mouth, the rush of all the sea filling his senses. Slowly the sound lifted, and he felt the wet deck beneath his cheek, smelled cordite and oakum.

The world started up again. Past his head feet were running.

Around him, the snapping of ropes whipped through the air.

He had been thrown to the starboard bow and lay in the scuppers beneath the netting. He turned over, up on one elbow, unsure whether he could stand.

The mainmast lay across the starboard bulwark. Fallen drunkenly, as the Campeche tree of its birth fifteen years ago.

Anderson was mesmerised by its size, gigantic in its latent power. He stared wide-eyed at the expanse of sky that the mast's absence had revealed above the deck – serene, vibrant blue – then he watched, frozen, as the ton of sail, spars and yards toppled it over the side with a noise like a surfacing whale, its snaking ropes grabbing men as it went down.

Most danced free; one cried out, his face sliced like beef from a slashing clew line. Another heard his back crack as it slammed into the breech of a starboard gun and his screams fell over the gunwale with him, swaddled in rope.

Only a third of the mast remained, tall as a man through the deck, insides crisp and fresh against its dark, worn skin.

The ship rolled with her trauma, the leeway enough to pull the larboard guns out of the port holes on their tackles as the crew grabbed for handholds.

Anderson stood with tremendous effort. Without thought he pulled his service pistol, then just as quickly tucked it back into his belt as he looked over the gunwale at the disaster.

The mast was boiling in the sea. He found young amusement in spying a few blue fish of excellent size floundering in her ropes and sails, then in horror at an arm doing the very same, still wearing its shirt sleeve.

He turned and yelled to as many men as he could see, 'Firemen to starboard! Cut her free – she's dragging us round!' and ten men with axes appeared from nowhere, barging Anderson back without a word. He carried on his backward path to the larboard guns and called for Howard and Dawson.

'Where away, Mister Dawson?' A powdery fog from the expired mast stifled his voice. Dawson merely pointed from the quarterdeck to the ship, now two hundred yards from the larboard bow, away from their guns. That would change in moments as the *Starling* turned, as if it were by her own design to lose her mast to heave her to bear.

'Mister Howard, fire as she bears.' Then he shouted upwards to the fo'c'sle, 'Mister Davison? Fire when ready.'

Davison tugged his hat. He had two nine-pounders right on the *Shadow*'s starboard bow and six men crowded with him to fire them. The trucks squealed as the men dragged them to the best degree to rake the deck with their loaded bags of grape. The linstock raised and Davison stood back as the guns fired in two heartbeats.

'*Down!*' Peter Sam hollered as the puff of smoke clouded from the *Starling*'s fo'c'sle. 'All hands! *Down!*' and he threw himself to the quarterdeck.

Eighteen pounds of pistol shot hailed hot across the deck. Two hundred spitting balls of lead sang off the cannon and whistled over the bodies of the pirates. Wood split from every corner of the deck, creating a world of dust, angrily firing splinters fore and aft. Cleats flew off the gunwale. Sheets were severed, springing away with glee, seeking to whip out any peering eyes.

The deadly rain stopped. Robert Hartley rolled over from where he had flung himself on his precious bags of powder, and immediately tossed a couple to Black Bill, who crawled fore to his guns.

Peter Sam checked over the gunwale. The empty space amidships of his enemy brought a coldness to his heart. He had seen the end now. The toppling of the mast would bring the men opposing him to their knees.

His pleasure ended at the firing of the next broadside towards them. Double-shotted. The starboard quarter exploded outwards and fell into the sea and the *Shadow* rolled in pain, toppling men over. Devlin would be picking oak out of his food for weeks if he ever returned to his cabin alive. Still the *Shadow* held. Holed above the waterline, her iron-walled bulkheads shook and shrugged off the barrage, the spent iron balls rolling, steaming along the lower deck.

'Good one, Mister Howard,' Anderson chimed. 'Next one the same, if you please. We'll have her yet.'

'Mister Anderson' – Dawson appeared by his side at the guns – 'we are stalled, sir! We have fore course and mizzen sails but no reach to draw! We are in a barrel, sir!' Dawson proffered the words with finality of his duty. He had made the sails. He had stolen the reach. With the wind behind him he could fly still. Now all he could do was turn.

Anderson nodded, understood. But the pirate had been holed for sure. The *Starling* had lost sail, momentum, but the pirates were still outgunned. The *Starling* could stand, hold fast, win the day by sheer firepower.

He turned to the helmsman. 'Hard to starboard, man!' he yelled aft. 'Bring all guns upon her!'

'Aye, aye, sir!' the cry came back. He placed all his weight against the wheel, then fell to the deck as it spun wildly away from him.

All turned to the sight of the wheel running free. The helmsman gathered himself back, then pulled it round in his hands, frowning. 'She don't answer, sir! The rudder chain's gone!'

Anderson tried to recall any shots to their stem or quarter that might have caused such an occurrence, but found his memory wanting. He opened his mouth to speak but could find no words, his silence broken by the next round of shot from the dark ship beyond.

The pirates sent them their own grape, from all their guns. It strafed the deck from a deadly angle, cutting through the capstan and mizzen like a thousand blades, whipping past their heads and thudding in to at least six of Howard's quarter-bill. Their duty was done.

Anderson rose from his crouch. The gun-crew cowered below the bulwark until slapped up by Howard and his Indian cohorts, and paid no mind to the dead men around them as they reloaded, exhausted, slipping in their own sweat.

Anderson sped to the quarterdeck, shouting to Granger to fire his guns, not caring if they faced open sea or not. He flung himself up the stair. The helmsman repeated that the wheel did not answer. Anderson jigged past him to the taffrail to look over the stern to the rudder chain.

His hands gripped the rail in an engulfing terror as he looked down to the two strange boats, empty, the open Great Cabin windows, the yellow coat hanging off a wedged sword and the rudder chain cut away.

He spun round. The words whispered from him, barely heard even by Granger, who stood only feet away with his gun-crew.

'Prepare to repel boarders...'

The cabin doors burst apart, thrown outwards by the roaring throats of the pirates. They poured out like rats, innumerable, hundreds of them surely by the blast of pistols and the swinging of axes. Swords still strung in their belts, they hacked at any head that dared try to scrape a cutlass free.

Anderson leaped to the rail of the quarterdeck. *'Pikemen! To arms! Repel boarders!'* He yanked his pistol free and fired down into the first waistcoat he saw.

The gun-crews at the foremast dived for the pikes standing round it. They turned to parry any blow and then stared into the barrels of the musketoons from the six pirates, firing from the waist, cutting them down in a moment, then swinging the butts into the skulls of any man near them, the smoke still trailing from the barrels. They moved fore, screaming, pulling blades and pistols.

Pistols from every nation, engraved for sons, bequeathed by fathers, grabbed from dead men, now hanging from their necks on silken ribbons, firing steadily into any body to the left and right of them.

Thomas Howard pulled his own pistol as two grenadoes bowled past him into the sailors around the foremast, the fuses sparking merrily and exploding bloodily into the huddle of men. He raised his armed fist with a cry, aiming to the crowd piling out of the cabin, only to have his arm stayed by the grasping reach of Dandon suddenly appearing at his side.

It took a moment for Howard to filter the face from the horde of others, the gold grin and moustache finally sinking in.

'Mister Dandon! Behind me, sir!' He tugged Dandon with his free arm, only to feel his movement cut.

'No, Mister Howard,' Dandon snapped, pulling him down, his French voice gone. 'Behind me is best, I venture you'll find.' And he brought the boy within his folded arms just as an axe was raised above both their skulls. The bloodshot eyes of the axeman looked once to Dandon, no longer seeing the boy; then he continued his sweep across the nose of one of the Indians and moved on, whirling madly.

Dandon shrunk below the bulwark, between the guns, with a struggling Howard in his grip. He pulled the boy's head to his chest, away from the carnage, and felt Howard's body go limp and shiver in his arms. He had none of the right words. All his world was wrong, he knew. He whispered as gently as his sordid tongue could.

'Good boy. Brave boy.' Then Dandon held his head high, making sure that every damned soul knew who he was as the blood flew around him.

Anderson drew his sword, and jumped over the rail to land behind the mizzen, the clump of his boots upon the deck drawing two wild faces to turn towards him.

He sprang forward, hacking at the two that singled him out. They wheeled away from his swings, once, twice, then picked up their hanging guns and fired together into his midriff.

He fell back to the mast in his own footsteps, slumped down the wood and stared to the spread of blood across his belly. His eyes drifted down to the tiny form of a translucent spider clambering upon him. He brushed at it weakly. He continued to brush at the spindly creature after the axe slammed into his forehead from an upwards swing and the bodies whirled away, pulling their swords, forgetting him at once.

The weight of the hatchet pulled Anderson's head to his chest, his wound spreading a soup of blood upon his lap, the spider, its path ill-chosen, drowning in the waterfall.

*

Peter Sam and Bill stood together on the quarterdeck, sharing a spyglass between them. They felt their blood rise as they watched the wave move through the waist of the ship until the madness reached the fo'c'sle, where Davison made a single swift effort to swing a swivel gun from the rails, only to be crushed by the onslaught that filled the deck. They watched the axes and cutlasses beat down again and again.

Their own crew crammed along the *Shadow*'s bulwark, craning for the sight of gore.

Then a new roar came over the sea. A victorious howl of raised cutlasses and pistol shot as the last of the *Starling*'s crew laid down and the *Shadow*'s brethren rallied to the cry and the howl echoed back.

Nine marines had died. Nine men had fallen with the yards, broken. Thirteen had been wounded by cannon and timber. Forty-nine others bowed or died to twenty-two pirates.

Dandon stood up, holding tight the shoulder of Thomas Howard. He threw his hat into the air and crowed once with the shouts of the others, then looked down at the terrified, mottled face.

'Oh, it'll be a fine day yet, Mister Howard.' He tugged the boy's chin. 'It was the "old game", just like you said it would be.' Then, quieter, 'You just didn't know the rules, lad, that's all.'

Chapter Nineteen

X

'*D*o not feel too bad, John.' Devlin slapped Coxon's back. 'You had no way of knowing that Dandon there was my very own *fidus Achates*.'

Coxon sniffed scornfully. 'Did you steal all my books as well, Patrick?'

Two hours had passed. The amber sun had begun to spread across the horizon. The pirates sang their bordello chords as they removed the trucks from the *Starling*'s guns and rammed nails into their touch-holes. Everything that could be swallowed, fired or rigged had been ferried across to the *Shadow*, Bill's pencil and paper marking it all. The remnants of the *Starling*'s crew were now employed to haul their wares over the boards at the fo'c'sle to the *Shadow*'s deck, their heads lowered, the songs of the pirates in their ears.

Peter Sam stepped onto the island from out of the surf, relieved now from the fire and the fury of the afternoon and preparing for the cool of night. He cast an eye to John Coxon, nothing more than a glance to his bloodied forearm, then strode to Devlin, almost with menace. He wrapped his huge right fist round Devlin's fighting arm and pumped it heartily.

'Cap'n,' he said, as if that was all that needed to be said in summary after weeks of separation. Then he looked beyond to the fat black chest standing on the beach. 'That be it, then?'

'Aye,' Devlin sighed. 'That be it. And ours.'

Peter Sam moved on towards the chest. 'Teague.' He nodded to Dan and likewise to Hugh Harris, who tugged a straggling forelock in response. He stopped in front of Gregory and Davies, who struggled to look into the cracked, powerful face of the quartermaster, with his leather rags that might for all their ruddiness be fashioned from human flesh. 'These men be dead, Cap'n?' he barked behind him, his hand already on his cutlass.

'Not for now, Peter. Let them be,' Devlin called back and walked to Coxon. 'John,' he said, 'we needs to talk now.' He gave no choice, taking Coxon's arm away with him. 'You have been mighty quiet this last act, John. This island was an Eden when the sun came up, I shouldn't wonder. Now it reeks of death. What say you on the matter?'

Coxon looked ahead as they walked, his voice flat. 'I have given it no thought,' he said. 'What has happened has been because of you. That is all I know. All I need to know.'

'Oh, it could have ended different now, let's be fair. I could be swinging in the breeze now, and you would have held the rope, and for truth I would not have blamed you.' He stopped them both and checked for earshot from his men, before drawing Coxon closer. 'But think on this,' he hissed. 'Those men of yours made you prisoner too. They came to take that there chest, not to protect it. On orders. And you were not part of their plan. Would you think that you were going back to England with them, or would you be of a mind to think otherwise?'

Coxon paused, looked to his wounded ship. 'I have thought not of their duty.'

'What of your duty? What would you do now for your precious board?'

He looked pitifully to Devlin and spoke like a bishop. 'I don't do it for them, *pirate*. There'll be a day when you'll know that.'

Devlin swung Coxon back to stroll across their sunken path. 'I will grant you back your ship and you will know that I spared you by my own grace. For it is only fair that someone as noble as yourself tells the court of what happened here, and I am only sorry that I will not see their faces boil as you tell them.' He waved a righteous hand. 'No need to thank me, John, I will hear no word of it. You may be on your way.'

Coxon's heels dug in and Devlin was pulled back a step. 'You will hear *this* word, Patrick.' He brought his face close. 'Mark me' – the corners of his mouth were white with hate – 'wherever I am in this world, when I hear tidings of your capture, I will make them wait and make you rot until I am there to watch you hang. You may lay to that!'

'You're welcome, John.' Devlin led him along again.

Coxon shouted now, for all to hear. 'Mark me! A year at best. That's all you've got! They are coming! There are acts penned every day for you all! For all your kind!'

'A year you say?' Devlin dropped Coxon's arm and joined his brethren. 'Couple of hours ago I thought I was dead. I have increased my span better than I had hoped!'

He left Coxon to the shore, contemplating the longboat and the anxious forms of Gregory and Davies. Devlin joined his men, hovering and leering around the chest like flies.

'Sate yourselves with a pocketful of coin, lads. Louis's face never looked so grand.' He trawled his right hand through the bitter smell of the coin, the music of it widening the pupils of all eyes upon it.

'What now, Cap'n?' Peter Sam asked.

Devlin dragged his hand reluctantly free. 'We shall take

the ladies back to Providence. The good Navy Board fellows will return to their ship. Tell England and their suckling allies of what has happened to their coffers.'

'Would we not be killing them all, then?' Hugh Harris voiced a frozen regret.

'No, lads. I'm of a mind that they will be most surprised to lay eyes on Coxon at all.' He looked back to the man beside the boat. 'Besides, I owes him at least for feeding me all these years.' Then, quietly now, 'My own father only fed me well the night before he sold me.' And he turned to the chest, burying his thoughts in the depths of the gold.

'*Shadow* fares well, Cap'n,' Peter Sam proudly remarked. 'Will Magnes has laid oakum and wood to all her holes.' He went on to reel off the goods hoisted from the *Starling*'s hold and the small counts of wounded and dead.

'We should leave now,' Devlin sighed. 'Leave the *Lucy* to her grave. And several more besides. Of which, Hugh, did you do as I made request?'

'Aye, Cap'n.' Hugh cocked a wink and clicked his tongue. 'All be prepared. Though our colours be rare now.'

Devlin smiled. He moved back to Coxon and took his bloodied hand.

'It was fair good to see you again, John,' he said. 'We will take you back to your ship now if you can bear to be borne away with us.'

'I do not lie, Patrick.' Coxon's voice was soft now, as sable. 'They are coming. There are scores of ships already in the islands. The colonies, the Americas, are the future. Whitehall talks of nothing else but sea rats and Jacobites. This age is at an end.'

Devlin lowered his eyes. 'That be as it may. And no doubt you will all be of one mind to forget that you taught every man his trade and reaped the benefit when it suited. But today I bested all of you. These men follow me and not because I own them. Be gone now, John, before I change my mind to you.'

May fell into June. The barque *Bellone* crept into the bay of the uncharted island, the crew still singing, laughing, of the nights spent ashore along the colonial coast.

Now they had returned to refresh the sentries and relieve the vavasour, Capitaine Bessette, from his laborious days of rest and solitude.

As the captain had anticipated after so many lazy days of flies and sun, a watch had not checked their passage. They approached the island unheralded. Unwatched.

His displeasure growing with every sweep of the oars from the gig, the captain followed the uneasy murmurs of his company as they ruminated on the spectre of the brigantine, still fresh, nestling amongst the eggshell coral.

Their rumblings grew as they stepped over the mosaic of footsteps that littered the path from the beach and still no guard greeted them.

They pulled their cutlasses at the eerie sight of the open gate of the stockade and the murder of crows that preened themselves along the walls, upon the watchtower, cawing at the approach of the strangers.

The captain stepped over the threshold, bolstered by the pressure of urgent curiosity behind him. He stepped aside, transfixed, and let the others filter through to share his shuddering dismay.

Despite the crowd of them, each one stood alone. Each one made his own peace and judgement at the sight before him. The crows cawed as they tore and scraped at the hanging flesh.

Someone had set ten poles ripped from the stockade walls into the ground beyond the gate. Sitting, straining forward as if still alive, bound by their fraying wrists, the black desiccated forms of what had once been their countrymen were fixed to each stake.

The tallest of the sitting corpses, still apparelled in a fine blue waistcoat and breeches, hung skeletal and eyeless beneath a black flag.

The grim design, now seared into their coldest memories, would slouch back, even years from this place, whenever the stench of decay or the gleeful writhing of maggots forced them to recall the grinning skull set in the ring of a compass rose, above the cross of a pair of pistols.

Epilogue

Proclamation of a King

George R

Whereas we have received Information, that several Persons, Subjects of Great Britain, have since the twenty-fourth day of June, in the year of our Lord 1715, committed diverse Pyracies and Robberies upon the High Seas, in the West Indies, or adjoining to our Plantations, which hath and may Occasion great Damage to the Merchants of Great Britain, and others trading into those Parts; and tho' we have appointed such a Force as we judge sufficient for suppressing the said Pyrates, yet the more effectually to put an End to the same, we have thought fit, by and with the advice of our Privy Council, to Issue this our Royal Proclamation; and we do hereby promise, and declare, that in Case any of the said Pyrates, shall on or before the fifth of September, in the year of our Lord 1718, surrender him or themselves, to one of our Principal Secretaries of State in Great Britain or Ireland, or to any Governor or Deputy Governor of any of our Plantations beyond the Seas; every such Pyrate and Pyrates so surrendering him, or themselves, as aforesaid, shall have our gracious Pardon, of and for such, his or their Pyracy, or Pyracies, by him or them committed before the fifth of January next ensuing.

And we do hereby strictly charge and command all our Admirals,

Captains, and other Officers at Sea, and all our Governors and Commanders of any Forts, Castles, or other Places in our Plantations, and all our other Officers, Civil and Military, to seize and take such of the Pyrates, who shall refuse or neglect to surrender themselves accordingly.

Given at our Court, at Hampton Court, the fifth Day of September 1717, in the fourth Year of our Reign. God save the king.

The Proclamation of Pardon sailed to Providence in a single unrated ship. Both ship and royal-sealed covenant were seized by the pirates that ruled therein and the captain and crew of the English ship were never heard of again.

In response, the Court and the Privy Council scratched beneath their wigs as to what manner of men scorned pardon and mocked their laws so.

In their attempt to fathom the depths of depravity and lawlessness that dirtied the waters of the Americas and sullied the reputation of the nation throughout the world, they turned to a man whom they held to be a privateer faithful to the king.

He had sailed the world several times over. He had journeyed with William Dampier, was an authority on the unknown lands to the south, and courted fame through the astounding story of the marooned Alexander Selkirk, whom he had found and rescued.

He had raided treasure ships and sent countless enemies to the dark bed of the sea. A pirate in all but name, if it were not for the brown oilskin that contained his letters of marque.

Woodes Rogers took the commission to become governor of the Island of Providence. He bowed before the Privy Council and apologised for the yellowing leer that rose up from one side of his face, a permanent legacy from the musket ball that had carried away a portion of his cheek and jaw.

He would take the proclamation back to Providence and, he gave promise with another bow, this time it would not be taken so lightly.

John Coxon had never been fond of Bristol. He stood by the entrance port of the *Milford*, the thirty-gun frigate he now captained under order of Woodes Rogers himself, taking the notion, frowned upon by his officers, of inspecting all the putrid souls tramping onto his deck.

Now it was early April, almost a year since he had limped away from the pallor the *Shadow* had cast upon him, and a painful winter past of his aching forearm from the pistol wound. The white scar marked upon him forever, from the pirate who sent him home to the shame and silence from Whitehall at the tale of Guinneys and the gold.

He had spent a Monday morning before the board with no gold to deliver, a broken ship and a butcher's bill of dead men. He had nodded to every damning recrimination and had not expected his sword to be handed back to him. But the Piracy Act was now in force and the Proclamation of September had failed. The Privy Council now estimated an approximate force of three thousand pirates operating in the Bahama Islands alone, and enough was enough.

Coxon was given the option to go back, his experience invaluable despite his failures. He had at least returned alive and, with a badge of loyalty for his efforts permanently star-shaped on his forearm, there had been no further mention of Jacobites and Stuarts.

Only once, as he sat before the table in Whitehall, did Coxon's eyes shift to the window to watch London trundle by as the Earl of Berkeley asked, with a cough, whether Captain Guinneys had shown any contradiction to Coxon's own particular orders.

Coxon looked back to the stern faces, scratched a hand through his hair, and declared that to the extent of his knowledge and recollection, Captain Guinneys had died at the pirate Devlin's hands in the execution of his duty to the letter of his orders as given.

But Bristol had too many hostelries for his favour, and the reek of stale ale mingled unpleasantly with the odour of death from the rolling slavers unloading their bales of cotton and loaves of sugar. Spars almost touched within the crammed harbour, the perpetual cries of gulls almost deafening, even amongst the throng of decks and bustling urgency of loading and endless hammering.

By the gangway he watched the passage of the men weaving their way aboard, every man tugging his forelock to him and ducking away as swiftly as he could. He appraised them all, noting the good ones amid the bad, and separating them mentally in an instant. Only one dragged himself through the port and dared to speak to him, a filthy red tricorne clamped to his skull.

'Ah, Captain.' He grinned, the effect of which was unsettling, as the smile snaked up almost painfully over a sunken, scarred left jaw. ''Tis a pleasure to be aboard such a fine vessel on such an auspicious occasion, commanded by such a man of the sea as yourself.'

Coxon sniffed at the dredge of a vagrant that stood pale before him. 'How came you by that jaw, sailor?' he asked directly.

'Well now, that would be in service to our good Queen Anne, no doubt on one of those fine mornings I would have shared with your good self some time ago. A world away it seems to me now, but it has never left me with a fear of the shot, Captain, if that be what troubles you.'

'Get below, man. And as for your jaw, you have that in common with Commodore Rogers himself. You are in good company.'

'Aye, Cap'n, fair sailing to us all back to the Caribbee.' The man tipped the cock of his burgundy tricorne to Coxon and sifted past.

'You have been to the islands before, then, sailor?' Coxon was now talking to the back of what had once been a fine brown twill coat. The coat turned round.

'Aye, Cap'n. Once or twice, to be sure.' He winked, then moved again to the companionway aft.

Coxon bellowed then, galled by the wink, stopping the sail hands in the yards above, their sail needles frozen in mid-stitch.

'You will remove that gentleman's hat, sailor!' he snarled, and the sailor turned, the burgundy hat now humbly in his hands, and bowed meekly.

Coxon's voice boomed again, 'It be straw or Monmouth wool for the hands on this deck, sir! You will stow that head-piece till I deem you worthy to go ashore!'

'Aye, Cap'n.' He promptly tugged his coarse blond hair, his evil smile thankfully gone. 'Beg your pardon, Cap'n.' The sailor bowed again as he turned, folding his hat into an outer pocket, then carried on his path.

As soon as he was below, he placed the dark red hat tightly back upon his head. He took in the cold faces of his companions staring at him in the gloom, and swung his canvas bag to land somewhere amongst the tables.

'Morning, lads!' He beamed. 'I be Seth Toombs and pleased I be to meet you! Ain't it a fine day to be heading to Providence, now?'

And as he slapped the backs of his new crewmates, he

almost forgot the dull throb that had haunted his jaw since the night Valentim Mendes had put a bullet through it.

He was sailing back. Back to the islands and his world. Home to seek the man who had stolen his ship and his crew and had left him for dead.

Back as happily as the dog, joyfully, to lap at his vomit.

Author's Note

*M*ost of what you have just read (or are about to read if you have flicked to the back of the book) is true. Let me repeat that first part: *most* of what you have just read is true.

The story takes place in what history refers to as the twilight years of the Golden Age of Piracy, the first quarter of the eighteenth century. The great wars between the powers of Europe, the same wars that kick-started the Golden Age, have ended. With peace (albeit limited) comes the grabbing and stealing by the victors of the islands of the Antilles and whatever pieces of America they can lay their hands on.

Spurred on by the weakening of Spain's dominance of the Americas, a tide of immigrants from Scotland, Ireland and France begin to descend upon the New World in their thousands, instead of the dribble over the last fifty years of convicts, gentry and hopeful pilgrims. It was this explosion in immigration to the New World, and the trade it brought, that made it a haven for the pirates who came into being at the end of the wars.

Although pirates have existed wherever man has sailed, and still very much do exist, it is this period of Caribbean piracy that epitomises the pirate to the modern world. These sea-rovers are the inspiration for Patrick Devlin and his men.

This is not the place to elaborate on the history of piracy but I hope the unfamiliar reader has been intrigued to learn more. For those who are familiar, there are plenty of references dotted throughout the story that will generate knowing nods and hint at things to come. It is to you I am cocking a wink across the pages.

It was never my intention to write a manual of seamanship. Ultimately this is an adventure story and I wanted the sailing aspects of it to be as accessible as possible and not alienate readers. You can toss the book across the room for other reasons but hopefully not because you couldn't follow the action. However, for the authenticity police, it would make me feel better to highlight a couple of things before the letters come in.

The ships: at the time of the story the majority of ships were still helmed by whipstaff for the larger vessels and tiller for the smaller. The ship's wheel had been around for about ten years but was not in widespread use. The *Lucy* has both, of course, but it was for easing the image into the reader's mind that I gave both the *Shadow* and the *Starling* a classic wheel. Also, unlike modern sailing ships' wheels, which act in the same way as a car's steering, in the Age of Sail when the wheel went left, the ship went right, and when the cry 'Hard to larboard' rang out, it was an instruction to the helm to push the wheel to larboard (port) and thus the ship to starboard. Confusing, isn't it? Thus, for clarity, when our heroes yell out, 'Hard to larboard,' the ship will go left. Trust me. I won't even mention that most of the steering was managed by the sails, I promise.

Other than those indiscretions, most of what transpires is true, as I promised at the start of this note. I have been faithful to the weapons, the methods and the spirit of these men as I interpret them to be.

Once, it was believed to be a fanciful notion of the pirate biographers of the eighteenth century that these supposedly raging, drunken misanthropes had codes of honour and conduct with which they policed their democratic crews, until evidence began to surface that confirmed it. Even buried treasure, one of the most romantic pirate myths, is slowly being uncovered, thanks to deforestation, oil testing and holiday landscaping of the coastlines of Central and South America.

Devlin's gold is not buried, however. The gold deposit outlined in the story is fictional, but there is much circumstantial evidence throughout history to suppose that governments did hide great gold caches throughout the Americas to fund their various armies. The legends of these troves inspire treasure hunters to this day.

On that note, as I am sure you are wondering just how rich Patrick Devlin and his men now are, I can average it out that they sail away with the modern equivalent of eight hundred thousand pounds and change. But they won't stop there. Again, you have to trust me on that.

Mark Keating, May 2009